BY DELILAH S. DAWSON

STAR WARS
Inquisitor: Rise of the Red Blade
Galaxy's Edge: Black Spire
Phasma
The Perfect Weapon

MINECRAFT: MOB SQUAD
Mob Squad
Never Say Nether
Don't Fear the Creeper

THE HIT SERIES
Hit
Strike

THE SHADOW SERIES
(AS LILA BOWEN)
Wake of Vultures
Conspiracy of Ravens
Malice of Crows
Treason of Hawks

THE TALES OF PELL
(WITH KEVIN HEARNE)
Kill the Farm Boy
No Country for Old Gnomes
The Princess Beard

THE BLUD SERIES
Wicked as They Come
Wicked as She Wants
Wicked After Midnight
Wicked Ever After

STANDALONE NOVELS
It Will Only Hurt for a Moment
The Violence
Bloom
Guillotine
Servants of the Storm
Mirrorverse: Pure of Heart

DUNGEONS & DRAGONS

RAVENLOFT
HEIR OF STRAHD

DUNGEONS & DRAGONS

RAVENLOFT
HEIR OF STRAHD

DELILAH S. DAWSON

Random House Worlds

NEW YORK

Random House Worlds
An imprint of Random House
A division of Penguin Random House LLC
1745 Broadway, New York, NY 10019
randomhousebooks.com
penguinrandomhouse.com

Copyright © 2025 by Wizards of the Coast LLC.

Penguin Random House values and supports copyright. Copyright fuels creativity, encourages diverse voices, promotes free speech, and creates a vibrant culture. Thank you for buying an authorized edition of this book and for complying with copyright laws by not reproducing, scanning, or distributing any part of it in any form without permission. You are supporting writers and allowing Penguin Random House to continue to publish books for every reader. Please note that no part of this book may be used or reproduced in any manner for the purpose of training artificial intelligence technologies or systems.

RANDOM HOUSE is a registered trademark, and RANDOM HOUSE WORLDS and colophon are trademarks of Penguin Random House LLC.

Wizards of the Coast, Dungeons & Dragons, D&D, their respective logos, Forgotten Realms, and the dragon ampersand are registered trademarks of Wizards of the Coast LLC in the U.S.A. and other countries. © 2025 Wizards of the Coast LLC. All rights reserved. Licensed by Hasbro.

LIBRARY OF CONGRESS CATALOGING-IN-PUBLICATION DATA
Names: Dawson, Delilah S., author.
Title: Ravenloft: Heir of Strahd / Delilah S. Dawson.
Other titles: Heir of Strahd | Dungeons & dragons.
Description: First edition. | New York: Random House Worlds, 2025. |
Series: Dungeons & dragons
Identifiers: LCCN 2024054759 (print) | LCCN 2024054760 (ebook) |
ISBN 9780593599778 (hardcover; acid-free paper) |
ISBN 9780593599785 (ebook)
Subjects: LCGFT: Fantasy fiction. | Novels.
Classification: LCC PS3604.A97858 R38 2025 (print) |
LCC PS3604.A97858 (ebook) | DDC 813/.6—dc23/eng/20241129
LC record available at https://lccn.loc.gov/2024054759
LC ebook record available at https://lccn.loc.gov/2024054760

Printed in the United States of America on acid-free paper

2 4 6 8 9 7 5 3 1

First Edition

BOOK TEAM: Production editor: Jocelyn Kiker • Managing editor: Susan Seeman • Production manager: Erin Korenko • Copy editor: Laura Dragonette • Proofreaders: Debbie Anderson, Emily Cutler, Julia Henderson

Book design by Alexis Flynn

The authorized representative in the EU for product safety and compliance is Penguin Random House Ireland, Morrison Chambers, 32 Nassau Street, Dublin D02 YH68, Ireland, https://eu-contact.penguin.ie.

For My Chemical Romance
because they get it

DUNGEONS & DRAGONS

RAVENLOFT
HEIR OF STRAHD

In a land of seemingly eternal twilight, a black shape sliced across the thick gray clouds. The air shivered, just on the cusp of frost. Far below, the valley spread open like the pages of a moldering, forgotten tome that no one wished to read, that perhaps no one should've written in the first place. The colors were muted, forever in shadow, the grass more gray than green. Stark cliffs held it hostage, stern and forbidding, looming over a deep, secret-heavy forest as sharply cut as a pierced tin lantern.

Keen golden eyes focused on a brown lump splayed in the dying flowers, but upon closer inspection, the lump proved to be only a stag torn asunder, its ribs open to the sky like fruitlessly praying hands, all its warm insides and organs already devoured. The raven soared higher, out of reach of the land-dwelling beasts that might be looking for a snack. It knew this realm, knew its dreary villages and sagging churches and barren fields and crumbling farmsteads. Very little ever changed here. And yet—

The Mists shifted like a living thing. Borders dissolved and reformed. The forest lost and gained ground. Sometimes the Mists brought strangers. And the strangers . . . they had a way of changing things.

Wheeling past the village gates, the raven skimmed over the hunched fir trees and eyed a far-off castle with spires that clawed toward the milky sun. Far below, thick white fog writhed among the trees, slithering like a thousand snakes, hiding the ground. The raven gently landed among the swaying branches of a towering cedar and hopped down, branch by branch, until the fog withdrew like a foul tide, pulling back just enough to reveal exactly what the raven sought.

Something new.

Five figures lay on the ground, so still they might be dead.

From one perspective, it was the lead-in to a joke.

A human, an orc, a tiefling, a kenku, and a drow walk into a bar . . .

Of course, in the nearest village, the barman would likely pull a weapon rather than greet and serve such a strange and motley crew. They all seemed to be relatively young—adults of their species, but only just.

There were no bedrolls, no banked fires, no one standing guard in case danger struck. These figures, each wildly different from the next, lay on their backs, their soft bellies bared to whatever might find and disembowel them first.

The raven's feathers fluffed with concern. These people—they were not from this place. The woods were chockablock with hungry beasts, werewolves and regular wolves and bears and all manner of unclassified monsters, for those who ventured into the forests and discovered the monsters rarely lived long enough to tell anyone else about what they'd seen. This camp was no camp; it had no protections, and no one kept watch. The only witness was a raven—a raven that wasn't exactly a raven. A raven that had little power in this form. A raven tasked with delivering a very specific message as quickly as possible.

The decision made, the raven settled as high as it dared in the swaying branches.

"Caw!" it shrieked with all its power. And when that didn't do the job, "Caw! Caw-caw-CAW!"

Five figures woke up, and all hells broke loose.

Well, perhaps not *hells*.
But definitely a sort of . . . limbo.

1

FIELLE

"Ten more minutes," Fielle murmured, squeezing her eyes shut. "Ten more minutes, Father, please. Zerina kept me up past two making more vibrato potions, as well you know." And in a softer voice, "Because who cares what Fielle needs if the Golden Zerina wants to warble like a sparrow until dawn . . ."

But still the loud voice called to her, and she finally sat up, scrubbing a hand through her cropped platinum hair.

"Honestly, it can barely be dawn—"

Oh.

She was not in her crooked room in the attic gables of the Dancing Dragon, the tavern her family ran in Baldur's Gate. This was not her cramped, child-sized bed. She was not sweating beside the sturdy bricks of the kitchen chimney that made up one wall, and she was not being barked awake to use her artificer's magic to turn yesterday's sugar cakes into today's tavern special.

And the voice that had awakened her?

Not her father.

These people around her were not her family members, which was both a gift and a problem. They were strangers, and none of them human like her. Even for strangers, they were stranger than usual. And the place around them was strangest of all.

Fielle was on the cold, hard ground, surrounded by imposing trees and hemmed in by swirling white mist. Shadows reached long, greedy fingers from the forest, and the sky seemed caught between night and day, the breeze as cold and tremulous as a dead man's dying breath. She felt as if all good things had withered and died, the air stolen from her lungs. This place was hung with foreboding, as grim and still as a funeral. And she was not the only mourner. The people around her seemed just as confused as she was. Luckily, if there was one thing she was good at, it was making people feel at home while taking charge of the situation.

"I'm Fielle," she said cheerily, turning to the blue-skinned female tiefling next to her. "What's your name?"

The tiefling had an otherworldly beauty, with twisting indigo horns and flowing hair of shimmering turquoise. But the moment her red eyes landed on Fielle, her wild, lovely face contorted with hatred. She scrambled to her feet in her clattering armor, a magnificent silver glaive in her hands. The metal flashed in what little light there was, showing crescent moon designs etched into the blade.

"Why should I tell you? What do you want? Where are we? Is this some dark plot of Shar, to bring me to this twilight hell?"

Fielle held out her hands in a calming gesture, giving her a warming smile. "Whoa there, friend. All I want is a road home and to stay far away from that glaive. I'm as lost as you are."

"This is not the academy," a deep and learned voice remarked, and Fielle glanced to her other side and saw a character who would've made her do a double take back home: an unusually scrawny male orc gazing up at the chalky sky like a confused baby bird. "Possibly not even Silverymoon." Despite his gray skin and the two sharp white tusks jutting from his lower jaw, he had an elegant, thoughtful cast to his features. His voice was cultured and erudite, and his auburn hair was shaved on the sides and unruly on top.

When she noted the burgundy wizard's robe, crystal-topped staff, and general lack of weapons, she offered the orc the same welcoming smile the tiefling had rejected. "It doesn't seem like home, does it?

We're certainly not near Baldur's Gate. It's summer there, and I've never seen trees like this before."

"Nor the Silver Marches. Perhaps another continent? Or another realm? If only it were night, and the constellations were visible, we would know more. I must consult the—" He fidgeted with a heavy iron ring on one gray finger. "Ah, but the archives are out of reach. I am Rotrog of Argitau Academy. Is anyone familiar with this place?" He looked to the next figure. "You, kenku!"

The kenku blinked at the orc, her thin shoulders hunched up and her iridescent black-violet feathers ruffling around her neck. She was just a little smaller than Fielle and shaped almost like a human or a tiefling, but up close, her birdlike features dominated. When she noted everyone looking at her, her lemon-yellow eyes dilated in terror, and she pulled the hood of her sky-blue cloak up with talon-like hands so that only her sharp black beak was visible. "Me? Yes? What?" she chirped.

"Do you know where we are?" the orc asked, although it sounded more like a demand. "It was a corvid's cry that woke us. Was it you?"

"Woke me, too," she said, hopping back and forth as if on the verge of taking to the skies. Not that she could, of course; her kind had lost their wings long ago. "A raven, that was. Don't know where we are. I'm Kah. From Waterdeep. This is not Waterdeep. Not Waterdeep at all." Her beak clicked with worry, and she bowed her head, her fingers wrapping around an amulet on a leather thong around her neck. "Akadi, Lady of the Winds, forgive your humble servant, and deliver me where I belong!" She waited, eyes squinched shut, but nothing happened. Disappointed, the cleric tucked her amulet back under her cloak and looked up at the sky. "The gods—their reach is infinite, yes?"

"Just because a god's reach is infinite does not mean they are listening," the orc said flatly. "Or that they care in the least."

"Selûne may tolerate blasphemy, but I do not," the tiefling spat, her tail twitching like a snake about to strike.

The orc looked at the sky. "Should the moon ever show her face in this strange place, I'll apologize."

Fielle next looked to the last figure in the group and the only one not standing: a male drow who was either in a trance or unconscious. He was large and muscular, his skin purplish gray under his many tattoos, and his long, lustrous hair was snowy white and neatly braided on the sides. He lay on his back, his hands on the sheaths of his weapons, a smile playing at his sculpted lips. Upon his chest sat what appeared to be a raw turkey, but as they stared at it, two leathery wings unfurled to reveal the yawning, golden-eyed face of a hairless tressym.

"Aren't tressym supposed to look like cats with long hair and feathery wings?" Fielle whispered. "And be . . . pretty?"

"Supposed to," the orc mused. "I do believe those words no longer apply." He cleared his throat, a fussy sound indeed from an orc. "You, drow! Wake up!"

The tressym blinked at him as if rolling its eyes and stood to arch its back, opening its fleshy wings wide. Tossing a disdainful look toward the four strangers, the beast put its face very close to the drow's ear and yowled.

"Yes, what?" the drow barked, sitting up suddenly as the tressym leaped off him and sauntered a bit away to slurp at its pebbled wings.

"Some warrior you are," the tiefling mused. "Surrounded by danger and still you slept!"

The drow stretched, his shoulders creaking, and stood, looking about himself with amused curiosity. His weapons were held easily in his hands, as if they were part of his body. "If I'd been surrounded by danger, I would've woken up."

The tiefling held up her glaive. "And what does this look like?"

The drow looked critically around the circle. "A bunch of odd folk standing around a clearing, bickering over stupid things?"

The tiefling's mouth opened in retort, but then she cocked her head. "Can't argue with that, I suppose." She looked at each person in turn as if marking them for later execution. "My name is Alishai Moonshadow, and I am not to be trifled with."

"I am Chivarion Dyrr, and I would very much like to be trifled with," the handsome drow said. "I had trifle once at a Midsummer festival. It was delicious. Very fluffy. Quite sweet." He pointed at the tressym. "And that is Murder. She does not eat trifle. But she would try."

With an uncanny intelligence, the tressym bobbed her head and resumed licking herself in a personal area, one bony leg flung behind her neck.

"Well, then, so much for introductions," Rotrog said; Fielle got the idea that he was fond of the sound of his own voice. "From what I now gather, we have been drawn here from all over Faerûn for reasons we cannot yet fathom. No one is familiar with this place, and no one knows how they came to be here?"

He was met with shaking heads and looks of confusion.

"I shall assume, then, that we have been victims of fortune's folly, and I will bid you farewell as I seek a way back to my home."

"We're not going to stick together?" Fielle asked, stepping closer to the group.

Everyone around her had at least one weapon, if you included the orc's staff. Even the tiny kenku cleric had a mace and a light crossbow at the ready. Alishai and Chivarion were both bedecked with weapons and seemed quite eager to use them. But Fielle had never managed a weapon in all her life outside of a small knife she mostly used to peel apples. All she had was a heavy skirt positively full of pockets and her artificer's kit, which wasn't going to help unless someone in the present company needed to speak with more volume, loosen up a congested throat, or bake the best muffins in wherever the hells they were.

"Stick together? What good would that do?" Alishai sneered at Fielle, making her draw back. "We don't know each other. We don't need each other. And frankly, you would only slow me down."

"But people need each other." Fielle looked at each of them and found only contempt (Alishai the tiefling), haughtiness (Rotrog the orc), worry (Kah the kenku), and—well, Chivarion the drow was ignoring them all completely, digging through a belt bag and then shoving the remains of a meat pie in his mouth. "We have a better chance of survival if we stay in a group. And I might not be much of a fighter, but I'm good at managing and organization and building things, and I can cook, and my muffins—"

"Muffins! Pah." Alishai snorted. "Muffins will not make this right."

"They wouldn't hurt," Chivarion murmured, wiping crumbs from his lips.

"What we need," Rotrog said slowly, as if speaking to children, "is information. A clear path forward, or a way to gain knowledge of this place. A trail, a road, an inn. Even a local shepherd with wool for brains might offer insight."

As if in answer, the thick mist pulled back like a magician dramatically whipping away a cloth. Just beyond the forest stood a building, and although it had clearly seen better days, smoke lazily rose from the chimney in a thin white curl, suggesting the presence of the local denizens Rotrog had requested. The structure was one story, made of sturdy wood with a lean-to on one side and well-built fences on the other. It seemed old, but Fielle could tell from the materials and style of construction that the builder was a craftsman who had planned this place to withstand the test of time. Chains over the door suggested a sign had once hung there.

"There we go." Fielle nodded once and put on her most agreeable smile. "It's a bit theatrical, but at least it's something. I'll go ask where we are and how we might find the road home."

As she walked toward the building, she shivered. Her grandmother would've said that a goose had walked over her grave, but her grandmother was dead, and there were no geese here. No animals at all, not even the usual birdsong. The farther she got from the circle of strangers, the smaller and more alone Fielle felt. Sure, she'd tried to appear brave and confident, but something about this situation didn't sit right. Despite the smoke curling up from the chimney, this place did not feel friendly or welcoming. The chains creaked lightly in a breeze Fielle did not feel. Inside the house, something moved, perhaps the gentle scrape of a boot on old wood floors.

Taking a deep breath, somewhat annoyed that she was the only one plucky and assertive enough to do something, she stepped to the door and knocked.

There was no answer.

But, well, there had once been a sign, and a sign meant a place of business.

Again, that scrape of movement within. Subtle. Muted. Why didn't they answer?

Fielle's fingers brushed the door's rusted metal handle, and the ancient wood swung inward with a complaining creak.

"Hello?" she called softly. "Is anyone home?"

There were no lights shining within, no cheerful fire or happily glowing lanterns. The hearth held only dying coals. Shadows pressed in from every direction. Straight ahead sat a thick butcher-block table with a gleaming meat cleaver stuck deep in the red-stained wood. Heavy hooks hung overhead on thick chains. Fielle shuddered to see a rib cage hanging from one of the hooks, the meatless bones lazily swaying.

So it was a butcher shop, she thought, one that had closed long ago. The sound she'd heard must've been rats scavenging. Her heart sunk. There was no help here, no jolly innkeeper to offer a bath and supper and a map drawn on a scrap of leather to guide her home.

There—

In the corner, the scraping noise. Something lay there, piled on the ground. An old blanket, perhaps, fallen over a broken chair?

She took a step inside.

A scream pierced the silence.

2

ROTROG

Rotrog watched skeptically as the oddly chipper human woman with the disturbingly large eyes strode up to the building, her voluminous skirts flapping, and knocked on the door. When no answer came, she shrugged and tried opening the door, which gave way easily. The moment she disappeared inside, a scream pierced the air.

Rotrog knew that sound, and strangely enough, it wasn't the woman who had screamed.

It was a pig.

If there was one thing Rotrog knew, it was a pig's scream.

Not because he'd killed a pig, because—ew. He had never killed a pig. He had never killed anything. The only fights he'd ever fought had been with his wits, and even those, to his dismay, he had sometimes lost. But his dormitory at the academy faced out onto Bloodbath Alley, where a plethora of pigs were slaughtered before each market day. He was fairly certain High Mage Argitau had placed him there on purpose, just one more obstacle on his path to greatness, the squeals and screams haunting his dreams even when he put a pillow over his head. The High Mage drilled into him daily that he was only a mush-for-brains adept who would never know true power, and yet Rotrog knew he contained greatness. Still, just now, in this strange place, he felt like a brittle, silly, foolish creature, cruelly flung into an eerie and hostile world.

Nothing made sense. For example, why would there be a pig in the abandoned building, and why was it screaming?

Ah, yes, there it was. The human woman—Fielle—was screaming now, too.

And that frightened him very much.

Perhaps a tempest of fear and worry raged in his heart, but to the outside world—and these three remaining strangers—he wore the heavy, angry face of an orc. Turning on his heel, glowering, his hand clasping his staff and his chatelaine of tools and spell components jingling against his hip, he strode purposefully into the mist as if heading toward an important meeting, away from the cacophony that spoke of slaughter. The moment he was out of range, he would break into a run and find someplace to hide. There was something very unpleasant in that building, and he did not wish to know more.

The Mists swallowed him, and his skin shivered at the clammy touch of air that should've been formless but that seemed to be . . . alive. It invaded his nostrils, clawed down his throat as if to squeeze his heart into pulp. He couldn't see in any direction, couldn't even hear his own footsteps. It was as if the world had dissolved around him, leaving him in a miserable, oppressive, choking nothingness. Not that this world had been a pleasant place before that. There was something wrong with it, something dark and twisted and fundamentally flawed. No matter which way he turned, Rotrog felt as if malevolent eyes followed him, a crossbow pointed at his spine. The Mists were like a living, twisted thing that delighted in containing him, strangling him, devouring him.

Even though he couldn't see, he kept walking. And walking. And walking. Wherever he was, he would be farther away from the screaming, farther away from the peculiar collection of people who'd woken up in the shadowy glade with no clue as to their location or destiny. As someone knowledgeable in the arcane arts, someone perceptive and canny and wide-reading, Rotrog suspected that he was not on

Toril anymore and that the rules had changed. The problem was that he had no idea what the new rules might be and how his powers might rise—or fall—to the occasion.

Finally, the mist began to thin, and he gathered himself to run.

Except—

He was back in the glade!

He had walked directly and briskly away from this place and should've been at least a quarter mile away by now, and yet here was the acerbic tiefling paladin with her glowing armor, tail lashing as she glared at the building, enormous glaive in hand, the weapon akin to a sword on the end of a long stick. There was the drow fighter with a magnificent silver blade swinging at his hip and a small crossbow at the ready, the bolts dripping with some sort of poison, as he noncommittally chewed a hunk of cheese. His tressym flapped overhead, hovering over him like a malevolent demon, its long tail lashing. Even the crow-like kenku cleric held a mace that seemed far too large for her slender frame. All three of them stood at the door to the cabin, on the cusp of stepping inside. The human woman within had ceased her incessant screaming, which was a mercy.

The tiefling rounded on him. "Where did you go?"

"And why in the name of all the gods did you return?" the drow asked.

Rotrog raised his chin. "I was testing the Mists, but I suspect there is no escape. It's possible that they are enchanted, and no matter how far and fast you run, you won't make any progress."

Rotrog felt a twitch along the nape of his neck and turned to find the Mists surging against his back, almost pushing him toward the house. A howl sounded, and Rotrog took a step forward. Then another. He did not wish to be enveloped by the Mists for a second time, especially if there were wolves with more pronounced senses stalking him therein. He twisted the ring on his finger, polished the orb set in his staff with the elbow of his robes, and took another unwilling step forward.

"Akadi, Lady of the Air, grant me wings," Kah whispered to herself. "Let me join you in the updraft. I'll do anything—"

"Less mumbling, more getting ready," Alishai barked.

"Ready for what?" the kenku asked.

"We're going to have to fight. Either the wolves in the mist or—whatever is screaming in the house."

"I choose wolves." Chivarion winked at the tiefling and strode boldly into the mist, his tressym riding on his shoulder.

Rotrog began counting in his head. When he hit thirty seconds, Chivarion strode right back out of the Mists, his eyes wide with shock.

"How—?" he murmured.

"This place has rules of its own," Rotrog assured him, his experience with the wicked fog now firmly replicated and his hypothesis confirmed.

The Mists were so close now that it was just the four travelers and the house. Everything else was swathed in thick, sickly white fog. But . . . the mist was changing, taking on a tinge of green. Rotrog's lungs began to burn.

"The Mists! They're poisoned now!" he cried.

Alishai coughed and barked a curse, and all four strangers edged toward the house.

"Help!" Fielle called from inside. "I can't—"

Her voice was cut off suddenly.

"Shouldn't she be running outside while she screams?" Chivarion asked. "What's the point of screaming if you just stand there?"

"Clearly something has captured her. I cannot let her die," the tiefling growled. Glaive at the ready, she ran for the house.

"And I can't let her have all the fun." Chivarion followed with Kah on his heels.

It was only Rotrog still outside now, and the sparkling green mist plucked at his robes, promising a slow death by asphyxiation.

"Fools," he muttered.

But of course he knew that he was the fool, and an untested one at that.

The green mist enveloped him, and he held his breath and charged for the building's threshold. He'd expected to find a fight within, but instead, he found the others standing over . . .

Something.

It looked like an old pig hide, but it was thrashing and shaking.

Fielle was nowhere to be seen.

Other than the strange hide, everything within the building was still and silent. It was an abandoned butcher shop, as evidenced by the chopping block, cleaver, and old hooks hanging from the ceiling. Barrels crowded one wall, while a brown blanket covered what had probably once been a display case for meats. There was a closed door to the lean-to and another door that probably separated the shop from the family quarters. No one had been here for many years. The wood was silvery and splintered, and the sagging roof overhead let in flashes of the cloudy gray sky.

"Let's find the human and leave," Alishai said. "This place is drenched in old sorrow."

"D'you think she might be under that skin?" the drow asked. "Playing around?"

The skin continued to undulate and thrash, a muffled voice barely audible from underneath it. Chivarion reached out one booted foot and gently prodded the hide—

Which curled around his foot, enveloping his boot and yanking him to the ground. He kicked it, hard, and it screamed, but it was not the scream of a human woman playing a prank.

It was the scream of a dying pig, ferocious and angry and filled with rage, the same scream Rotrog had heard from outside.

"Get it off!" Chivarion cried.

Alishai lifted her glaive overhead, preparing for a mighty swing that might or might not take off the drow's hide-wrapped foot, but Rotrog stopped her with a hand.

"No. If you hit the drow's leg, we're down a fighter. And if the human is inside—"

"I have forsaken my vow," the tiefling finished. She lowered her glaive. "Thank you for stopping me, but do remove your hand if you wish to keep it."

The drow had his knife out and ready but didn't know where to cut to avoid hitting his own leg. As for the kenku, she waved her hands in the air, eyes closed, and murmured quiet words. Flames burst from her fingertips and enveloped the heaving hide, causing its porcine screams to ratchet up to an earsplitting level. The scent of barbecued pork filled the air. The hide quivered and shook, releasing Chivarion's leg and slithering off a thrashing form—

Fielle.

The human gasped for breath and struggled to sit up, panting and striking out with her hands as if she couldn't quite believe she was free of the flesh cocoon that had trapped her.

"What is it?" she gibbered. "What is it?"

Rotrog watched the thing squirm into a corner. It was a pig hide, with the head still attached and screaming. It moved jerkily, unthinking but desperate, trying to put out the fire that made its skin crackle like fatback in a pan.

"A pig, but . . . boneless," the orc said, horrified and yet still curious, in the way of wizards.

"It attacked me." Fielle's eyes bounced everywhere like a rabbit with no hole to hide in. "Wrapped me up. Crushed me. I couldn't get out. Couldn't breathe. Couldn't even grab my knife."

Alishai again raised her glaive, but this time, there was no drow leg, no missing human, just a hideous, boneless monster already turning to attack again. The glaive slashed through the tough hide and into the wooden floor. As the tiefling tried to yank the glaive back out of the boards, the hole in the flayed skin contracted around the glaive handle, wrapping steaming pigskin around Alishai's hands.

"Get out!" she screamed. "This is a place of death!"

Rotrog turned to find that the door had closed behind him. When he pulled on the handle, it wouldn't budge. Being a creature of desperation and cleverness, he ran to the door that had to lead to the lean-to. That door, at least, opened easily, and he charged through—

And ran face-first into something.

Someone.

A human, but . . .

Wrong.

Why was everything here so *wrong*?

The human was as solid as a tree trunk and smelled of mold and rot and the iron tang of old blood. Rotrog stumbled backward in the darkness, holding out his staff like a weapon.

The man—the dead man—

Shambled after him, groaning. The moment the tall, lurching figure stepped into the weak light, Rotrog knew he had finally discovered the missing butcher, and that the butcher had been dead for a long, long time. He wore a heavy leather apron over his faded, decaying clothes and carried another cleaver in a hand that was mostly bone. Half his face was missing, the wounds jagged, like the flesh had been eaten directly off his skull.

Rotrog had heard of this, had read about this in the academy's grimoires.

"Zombie," he breathed. Then, louder, so everyone would know, "Zombie!"

The zombie butcher took another uneven step, moving as if unseeing but still determined, blindly drawn to his prey. His eyes were gooey, hollowed-out cups, and his body moved with a disjointed, unnatural hitch. He staggered toward Rotrog, groaning, but one of his legs was at an odd angle. The moment he bumped into the counter, a second pig began screaming. What had looked like an old, moldering blanket was actually another boneless pig. It heaved and flapped to the ground, revealing a rotten face covered in maggots, its mouth open and squealing around a blackened tongue.

"Try the other door!" Rotrog shouted.

And Kah did, but that door, like the first door, refused to open.

They were trapped in here, trapped in the butcher's foul and blood-steeped workshop, and the butcher, for all that he was dead, still knew very well what to do with the weapon in his hand.

Rotrog was terrified to his very bones, but he would not simply lie down on the stained floorboards and die. He was a wizard! An adept of Argitau Academy! In no world did some shambling corpse best a wizard, even one whose skills, thus far, were mostly conjectural. With a mighty roar, Rotrog pointed his staff at the zombie, waved his fingers, and murmured a spell he'd never actually used with any success.

A bubble of acid slammed into the zombie's arm—

Where it exploded and hit the tiefling as she tussled with one of the pigskins.

She screamed and glared at him, her cheek blistered and raw. "Was that on purpose?" she demanded.

"Collateral damage," he corrected, realizing that he needed to practice his aim.

The acid was eating away at the zombie, but the main problem was that, unlike Alishai, the zombie did not care. It continued to shamble forward, and Rotrog stumbled backward, but then he heard one of the pigskins screaming nearby and decided that he'd rather face the zombie. After fumbling for the right page in his beloved spell book, he lifted his staff high overhead, where it got tangled up in the rib cage dangling from a hook. He struggled to regain control of his one true weapon, watching with growing terror as the zombie mindlessly stumbled toward him, the rusty cleaver raised in fingers of bone corded with blackened tendon.

But before the cleaver could fall, a silver blade slashed in sideways, neatly slicing the zombie's hand off at the wrist. The hand fell to the floor, taking the cleaver with it, and Rotrog jumped back to avoid losing his toes.

"You're welcome," the drow said, making a face at the gore marring his glorious blade. His tressym, Rotrog noted, was perched in the rafters. With another clean slice, Chivarion took off the zombie's other hand.

"Less manners, more fighting," Alishai snapped. "Help me with this boneless thing! It's got the human again."

"My name is Fielle!" the human said, punctuated with grunts as she struggled against the animated pig's skin. The hole sliced in its center had not lessened its rage nor its hunger. The pig's head jerked toward Fielle, ivory teeth snapping, and she put a boot in its eye, which exploded with black ooze and pus.

The other boneless pig was half crawling, half rolling across the floor toward Kah, who held a mace in both hands and muttered prayers as she gathered the courage to swing. Rotrog couldn't be certain, of course, but it looked like perhaps she had never been in a fight, either. When she finally brought the mace down, it struck the pig's face in the cheek, which erupted in a shower of degraded muscle, rotten teeth, and black bile. Taking heart, the kenku prepared for an even bigger swing, but as soon as she raised her mace, its sharp point drove directly into Alishai's shoulder as the tiefling murmured a cantrip. Alishai dropped her glaive and grabbed her shoulder.

"Oh, so sorry, this space—so much going on—" Kah chirped.

"Learn how to fight, blast you all!" Alishai growled. "Have some situational awareness! My cheek dripping acid, my— Have you broken my shoulder?" She shook her head. "Fools."

While Kah was apologizing, the pigskin monster wrapped a flopping trotter around her leg and jerked, dragging the little kenku to the ground. Alishai pulled out a knife and tried to find a good angle. There was a squeal and a thump, and Rotrog spun to see Chivarion slice off the head of the charred and boneless pig that seemed to have taken a particular liking to Fielle. Even with its head sliced away, the pig's flesh continued to writhe and flap, trying again to cover and smother the poor woman.

"Unggh."

The zombie—it was still crawling toward Rotrog. There was no one available to save him. Heart stuttering, he racked his brain for the right words, the right movement. This was a more advanced spell, one he wasn't accustomed to, but it would have a bigger effect. Magic Missile, High Mage Argitau said, never missed.

And it didn't.

The only problem was that in his haste and under such stress, Rotrog confused his two newest spells and instead cast . . .

Grease.

A spray of slippery liquid splattered over the tiefling, the drow, the human, and the kenku. And, yes, the two writhing, screeching pig corpses and the shambling zombie. What had been a fight to the death, a fight they were losing, became a fight merely to stay upright. The drow's sword flew from his hand. The tiefling tried to stand, slipped, and fell, her ankle making a horrific popping noise. The poor kenku's feathers were instantly sodden, weighing her down. The drow was calling Rotrog epithets from the Underdark that the orc had never heard before but that he was quite certain were the worst words in that unfamiliar language.

"Pick up a weapon and do something useful!" Alishai shouted from the ground. "Forget your stupid magic and hit something!"

But—no. All the weapons were covered in grease. Rotrog clutched his staff and swung it into the face of the zombie. The dead butcher absorbed the hit and slipped in the grease, falling onto its back, where it thrashed about like a diseased tortoise. As the tiefling struggled to stand, Rotrog swung his staff again and again, grimacing each time the crystal orb smashed into the zombie's skull. Fetid brain matter and black blood sprayed across his beloved robes, but the zombie—

He had to—

It had to stop.

There was a grunt to his side, and he found Fielle holding the drow's short sword in two hands, wrapped with a bit of her skirt. She clearly had no idea what she was doing, but she swung the blade at the nearest pigskin, slicing off a heavy trotter. The more cuts in the blanket of skin, the less harm it could do, apparently, as it was flapping and flailing but no longer had the same tensile strength. The drow, realizing he couldn't stand, crawled into the lean-to with his tressym right behind him, a look of absolute disgust on his sharp features as he kicked a chewing, chomping pig face out of the way.

The zombie was thrashing on its back. One pigskin had been reduced to flapping ribbons of disintegrating flesh. The drow was out of the picture, the tiefling was badly wounded, the kenku was scrabbling in the grease to pick up her mace, and the human was doing her utterly ineffectual best. Rotrog had to prove himself. He had to finish this.

Shifting his grip on his staff, he reared back and swung it at the remaining pig head with all his might.

3

ALISHAI

The idiot wizard swung his club like he was playing a game of stickball, slipped in his own blasted grease, and landed in a heap, tangled in his own oily robes. The animated swine corpse flopped forward and yanked viciously at the dark red fabric. It was a comedy. A tragedy.

Fools. They were all fools.

And they were going to get Alishai killed.

They'd already accidentally injured her—two of them!

She was the best in a fight—although admittedly the drow had merit—but she was injured. The pig thing was all torn apart, but still it tried to wrap her up like a rotting blanket.

The thick-headed drow would soon crawl right back out of the lean-to, she knew, looking bewildered even though they'd all tried various forms of escape by now and failed. These doors, like the Mists, were magical somehow, impassable and malevolent. The world had pushed them into this fight, and it was making damn sure they would finish it, no matter the cost. And now the grease made their weapons impossible to hold. Not only that, but Alishai's ankle was broken; she'd felt the bone snap. Her cheek still burned from the acid, a dull thud that made her skin swell with every heartbeat, and the mace had shattered her shoulder. She'd never known pain like this, and she'd known quite a lot of pain. At least this kind of pain, she thought, wasn't personal.

"Kah!" she cried. "Can you heal me?"

The kenku's head swiveled toward her and nodded eagerly. Her hands raised, dripping grease, and her black beak opened—

Right as the zombie, now standing and missing the top of its head, reached for her with handless arms and slipped in the grease, knocking her back to the ground. The crunch and gasp that followed suggested the slender kenku had broken some ribs, if not her back. Her hands were at the zombie's chest now, holding its blackened teeth away as they snipped and snapped in the air, ripping out a few facial feathers.

"Someone do something!" Alishai screeched. "I'll not die here, now that I'm finally free!"

Gods, she'd never been so furious. Whatever this place was, it was better than where she'd come from. Maybe it felt all wrong, maybe the air held a tang of darkness that she couldn't quite swallow, and maybe the sky would forever hide Selûne's face, but at least she was no longer trapped and caged, a tool of a cruel master. At least she hadn't—

No.

It was too late to feel regret.

Either she'd live or she'd die, and if she lived, she could worry about that later.

"Human, use the sword!" she barked.

Fielle obediently ran over and slashed at the animated pig corpse, but she might as well have been jousting with a butter knife. She clearly had never held a sword before, had no idea how to leverage a thrust or use her legs to improve her power. And because she was fighting a glorified chunk of skin, stabbing wasn't going to do much.

"It's not a broom!" Alishai shouted. "Swing like you mean it! Slash it to ribbons!"

Nodding with determination, Fielle looked at the sword . . . and threw it away. She reached for one of her pockets and pulled out a paring knife. Throwing herself onto the pigskin, she whittled away like it was an apple that needed peeling.

And much to Alishai's surprise, this tactic . . . was successful.

As each chunk of the skin was cut away, it ceased moving. Even as the greater piece kept bucking and slapping, Fielle would simply grab whatever reached for her and slice it nimbly off. This worked quite well until she got too close to where it held Alishai, and as the flesh ripped free, viscous blood splashed from the cuts. It was in her eyes, blinding her, burning her. Gods, what terrible luck was ruling over them today.

"Has the drow returned?" she asked.

"I suppose I never left," Chivarion said. He snorted. "I think I hate this place."

"You're going to die here if you don't get down to business. You're a warrior. So start—!"

"Warring?" He stood over her, looking down. "I might say the same to you."

"My ankle is broken, my shoulder is destroyed, and I'm blind with rotten blood!"

"Yes, well, everyone makes mistakes."

A feline yowl made him look away, and whatever he saw changed him utterly, filling him with a fiery rage. His teeth ground together so loudly Alishai could hear it.

"Murder!" he screamed, running off.

The thumps and tears she heard for the next few minutes told Alishai that whatever he could do with his sword, he could also do with his hands and teeth when the barbarian rage took him. There was one more groan, and then the room went blessedly silent of undead grumbles. She grimaced as she pushed herself up on one elbow to see the drow holding the zombie overhead, its body nearly torn in two and leaking foul, black tubes of intestines. The tressym sat on the ground nearby, licking at a small cut on its wing.

Lesson learned: Don't mess with the tressym.

An eerie clacking sound brought Alishai's attention back to the pig head that had once been attached to the hide Fielle was paring to shreds. Even unattached, it was using its putrid tongue to push itself toward her, its teeth chittering hungrily.

"Drow!" she barked.

But he didn't answer.

Ah, because he was murmuring sweetly to his stupid pet.

"Chivarion, a little help?"

"They hurt Murder!"

"They're going to hurt all of us!"

Alishai dragged herself along the ground through what was left of the grease. It had mixed with the dried blood on the floor to make a crumbly mud. She couldn't stand, could barely sit up. She could see only a little, if she squinted, but just as she'd known from the start, no one here was going to save her.

The drow was attending to his stupid pet. The kenku was struggling with a hanky-sized flap of pig flesh, her feathers so matted down that she could barely move. The wizard was jabbing at half of the zombie with his staff as if afraid to mar the shiny orb. And Fielle was crouched with her knife, looking like any kitchen maid working through a bin of potatoes.

"Selûne, Moonmaiden, She Who Guides," Alishai intoned. "Give me your strength, that I might live to prove myself to you. On my oath. By my steel."

The pig's head lunged at her, and she barely grabbed her glaive in time. The hot snout scraped against the glaive's handle. The fetid tongue felt around feverishly for flesh to devour.

Alishai was in so much pain that she could barely put words together. The world went red and began to spin, but the words fell from her lips in a slurred string.

"Moonmother, I know that I have transgressed, but I am your daughter, and—"

There were two pig heads now, degraded and eyeless but seeking and hungry. Back home, they would've been no match for Alishai Moonshadow. She wouldn't have even needed her glaive. She could've punted them like a child's ball, could she but stand. Here, in this strange place where the regular rules didn't work, weighed down by her sins, confused by the Mists, surrounded by clumsy oafs, coated in grease, broken, burned, hurt, bleeding—

Did she even want to fight?

Did she really deserve to live, after what she had done?

Perhaps this was what she deserved.

"Maybe this is my answer, then," she whispered, fingers gone sky blue where they clenched the glaive. "Maybe this is my just reward."

Somewhere outside her field of vision, someone began to mutter, almost as if they were chiding lazy children. A strange sound filled the room, a rhythmic flapping and slapping.

"Well, I never!" the orc wizard said fussily.

The world came into focus, and Alishai was amazed by what she saw. The useless human woman was waving her fingers like a conductor leading an orchestra, and all the little chunks of pigskin were acting like animated napkins, mopping up the blood. There was a jaunty energy to their work, as if they danced to a tune only Fielle could hear. Dozens of bits of skin wiping up the gory mess, sweeping it into corners to make rancid piles.

"Well, this is looking better," the drow said. "Time to pillage!" He went to one of the barrels collected in the corner of the room, and Alishai shouted, "No—!"

But it was too late.

The moment the barrel was open, Chivarion stumbled backward. With a loud, slurping plop, a . . . thing oozed out and landed on the floor. Alishai could see trotters, hooves, horns, skulls, legs, tails, organs. All the leftover parts of an animal a butcher might stow away to sell as dog food or soup bones. And just like the boneless pigs, just like the zombie, this swarm of animal limbs was hungry and filled with voiceless rage. It scrabbled and galumphed across the floor, a goat's mouth opening to spill black bile with a shrieking bleat.

And in that moment, Alishai decided she had had enough.

Enough.

Energy flowed into her muscles, and her pain ebbed away like the tide. She struggled to her knees and then her feet and prepared herself for the final standoff. Grunts and growls and whimpers and thuds emanated from the hideous ball of offal as it scuttled toward her. Her glaive felt solid and heavy in her hands, and she muttered a spell under her breath and put her entire body into the downward swing.

The silver blade glittered as it fell, and the moment it hit the meat swarm, thunder shook the room, along with a blinding light. The hooks and chains overhead clattered and danced. The pile of flesh and fluids was reduced to a crispy black cinder. All the while, Fielle's magic continued, the bits of skin cleaning as one with a rhythm that felt like the world's heartbeat. Alishai pivoted toward the next barrel, waiting to see what would happen, but apparently as long as no one bothered the barrels, the barrels would not bother them.

The wizard looked to be dead, just a gray lump under burgundy robes. The drow, at least, was doing something useful, stomping a pig face to death. The kenku was sitting, staring off into space, probably living through trauma for the first time and finding herself quite lost.

They'd won, Alishai thought. They'd fumbled, and they'd made plenty of mistakes, and she'd taken most of the damage, but they'd won.

And that's when something fell through the hole in the roof, wings flapping, and aimed for her face. She batted it away, and it landed on the ground, shook itself, and ran right back at her. It was—

Gods. A headless zombie chicken?

What had this butcher done in his life to steep this place in such fury?

"Here, chickie chickie," Alishai murmured as she stalked toward the ball of black feathers. They were coated in gore, sticking out at strange angles. The head was missing, accentuating the skinny strangeness of the neck. Alishai raised her glaive, and—

"Look out!" Fielle called, and Alishai spun just in time to stop a zombie from grabbing her.

This one was a woman—the butcher's wife? She wore a similar leather apron, and her face had likewise been eaten half-off. Alishai held her glaive against the zombie's chest, but still it managed to push her backward. She tripped on the chicken and fell on her back. Her glaive went flying and she landed hard, breaking something else. She felt every pain now, every bruise.

This place! Why did it hate them so?

Nothing back home had ever been so hells-bent on destruction; it was as if all the undead things were merely puppets dancing on someone else's strings.

Alishai struggled to keep the zombie from biting off her face. Undeterred, it changed focus and managed to get teeth around Alishai's wrist—

Gods, that was tooth on bone, scraping, burning, and—

She couldn't stop herself; she screamed bloody murder as a chunk of flesh was ripped off her wrist in a hot spurt of blood. An artery. She was going to bleed out here under unfamiliar skies, far from the moon and her comfort, far from everything.

"Hold still!" Fielle shouted.

"Tell that to the zombie!" Alishai shouted back.

With a grunt of effort, the human swung Alishai's glaive into the zombie's back, the blade nearly emerging from its rotten-pumpkin chest to slice into Alishai herself. The zombie's mouth flew open, releasing its grip, and Alishai managed to shove it off her with one arm. She tried to stand, but she couldn't even roll to the side.

The human woman just stood there like a fool, trying to pry the glaive out of the zombie, one foot on its back.

"Put down my glaive, damn you! Can you heal, or do you just make things worse?"

Fielle nodded and attempted a healing spell. Whatever concentration she needed, whatever energy was required, she didn't have it. She began to paw through her skirt, which seemed like a very ridiculous thing to do.

Everything hurt. The pain only grew worse.

"Heal me!"

"I'm trying, but—"

"Shut up."

Alishai attempted to heal herself, but she had so little energy left. The severed artery, at least, stopped pumping her blood onto the floor. Her head fell back, her hands in fists. The world was getting a bit . . . spinny.

"You might like to know the last zombie and the chicken are dead," the drow said from somewhere overhead. "I mean, they were already dead, but now they're . . . deader."

Everywhere here was somewhere else and nowhere and Alishai couldn't see much anyway. It was as if the mist had gotten into her eyes, her bones, her lungs. She felt so heavy, so slow, so tired. Her body wanted to sink into this strange, cold earth and rest, far from the reach of the undead butchers and their victims, far from everything Alishai had ever known and loved, although she'd honestly hated more than she'd loved.

From an eternity away, Alishai heard the drow say, "You, wizard. Heal the girl."

And then she heard the wizard say, quietly, "That's not how wizards work."

"Then the bird-person."

"She, too, is injured."

"So do we just watch them die?"

The wizard sighed. "The Mists have surrounded us, and the doors are closed. There's not much else we can do, I'm afraid."

"Bother. This is not what I wanted to do today."

"Not my first choice, either."

It filled Alishai with a ridiculous sort of anger, that her final moments might be spent listening to a drow and an orc complain about how boring her death was.

"I'm not dead yet," she whispered. "So please stop talking about me like I'm a bad play."

Warm glass touched her lips. Sweet liquid flowed down her throat, making her choke. She swallowed on reflex and was rewarded with a swell of warmth that traveled down her spine and into her veins, spreading with the soft pleasure of hot tea on a cold morning. It was like sinking into a perfectly steaming bath, and she closed her eyes and tried to savor it as every part of her went warm and numb and fuzzy in a wave from her head to her feet.

And then . . .

Nothing hurt.

She opened her eyes, expecting to learn what the afterlife was like, but instead, she found the worried face of the human staring down at her from overhead.

"You . . . you saved my life," Alishai croaked.

"It was my only healing potion, but it seemed preferable to the alternative. I'm sorry—"

"If you tell me you're sorry again, I'll give you something to be sorry about," Alishai whispered, fumbling over her tongue.

"You sound like my father." Fielle smiled, relief shining in her eyes. "Hopefully you won't swat me with the soup ladle. Do you feel better?"

With a shaky breath, Alishai closed her eyes to do a body inventory. Zombie-chewed arm? No longer pulsing with every heartbeat as her blood gushed onto the greasy floorboards. Ankle? Better, the bones no longer grinding. She could wiggle her foot. Cheek? If the acid burn was still there, it didn't hurt as much. Right shoulder? Didn't feel like a mace had shattered the bone.

But when she tried to sit up, the world spun, and she lay right back down.

"Better, but not to my usual degree."

Fielle sighed. "I'm—" She cleared her throat, thinking better of apologizing. "I'm not much of a healer. Not a lot of life-threatening wounds at the tavern. Just an occasional soup burn or twisted ankle. Maybe Kah has better skills."

The human disappeared, and Alishai had to be content with staring up through the holes in the roof at the gloomy gray sky. It almost felt as if someone else were looking down, watching her in return. There was no sun, no streak of blue, no cheerily singing birds. It felt as if the day were holding its breath and preparing, like a sullen child, to do so until it went unconscious.

If she twisted her head, Alishai could watch Fielle standing worriedly over the kenku, who seemed stunned. The human knelt and helped Kah to sit up, murmuring softly to her. Kah gave her thanks and fluffed her feathers before placing a hand over her heart. She said an unfamiliar word, and a light golden glow briefly shimmered around her. With a sigh of relief, she scrambled to her feet, good as new. Alishai was annoyed that she could not currently accomplish the same feat. At least it seemed like they were out of immediate danger. The drow had his sword in hand and was checking the newly opened closet door for further danger. At each thick-glassed window, the Mists curled close like a curious stranger, a solid wall of white enveloping them all.

"May I?" the kenku asked, appearing over Alishai with her hands outstretched.

Alishai had never felt so vulnerable in all her life, her entire existence held in the hands of a naïve artificer and a sky cultist. "I'll take what I can get."

Kah's hands were bony where they clutched Alishai's head, well away from her horns, and then she felt again that spreading warmth. The broken bones, the acid, the bite—it was as if they'd never happened. Between the potion and the cleric's touch, Alishai was as good as new. She quickly stood, her ankle solid and her wrist unmarred by so much as a scar.

"That's handy magic," she said approvingly. "As good as any I can do."

Kah bobbed her head. "Akadi bids us help our fellows."

Fielle held up an empty glass bottle. "Well, if we're going to be stuck here together in this malevolent place, it seems like we're going to need all the healing potions we can get. Anyone have a spare gemstone? Doesn't have to be fancy."

"We're not stuck here together, we're just stuck here," Alishai muttered. "And I, for one, am ready to find a way out. If only the doors would open, and the bloody Mists would go back where they came from."

As if on cue, the door opened, and the Mists pulled back almost as if creating a hallway, revealing a tunnel through the crepuscular woods beyond. A chill breeze swept in, ruffling Alishai's hair and making her teeth chatter and her tail twitch uneasily. A wolf howled, and then another. She knelt and grabbed her fallen glaive, its blade slick with various rancid fluids, and stared into the forest. The trees trembled, and the sky darkened as a figure strode toward them out of the shadows. The wind seemed to whisper around him with a tremulous groan.

It was a man, tall and sinewy with pale skin and long black hair, powerful and haughty. The cut of his clothes suggested he was wealthy, possibly royal. He paused just outside the door.

"Welcome, travelers," he said, his voice smooth and cultured. "To Barovia."

4

CHIVARION

Something was wrong, but Chivarion Dyrr couldn't quite put his finger on it.

Well, yes, most things were wrong in this place.

Everything, in fact.

It looked wrong, it felt wrong, it smelled wrong, it sounded wrong.

Hells, it even tasted wrong—he'd accidentally gotten some dirt in his mouth, and it was sour and full of rot.

Chivarion made a living as hired muscle. He'd been in so many fights with so many kinds of creatures that he'd given up remembering them all. He'd tasted plenty of blood, strictly by accident, as it tended to spray a bit. And yet, those wretched things they'd faced today, dead people and masses of dead animals and empty skins powered by rage—

He'd never seen anything like it, not aboveground nor below.

And now here came a strange man striding through the Mists—no, not a man. An elf! But not the normal sort of hideous aboveground elf, and not a beautiful drow; more like something in between. He'd appeared like an actor strutting onstage from betwixt parted curtains as if this were a perfectly normal thing to do. Chivarion looked him up and down, noting the well-crafted leather armor, the swirling gray cloak, and especially the shining scimitar hanging at the stranger's belt. There was something unusually dangerous about him, some animal sense that walked cold fingers up Chivarion's spine, screaming *Predator! Predator!* and keeping him on high alert. He would not turn his back on the newcomer, he knew that much.

"Who are you and what do you want?" Alishai all but spat, her glaive in hand.

"Have you learned nothing?" Fielle said softly, like a scolding mother. "Or must you still see everyone as an enemy?" Stepping forward, she dropped a passable curtsey, for a human, and said, louder and with a smile, "Greetings, sir. We thank you for your fine welcome."

The man suddenly stood before Fielle, for all that Chivarion had not seen him move through the butcher shop's open door. He reached for her hand and swept a bow as his lips brushed over her skin.

"Your beauty and grace bring honor to my lord's domain. I am Rahadin, chamberlain of Count Strahd von Zarovich, he who is master of this realm."

"A chamberlain! I've never met a chamberlain before, milord. Or is it my grace? Your grace?" Fielle shook her head girlishly, blinking her big eyes.

She was indeed very pretty, if one liked a woman to be diminutive and fragile, as most humans were. Chivarion preferred a little meat himself, but he was fairly certain the tiefling would bite off his fingers and the orc seemed terribly clumsy—not that that would stop him from flirting a bit when they weren't quite so distracted.

"I'm sorry. We've just barely survived a fight with—with monsters, and I haven't quite recovered. My name is Fielle Goldennote."

As if on cue, a wolf howl went up somewhere nearby. Rahadin nodded knowingly.

"There are indeed many dark creatures haunting these forests, Fielle. My master would hate to think of you facing such dangerous beasts."

"The wolves' howls are longer than usual," Rotrog said, sounding very much like a schoolboy taking notes. "And of a different tone. A local subspecies, perhaps? What is this place?"

Rahadin's eyes flicked to the orc in annoyance. "As I said, the land is called Barovia. We are in the Svalich Woods. And perhaps you are hearing our dire wolves. A large, hardy breed admired by those who enjoy the hunt."

"Oh, but they sound terrifying!" Fielle said as if conversing with a neighbor by the garden gate. "Is Barovia near the Sword Coast? My family will be looking for me, and I'd like to rejoin them as soon as might be possible. Not that your master's land isn't a . . . lovely place . . ."

The pause revealed the lie, but Chivarion understood. When conversing with little kings and their little men, it was best to compliment their holdings, no matter how pathetic. He'd learned that after a few rat-filled dungeon stays, and although he'd been told he was not an intelligent man, he knew well enough when to shut up.

Rahadin looked around as if noticing their surroundings for the first time. He raised one sharp eyebrow. "This derelict building does not show our land to its greatest advantage. It would seem you have a kind and generous heart, Fielle. I feel certain my master would wish to meet you and your friends himself." The scowling elf considered the strangers in the room, not quite meeting anyone's eyes but making it clear that he had marked each of them. "A storm is coming, and the forest will be treacherous at night. I would hate to think that something unfortunate might befall you. Please allow me to extend my master's invitation to join us at the castle."

"No!" Alishai barked.

Everyone stared at her.

She was trying very hard to say something with only her eyes, but they were all strangers, and thus her facial expressions were in a language Chivarion could not read.

"Let's not be rude," Fielle said, trying to smooth things over.

"I want to go home, not to a castle." Alishai's fingers gripped her glaive in an unfriendly manner. "Is there a port nearby? A road? Even an inn?"

Rahadin drew himself taller, glaring imperiously. "There is not. And I would urge you not to refuse my lord's hospitality. His displeasure carries certain . . . consequences in this realm."

Alishai glared rebellion at him. "The displeasure of some puffed-up, inbred lordling is not the only cause for consequence."

"Please!" Fielle said, glancing from one to the other. "Please. I'm so tired. We're not safe here. Let's go to the castle and eat and rest, and then we can consider our next step, whether together or individually."

"Do you have archives?" Rotrog asked, his eyes alight. "A library, perhaps?"

"My master keeps a study," Rahadin allowed. "And the castle's accountant has many tomes on hand."

"Mmm." Rotrog sighed blissfully. "Tomes. Surely we will find an atlas therein, and thus we might discover the most expeditious route home."

"Home," Kah echoed. "Yes, home."

"I still say no." Alishai slammed the butt of her glaive on the ground. "It's a waste of time. And what does some lordling want with the likes of us?"

Rahadin stepped back and bowed. His smile, Chivarion thought, was more threatening than his frown. "Count Strahd only wishes to offer tired travelers the warmth of Barovian hospitality. But of course your freedom remains your own. I'm sure you'll eventually find your way out of the forest. The village of Barovia is to the east. Perhaps the village inn will supply what we at the castle cannot." He reached again for Fielle's hand and held it as if to kiss her knuckles, but he seemed only to inhale her scent. "My lady, whatever you choose, we wish you a safe journey."

He bowed again—so many bows, honestly!—clicked his heels, and strode firmly out the door, disappearing as the opaque white fog fell like a curtain behind him.

"Must you be so aggressive, tiefling?" Rotrog whined, and Chivarion smothered a laugh.

"I know evil when I see it." Alishai glared at the mist like she might burn it away with pure hatred. "Something about that Rahadin is dangerous. His master probably more so."

"People in power are always dangerous," Chivarion said. "Especially when you make them angry. Insulting them, say. Turning down their invitations and such." He cocked his head at the tiefling and gave her his most flirtatious grin; she was acting so feisty, and he liked that. "Speaking of invitations . . ."

"The answer is no." The tiefling pulled a compass from a bag at her belt and turned until she was facing east. "This way, then. East, toward the village."

"Into the Mists?" Fielle asked softly. "The Mists that make my throat close up, like I might never sing again? The Mists that keep turning us around and around until we're dizzy and then spitting us right back out into this same clearing? The Mists that are sometimes poisonous? *Those* Mists?"

Alishai rounded on her. "If you haven't noticed, those Mists have completely surrounded us. So by your logic, going to your new beau's castle is just as impossible!"

"Beau!" Fielle squawked indignantly. "He's a chamberlain, and I'm a glorified tavern maid! He was being polite!"

"You're the only one he kissed."

"It was my hand! And I'm the only one not covered in blood."

"Because you can't fight!"

"I have other skills!" Fielle held up her hands, took a deep breath, and centered herself. "But as it stands, we needed a path, and you just told that path where to shove it."

"Look, you've done me a good turn, and I appreciate it, but our connection is done. The path lies east. For me, at least." Alishai's nose wrinkled up. "Ugh. Rhyming. That was an accident."

Thunder pealed overhead, heavy as a gong. The clouds darkened. They hung low, pendulous, threatening. Chivarion couldn't tell if it was due to night falling or the incoming storm. Probably both. He was well accustomed to being rained on, seeing as how he spent most of his time as hired muscle, guarding creaking wagons full of coin or cabbages, but he would've appreciated a drier, less blood-coated place to lay out his bedroll. And Murder's bedroll. And a roll, possibly full of cured meats and fine cheeses, although he wasn't sure he'd want to smell fresh pork for a while after today.

"I'll try for the village, too," Chivarion said, moving beside Alishai. Even if it wasn't the best plan, she was by far the strongest when not encumbered by idiots, and he would rather follow her to an inn than babysit the other three fools in this rotten abattoir. Plus, once she got away from them, she might warm up to *him.*

Alishai looked to Kah. "And what of you?"

Kah glanced nervously up at the disintegrating roof, but then again, she did most things nervously. "No birds fly in this forest," she chirped. "A bad sign, that. The village."

"Well, I'm for the castle," Rotrog said, although no one had asked him. As far as Chivarion was concerned, the wizard's bumbling with the grease had nearly killed them all. Maybe the inn would have a washerwoman who knew what to do about grease stains.

"I'm also for the castle." Fielle stepped closer to Rotrog. They looked absolutely ridiculous together, an enormous orc and a slight human woman, both equally useless.

"Ten minutes," Chivarion said.

Alishai's brows drew together. "Until what?"

"Until they're eaten by wolves if they go it alone. Would anyone care to wager?"

The moment he said it, he flinched, but no one noticed because the wolves had begun to howl again, right as the first splatters of rain plopped through the holes in the roof. It was like being pelted with tadpoles, and moving directly out from under the holes didn't help a bit. Within moments, the rain was unrelenting and slanting in every direction. There was no dry place in the butcher's cabin. The floor was turning into very bad soup. Chivarion desperately wished he'd brought a cloak.

"Well, then." Alishai nodded to Fielle and Rotrog and strode out the door and toward the misty forest, holding her compass out before her with an air of grim determination. Kah threw them a worried glance and hurried after her.

"Good luck. Happy hunting. Try not to die." Chivarion saluted the orc and the woman and took a deep breath before stepping outside.

As before, he was immediately encased in solid white mist. He put his hands out before him and threw out his senses, hoping to hear the tiefling's firm footsteps or the kenku's claws in the leaf litter. He heard nothing, nothing but the howls of wolves and the rumble of thunder.

"Where are you, pretty tiefling?" he called to Alishai, but there was no answer.

"Kah?" he tried next. "Anyone?"

The next bout of thunder shook his chest and rattled up through his soft boots. How had he not run into a tree yet or stumbled over a stump? How could the fog hide both the ground and the sky? Murder's claws dug nervously into his shoulder, and he reached up to rub the tressym's head.

"I'm sorry about this," he murmured. "Don't tell the tiefling I said so, but . . . well, this place—"

His next step brought him out of the Mists and into the clearing where they'd originally awakened. The rain fell in dingy gray sheets, slanting in sideways, soaking through his hair and making Murder growl. Alishai and Kah emerged on either side of him, and they all stood there in utter shock. Standing by the butcher shop was the last thing Chivarion Dyrr had expected to see:

A grand coach pulled by four black horses, stamping their feet as they waited.

5

KAH

Kah almost enjoyed the Mists. She had always dreamed of flying through a puffy white cloud, and this was as close as she would likely ever get. She held out her arms and gracefully waved them up and down, pretending they were real wings, covered with primary feathers that gleamed iridescent indigo in the sunlight. She could almost feel the swell of an updraft, the wind rippling through her cloak, the world spread out below her as she soared, free and unencumbered, finally truly blessed by Akadi—

She stepped out of the mist and into a fierce squall. Her arms went instantly, sheepishly to her sides. Luckily, no one had noticed her foolishness. They were all shielding their eyes from the onslaught of stinging rain, staring at a coach that had no business in this forest, no business at all.

"Where did that come from?" Alishai asked as she stormed out of the wall of white.

"From the Mists, same as you," Fielle said smartly from the door of the butcher shop, shouting against the rain.

Kah admired that—the way the human woman just said whatever she liked. Even though she was practically defenseless, still she stood up to the fierce tiefling. Assertiveness was not a trait Kah possessed. Whenever Alishai looked at her, she wanted to pull her hood down and disappear. Not only was Fielle confident and friendly, but she had done her best in the fight even though she had no skills with weapons or defensive spells. And she had given Alishai, an aggressive stranger, her only healing potion. She was kind, and this was not a kind place. That was worth something.

"How long has the carriage been here?" Alishai demanded.

"Only just arrived," Rotrog said.

As if he didn't even feel the rain, Chivarion walked around the coach, which was fancier than most of the ones Kah had seen back home in Waterdeep. The ink-black horses were sleek and well mannered, barely twitching their tails as they waited in the raging storm, which was good, because there was no one holding their reins. Kah didn't know much of horses, but she understood that this was unusual.

"Does a ghost drive it, do you think?" Chivarion asked, running a hand down a horse's sleek wet neck.

"Does a ghost," Alishai asked slowly, "drive the coach? Because I would humbly suggest it is more likely magic."

Chivarion held up his arms to the storm. "Magic—bah! Does this place not seem haunted to you? Does it not constantly feel as if a dagger is aimed at your heart? Were those not zombies?"

Alishai blinked against the rain. "I want to argue that, but I cannot."

"It is magic," Rotrog admitted, "but that is no less sinister an answer."

"It isn't a nice bit of magic," Kah agreed. "Mean magic, that."

Thunder growled overhead, and a spear of lightning arced down to strike a nearby tree in an explosion of white-hot heat that made Kah double over, her arms shielding her face. The tree split in two with a screech as flames bloomed from its heart. Half of it slowly, slowly fell, and she and the drow and the tiefling were forced to run closer to the coach unless they wanted to be simultaneously crushed and set afire. Oddly, the horses did not react. To anything.

"Back into the murder house, or do we prefer the ghost-driven fancy man wagon?" Chivarion asked.

Another grumble of thunder, and lightning struck the roof of the butcher's cabin, setting it aflame. Rotrog and Fielle ran out the door and were instantly soaked. Rotrog stopped just beyond the threshold, but Fielle took a few halting steps toward the coach as the cabin's fiery roof collapsed with a mighty whump. Two doors swung open—one on either side of the coach—and the human stuck her daisylike yellow head inside.

"There's a note," she said, holding up a heavy white envelope, careful to keep it inside the coach where it wouldn't get soaked by the rain. She leaned inside to read it and then clambered up the step and into the interior, where she peered out at them. "It's from Count von Zarovich himself," she called. "Extending a more formal invitation. And I think we should take him up on it."

"That's only because you're soft and weak and will die out here tonight, otherwise," Chivarion called over the steady thrum of the rain.

"Seems like a good enough reason," she replied. "We've nowhere safe to rest. There's enough room for everyone inside. Let's at least stay at the castle tonight. Perhaps things will look different tomorrow when the sun is shining. Nothing good can come of remaining where we are."

Kah did not need further inducement. She scrambled up into the carriage, settling into a far corner. It was an immediate relief, being out of the rain. Akadi was the goddess of fair skies, but also of tempests, and Kah understood that this weather was a message that could not be ignored. As Master Ondraz said back home, one must remain as flexible as the willow if one wished to bend in the winds of the harshest storms. Master Ondraz also said that life was a journey and the traveler an artist; Kah had never felt much like an artist, but she knew that creativity was important, and it just seemed uncreative to stand outside by a burning building when a more pleasant method of travel was available to take her on an adventure. Besides, Fielle was right—nothing worse could possibly happen to them, not after being attacked by undead swine and angry butchers.

The coach was an opulent treat, with seats of rich red leather. Heavy drapes covered the glass windows, blocking out their view of the gloomy rain, and lanterns lit the space warmly. There was plenty of room, even for the orc. He was the next to struggle up into the conveyance, tripping on his robes as he did so. Settling into his own corner, he dragged his thick gray fingers over the tassels and woodwork, humming with pleasure at their beauty. The drow joined them shortly thereafter, throwing himself into the center of a bench seat and settling back with his knees spread wide. His tressym crept down from his shoulder to work its claws against his leg, making him wince as the beast settled in.

Only Alishai was left, scowling at them from the rain, the tree merrily on fire behind her. As Kah watched, a wolf materialized out of the mist, then another. Alishai looked over her shoulder and startled. It was perhaps the first time she'd seemed . . . scared.

"Fine, fine," the tiefling grumbled, feigning insouciance. "I get the message."

She climbed into the carriage and took her seat, but she crossed her arms and scowled, making it clear that she wasn't happy about the situation. Kah had seen this attitude in so many people over the years, as if they wished to argue with reality and didn't understand that reality would always win. The Companions of the Summer Wind— Kah's particular sect of Akadian worship—preached that change was constant, freedom was the right of all, and you couldn't fight air, much less a storm. Alishai had not learned that lesson, and perhaps she never would. Both carriage doors gently closed and latched themselves, and with a jangle of traces and the squeaking of wheels, the coach took off despite lacking a driver.

"So do we all agree that this is dangerous?" Alishai said.

Chivarion leaned his head back, his arms across the back of the seat. "I just assume everything is dangerous, darling. Saves time."

"In such a rural area, perhaps it is the custom for a lord to invite newcomers to his manse?" Rotrog said. "It does seem hospitable."

"It's not normal," Fielle said. "I've never heard of a single nobody invited to meet a count. But then again, I've only ever lived in a big city, so, as you say, maybe it's a country thing." She read the note again, and Alishai snatched it from her hand.

"Unto the visitors in my land, Count Strahd von Zarovich, Lord of Barovia, sends fondest greetings." Alishai shook her head. "Fondest? A driverless

carriage and a creepy chamberlain don't seem fond to me." She continued reading, adding a stilted tone, *"Fairest friends, I pray you accept my humble*—yeah, sounds real humble—*hospitality and dine with me tonight. It is rare we receive visitors, and I do so endeavor to make your acquaintance. The carriage shall bear you to the castle safely. I await your arrival with pleasure. Your host, Strahd von Zarovich."* She tossed the heavy paper to the carriage floor. "Fondest? Fairest? I didn't know the aristocracy was so very fond of hyperbole."

Rotrog eagerly picked up the note and inspected it, going so far as to sniff it. "An unfamiliar scent in the ink. Gall and . . . iron? Perhaps he will share the recipe." The orc tucked the note into his robes, Kah noticed. Perhaps, like her, he enjoyed trinkets. The chatelaine hanging off his belt with all its bits and bobs had definitely caught her eye—she saw sticks, wire, bottles, scissors, and several small velvet bags.

The party went silent as the carriage rolled swiftly along. Kah reached for her curtains to look out, but she saw only the swirl of the menacing fog. She wondered for a moment if it might spit the carriage right back out at the butcher's cabin, but soon they emerged from the mist and into an entirely different sort of evening. The rain and storm were gone, although the heavy gray clouds remained, pressing down overhead. There was no paving, but the trees grew around a natural sort of path, just wide enough for the carriage to avoid having its paint scraped by rogue branches. Up ahead, Kah saw another clearing and a gray stone road. She also saw a village, small and sad looking, not lively at all. The horses turned right, away from the village and onto the road.

The furtive noises of the forest were replaced by the heavy clatter of iron wheels on stone. The horses trotted faster now, as if just barely held back from a run. The carriage bumped over a bridge, and the forest closed in again. Kah preferred open air to the way these trees loomed overhead. She longed to be up in the wide skies and hated any reminder that she was cursed to the ground. She let the curtain fall closed and slid down in her seat.

"Would anyone care to exchange riddles?" the orc asked.

"Yes. I'll begin. Why won't the orc shut up?" Alishai spat back.

Chivarion raised his hand. "I know, I know!" He paused, thinking. "Because no one has cut out his tongue?"

Rotrog sat back and caressed the orb on his staff as if he were petting a cat. "I am accustomed to less aggressive company."

"Is that why you nearly got us all killed in there?" the tiefling asked. She rolled her shoulders back as if testing to see if they still hurt.

The orc's eyes widened. "Spells sometimes go awry. That is the way of spells."

"That is the way of the *spellcaster*," Alishai corrected. "If you do a grease spell, you're going to get grease."

"We all made mistakes," Rotrog continued. He nervously twirled the large ring on his finger.

"Well, some more than others." Chivarion put a possessive hand on his tressym's back. "Say, what's that big ring you're always fiddling with?"

The orc shoved both his hands into his robes. "Just a ring, and none of your business."

"Testy!" the drow said with a laugh. "I guess you can bite, when you want to. Not that I mind."

Fielle leaned forward, hands out in a calming gesture. "Friends, there's no point in arguing over the past. We were all caught off guard. Who could expect . . . what we faced back there? I'll be the first to admit that I've never been attacked before, and that it seemed especially frightening because our opponents were undead and couldn't listen to reason. I know I made mistakes, and I'm sorry for any pain I caused anyone."

"You did your best," Kah said, because she could tell the human woman really was sorry. "And you cut up the skin-thing. Clever with a knife, you."

Fielle's smile was radiant and warm. "Oh, that is kind of you to say! If you can carve bacon, I suppose you can carve, um, pre-bacon."

"Speaking of which, how did you end up wearing that pigskin like a caul?" Chivarion asked.

"It fell from the hooks." Fielle looked away. "It was awful. Like being suffocated by—"

"Ham?"

"More like an angry blanket. I couldn't breathe. And it was crushing me."

"Why didn't you just slice it open from the inside?" Alishai asked.

Kah didn't think the tiefling meant to sound accusatory, but almost everything out of her mouth was sharp and acerbic.

Fielle looked down at her hands. "I panicked. It was dark. There was no air. I was being squeezed half to death. My hands were nowhere near my knife pocket."

"Well, don't you know any cantrips?"

"Like I said, I panicked, and most of the spells I know off the top of my head are to help around the tavern back home. I suppose I could've made the dead pig sing soprano, but it wouldn't have done me much good! By the gods, you're cruel." Fielle put a hand over her mouth as if surprised that she'd said anything spirited at all. *Good for her*, Kah thought. "Now, I understand that you're angry, and that the fight did not go the way that you, personally, would've preferred, but we're trapped together for the time being, and I'd appreciate a little less blame and a little more understanding. Is Selûne not a goddess of compassion and grace?"

Alishai's lip curled. "Do not speak of my lady—"

"Let all on whom Selûne's light falls be welcome if they desire," Fielle said.

The tiefling glared, her brow drawn down. "You are no Selûnite."

"One does not have to follow a god to believe in her. I have heard enough of Shar's darkness to know that Selûne is good and true."

Alishai looked as if she wished to retort but could not; there was nothing to fight in the human's statement. Kah had heard of Selûne and had to agree that she seemed a pleasant enough deity, although she was nothing compared to Akadi. The human was good at defusing conflict.

Kah stole another look outside and saw that night had fallen. The darkness was impenetrable, and there were no stars, no hint of the moon, no sparkle of lanterns in castle windows. It had been such a long, strange day. She had awakened at dawn in the dormitory, gone to morning salutations to chant with Master Ondraz, taken her turn in the monastery gardens, gone out into the busy afternoon streets to find—

No. Best not to think about that.

It had almost happened, but it hadn't happened, and then she woke up here.

Could the two things be connected?

No. Surely not.

Perhaps this was a dream.

Or more likely a nightmare.

All Kah could do was keep moving forward. She would eventually learn what Akadi, Queen of Air, had in store for her faithful follower. Perhaps this was a sort of test. Maybe this was her life experiment. In any case, Kah would do her best to remain free and pursue her dream, as that was what her lady commanded her to do.

This count, this Strahd—perhaps he had unique powers that could help her reach her goals. Perhaps other places had other rules.

Kah settled back into her corner and let the pleasant rumble of the carriage lull her to sleep. If her companions were determined to argue, she wasn't going to miss anything anyway. This was a new adventure, she told herself. A dreary one, but an adventure still. She would know more when they arrived at the castle. It couldn't possibly be worse than the forest.

6
FIELLE

The air inside the carriage was as thick and gloomy as the clouds outside. The tiefling seemed determined to be angry and blame others for their chaotic afternoon, while the drow seemed to possess that unique combination of density and danger that made him truly enjoy stirring the pot. The orc watched everything play out with his priggish nose in the air, which reminded Fielle all too much of her sister, the great Golden Zerina. But Zerina, for all her many faults, had genuine talent, whereas the orc seemed puffed up for nothing. Even though she preferred to look on the bright side of things, him spraying the room with grease during the fight had very nearly been the end of them all—and it had already been a rather horrid day that had begun in annoyance after far too little sleep. Fielle, like the orc, had no experience fighting, and yet she felt that she'd at least redeemed herself, thanks to her healing potion and experience with paring potatoes. She wanted to stay awake and keep tempers at bay so that no one would get too bent out of shape, but she was exhausted to her aching bones. The kenku had the right idea, going to sleep.

Except whenever Fielle closed her eyes, she saw the blood-flecked pig corpse reaching for her, heard its rage-filled screams, felt the bone-crushing embrace of its sour flesh and the renewed terror of being trapped in the darkness of its embrace. There was something wrong with this place—this world—where they had all awakened together, surrounded by mist. It was dark and rotten and weirdly theatrical, as if they were all acting out parts in a play directed from the shadows. Was it some kind of afterlife—a place of punishment? Was she here because of what she'd done—

Perhaps.

She'd let her baser instincts and long-simmering jealousy take over, and even if the deed had not seen completion, the damage had been done. After years of contemplation, she'd made a choice that could not be unmade.

Maybe she deserved what she'd faced today.

Maybe being caught in this nightmare was her punishment.

Or maybe, and yes, this was her optimism talking . . . maybe it was a chance to start over.

Here, there was no Golden Zerina, there was only Fielle.

Here, there was no family hierarchy, no money-hungry patriarch, no shouting, no endless list of chores.

Here, she was in the fanciest carriage she'd ever seen, on her way to meet a count.

A count!

It was time to look on the bright side. Fielle loved a good romance story, and if the chamberlain was that dashing and well heeled, she imagined this Strahd must be an even finer specimen. She pictured him as a lonely young man, willowy and fair, with kind blue eyes like the sky and honey-gold curls. His castle would be a lively place of beauty, peace, and freedom. Someone else would scrub the ovens, bake the food, wash the dishes, peel the potatoes. With no Golden Zerina, there would be no reason to keep Fielle up all night crafting potions and creating machines to help the family star shine all the brighter, draining Fielle's youth and beauty so that her sister might earn a few more gold coins for their father's hungry purse. Here, Fielle might be the— What was a count's wife?

A countess?

Yes, and she would grow her hair out long and have fat babies and go on picnics.

That was a better future than she'd ever dared to dream about back home.

So what if today had been gloomy?

The sun would come out eventually.

Spring would gently fall, and flowers would run riot in Barovia, and they would travel the glorious countryside together, stay at the count's seaside manse, ride side by side on snow-white horses, laughing.

"Why are you grinning like an idiot?" the tiefling asked.

"What?"

Fielle blinked herself back to reality.

Everyone was staring at her, except for Kah, who was now sleeping with her head against the drow's beefy shoulder. He and his tressym did not seem to mind, and the kenku's fluttery snores sounded like a dove cooing.

"I asked why you're smiling like an absolute fool?"

"Was I? I was just lost in thought, I suppose."

"Nothing in this general area is worth smiling about. Do you know something we don't know? Is that it? Do you know this Strahd?"

Fielle crouched back in her seat, away from the tiefling's fury. A tiny spark of rage flared in her own heart, but she ignored it and met the tiefling's gaze. She saw pain there. "Why are you so angry?" she asked softly. "Why are you lashing out? I'm on your side."

"Not necessarily." But Alishai looked away, discomfited.

"I am, believe me. Bad things happened to you today, but they were accidents, and cruelty is not the answer. You're like a dog with its leg in a trap, snapping at everyone who comes near. What can I do to prove to you that I mean you no harm?" Fielle reached into one of her skirt's many pockets and produced a bit of jerky.

After a few moments, the tiefling snatched it away and tore at it with her teeth.

As she chewed, Fielle went on. "Of course I don't know what's happening. I don't know this count any more than you do. I told you—I'm from Baldur's Gate, and we don't know where we are now. I just know that castles generally mean safety and resources, two things we desperately need."

Alishai had finished the jerky, and she slumped down in her seat. Fielle handed her another piece of jerky, and she considered it. "This is good jerky."

"I'm a good cook."

The tiefling heaved a sigh. "I get mean when I'm hungry. I . . . offer my apologies. I've been rude. You did save me today, and none of what happened was your fault." She said it like each word cost her, but Fielle immediately brightened up. If the surly paladin could be plied with food when angry, that made Fielle's life a lot easier. She had long ago learned how to butter up the regulars of the Dancing Dragon, and she would find a way to win over Alishai's hard heart, especially if they were going to be stuck together.

"I appreciate that," Fielle said with a warm smile. "I'm glad we're on the same side."

The group was quiet for a while; heavens knew they all had to be exhausted. The drow dozed, and the orc muttered to himself; Fielle thought perhaps he was running through spells. Alishai seemed far more relaxed now that she had some food in her.

In the pleasant quiet, Fielle thought she heard violins and drums, and, perplexed, she peeked out the curtains of her window. The road ran alongside a shimmering lake of black water that filled the horizon. The only source of light was a single bonfire. Colorful wagons ringed it, and people sat on benches and logs, eating and drinking and tapping their feet to the lively music. One old woman's thready voice sang in a pretty, guttural language. It was an enchanting scene right out of a pastoral painting, and Fielle was a little disappointed as the carriage hurried onward, leaving the warm scene of family and celebration behind.

They were back in the woods now, and to a city girl gazing upon them on a moonless night, they looked like any other woods, all the trees looming like ruffians in dark alleys. She could've sworn she saw a giant spider at one point, but it had to be a trick of the light, just a jumbling of branches, perhaps. With a little swoop, the carriage went over a curved stone bridge, and Fielle heard the thunderous gush of a waterfall. Unfortunately, she was on the wrong side of the carriage to see the falls herself, and since Kah was asleep and Rotrog was lost in his muttering, she couldn't politely ask them to open their curtains.

On the other side of the bridge, they entered another blanket of mist. For several long minutes, Fielle saw nothing but solid gray. She put a hand to the window and felt the chill seep through the glass and into her skin. Moments later, the mist dissipated, revealing a land that had become entirely more threatening. Sharp, stark mountains rose up, and if before the trees had loomed, now the mountains took that to a whole new level. Everything here seemed to press down, to lean, to threaten. Dark sky, dark mountains, dark trees, dark lake, dark dark dark. No stars. No moon. The opposite of what was in her heart. Fielle loved nothing so much as a sunny morning, a blue sky, birds merrily singing as she tended the herbs she cultivated in window boxes all over the tavern for use in the kitchen. She was a bright, happy creature, and this domain seemed uniquely created to oppress her and make her feel . . . other.

She let the curtain slip closed. These mountains suggested the count's castle was not, in fact, in a verdant valley carpeted in flowers. Fielle's hope began to die a slow and agonizing death. The clop of hooves on road changed abruptly to the scrape of stone and scree. The carriage bounced, wobbling a little. Fielle closed her eyes and gripped the edge of her seat, quite certain that if she looked out the window, she'd find they were hanging off the side of a mountain, leaning over an endless drop. Something in her heart grew more and more frightened the closer they came to the castle, and she could not point to a real reason why.

"What has scared you?" Alishai asked. "Something outside?"

Fielle shook her head. She was getting queasy. "I don't know. I'm just filled with this strange foreboding. There's a . . . theatricality to this place, have you noticed? As if we are but mice being herded into a trap by a bored cat with all the time in the world. As if everything has been planned around us, for us. The magic does not feel very nice."

"Nice? When has anything ever been nice?" Alishai opened her curtain and looked out, then swiftly shut it. "If what you say is true, then whatever magic this carriage possesses will keep us safe. It has to. Wizard, is that not the way?"

Rotrog's eyes flicked to her as if she were an annoying fly. "I do not often say this, but this kind of magic is outside of my bailiwick. Considering the horses are calm and the carriage is old but in good keeping, one must assume that they have made this journey before." He peeked out his own window. "The road forks, and there are massive iron gates in the other direction. Closed. So this Strahd must appreciate his privacy. He has taken care to make the path to his home treacherous."

"I knew this was a bad idea," Alishai muttered.

Fielle had thought it was a good idea, but that was a lifetime ago. All her pluck had drained away, and she simply felt like a rabbit huddled in a hawk's shadow. The moment they'd passed through the mists near the waterfall, she'd felt . . . repelled.

And yet . . . she had to look out the window again. She had to see what was coming.

Right as she risked a glance, the road curved around a peak, and Fielle was greeted by the stark visage of the most horrid castle she could imagine. It looked . . . gods, it looked like it was clawing at the sky, its sharp shadows stabbing into the gray clouds, piercing the sky's very heart. These pointed towers and heavy ramparts suggested not a life of joy and plenty, but of constant attack and defense. Fielle could almost feel the blood soaking the stones, the many lives that had been lost here. The road straightened again, the castle disappearing, and she wished she could close her eyes and make it disappear forever.

There would be no verdant valley, no white destriers, no fond picnic.

And Strahd, whoever he was, could not possibly be some innocent boy with a heart full of love. There was no way anything sweet and innocent could dwell here long.

Soon the horses' hooves clattered on stone again, and then the carriage jolted to a stop. One of the horses stamped a foot imperiously, and both doors sprung open.

No one in the party moved.

"I take it the horses won't return us to the murder cabin?" the drow said, waking and stretching and taking up a great deal of space doing so. He tapped Kah on the arm, and she blinked sleepily and rubbed her eyes.

"I worry that if we don't get out, the foul magic will force us to do so. Unpleasantly." Rotrog sighed and was the first to exit the carriage.

Alishai followed him, then Chivarion and Kah. At last only Fielle was left within. The horse stamped again, and the carriage jolted with equine annoyance. Fielle did not think herself a brave person, but she had never been so terrified of anything as she was of setting foot in the castle.

Something tickled her shoulder, and she turned to find a giant millipede crawling down from the red leather seat. With a shriek, she fell to the floor of the carriage, batting the hideous thing away. Another one plopped down from—somewhere—and crawled toward her, jaws clicking. She practically tumbled out of the carriage in her haste to escape it, landing hard on her hands and knees. The moment she was on the ground outside, the horses took off at a terrified gallop, the carriage jouncing along madly behind them.

Chivarion held out a hand and pulled Fielle up to standing. The world was not any more comforting from that height. They stood before a stone guardhouse and a rotting wooden drawbridge, which spanned a chasm Fielle didn't want to consider. Winds whipped at her skirts as if trying to pull her down off the cliff. Beyond the rusted chains of the drawbridge, the entrance to the castle offered no comfort. This was no grand, welcoming edifice, no vaunted, well-scrubbed entryway. It looked abandoned and unloved. Even the raised portcullis appeared to be rusted in place, and yet, at the same time, seemed as if it might suddenly fall down as unwary travelers passed beneath it, hungry for their blood.

"Is there no other way in?" Fielle whispered.

"I could carry you," Chivarion said, looking her up and down. "You can't weigh more than a sack of feathers."

"Or we could just leave." Alishai turned to look back at the road. "We could probably walk back down the mountain by morning. We could stop at that encampment we passed with the wagons around the fire. They will likely know more of this place. And have food."

"Yes," Fielle quickly agreed, remembering the golden warmth of the campfire and the merry tune of the songs. "Please."

A howl went up, and slinking figures appeared from the shadows of the road: four wolves, and large ones, their heads down and their green eyes glowing. They stalked forward on stiff legs, growling, and spread out as if to cover all known methods of escape.

"I see it now. Your theatricality. There does indeed seem to be some intelligent force at work," Rotrog said thoughtfully. "At each point, we have been herded from one location to the next. If this is a play, it's a very bad one."

"I, for one, do not like to have my hand forced." Alishai held her glaive at the ready.

Chivarion shrugged and gamely drew his sword. "Killing things is my job. No force required. And although I am fond of dogs and animals in general, wolves tend to be quite bitey. A nice stretch of the legs after that cramped journey wouldn't be all bad."

"No!" Kah squeaked. "No, there are more. Look up, look up!"

They were surrounded by wolves. The sly creatures were perched on promontories, peeking out from behind boulders, slithering up from every crevice. There had to be dozens of them.

Alishai hooked her glaive onto her back. "Four wolves is a pleasure; four dozen is a death sentence. That's it, then. Your 'intelligent force' of theatricality"—she glared at Rotrog and then Fielle—"has made its preference known." The tiefling spun on her heel and tested the drawbridge with one foot. "Seems solid enough." She walked across the drawbridge heavily, angrily, her tail lashing.

Kah followed close behind her as if recognizing that it was safer to be in Alishai's orbit than virtually anywhere else. Rotrog went next. The drawbridge held, the chains barely clinking. Finally it was only Chivarion, Fielle, and the tressym, which leaped from the drow's shoulder to the ground, ears flat as it regarded the wall of wolves.

"Shall I carry you?" Chivarion held out his arms like a fond uncle offering uppies, but Fielle refused to meet her fate being carried like luggage.

"Thank you, but no. I . . . I have to do this myself." Taking a deep breath and fighting every nerve in her body, she turned and ran across the bridge as quickly as her legs would take her, certain that every step brought her closer to her doom.

7

ROTROG

Rotrog had never been in a castle before. He had never ridden in a fine carriage. The highest-ranking person he'd met thus far was High Mage Argitau, and even he commonly had mustard stains on his robes. Although Rotrog had originally been impressed and charmed by the attentions of a count, he now began to understand that he was just a pawn to someone with powers the likes of which he'd never beheld. He did not like feeling insufficient, but it was becoming a habit. Whoever owned this castle—and the magical driverless carriage and the powerful chamberlain—certainly had this small group of strangers over a barrel.

The drawbridge had quaked unpleasantly under Rotrog's boots, and now they stood in an entryway designed not to impress, but to depress. The orc could smell wet mold dripping down the walls, decay eating away the mortar, metal rusting to powder. What was the point of having such resources, he wondered, if you lived someplace so pathetic? Perhaps this Count Strahd had loftier concerns. So long as he had a library, an atlas, and a reasonably set table, Rotrog would be content.

The angry tiefling led the way, seemingly unperturbed as they wandered into an imposing courtyard. Grotesque gargoyles gazed down from every crevice, lit here and there by moldering torches. The tressym wound around the ankles of the dim-witted drow, meowing complaint. Rotrog found the animal hideous and insufferable. He was grateful to know that, if times were tough enough, there would at least be a little meat to keep them going.

Now in a position to fully appreciate the massive castle, Rotrog took in its soaring heights. These Barovians certainly had a style to their building; the castle ranged from some dumpy towers to one pointy peak that had to be thousands of feet high. The grandness was nearly canceled out by the shabbiness. The castle was obviously ancient, and it seemed entirely neglected. Dead greenery clung to the blackened stone, and the stained-glass windows shone dully. The massive front doors, more than twice as tall as Rotrog himself, were covered in intricately carved scenes of humans murdering one another. He approved of this show of force; perhaps whoever lived here didn't keep up appearances, but they knew how to massacre an army. For all that he hadn't been trained to wage war, he still admired power and wanted to gather as much of it as he could. He fiddled with the ring on his finger. The library here was sure to have spell books somewhere, and its neglectful master was unlikely to notice if they went missing.

"Do we just . . . knock?" Chivarion said. With a finger, he prodded one of the raven-shaped brass door knockers. Its eyes shone like living things in the light of the nearby torches, and Rotrog longed to pluck out those jewels and tuck them into one of the little velvet bags in his magical chatelaine.

"You'd think the master who commanded our presence would have someone here to greet us," Alishai complained. "Not leave us wandering about in the gloom."

"Those of you who can't see in the dark aren't missing anything," Chivarion offered. "All you're missing are hideous statues and mold."

"Perhaps he enjoys our fear," Fielle said softly. "I feel like we're being watched. Don't you?"

Yes, Rotrog felt that way. He had felt that way ever since opening his eyes in this blasted realm. He suspected that their host was playing with them. This knowledge did nothing to improve the situation, and he did not speak it aloud for fear the others would find it laughable.

"We are being watched. By the wolves waiting on the other side of the drawbridge. So I'll take the door." Chivarion grasped the knocker and banged it three times against the ancient wood. The sound echoed across the mountains like a death drum.

After only a moment's pause, the door swung inward with a creak of protest to showcase a vaulted foyer. The tiles underfoot were crumbled and, in some places, shattered. More sconces lit the walls, revealing four stone statues of dragons glaring down in judgment from above. Directly ahead stood . . .

"More doors," the tiefling said. "How very welcoming."

This next set of enormous doors swung open almost reproachfully at this comment to reveal a grand hall—or a once-grand hall. Organ music filtered in from somewhere deeper in the castle, but it sounded more like a funereal arrangement than something celebratory or meant for dancing. Cobwebs trailed from the columns, and eight scowling gargoyles presided from perches on the rim of the domed ceiling. Long ago, someone with great skill had painted glorious frescoes across this artificial sky, but now they were stained and darkened, cracked and crumbling.

"Little too bright for my taste," Alishai said. "Far too jolly and frivolous. All it needs is a coffin and, I don't know, a pile of bones to really liven up the place."

Rotrog did not speak; sound carried here, and he did not wish to offend any who might be listening. Directly ahead were yet more doors, tall and brass and tarnished, while a grand stairway on the left suggested, perhaps, family rooms.

"We are so very sorry to disappoint," someone said, sounding in no way apologetic. Rotrog immediately recognized the voice and was glad he'd held his tongue; it was the elf chamberlain, Rahadin, who had approached them in the forest. He materialized from the shadows of the sweeping staircase wearing a cold and calculating smile. "My master is expecting you. Please, follow me."

With a bow, Rahadin gestured toward the bronze doors, which

opened as if by unseen hands. The slow, dismal music swelled, and Rotrog noticed a figure seated at a large instrument composed of dozens of brass pipes that ran up into the ceiling. If this was what passed as Barovian music, then, like their architecture, weather, and roads, he did not care for it.

Alishai stalked into the room and headed directly for a long table heavily laden with a variety of prepared foods. Mounds of steaming meat, tureens of soup, bowls of vegetables, odd confections of fruit and cream, all waited tantalizingly on a shiny white cloth. Five places were set, each with a gold-rimmed plate, an annoying number of tiny human utensils, and a delicate goblet of amber liquid. Once the tiefling was in the room and plucking a leg of fowl from a platter, the rest of the party moved in behind her, almost unwillingly. When Rotrog went to ask Rahadin about the promised study, he found that the chamberlain had mysteriously disappeared. Instead, he headed for the figure playing the organ.

"My lord, we are appreciative of your invitation," he said. "For we are lost—"

The music stopped abruptly, and elegant white hands dropped from the keyboard. "We receive so few visitors to the castle, I fear I have forgotten my manners." The figure stood and turned, and Rotrog felt the blood freeze in his veins.

So this was Count Strahd von Zarovich, ruler of this strange land.

Rotrog took one look at him and knew the count didn't fear having forgotten his manners. This Strahd did not fear *anything*.

He stood more than six feet tall and possessed the lithe, contained danger of a displacer beast. His clothing was clearly very fine, cut to suit him and highlight the width of his shoulders, the narrow aspect of his waist. A red cravat made his skin seem all the paler, and his ears were slightly pointed. His eyes and hair were black, his smile a threat.

"I am Strahd," he said simply. That one word, that proud confidence, said more than all the titles in the world. "I welcome you to Castle Ravenloft. Please, sit and enjoy my hospitality."

Rotrog looked to Alishai, not because he ascribed her any authority, but because she seemed the angriest and the most paranoid, and if she had plans to attack, he wanted to get out of her way.

But no. She held the goblet in both hands, greedily drinking down its contents.

Ah, yes. All this time, and there had been nothing to drink.

She'd had two strips of dried meat and no water.

Whatever danger she felt here, she had made her choice.

Strahd sat in a tall chair at the head of the table and reached for his goblet, which was made of heavy metal—tarnished gold? He held it up to them in a toast then drank, his canny eyes watching them over the rim.

"A marvelous repast," Chivarion said. He was already eating, with a bit of fowl in one hand and a glass in the other—probably not poison, then, although it might take a prodigious amount to kill the oaf, in any case. "I'm a bit peckish after all we've been through today."

Giving in, Rotrog pulled out a seat and made himself comfortable. Kah sat beside him, and Fielle sat beside her, as far from Strahd as possible. Rotrog considered the platters nearest him. He understood that Strahd was powerful and dangerous, and yet . . . why would someone call for a feast, invite visitors, and then cause them harm? It made no strategic sense; Strahd was clearly wealthy and powerful, and their clothes marked them as commoners and outsiders. If Strahd didn't want them here and if he wanted to hurt them, he could've accomplished that easily as they stood in the forest. They had to be safe here.

Surely they were safe here.

For now.

Rotrog reached for the platter of roast and selected a thick slab of meat, then added a leg of fowl. However strange this place, the meat was savory and delicious. Alishai, Chivarion, and Kah were eating as well, but Fielle merely huddled in her chair looking miserable and staring at her empty plate. This was puzzling, as she had previously been so open, curious, and warm.

"My dear, are you not hungry?" Strahd asked her. His voice was like music, but the kind of music that makes people dance until they die.

In response, Fielle merely shook her head.

"Are you too cold? Would you like a fur-lined cloak? I do wish you to be comfortable, and I will do all in my power to please you."

"I don't feel well," she whispered.

Strahd stood and moved so swiftly around the table that Rotrog had to blink.

Yes, this count was definitely a student of spellcraft.

Fielle gasped at his sudden nearness, and Strahd reached to put a concerned hand on her shoulder. She flinched and went stock-still.

"My poor girl. You must be exhausted. I will have my chamberlain show you to your room, where you can rest. We'll have a meal delivered so that you might eat in privacy. I imagine today has been an especially trying day."

He removed his hand, and Fielle came back to life as if she'd been frozen. She couldn't speak, but she nodded and stood. Rahadin appeared out of nowhere—gods, was he a wizard, too?—and glided to Fielle's side.

"You all right?" Alishai called, scooting her chair back like she might leap up to follow.

"Yes. I'd like—I'd like to go to my room." Fielle's voice was barely a whisper. The human had been so lively and friendly before that Rotrog couldn't imagine what had come over her. Like Alishai, he felt protective of her, and yet . . . well, what was there to protect her from? They were perfectly safe, in the heavily fortified palace of a count. The food was good, drink was available, and they weren't being chased by dead things and harried by storms. Perhaps she had simply reached her limit. Humans, Rotrog had learned, were fragile creatures, and Fielle looked like she could be torn in two like a piece of bread.

Rahadin put a hand on her shoulder and steered her out the imposing brass doors. Strahd returned to his chair, and Rotrog applied himself more fully to the fine repast. The count watched them eat but, Rotrog noticed, ate no food himself. He did sip from his goblet occasionally, and it must've contained red wine, as it tinted his lips a dark mauve.

"So you're the lord, eh?" Chivarion said, once he'd placed some meat bits on a plate for his tressym, which sat at the table, making mumbling noises while she ate. "And what sort of place is this? Are we close to Neverwinter? It's a little like the High Forest, but . . ." He made a face. "Then again, nothing like it."

"Barovia is a place all its own," Strahd said with a cloying smile as he leaned back in his chair, fingers steepled. "A difficult place to find. Not on many maps."

"But surely you possess an atlas," Rotrog said between handfuls of grapes. "Every place exists at some fixed point."

"I do not fashion myself an expert on cartography." Strahd's eyes danced with amusement. "But you are welcome to look for what you seek in my library. While you are here as my guests, you are free to enjoy the grounds of the castle. Certain places are private, but I'm sure you will recognize their nature."

Rotrog put down the remaining grapes and pushed his plate away. "I'm very eager indeed to see this library." For all that he was exhausted and slightly concerned for the human, he had never yet had the privilege of enjoying a library outside of the carefully pruned one the academy provided for its adepts, and he wanted nothing more than to get his hands on any magical tomes that might add to his wizardly prowess. Once he had absorbed any new spells he might find among Strahd's collection, then he would find an atlas and plan his route home.

Strahd stood and gestured toward the tall doors. "If you like, I can show you the way, that you might peruse it at your leisure."

Rotrog likewise stood. "It would be an honor."

As Strahd led him toward a spiral staircase, Alishai repeated, "You all right?"

Rotrog gave her a warm smile, showing his tusks. "If I am headed toward books, rest assured: I am good."

The spiral stairwell was a tight fit and poorly lit. Not wanting to tread upon Strahd's heels or threaten him, Rotrog gave him plenty of space.

"I immediately understood that you were the leader," Strahd said quietly. "A person of intelligence and wisdom little understood by his traveling companions."

Oh, the joy this lit in Rotrog's heart, to be seen!

"Indeed. They are not friends, you understand. We only met today, thrown together by curious circumstances which we have not yet begun to fathom. They are strangers, all."

"The drow seems especially dim, and the tiefling—"

"Brash and paranoid," Rotrog agreed. "Aggressive, even when no aggression is warranted."

"And the kenku appears to be a timid soul."

Rotrog nodded. "Timid and nervous. I've never met one so skittish."

Strahd sighed in understanding as they passed a landing to the second floor. "It is challenging, is it not, to deal with those who are lesser? I suffer many fools in the villages of Barovia and rarely meet anyone I might consider an equal. It is good that you have arrived. Tell me—" He paused.

"Rotrog."

"Tell me, Rotrog, do you enjoy games of strategy?"

Rotrog had never played a game of strategy and thought such games beneath him, but he would not say that to Strahd. "I enjoy a game of wits, and I am always eager to learn."

A chuckle. "Then perhaps I shall teach you Hawks and Hares, and we shall see who is more cunning. Ah, here we are." Strahd stepped off on the next landing, and Rotrog followed him into a charming study.

The rooms downstairs had been neglected and abused by time, but the study seemed better kept. A fire roared in the massive hearth, its warm light glittering on the gilt titles of hundreds, perhaps thousands of books arranged on floor-to-ceiling shelves. Not a single tome seemed out of order, and every leather spine appeared well oiled and well loved. A long, low table was thoughtfully arranged in the center of the room so that a scholar might have a pleasant place to sit and spread out various books for perusal. Overstuffed couches, swooping divans, and tall-backed chairs were placed just so. It was the most pleasant room Rotrog had ever encountered.

Well, except for one thing. A human woman stared down from an enormous painting hung over the mantel. Something about her bothered Rotrog, but he couldn't quite put his finger on it. Most humans looked the same to him, and yet there was something familiar about this one, with her auburn hair and large eyes that seemed to follow him around the room.

Strahd brought out a wooden game board and a collection of polished stone. He set up the board on a small table between two burgundy chairs and explained the rules, which of course Rotrog had no problem learning. As they played, Strahd showed great interest in his guest, asking him all sorts of probing questions about his family, his academy, and his history learning magic. Rotrog was careful to speak the truth, but he certainly left out many important points of his life story. He wanted Strahd to think only the best of him, and he was flattered by the attention. He may have embellished a few points, but what of it? Wherever they were, Silverymoon was quite far away indeed, and the count would never know the difference.

As the fire merrily crackled, Strahd asked about the afternoon's affairs, and Rotrog told the story of the abattoir in a way that painted him as the strongest fighter, rather than the one who botched a spell. In his retelling, there was no grease, and the magic missiles hit their mark, and three extra zombies were mowed down, never to groan again. Although he was unable to answer the count's every question about the other visitors in the castle, Rotrog was more than happy to offer his thoughts on their personalities, strengths, and weaknesses. Strahd was an excellent judge of character, and he agreed with every proclamation. It wasn't terribly long before Rotrog had bested the count in his first game of Hawks and Hares.

"You certainly are as intelligent as I had dared to assume," Strahd said, shaking a handful of gray stones and looking mightily impressed. "Very few players can beat me. This study is yours to enjoy while you're here, and I hope I might prevail upon you to play again sometime."

"Gladly, my lord," Rotrog said. Next time, he would beat Strahd in fewer moves. He already had some ideas for a better opener.

"Now, if you'll forgive me, I require rest. Let me show you to your chambers."

Rotrog was sorry to leave the study, but he would return as soon as he woke in the morning. It had been a marvelously pleasant evening for him. Never before had he met anyone who recognized him as an equal in intelligence, education, and savvy. When Strahd showed him the room reserved for his use, he was even more pleased; it was fit for royalty, decorated in rich shades of burgundy with a sprawling four-poster bed.

"It's been a pleasure making your acquaintance," Strahd said, giving a little bow. "I feel sure we shall come to know each other better while you sojourn in my domain."

"It has indeed been a pleasure," Rotrog said, returning the bow.

Only as he settled into his massive bed and struggled to get comfortable on the strangely soft mattress did Rotrog realize why the portrait over the study hearth had bothered him so.

The auburn hair was the wrong color, but the eyes, so big and so sad—they looked exactly like Fielle's.

8

ALISHAI

Fielle's jerky kept Alishai from turning into a monster and making people cry, but the banquet made her feel like herself again. Spiced meats, unctuous cheeses, ripe fruits—so many luscious flavors and textures, foods she couldn't even identify after a life of asceticism. She ate until her belly was round, a freedom she'd rarely enjoyed back home in the Sanctuary of the Fullest Silver Moon. Food was fuel, not something to be enjoyed, Silverstar Narelle always told her initiates. They were given appropriate portions, unseasoned but for a sprinkle of salt from the Sea of Fallen Stars. Those who took too much food were gluttons who would deny the needy, and gluttons were disgusting to Selûne. Alishai had always believed everything Narelle told her.

But then she'd learned better.

Now she would not deny herself the enjoyment of her senses. If delicious food was offered, she would take as much as she wanted. This was no sin. It was foolish to ever think it was. Why would a goddess care if she had one bite too many? All Selûne cared about was her faith. Her oath. The strength of her conviction.

And her conviction was stronger when she wasn't starving.

"What now?" she asked, regarding her remaining companions.

With Fielle retired to her chambers and Rotrog enjoying Strahd's company and probably puffed up like a bullfrog with smugness, that left only Chivarion, Kah, and Alishai herself in the banquet hall. There were no visible servants, no further instructions. She wanted nothing more than to unbuckle her heavy belt and harness, remove her armor, bathe, meditate, and go to sleep, but unless she wanted to wash her nethers in a tureen of consommé and sleep under the massive table, she didn't know how to make that happen.

Chivarion yawned, and his tressym followed suit. "Floor's fine for me. I haven't seen a rat yet, so it's better than plenty of other places I've bedded down." He stood, scooted his chair out, and dug through his bag.

"Wait, shouldn't we wait?" Kah asked, looking around the dining hall with bright, curious eyes.

"Why's that?"

Kah blinked at her. "The chamberlain will show us to our rooms. We shouldn't wander." She leaned in. "Traps. Protections, you see."

Alishai did not see. "Strahd said we had the run of the castle, didn't he?" She stood and stretched, walking around to peer into the count's golden goblet. A single drop of red was left in the very bottom, and when she smelled it, it was so heavy with tannins and iron that it nearly turned her stomach. Landed gentry surely had peculiar tastes, not that she had encountered any gentry before. Or anyone, really, outside of the small sect—no.

Not a sect.

Cult.

The small, secluded *cult* in the plains of Sembia where she'd lived all her life in complete ignorance.

She walked over to the musical instrument Strahd had played and pressed one of the keys, jumping back when it made a loud, sonorous tone. There were so very many keys and tubes that she wondered how anyone might learn to operate it. A chair scraped, and then Kah skittered over, likewise curious.

"Organ," she said, touching a key so lightly that it made no sound. "But this is not a chapel. No, no, not a chapel at all." Her bright yellow eyes, ruffling iridescent feathers, and twitchy movements were so nervous that it made Alishai feel nervous by extension. "Oh," Kah said, cocking her head at the floor.

Alishai looked down, and Kah ran her foot—talon?—over a deep scratch mark on the stone. Their eyes met in understanding. The organ, somehow, could move, suggesting that there was something hidden behind it.

"Admiring the master's instrument?"

The haughty voice carried across the room with a tone of accusation.

"Never seen one of these things before," Alishai said, knowing Kah was both too panicked and too honest to hide the fact that they'd noticed some chicanery. "It's a bit . . . bleaty."

Rahadin stared at her coldly. "Bleaty?"

"Bleaty. Like a sheep. *Bleeeeeeh.*"

The chamberlain did not seem amused by her best imitation of a sheep, but Chivarion chuckled.

"Well, if you are finished *bleating*, I would be pleased to show you to your chambers." Rahadin's sharp eyebrows rose, and Alishai understood that this man was not accustomed to waiting—and that he was likely not pleased by anything.

She touched one more bleating key to show she could not be intimidated and met him at the door. Kah hopped along behind her, and Chivarion picked up his tressym like it was a sleepy child and joined them. Rahadin led them up the grand stairwell they'd passed on the way in. Up and up and up they went behind the silent elf, passing multiple landings that suggested other floors.

"We're not sleeping on the roof, are we?" Alishai asked, only half joking.

"Only our finest rooms with the loveliest views will do for such illustrious guests."

Still upward they clambered. Alishai was already tired, but now her legs were aching. She could feel Kah keeping close behind her, so she was careful not to smack her in the face with her angrily twitching tail. Chivarion came last, murmuring to his tressym, assuring her that they would soon be somewhere cozy and asking her, politely, not to leave a dead mouse on the count's pillows because *some people* didn't consider that a gift.

Finally they stepped off onto a landing, and Rahadin opened a door to reveal a chamber that seemed enormous to Alishai because she'd only ever lived in a tiny cell. Moldering tapestries sagged on the walls, and two long, thin beds with heavy coverlets slumped in opposite corners.

"For the females," Rahadin said, which made Alishai silently shudder. "Compliments of Count Strahd. He hopes you will be comfortable here and wishes to remind you that you are free to roam the castle grounds but should be wary of any warnings that suggest an area may be off-limits."

"What kind of warning?" Chivarion asked.

Rahadin raised an eyebrow at him. "You will recognize the signs."

At that, the drow perked up. "Oh. Well. That does sound fun. We'll have to go poke around some corners tomorrow and see what we can drum up, eh?"

The chamberlain shook his head as if he wearied of talking to children. "The cemetery is extensive, and the catacombs can hold untold corpses, so I suppose that is acceptable."

"Wait," Alishai said as Rahadin turned from the door. "Are there not enough rooms for us individually?"

Kah's feathers flattened in reproof, but Rahadin merely inclined his head in the negative. "Sadly, much of the castle has fallen to disrepair. You should have everything you require. I wish you a good evening."

He all but slammed the door in his haste to leave. Alishai wondered whether Chivarion might be roomed on the same floor; there were several doors, after all, and judging by the size of the castle, she had to assume Rahadin was lying about there being too little space to accommodate separate lodgings.

"No offense," she said to Kah. "I like my alone time."

Kah fidgeted, looking around the room a little sadly. "I'm used to a flock. Nice to have someone around. Nice to not be alone here." She shook her head, fluffing her feathers. "Dreary place. Dark. It wants to suck us dry."

"A bit melodramatic," Alishai murmured, mostly to herself. She chose the bed farthest from the door and flipped back the coverlet.

A cloud of dust rose up, making her cough. "Only the finest guest rooms, my rump." At least there were no vermin.

Walking around the room, she looked out the window to find a night so dark it was impenetrable. She still saw no sign of the moon here, and it made her uneasy, as if her goddess had been erased from the heavens. Next she moved to a wardrobe, finding only a collection of old, musty dresses inside, the fabric moth-eaten and faded. Several clumps of leather on the shelf must've once been shoes, before the mice had discovered them. She checked behind every tapestry to make sure there were no hidden doors, looked under both beds, and was immensely relieved to find a bath behind the only other door. Of course, there was no water in it, but surely there were servants somewhere. She poked her head out into the hallway, but Rahadin was long gone. The thought of him carrying water up all those stairs was beyond amusing.

"Hey, do you think—"

But Kah was already asleep, a gently snoring lump under cobwebbed covers.

Oh, to be able to sleep like that! But Alishai had always had trouble quieting her mind and finding peace. She was kept so busy during the day back home that generally the only time she had truly to herself was after midnight. Even though she knew the morning would punish her, still she would rebelliously stay up to watch the moon through the tiny window of her cell and speak to Selûne of her worries and fears and hopes. There had always been more worries and fears and very few hopes, but now that she was finally free, the moon was nowhere to be found, and she missed her best conversation partner.

Alishai divested herself of weapons and removed her armor and thick boots. Gods, she wanted a bath! She stilled her heart and meditated on her oath and flopped on top of her covers, then underneath them. She lay on her back, her belly, her sides. She breathed along with Kah's fluttering snores and then counted up by sevens and down by sixes, but her mind was far from sleep. Finally, she gave up and went outside to the landing.

"Hello?" she called.

Hello, hello, hello, the spiral staircase echoed back.

She tried the other doors on the floor, but they were locked. Whether Chivarion was within one was anyone's guess. Contemplating the dark stairwell, she reasoned that she was more likely to find a servant downstairs cleaning up the banquet than she was going even farther away from the heart of the castle.

"This is how badly I want a bath," she muttered to herself.

She had not counted the stairs on the way up, so she had no real idea how many landings she had to pass on her way back down; she knew only that it felt tremendously far. Despite her ability to see quite well in the darkness, these shadows were . . . almost palpable. It reminded her of the Mists in the forest. So cold, the air—so thick. As her fingertips trailed along the stone and her bare feet found each next tread, dread built in her chest. It felt as if someone tiptoed just behind her, hands hovering over her back, ready to push. She could imagine tumbling down the endless stone, feeling her bones snap yet unable to stop her momentum. It made her go all the slower. She wished she could sit down and scoot down, step by step, but even alone, she wouldn't allow herself to appear so weak.

"No one here," she reminded herself. "Keep going. The only way out is through."

When Alishai emerged on the next landing, a great sigh of relief gusted out of her. Maybe she didn't need to go all the way down to the banquet hall. There were torches on this floor, and it appeared much bigger than her own floor. She followed the light down a long hall filled with shadowy alcoves. At first, she thought rows of soldiers were staring at her, their faces frozen in horror. Then she realized that the alcoves merely contained statues. They were fine likenesses of elegant humans, almost like at a museum. What a strange way to spend money—hiring an artist to carve dozens of statues that few would ever see.

"Do you know where all the servants are?" she asked the nearest statue jokingly.

"Dead."

Alishai drew back.

That creaky, breathy voice—surely it was her imagination?

"What did you say?"

But the statue gave no reply, if it had ever spoken at all.

She hurried out of the hall and took a right, headed toward a crackling fire in a large hearth. At a long wooden table in the middle of the room, Rotrog was asleep, his massive gray head pinning down a leather-bound book. He was drooling a little, his spittle dripping down from a tusk and smearing the ink. The entire table was covered in such books, and there were empty places in the many bookshelves covering the walls. A drained chalice lay on its side by his hand.

"Rotrog!" Alishai called.

The orc did not stir.

She put a hand on his shoulder, expecting to jump back to avoid being cuffed, but Rotrog didn't even twitch. When she called his name again, still he remained stubbornly asleep, his breathing shallow. Was he sick, perhaps?

"Our friend the orc is drunk."

Alishai's hands went for weapons that were not there as she located the source of that now familiar voice. Strahd sat in a tall brocade chair pulled close to the fire, hidden from view.

"Then your wine must be uncommonly strong," she replied.

The count rose smoothly and strode to where Alishai stood at the table. He was so close now that she could feel the fire's warmth seeping off his body. People did not generally get this close to her, whether because she was a fighter or a tiefling, and she went very still, waiting to see what the count would do.

"My cellar is indeed filled with an uncommon vintage." His voice was low and genteel and as intimate as a caress. "But I rarely have guests with whom to share it. Will you have a taste?"

A goblet appeared in his hand, brimming with sweet red wine. He held it to her lips, and she wanted to turn away, wanted to leave, but something held her there, her body locked in place. When he tipped the goblet up, she had no choice but to drink or drown. The liquid was warm and soft as velvet, sweet and syrupy, and it slid into her like a poisoned blade. When the cup was empty, it disappeared, and things became very strange.

Strahd was right across from her now, holding her face in both hands. His eyes bore into her own quite fiercely, as if he were looking into her soul. She thought he might kiss her, and a foolish thing that would be, but he merely shook his head sadly and stepped away.

"You don't like what you see?" she asked, emboldened by the wine— and a little insulted.

"I cannot see what is not there. Tell me, Alishai. What do you most desire?"

She was tipsy, perhaps, but not so drunk that she was willing to spill her secrets, especially not to a stranger.

"I want to go home."

He chuckled and used his thumb to swipe away an errant bit of wine on her chin. "That is true, but it is also a lie. You want something more than that." The hand tightened on her chin, holding her head back, exposing her throat. "You want to be wanted."

She tried to pull her head away, but his grip was iron. "I want to be free."

"Not as badly as you want to be wanted. All your life, you've been a discard and a disappointment. No matter what you did, it was not good enough. You think if you are strong enough, vicious enough, then no one can ever reject you again. If you were truly free, you would be beyond such desperation. I can give you that freedom. I can make you powerful beyond your wildest dreams."

She jerked her chin away, feeling his thumbnail scratch her skin. "And then I would be beholden to you, just another master. No, thank you. Good evening, my lord." She cut a mocking bow and strode out of the room. She expected to hear sharp footsteps or a sharper rebuke, but none came. When she looked back, Rotrog still slept, but Strahd was gone.

How did he know— Why did he—

She shook her head. What had just happened made no sense. It was almost as if her mind had conjured it. Why would a count care a fig about her? What had he searched for when he looked into her eyes? What was it he had failed to find? How was she still not enough?

Annoyed, and a good bit tipsy now, she turned her attention to the room she'd randomly entered. Immediately, her stomach turned. An enormous, many-tiered cake rested on another long table. The frosting was green and moldy, the entire thing listing sloppily to one side. The room reeked of sweet decay, and dust covered every horizontal surface like a shoddy carpet. Not even footsteps disturbed the scene, suggesting no one had been there in months, perhaps years. And why would they? It was disgusting. An enormous iron chandelier hung overhead, draped in cobwebs, and a tall harp rested in the corner. Alishai would've abandoned this room immediately, except that she could see what waited in the chamber beyond, and it had utterly captured her attention.

An enormous bathtub!

She shuffled through the dust, carefully holding her tail up, hating how dry and dirty the detritus felt on her bare feet. She would fix that soon; she could already see fragrant steam rising from the clawfoot tub, and the scent of fresh cleansing herbs perfumed the air.

"Hello?" she called.

There was no answer. Carved double doors waited across from the bathtub, and she wondered if perhaps this was Strahd's chamber, Strahd's bathtub. He had just been nearby, after all. But why would it just be sitting open like this? And why would hot water be waiting? There was even a towel and a ball of soap. Rahadin had said the visitors were free to roam the castle, and that they would know when they'd entered an area where they weren't welcome. Alishai felt very welcome at that moment, as if this grand bathing chamber had been waiting just for her. She checked the area but found only a closet behind closed red velvet drapes. If the count was still around, surely he would've answered her.

"Hello? I'm going to use this bathtub. Speak now or give me a sign if that's not okay."

The castle was heavy with silence.

Which was her answer.

Sloshed and giddy and firmly trying to forget her confusing interlude with the lord of the castle, Alishai closed the door to the dusty cake room. She swiftly undressed and climbed into the bathtub, ducking all the way under the perfumed, heated water: her body, her head, even her horns. For a long moment, she stayed there, eyes closed, and enjoyed the womblike sensation of being totally immersed. When she couldn't hold her breath any longer, she surfaced and slicked her hair back with her hands.

But something was wrong. The water was no longer steaming.

It was . . . lukewarm. Almost tepid. Thick. Syrupy, like Strahd's fine wine.

It no longer smelled of fresh herbs and flowers.

She opened her eyes.

The bathtub was full of blood.

Alishai lurched up and scrambled over the edge of the tub, sliding in wet red gore. She landed on the black-and-white tiles, her feet slipping as she stumbled away, drunkenly knuckling blood out of her eyes for the second time that day.

But there was something wrong with the bath—with the blood. It was bubbling, heaving, slopping over the sides of the tub. The liquid erupted, and a monster burst from its depths with a scream of fury and flew to the ceiling, sinking in its claws to cling there.

With slow menace, its head turned all the way around, white eyes glaring rage at Alishai as its mouth opened to show long yellow fangs.

9

CHIVARION

Like all drow, Chivarion Dyrr did not sleep. When rest was required, he would lie down comfortably and go into a trance. But he was not one to meditate on the past or contemplate the future. No, for him, trance—like life—was a sort of pleasant limbo. As he lay in his bed in Castle Ravenloft, he was blissfully unaware that his beloved pet tressym, Murder, sat vigilantly on his pillow, guarding him from threats the drow couldn't see. The castle was full of things—dark, secret things—that only certain creatures could discern.

In the morning, Chivarion woke with a smile and stretched. He had slept entirely nude in the sprawling bed, and his only complaint about this chamber was that someone had boarded up the window and sealed the cracks with pitch, making it quite a dark and airless place. Yes, well, that was easy enough to fix when one was a barbarian. He simply curled his fingers under the wood and pried it off, revealing thick, milky glass and views of the Barovian forest. Strange way to decorate a room, that. At least the mattress was comfortable.

All of his new companions were disturbed by this place, and quite a strange place it was, but Chivarion had long ago gotten used to strangeness. He barely remembered his childhood days in the Underdark and had spent most of his conscious life running wild in the streets all over Toril as first a beggar child, then a particularly bad thief, then, once he hit his growth spurt, hired muscle. It was honestly just easier to get along than it was to make a fuss. He stored his rage inside like squirrels stored nuts in hollow trees, and when necessary, he could pull out the stopper and just let the nuts flow. Until that time, his general attitude was "Oh, well." That could range from "Oh, well, zombies are attacking; time to fight!" to "Oh, well, gruel for dinner again; at least there are no weevils" to "Oh, well: weevils."

He understood Alishai's general annoyance, but honestly, being annoyed took a lot of energy. It was just more work. Better to save that energy for fighting, feeding, and f—

Well. The pretty tiefling would warm up to him. Eventually.

And if not her, perhaps Rotrog? Or Rahadin? Chivarion was easygoing in that area as well. He was attracted to passion, not gender or species.

With no way to know where anyone else was, he decided to head downstairs. Either last night's food would still be there and hopefully in decent shape, or the count's servants would serve something new.

"You ready?" he asked Murder.

The tressym slept soundly on his pillow.

"Murder!" he shouted.

Murder opened one baleful eye, closed the eye, and went back to sleep.

"Lazy beast," Chivarion muttered. "Keep sleeping, then."

Now, for a muscular drow warrior, opening a door should've been a spectacularly easy feat. Chivarion was quite certain he had opened thousands, maybe millions of doors in his lifetime. This door, however, refused to budge. No matter how Chivarion pushed, pulled, shoved, or kicked, no matter what rage he brought down upon it, the door remained annoyingly stuck in place. Oh, how he wished for the tiefling's glaive! He hated to think of dulling the blade of his beloved sword, Liversliverer.

He looked around the room, but there was nothing heavy that might be used to bludgeon the door. Although he found it distasteful, he tried one more thing.

He knocked.

Well, slammed his fist, really.

"Hello? Anyone? My door doesn't seem to be dooring," he shouted.

There was no answer. And, quite honestly, banging on the door didn't feel like banging on a door. It felt like banging on a wall. Like perhaps there was no opening on the other side, but merely solid stone.

With a sigh of annoyance, Chivarion stood before the recently revealed window. He could deal with heights, but he didn't *want* to deal with heights, especially before breakfast. Perhaps there was a hidden door somewhere. Every room had a door, after all, even if sometimes those doors misbehaved.

He walked the perimeter of the large room, looked under the bed, pulled back every rug and tapestry. Dust filled the air and tickled his nose as he opened a wardrobe filled with fine clothes that seemed the right size and shape for an elven sort of person, if a few centuries out of date. Pushing the capes and tunics aside—and tossing one fine cloak on the bed for his personal use—he ran his fingers over the back wall of the wardrobe and was beyond pleased to find a hook.

"Bothersome place for a door," he said to the room as he undid the catch.

Behind him, Murder hissed a warning, and then the secret door burst inward. Some sort of creature sunk its claws into Chivarion's chest, and he stumbled backward, already reaching for a neck, or whatever it had that might be useful for strangling. The thing evaded his hands and skittered onto his back using needlelike talons. Twisting, he reached for it, but whenever his fingertips brushed it, it slipped in a different direction.

"What in the Nine Hells—" he muttered.

In response, whatever it was sunk teeth into his shoulder and held on, digging in deeper like it was trying to take out a chunk of the muscle Chivarion worked so hard to maintain. With a hiss of rage, Murder leaped into the air and flew directly at her besieged drow friend, who helpfully turned his back to allow the tressym a clean shot at the beast. The teeth released Chivarion's shoulder, leaving behind a hot well of pain and a gush of blood, and the creature used his shoulder to catapult into the air. Chivarion spun, pulling his sword, to find the tressym rolling around on the floor with—

Ye gods, it was hideous.

Not another tressym, not a cat, but some sort of ugly, twisted nightmare cat? Like Murder's hideous, monstrous twin.

It was soot gray and hairless with huge pointed ears, enormous spreading claws, and a long, bare, sinuous tail like a dead snake. Its beady yellow eyes flashed coldly at Chivarion as it grappled, the two beasts rolling around on the ground, hissing and spitting. The cat-thing got its teeth into Murder's skin, but this was one of the tressym's clever defenses. As soon as the beast latched on, Murder twisted inside her overabundance of wrinkled skin and got the thing's throat in her teeth.

Chivarion did not want to steal Murder's fun, but neither of them knew what this thing was, and it might have venom or more defenses or friends waiting in the wardrobe. He had to end this fast so they could find someone to heal them both. He reached into the hissing, spitting mess and grabbed the offensive nightmare cat by the scruff of the neck. Murder narrowed her eyes in annoyance but released her prey, and Chivarion didn't so much as pause. He sliced the thing in half before it could react.

Instead of swiftly dying in two bloody pieces like a sensible creature, the cat-thing dissolved into two piles of scaly chunks. Chivarion opened his fingers, eager to stop touching whatever it had become.

"Stinks of magic," he said. "Have you ever seen anything like that before?"

Murder was on the ground, licking at her wounds. The tressym, of course, said nothing, but her eyes flicked to Chivarion briefly and blinked once. That was a no.

With his sword still in hand, the drow strode to the wardrobe and glared through the hidden door. On the other side, he found the hall he remembered from last night.

"Shall we go find Kah?" he asked the tressym.

Murder stood and walked gingerly over to the wardrobe, nimbly leaping through. Confident that there were no more magical cat-beasts on the other side, Chivarion squeezed through and followed the tressym into the hallway. They took the steps down and found three doors on the next level. When Chivarion knocked on the one he remembered the women entering, he was greeted by Alishai's annoyed voice.

"Go away. S'too early," she called weakly.

"If we wait too long, I might die of poisoning," he called back.

"Good."

Kenku talons clicked to the door, and Kah let them in. She noticed his wound, grinding her beak as her golden eyes dilated with curiosity.

"What did this?" she asked. "Too many teeth!"

"Please see to Murder first," Chivarion told her. "If you're willing to help us."

Kah looked toward a narrow bed in the corner and called to the lump within it, "Come, come help heal. Looks bad, it does."

"Maybe later." Alishai sounded . . . drunk? Sick? Definitely not her usual self.

Chivarion pointed at the bed lump. "Does she need healing, too? How much did you drink last night?"

"Nightmares," Alishai muttered. "So many nightmares."

He nodded knowingly. "Ah, yes. Orcish moonshine. I know it well."

Kah was done waiting. She held her hands over the tressym and muttered a musical word, and the bite marks and claw marks sealed up, leaving only more faint scars on the dimpled skin. Chivarion didn't think his feline friend minded that she was covered in similar marks; in fact, he was fairly certain Murder was proud of her many battle scars.

Although he couldn't see the damage done to his own back, he wasn't quite as eager to mar his tattoos or have to explain to a lover one day in the future that he'd been attacked by a greasy magical cat-bat hiding in a closet. Kah gestured for him to bring his wound closer to her own height, and he obligingly dropped to his knees. She gasped when she saw the mess of his back and performed her spell. Chivarion was a connoisseur of healing, and he was always grateful when there was someone around with the ability to magically fix the stupid things he ended up doing to himself. The moment the kenku spoke her chirpy words, the searing heat of a raw bite became the warm touch of sunlight. He exhaled in relief and rolled his shoulders, glorying in the suppleness of his reknitted flesh.

"Many thanks," he told Kah. "You're quite good at that."

"Oh, no," she said, fluffing up her feathers and looking away. "Just a little spell. Not much at all."

But she seemed pleased, Chivarion thought. Now that he did not have a ragged hole in his body, he focused on the lump in the bed.

"Alishai, are you dead?"

"A little," she admitted.

She threw back the covers, and Chivarion screeched.

"You look horrible!"

She blinked at him. "Thanks?"

"Well, it's mainly because you're covered in blood. And very pale. Kah, what do you make of this?"

The kenku hurried over, and Alishai glared at them but seemed too sleepy to actually do anything about it. Her indigo hair was crusty with red where it lay on the blood-soaked pillow, and splashes of rust stained her cheeks, her eyelashes, her horns.

"What happened to you?" Chivarion asked.

Alishai struggled to sit up and failed. She ran her hand through her hair, her fingers got caught, and she grunted in annoyance. When she saw the red rimming her nails, she gasped and hurriedly sat up. "I thought I'd dreamed it."

"Dreamed what?" Kah asked, creeping closer.

Alishai looked off into the ether and blinked as if searching for something. "I was wandering the halls, and then our odd host was there, and he made me drink some wine. I escaped him and found a bathing chamber. It was just magnificent. Huge bathtub full of hot water, red velvet curtains, soft towels. I called out to make sure I wasn't trespassing, and there was no answer, so I got in the tub and went under. But then it got all . . ." She grimaced, shaking her head and squeezing her eyes shut. Rusty flakes fell from her lashes like snow. "Cold. Sludgy. I opened my eyes, and it was blood. Just . . . a tub full of blood. I—I scrambled out, slipping and sliding, just blood everywhere, and the moment I was out, this mad thing burst out of the blood, some kind of twisted creature. It was crawling on the ceiling, scuttling like a bug, cackling like a hag. And then it disappeared through an archway, and . . ."

"And?" This was the strangest nightmare Chivarion had ever heard, and he was curious.

"And . . ." Alishai rubbed the back of her head. "I slipped in the blood and hit my head. So maybe it wasn't a dream? There's a bump back there—I know that much is real." She held up her fingers, rubbing them together and watching dried blood fall like pepper. "And apparently the blood is real, too." She squinted. "Or maybe it's something else?" She touched her tongue to a patch of red on her arm and shuddered. "No, definitely blood."

"How did you get back to the room?" Chivarion asked. "I saw no bloody footsteps in the hall."

"That's the weirdest part—the reason I thought it must've been a dream. I was lying on the floor by the bathtub after the blood-creature had skittered away, thinking that if my head was bleeding, there was no way to tell. And then the count walked in and stared at me from overhead. He said something, I don't remember what, and picked me up as if I was an infant, as if I weighed nothing. He carried me all the way back up here and put me to bed."

"The count?" Chivarion asked. "Count Strahd von Zarovich, ruler of the land, the guy in the fancy suit? I can understand him giving you some wine, but now you're saying he picked you up when you were covered in blood and carried you up a bunch of stairs?"

She nodded. "It was pitch dark. For me, it was dim, of course, but for him, with no darkvision? How could he have navigated that? And, let's be honest, my size is not insignificant. Plus, I was naked in the bath, and now I'm clothed. It makes no sense." She plucked the sticky undershirt away from her chest. "Gods, I need a real bath. And a hangover cure."

She sat up and swung her feet to the floor, confirming that every bit of her was covered in dried—and in some places wet—blood. Red smears appeared under her feet the moment they touched the stone floor, and yet there were no other stains in the room. Her fingers clutched the edge of the bed, and she wobbled back and forth as if not quite strong enough to stay upright.

"Need food," Kah said. "Food and drink."

"And healing, perhaps?" Chivarion suggested. "In case it really all is from a bump on her head."

Kah stared at her hands sadly. "You and the tressym are two. That is all Akadi grants me."

"A girl's got to do everything for herself, eh?" Alishai closed her eyes and raised her hands, a look of steely determination turning her face to stone. "On my oath," she muttered. "By my steel." A moonlit glow shrouded her body, and when she opened her eyes again, she looked a lot more . . . alive. And awake. And less hungover. Still bloody, though. Chivarion stepped back.

The tiefling stood and jumped up and down as if testing her body's sturdiness. "Right. Food. Shall we all go together just in case something disgusting explodes out of a bathtub?"

Chivarion took another step back. "I'm all in, but we really do need to find some water. You look like— Well, I mean, you're . . . kind of purple, honestly. It's very strange."

Despite the blood soaked into her clothes, Alishai buckled on her armor and hung her weapons in their right places and put on her boots. Chivarion was, of course, always well armed. Kah fetched her mace and crossbow. They moved into the hall in fighting order, with Chivarion in front, Alishai in back, and Kah in the middle alongside Murder. It was funny, Chivarion thought, how last night he had gone to sleep thinking that they were safe and cozy, under the protection of a generous lord with grand holdings, but now they were traversing the spiral staircase as if expecting a fight at any moment.

"Your shoulder!" Alishai said, just noticing the wreck of his tunic. "Wait. Kah was healing you while I was waking up. What happened?"

"Oh, an ugly cat-thing leaped out of the secret door in the back of my wardrobe, which I found because the proper, me-sized door was magicked closed and the window was sealed up. The cat-thing climbed onto my back and attached itself like a leech."

After a few moments, Alishai said, "That is not normal."

"No, I didn't think so. This castle is odd."

When they hit the first landing, Alishai stepped off and pointed. "This floor. This is where it happened. There's a sort of gallery of statues, and a cozy study, and a melting cake, and then the bath chamber."

Chivarion took his sword in hand. "We have to go see the blood tub, right?"

Alishai sighed. "I suppose we must. Can't wait to see what a mess I made, flailing out of the tub and falling on my arse."

She moved to the front, and Chivarion obligingly moved behind Kah. He was already accustomed to always sandwiching—mmm, sandwiches! He was so hungry—himself between the most vulnerable members of his current team and all the horrible things in the world that wanted to kill and/or eat them. Kah had her mace in hand, but so far, she had not proven herself to be a talented fighter. Perhaps Alishai had botched that first fight, but Chivarion could see that she was trained and powerful, and also that she had an enormous glaive, and he respected that.

The next room was indeed a lavish study, although there were altogether too many books for Chivarion's tastes. They covered the walls and were strewn across a large table. Flopped across this table, seeming quite dead, was Rotrog the orc.

10

KAH

This place!

This place was so strange, and it was doing strange things to people, and the poor orc—

Kah hurried to his side and put two fingers to his neck. There was his heartbeat, heavy and strong but slower than she would've expected. He was breathing, but again, so slowly. Oh, if only she could use her healing spells on him, but Akadi granted her only so many gifts, and she was not accustomed to healing so many people in such a short time. She would have to be careful, in this peculiar place, not to expend herself too quickly. It would be a terrible thing, letting her new friends down or causing them pain.

She'd thought herself safe here. She'd fallen asleep, so cozy and protected. And then she woke up to everything going sideways.

"Not dead," she said, looking up at Chivarion and Alishai. "But something is wrong. Poison, maybe?" She sniffed the goblet.

Alishai hurried over, rubbing her hands together. "I checked last night, but I did not see evidence of foul play. Then again, a lot has happened since last night, and I was perhaps not in my right mind."

Together, they looked closely at the orc, from his rumpled auburn hair falling over the contours of his wide jaws and jutting tusks to the drool pooled on the table underneath his pale cheek. His eyes were closed, and his robes, at least, weren't covered in blood. Kah hadn't smelled any poison, but there wasn't an obvious wound, and his neck didn't look broken.

Alishai held out her hands and murmured a spell Kah didn't know, and after a few moments, Rotrog's head jerked up, his eyes wide and crazed.

"How dare you?" he barked. "Can't you see that I'm studying?" He reached for a nearby book, slammed it shut, and pulled it close like a jealous lover.

"I think you mean 'thanks,'" Alishai said.

"For what? Disturbing my rest? I was up quite late, poring through these valuable tomes. Our host keeps a glorious library. And a better wine cellar. Such a learned man. We spent many an hour conversing over a bottle of wine while you slept."

That got Alishai's attention. "At what hour?"

"I— Well, quite late! After that marvelous repast, we retired here to play a board game of his own devising. I drank nearly an entire bottle of the most glorious red wine, and then he showed me to a sumptuous chamber just through those doors. The King's Chamber, he called it. I was a bit tipsy, but intellectual curiosity waits for no orc. He graciously gave me full access to the study, and here I've been ever since."

"But when did Strahd leave you?"

Rotrog looked about. "How could I know? There are no windows here, and it seems always to be dusk. Why are you concerned with our host's whereabouts?"

"Because I thought . . ." Alishai walked to the closed doors Rotrog had indicated and pushed them open. "What the hells?"

Kah scurried to her side. The room had to be twice the size of the one they'd been given and truly fit for a king. The bed was big enough for five orcs, and sumptuous red velvet hung around arched doorways, the crimson fabric far less moth-eaten than the tapestries that shed dust with every breath of air in their smaller room. A grand window let in a chill breeze that smelled of sturdy pines and possible snow. Tall white candles in golden candelabras shed the brightest light Kah had seen since waking up in Barovia. Why, this room was almost pleasant!

"He must like you," she said.

"I believe our count sees in me a fellow intellectual." Rotrog, now back to himself and no longer the pale green of lichen, puffed up a bit and stroked his chin. "He is a thinker. A strategist. And a student of the magical arts. We have much in common." The orc looked much better; his eyes were no longer red. He'd just been hungover, apparently. And here she'd thought him on the verge of death. This place made her paranoid.

Alishai turned to Chivarion. "What's your room like?"

"Not like that," he admitted. "Not as shabby as yours, either. The bed is big and nice, and the atmosphere was jolly enough once I'd ripped the boards off the window and killed the murderous cat-bat."

"I want to find Strahd and ask him why—" The tiefling's red-tinted head swiveled to the left, and her face flushed nearly purple. "Wait. Wait. No." She stomped out of sight, and Kah and Chivarion moved into Rotrog's bedchamber to see what had upset her so. The furious tiefling stood before yet another grand set of doors and shoved them open to reveal a luxurious bathing chamber. "This! This is the bathtub! It was full of blood!"

"Oh! I wanted to see that! It sounded like an impressive amount of blood." Chivarion practically jogged over, with Kah following. Rotrog reluctantly joined them.

"Please do not disturb my personal spaces," he said stiffly.

Alishai rounded on him, bug-eyed. "Last night, I dreamed that I entered this bathing chamber and found the tub full of hot, perfumed water. I climbed in, and then it turned to blood, and a hideous monster exploded out of it and scurried across the ceiling. And then I woke up like this." She held out her arms, and Rotrog actually looked at her as if for the first time. He grimaced at the rusty red coating every inch of her.

"That is unacceptable."

"I know! The blood—"

"Not that! You had no permission to be here, in my quarters,"

Rotrog growled. "And now you're shedding"—he shivered with disgust—"flakes."

The bloodstained tiefling faced off with the orc. "I thought I was dreaming," Alishai said. "But it must've been real. I didn't know the fancy lordling had given you the special room. I came through this other door. When I open it, you're going to see a long table with a moldy cake—" She opened a single door to reveal a banquet hall that had been poorly kept. The sickly-sweet smell of rot nearly turned Kah's stomach, and she didn't look too closely at the cake in question. "Yes! So you see, I didn't even notice the bedroom."

She walked back to the tub and stared down into its depths. When Kah joined her, she couldn't find one droplet of blood, not a single reddish stain. The tub was gleaming as if freshly cleaned. The entire chamber was tidier and better kept than anything else they'd encountered since arriving.

"You slept through it, Rotrog. I'm surprised you didn't wake up when I started screaming. You must've been deeply, deeply drunk."

Rotrog bared his teeth and wrinkled his nose. "And what if I was? We had quite the day, and it's rude to turn down a count's finest vintage. I promise you this: Had I heard you screaming in my bathing chamber, I would've definitely responded, and not politely. Perhaps you did dream it."

"Explain the blood in my ears, then!"

The orc looked away. "I know little of the tiefling anatomy—"

"That is so ignorant!" Alishai cried.

"But I must assume you stumbled into something you shouldn't have," Rotrog finished fussily. "Normal people do not simply wake up covered in blood."

"She didn't wake up. I woke her up," Chivarion said helpfully. "Hard as hells to wake her up, actually." He squinted at her. "Was everyone drunk but me? Because, rude. That mead at dinner barely took the edge off."

"I wasn't that drunk," she admitted, tail lashing. "But I don't feel right. Even after healing myself. I'm tired. And perhaps a little grouchy."

"Need food," Kah said, reminding her. "Need food, need to find Fielle."

Alishai took one last look in the tub, then stared up at the high ceiling. There was no blood there, no trail anywhere in the room from a tired tiefling or scuttling beast, and such a thing would've been terribly difficult to clean. "The creature that burst out of the tub went straight up, then it skittered that way, and through those curtains. It was humanlike but almost skeletal, with stringy hair. Naked."

"That description does not reflect any creature I've ever read about, much less encountered," Rotrog admitted.

"Nothing here does." Alishai peeked behind the velvet curtains as if making sure the thing wasn't waiting in the wings, but she seemed satisfied with whatever she found there. "I mean, have you ever heard of Barovia? Or seen it on a map? Met someone who claimed to hail from here? Let me stop you there because the answer is no. Now, let's go find some food before I get *really* grouchy."

With her glaive in hand, she led them down two floors to the dining hall. Another repast awaited, complete with cider, watered wine, a platter of breads and sweet rolls, eggs and sausages, porridge, and even some sickly berries. They all helped themselves and sat in their same chairs from the night before; no place was set for Strahd, and Fielle's chair was empty.

Once she'd eaten her fill of porridge—Kah found eggs in poor taste and did not want to taste pork ever again, after yesterday—she rose and went to the grand organ. Last night, she'd noted the scratches on the floor, and this morning, they were even more obvious. Kah loved a puzzle, and now that she knew there was something hidden behind the instrument, she was determined to find it.

She started by feeling all around the edges of the organ, but there was no obvious catch. Next, she touched a few random keys, but they merely made that awful bleating noise Alishai had described so well.

"Perhaps I'm no longer hungover, but that is not the apex of musicality," Rotrog complained.

Kah didn't particularly mind annoying the orc, but she was aware that if she made too much noise, she was likely to attract the attention of Rahadin or some other disapproving servant. Although they'd been given full run of the castle, it was unlikely the count was eager to have all his secrets laid bare, and Kah did not like being yelled at. Instead, she considered the pedals on the ground. When she tapped one with her claw, it made almost no sound, which was a great relief.

She pressed every pedal, then tried them two at a time, and after a few minutes of working through the various combinations, she was rewarded with a click. With a meaty scrape over the stone floor, the organ slid out only a few feet, just enough to admit a person. Kah trilled in triumph, and Alishai swiftly joined her, bringing along a sausage stuffed in a sweet roll.

"Clever," she said, and Kah preened a little.

The space beyond the organ was dark, with long arrow slits offering the only source of light. Kah would've been frightened to enter, but she did not sense any traps, and she was comforted by Alishai's sturdy presence—and her array of weapons and spells.

"What's back here?" Rotrog appeared, squinting around the small room as he stepped inside.

Chivarion, too, had joined them. "Anything fun that wants to fight?"

But Kah was puzzled. In a secret room like this, she would've expected treasure, or hidden magical items, or something exciting. Instead, there was only a sad collection of mirrors leaning against the wall, dozens of them. Big mirrors and small ones, gilded monstrosities and cheap brass hand mirrors fit only for a maid's morning ablutions. Kah ran a finger over the top of a mirror nearly as tall as herself; it came away coated with dust.

"You know, I haven't seen a mirror in the castle, now that I think about it," Rotrog said. "And our fine host is quite handsome. Why the aversion, I wonder?"

Kah did not know what other species found attractive about one another. They had no feathers, no sharp beaks, and their eyes were unforgivably dull and inexpressive. Living without wings was difficult enough, but living without feathers, naked for all the world to see? The thought made her pull up her hood.

"Breaking a mirror is bad luck," Chivarion said as his tressym sat before a mirror, regarding her angular face. "Seven years of it, I've heard. For humans, at least. My kind is so long-lived that it might be longer for us." He snatched the tressym up by her armpits and stilled the mirror the creature had nearly knocked over with her tail.

"So maybe our host is superstitious. Or cursed." Alishai poked at her crispy red hair in a mirror, and it made a terrible crunch. "Gods, I still need water. My hair is hardening to stone."

Rotrog went to an arrow slit and looked out. "Strahd is a man of reason. Of science. He told me the locals are indeed a superstitious bunch of fools, but I do not believe the count is frightened of some irrational make-believe. If he did this, he had a reason." He stroked his chin. "Although I could see, perhaps, him following the local beliefs to calm his people. He is a concerned leader, after all."

Kah, too, looked out an arrow slit, but all she saw was gray, cloudy sky and the reaching gray spires of the mountains. If she lived somewhere this dreary, she might develop some superstitions herself.

"You know, he may not like mirrors, but there's a portrait of him outside my room." Chivarion clutched the tressym to his chest as the creature fought to obtain her freedom, probably to knock over a mirror. "When he was younger, I think? He looks a little different, but not much."

"So maybe the rich prefer images they can control to images they can't," Alishai said.

"I'm sure there's a perfectly rational explanation. A person can store old things away. Perhaps mirrors are no longer the fashion here." Rotrog seemed desperate for any story that showed Strahd in a good light, but Kah wasn't so sure. People didn't tend to build secret rooms and go to the trouble of hiding things there for altruistic reasons.

"That's it. I'm going to find a servant if it kills me." Alishai gave the mirrors one last headshake of disapproval and swiftly fled the secret room.

"And I could use some more meat," Chivarion said, still wrestling his pet. "Muscles, after all, do not grow themselves."

"You can just leave the room without explaining why," Rotrog huffed, following them out.

As the others made their exit, Kah caught her reflection in one of the big mirrors. She'd not encountered many mirrors in her life, as there were none among Akadi's flock back home; being too vain was considered a distraction. She pushed back her hood and shyly admired her bright eyes and shimmering feathers. Holding up a hand, she watched how her reflection moved in tandem with her. It was like a game: turning her head, opening and closing her hands, watching her feathers shift prettily to show a rainbow of oily colors. But then the Kah in the mirror—something about her changed. Her eyes were not so kind. She held up both hands to the mirror, curling her long black fingers like she wanted to reach through and grab Kah—

Or something else.

Something she was never supposed to touch, much less take.

She stepped back to find every mirror held the same image, the same cruel Kah with reaching hands.

With a squawk of fear, she turned away, squeezing her eyes shut. She didn't want to remember this moment. She had to get out of this room, away from the mirrors. But as she hurried toward the dining hall's golden shine of candles and a welcome second bowl of porridge, the unthinkable happened. The organ swung into place, the secret door slamming shut, and she was left alone with the mirrors—and what the mirrors revealed.

11

FIELLE

Fielle didn't quite remember how, but she was currently sitting at the dining table. Alone. Someone had filled a plate for her, selecting more food than she could eat in a week. She longed for some good, strong coffee, for the way it always helped her wake up and face the day, but it would appear that all the drinks here were cold. She would've asked a servant, but there were none to be found. Only Rahadin, who—

Oh, yes. He had walked her here. Or carried her? Yes, he must've carried her. She had never been so tired in all her life, as if her limbs were fighting her. She wanted to sleep, and she wanted to run. There was no in between. Rahadin had ordered her to eat, and so eat she must. She selected a piece of toast and nibbled at it, but it dissolved to ash in her mouth. She choked it down, but it wanted to come up again. Was even her own throat going to rebel against her today?

"Fielle!"

Alishai appeared from behind the organ, and Fielle gasped when she saw the dried blood coating the tiefling's skin and hair. Despite her exhaustion, she stood and hurried over, hands out.

"Are you hurt?" she asked, not that there was much she could do.

To her surprise, Alishai laughed. "No wound. There was this tub full of blood, and . . ."

"It's not full of blood anymore," Chivarion said, strolling out behind her.

"Well, it was a long night," Alishai continued. "I still can't find any water to wash with."

"I don't understand—"

"No one does," Rotrog said sourly, emerging from behind the organ and sitting down to a plate overflowing with breakfast meats. "I don't know which is worse, the smell or the sight."

Fielle held up her hands and wiggled her fingers. "May I?"

Alishai drew back as if startled but then relaxed. "I suppose it can't hurt."

Fielle murmured a word and swirled her fingertips through the air, and a sudden wind whirled around Alishai, starting at her feet. Her boots, dirty and dull, were left polished, the leather smooth and supple again. Her red-spattered armor now looked brand new. Best of all, the cleaning cantrip scrubbed away all the crusted blood and left her turquoise hair squeaky-clean with a pleasant bounce and a little curl. It was immensely satisfying to see such an improvement in someone who had been so conspicuously miserable; back home, Fielle had been required to use her magic mostly on pots and pans that no one else ever saw. As for Alishai, she . . . actually smiled.

"By the moon, I feel fresh as a flower!"

Chivarion leaned in, smoldering. "And you look—"

"Disinterested in compliments." Alishai's glare didn't seem to bother Chivarion in the slightest. In fact, he only seemed more amused by her disdain.

Fielle chuckled—

Then swooned.

The world went woozy around her, and the tiefling caught her gently before she could tumble to the floor.

"You good?" Alishai's voice sounded like it was underwater.

"Just tired. They always tell me I should eat more. You get angry when you're hungry, but I faint like a goat." Fielle tried to make it into a joke, but even she could tell it just sounded pathetic. Alishai guided her back to her chair.

"Eat, then. Drink. And where'd the dress come from?"

Fielle looked down.

This was not her colorful skirt of many pockets with soft leggings underneath, nor her shirt and vest and belt of potions and tools. She was in a formal gown in various shades of violet, tightly fitted and perfectly handmade for someone of her proportions, and warm enough to cut the castle's bone-deep chill, thanks to a furred cape. She did not remember changing clothes. She . . . did not remember being unclothed at all.

This was disturbing.

As was the fact that she'd lost time.

She remembered dinner last night, remembered Rahadin guiding her to a chamber on the same floor, up just a few steps. The room had smelled of lavender and seemed freshly scrubbed, with clean blankets and mounds of sumptuous pillows. She'd lain down to sleep and had the strangest dreams. Something about a prince, a wedding, a high parapet? Wind and a green valley. Flying. Someone had held her hand and whispered to her, brushed cold lips across her throat.

She shivered, struggling to put the pieces together.

Dreams were strange things, after all.

"The dress was in my room," she said, because what else was there to say? She didn't want to cause problems. If she told the others that she had no idea where the dress had come from or how it had gotten on her body, they were likely to overreact and cause a situation. It all just sounded so very tiresome.

She forced herself to eat bigger bites, washing down the bread with cold cider. She wondered if anyone else was struggling and looked at each of her companions in turn. Alishai had recently been covered in blood from horns to tail. Rotrog seemed fine if a little pale. Chivarion had a large hole in the back of his shirt, through which his muscular gray shoulder was visible. Fielle ached to mend it, but . . . she needed more energy before attempting any magic, or she would certainly faint again.

And—

"Where is Kah?" she asked.

The others looked around in confusion. Chivarion stuck his head under the table as if the kenku might be playing a game of hide-and-seek.

"Blast! The organ!" Alishai hurried to the instrument and stared at it. "It closed on its own! How did she open it? Was anyone watching?"

"A few off-key blats and then there was a door," Rotrog said between sausages.

Chivarion strode over and tried to pull the organ away from the wall with only his strength, but it resisted him. Alishai touched a few keys, muttering to herself, then fell to her knees and pressed on various pedals. Feeling utterly useless, Fielle struggled up from her chair and knelt by Alishai, her gown pooling around her. It took far too much energy, but she somehow knew exactly which pedals to push at the same time. There was a click, and the organ slid away from the wall.

Kah burst through the narrow space, panting. Cobwebs covered her feathers like a cloak, and her eyes were dilated, her pupils tiny pinpricks in the lemon yellow. "Spiders," she whispered. "Don't like spiders."

Fielle plucked an enormous eight-legged tarantula off the kenku's back, and Alishai knocked it from her hand before stomping it multiple times. Fielle flinched; the poor spider. She had hated spiders once, but not now.

"What do you need?" Fielle asked, one hand on Kah's shoulder.

Kah shook her head, ruffling her feathers. "Food. Fewer spiders." She shivered. "This place. It's always watching."

After swatting at her cloak like it might still be covered in invisible arachnids, the kenku took her seat. Alishai made sure Fielle got safely to her place, and Chivarion scraped up the squashed spider with a spoon and tossed it to his tressym. Rotrog continued to shove sausages in his face as if it were all perfectly normal. Just five average strangers having a delightful feast in a moldering castle.

Kah was right, though. It always felt as if someone were staring at Fielle, as if a weapon were pointed right between her shoulder blades. There were never quite enough torches and candles, and wherever she went, her shadow wouldn't quite behave, as if it wasn't certain where the light was coming from. Even now, in a room lit by a grand chandelier and multiple candelabras, their shadows seemed to fight on the stone walls, clawing at one another, tearing at the very weft of reality. Fielle felt like that—like something was in her chest, tearing her heart up like a piece of paper, ripping it in half.

This was ridiculous. She needed to eat.

She bravely took a sausage and some eggs and decided that she would get them down no matter the cost. Feeling weak and silly did not suit her. She would not faint again, would not make these poor strangers pick up her slack.

After a few moments during which the sound of chewing filled the room, Alishai leaned in. "Look, a free bed has its place, and the food is plentiful, but does anyone else feel like we might do better in the village? If what we really want is to find a way home, I don't think we're going to discover it here."

"But our host has offered me use of his atlas," Rotrog exclaimed. "I just need to find it—"

Alishai aimed her fork at him. "That's just it! Who can't find an atlas? Has anyone offered us any help at all, or are we all having horrible dreams and fighting strange monsters and getting stuck in secret rooms? This is some kind of—I don't know. Nightmare? It feels all wrong."

"The village will at least have a road that goes to a bigger city," Chivarion pointed out. "And likely a coach delivering people and mail. Any tavern keeper worth their salt should be able to point us toward Baldur's Gate."

"The ruler of a bit of land should be able to do that, too," Alishai noted. "Does this Strahd not send letters? Or ship off to a bigger city for artisans or a change of clothes? Any landowner knows how to find a bigger road."

"Well, I wish to stay." Rotrog dabbed at his lips with a napkin. "This place suits me fine in every particular, and my studies are not yet complete."

Alishai rolled her eyes at him. "Your main area of study is kissing the count's rump. Anyway. All in favor of slipping out to the village to ask about travel routes, raise your hand."

Four hands went up: everyone but Rotrog. Although Strahd had been nothing but kind to her, Fielle was uneasy and off-kilter. Ever since she'd arrived in the castle, it felt as if she were floating through a dream, or perhaps drifting in and out of a fever. Time was as flimsy as a dandelion puff, and space no longer followed the proper rules. At least in the monster-filled butcher shop, she'd felt like . . . herself.

"Rotrog, feel free to stay. We're going down to the village. If we find out anything more, we'll send word. Right?" Alishai looked around, and everyone nodded.

"And the word we'll send will be: bye." Chivarion waved at Rotrog like he was an infant and stood to stretch. "Out the same way we came in?"

Fielle gathered her strength and stood. She noticed Kah dumping pastries into her cloak's pockets and Chivarion nodding in appreciation and swiping yet more food into his own bag. If only she still had her skirt of many pockets and her bandoliers and pouches. The dress she wore now was heavy and cumbersome, the waist tight enough to make breathing a challenge. Her rib cage felt crowded. Hopefully they wouldn't run into any trouble on the long walk down the mountain. Hopefully she could actually *make* the long walk down the mountain.

Alishai went first, then Kah, Fielle, and Chivarion and his tressym. The beefy drow's presence there was a comfort to Fielle. If she faltered, he had quick reflexes and was likely to catch her before she fell and hit her head. They took a left out of the dining room and into a hall guarded by a suit of armor. The metal gleamed in the candlelight, and Fielle would've sworn someone watched her from the eye slits in the closed helmet.

But the moment Alishai set foot in the entryway, the sound of cracking stone echoed down the hall. Fielle watched in horror as all eight gargoyles perched around the ceiling came loose from their moorings, twisting their hideous heads and spreading their bat-like wings. As the first gargoyle launched itself into the air, Alishai pulled out her glaive. It swooped toward her, and she shouted and swung the silver blade. Thunder filled the room as her weapon connected with the stone monstrosity, knocking it to the ground. Behind Fielle, Chivarion already had his sword drawn and was beginning to shake with rage, and in front of her, Kah was praying as she clutched her mace. The air was full of swooping creatures screeching and gibbering, and then the gusts caused by their wings snuffed out every torch and candelabra, leaving Fielle in complete darkness.

She was without her potions and magic, without any defenses at all. She couldn't see, and she'd gotten so turned around that she didn't know where the doors were.

"Fielle, duck!" Chivarion called.

Dropping to her knees, she landed roughly on the stone and felt air whoosh by overhead. The heavy thud of metal striking something like stone made her grimace, and she buried her head under her hands. She didn't know where to go, didn't know what the others were doing, where their weapons were. The darkness all around her was alive with fighting, spells, muttering, slashes, sick thuds. The drow snorted like an angry bull. Kah called out a prayer, and light filled the room, giving Fielle the brief and terrible gift of sight. Everywhere she looked was a leering gargoyle. One saw her; its slitted eyes lit with fiendish glee as it charged at her, and Chivarion's pet tressym used her back as a springboard to launch her leathery body right at the beast, her claws digging into Fielle's flesh even through the thick dress.

"No, no," Fielle muttered from the floor, tears streaming down her face. She didn't even have the energy to stand. "Please help." Somehow, impossibly, it felt as if cold fingers caressed her cheek in apology.

But then the ground right beside her shook with a mighty crack, and hard stone claws latched around both of her upper arms. The gargoyle snickered as it pulled her up from the floor, its fingers bruising her ribs. Fielle fought with everything she had, writhed and kicked and spit, but the gargoyle's grip was as hard as stone—*was* stone—and she had never been so weak in her life. She felt a sick pop as something terrible happened in her shoulder and that entire arm went numb. As the gargoyle began to drag her away into the darkness, Fielle did the only thing she could.

She went unconscious.

12

ROTROG

The silly fools, Rotrog thought. What kind of an idiot would look at the generosity of a count, at the delectable table set in a castle, at the enormous study filled with books and stocked with fine wine, and think, "No, thank you very much, I'd prefer a filthy village of small-minded yokels and a straw pallet on the floor near the rats; extra fleas, if you please." He himself would be perfectly happy to dwell here for many years, learning from the count and mastering new spells until he was even more powerful than High Mage Argitau. Rotrog was still embarrassed about his showing in the abattoir fight, but he was certain that with a little training and practice, with just a bit of confidence, he would reach all of his loftiest dreams.

He reached for yet another sausage, waiting to hear the screech of the portcullis rising, but instead, he heard cracks and thumps and thunder. He got up from his chair and took his orb-topped staff in hand, peering around the corner past the entryway. The room beyond was pitch dark, the big doors closed. The noises coming from the enclosed hall made him want to sneak right back up to his room and close all the doors in between. His friends—no, the strangers with whom he'd been traveling—were seemingly caught in the fight of their lives.

As Rotrog tiptoed past the door, it exploded outward. Chivarion, covered in cuts and bruises, had an unconscious Fielle tossed over one shoulder like a bag of grain and his gleaming sword in hand.

"Run!" he shouted when he saw Rotrog, gesturing for the orc to go ahead of him up the staircase. Not sure what else to do, Rotrog actually did as he'd been ordered. He was tired, and perhaps such fights were not his bailiwick. Running seemed like the proper answer. It was always better to have Chivarion between him and whatever wanted to hurt him.

With no better options, he bounded up the grand staircase.

"Faster! They're coming!" Chivarion growled.

"Who is?"

"The nasty rock things! Like if a statue and a demon had an ugly baby!"

That wasn't helpful, but if Chivarion thought something was nasty, Rotrog did not want to meet it. He scrambled up the steps, and Chivarion's tressym darted past him.

"Are they following?" Chivarion called back.

"I don't think so."

That was Alishai, so she, at least, had also survived the encounter. Rotrog glanced back over his shoulder. The tiefling, so recently cleaned up, again looked like she'd been in a war. Rotrog wondered if Kah was dead and had been left behind, but then a radiant light burst out of the room, followed by the heavy clunk of stone hitting more stone. The kenku darted out, mace in her hands, and ran up the stairs, shedding feathers in her wake. Satisfied that everyone was accounted for, and that the enemy would have to get through four people before it reached him, Rotrog redoubled his efforts to reach the study.

By the time he collapsed in an overstuffed leather chair, he was out of breath and regretting his decision to eat so many sausages. The rest of the party ran inside, and once Kah had joined them, Alishai pulled both of the study doors closed, yanked a fireplace poker from its stand, and shoved it through the door handles. Chivarion carefully placed Fielle on a sofa, and he and Alishai stood before the closed doors, weapons in hand, waiting for the sound of stone-clawed beasts ramming into the sturdy wood. Not wanting to show any fear despite the fact that his heart was galloping, Rotrog stood, his staff aimed at the door, the right spell running on repeat in his mind, the spell that was most definitely not for creating grease.

"Were they not following us?" Chivarion asked Kah, the last one out of the foyer.

"Not sure," she chirped as she looked over an unconscious Fielle. "Stunned them proper, didn't stop to check. Alishai, can you help?"

Alishai stepped toward the door and listened hard before shrugging and joining Kah beside the couch. Rotrog could see that one of Fielle's arms had been pulled out of its socket, and her face was covered in violet bruises that clashed with her dress.

"Poor thing," Alishai murmured before turning to Kah. "Hold her up, and I'll reset it." Together, they maneuvered Fielle to sitting, and with one sickening crack, the frail human's arm was back where it belonged. After they'd laid her back down, Alishai held up her hands, closed her eyes, and growled, "On my oath, by my steel." White light surrounded both women, and then the bruises melted back into Fielle's pallid skin. Somewhere along the way, she'd lost her furred cape. "What were those stone things?"

"Gargoyles," Kah offered.

"What an awful word. Like gargling," Chivarion said.

Alishai gave him a look. "Well, I hate them."

"I don't think anyone's a fan." In all this time, not so much as a pebble had plunked against the door. Chivarion reached for the poker and withdrew it from the rusted handles. After peeking outside, he shrugged. "I suppose they didn't follow."

"Gargoyles are guardians," Kah said thoughtfully.

"So what are they guarding?"

Kah's head hung, and a single feather fluttered to the stone floor. "Us. Keeping us in. That's the way out."

"But why would— Wait. Look!"

Chivarion's giddiness caught everyone's attention, and they all turned from the doors to the fireplace. The drow stood before it, holding the poker, but Rotrog could not see why he was so excited.

"Are you an aficionado of the fine arts?" he asked, gesturing to the painting.

"A what of the— Ew, no. What? No." Chivarion wrinkled his nose and tossed the poker to the floor. "When Alishai pulled the poker out, a secret door opened. Beyond the fire. Don't you see?"

Rotrog stepped closer, and that's when he noticed that the soot-stained back wall of the hearth had been replaced by yawning darkness, with a subtle breeze that whispered at the flames. He had suspected that Strahd had spell books squirreled away somewhere nearby, and what better secret cache than a hidden room?

"We must douse the fire," he said, nose in the air. "We need water."

"I spent most of my morning looking for water, if you don't recall," Alishai said, still a bit sour. "I found none outside of the liquid in our breakfast beverages."

Rotrog had a sudden idea, and he was certain he could pull it off.

"There is a cistern outside my chamber," he said, pleased with how smoothly the lie fell from his lips. "I couldn't lift it, but—"

Chivarion stretched and sauntered in that direction with Alishai and Kah on his heels. If there had been a cistern, Rotrog could've easily lifted it; he was an orc, after all. But he merely needed the fools out of the area. As soon as they were in his chamber, he slammed the doors closed and slid the discarded poker through the handles, then hurried to the fire. Taking a deep breath, he held out his hands and performed a spell he'd never actually managed before. With a single word, the fire in the hearth was extinguished, leaving only a steaming pile of soot. He held up his robes and hurried through the open space behind the hearth and into the secret room beyond, quite pleased with himself and ready to claim whatever books Strahd had hoped to hide from him.

"Is that you, Guzzlegut?" asked a harsh, scratchy voice. "Trying to sneak up on me?"

The moment Rotrog saw the witch standing there, grinning with broken, browned teeth, he knew he was in trouble. She was naked, her skin the pale white of a grub, stretched in some places and wrinkled up in others like an ill-fitting suit she'd hastily put on over too-sharp bones. Wisps of wet black hair struggled around her face, and her eyes were cast over white with writhing movement beneath as if worms were struggling to break through. In one hand, she held a knife carved of bone, and with the other, she pointed a gnarled finger at Rotrog.

"You're not my little Guzzlegut, no no!" She cackled. "Just a toad that learned how to walk upright." She stepped closer, cocking her head as her nose twitched. "A poison toad, sent here as punishment for some foul deed, I'll wager. I can smell it on you, rotting within. Tell me, does Strahd know of the chancre in your heart?"

Rotrog was frozen, his clever mind, for once, empty. What did this witch know?

He licked his lips nervously. "I am but a humble visitor to the castle," he said.

"You are a creature of obscene hunger," she corrected. "You crave power. You think you can just take what you desire, but there are consequences, little poison toad. We who protect our master will not let you steal again."

She raised her hands and threw back her head, and Rotrog raised his staff, but he wasn't fast enough.

"Take that, toadling!"

The witch tossed something small at him as she murmured a curse, and Rotrog felt the magic slam into his body.

She was right—he was just a large toad!

It was the funniest thing he'd ever heard in his entire life!

He, a fully grown orc male, greatest adept of the academy, was nothing more than a large amphibian, tall and boggle-eyed with skinny legs!

Rotrog laughed and laughed. He laughed so hard that he couldn't breathe. His stomach muscles ached, his lungs burned, and tears ran down his face.

But—well, it wasn't that funny, actually. He was nothing like a toad. The witch's spell was good but not great. Rotrog was doubled over as the last laugh gusted out of him, and he pointed his staff at the witch and returned his own spell, the one with which he was most familiar. A bubble of acid slammed into the witch's leg, the vile green liquid sizzling against the wet white skin, peeling it back like the flesh of an overripe fruit.

"You do not know my heart," Rotrog said as she danced around, trying to push her lumpy skin back down over the wound. Just for good measure, Rotrog darted forward and smashed his staff into her head while she wasn't paying attention, then jumped back.

Unfortunately, he tripped on something—

The witch's familiar, a patchy black cat.

She cackled anew and hit him with a ray of frost. Rotrog rolled to the side, and the glancing blow of frozen sleet rendered his left arm completely numb and mostly useless. That didn't matter. He could still beat her with his right arm. He was Rotrog, and he was powerful! He had studied for this day, poring over the academy library's tomes in his search for—

The witch landed a kick in his ribs as her cat sunk claws into his calf. Rotrog flailed and thrashed and scrambled to his feet, lashing out with his staff but missing them both. He hurled a firebolt at her and missed. The firebolt crashed into the wall, shaking the stones and leaving a scorch mark.

"Oopsy doopsy, little toad!" the witch rasped. "Let's get you back in the cauldron where you belong."

She cast a spell Rotrog had never seen before, and he braced himself for fire, ice, acid. If the spell had hit him, he didn't feel it.

"Looks like you—" he began.

And then he vomited.

A wave of illness rippled over his body. His head was burning and feverish, his stomach was roiling, his legs were weak. He held out his staff to hurl magic missiles at his opponent, but all that came out of his mouth was acid swimming with sausage bits. The witch reared back, cackling madly, as her black cat cavorted around her bony white legs.

Rotrog wanted to hit her with a spell, but every time he opened his mouth to speak, it was filled with bile. He wanted to rush forward and strike her, but he was too weak to stand. Whatever that spell was, it was stronger than anything he'd ever felt.

That was the problem with the academy, he thought. High Mage Argitau focused so much on theory and so little on spellcasting that Rotrog was utterly unprepared for a duel. Sure, he'd practiced magic alone in his dormitory, but facing off with an enemy who also knew spells—who knew *more* spells—turned it from a pleasant exercise into a life-or-death situation.

"Come now, little toad. Don't you have any more magic? Some wizard you are!"

Rotrog's hands went into fists, his ring digging into his knuckle. He was an excellent wizard, but this was—

Oh, gods. His guts were twisted in knots; his brain was on fire! He couldn't think.

The witch stood over him, triumphant, fetid, dripping acid, cackling. She smelled like corpses rotting in the swamp, which only made Rotrog more nauseated. She raised her hands and grinned down at him with worms in her teeth. "Toodle-oo, little toad," she said.

"Toodle-oo to you!"

Two crossbow bolts sunk into the witch's chest. She looked down, confused, and stumbled backward. Chivarion Dyrr, thundering with rage, stomped across the room and picked up the witch, throwing her into the stone wall. She hit the blocks and crumpled into a heap, her cat caterwauling around her. Chivarion's sword was in his hand, and with one glorious slash, the witch's head went rolling away like a ripe melon.

Chivarion looked at the cat. "I don't like to kill animals," he told it, as if it could understand him.

Murder ran into the room and jumped on top of the cat, hissing and spitting.

"But my friend does."

Turning away from the catfight in which Murder was currently living up to her name, Chivarion reached a hand down to Rotrog and then grimaced.

"You're covered in sick," the drow said.

"I'm—"

Rotrog vomited.

"Sick," Chivarion finished for him. "Anybody got any healing left? Maybe a cleaning spell? Or at least one of those corks they put in wine barrels?"

"That was the last bit," Rotrog told him. "It's wearing off."

"Well, the smell certainly isn't."

"Help me through?" said a faint voice.

Soon Fielle and Kah appeared, with the kenku supporting the human woman as they picked their way around the puddles of acid and sausage.

"It would help if you could stand and move away from the sick," Fielle explained. "Otherwise I'd just have to do the spell again, and I'm so sorry, but I don't think I have the energy."

Rotrog took a deep and cleansing breath—well, it would've been cleansing if not for the smell—and pushed up from the floor. His legs were no longer shaking and wobbly, but he certainly wasn't up to his usual strength. It was no coincidence that he chose to lean against the wall nearest a pile of books. On top was the very thing he'd been looking for—an old and well-used spell book, open to a spell called Ray of Sickness. Rotrog reached for the book, his eyes alight, and the moment his hands connected with it, he felt as if he'd been hit in the head with a hammer. He fell to his knees. Images of witches dancing around a cauldron filled his head. Green fire flickered; cats and toads gathered. A human infant was laid out on a table, a bone knife flashed in the candlelight—

"No," he rasped.

In his head, the witch's cackles echoed and echoed, rattling around his skull.

"No?" Fielle stood before him, the picture of innocence and fragility.

"Just a headache," Rotrog said weakly. He slid the rotting spell book into his robes. To gain these spells for his own, to master the laughter and the illness and wield them against his next enemy—it would be worth it.

Fielle performed her cleaning cantrip, and Rotrog had to admit that for a quotidian little flit of magic, it was handy. He was annoyingly fussy about tidiness, and he'd been unhappy about the soot even before vomit had entered the fray. Now he was clean and crisp and dry, and the air smelled faintly of flowers.

He noticed everyone was staring expectantly at him. Kah jerked her beak toward Fielle.

"That was rather pleasant," Rotrog said.

"You just can't say the words 'thank you,' can you?" Chivarion shook his head. "Not that hard, mate. It's just two words. You can even take it down to 'thanks,' if that's too difficult for you."

Yes, Rotrog hated those words. He hated feeling like he owed anyone anything. But he had to admit to himself that he had lost the fight with the witch and had been about to die covered in vomit, if they hadn't burst in. Which—

"How did you get in here?" he asked.

Chivarion pointed at Fielle. "After you locked us out, for some insane reason of your own, Fielle heard us pummeling the doors and pulled out the poker. I could've busted them down, but that seemed rude."

"And why'd you lock us out in the first place?" Alishai asked from beside the hearth. She had her glaive out, ready to defend them from anything else that might show up.

Everyone stared at Rotrog.

Rotrog stared right back.

At first defiantly, and then . . . guiltily?

He thought of at least ten different lies, because he didn't owe anyone anything.

Oddly, he opted for the truth.

"I thought there might be a spell book in here and I wanted it for myself. I recognize now that this was not the correct way forward." He kept his chin raised, his eyes cold.

"And?" Alishai demanded.

Rotrog looked down at his clean robes, his polished staff.

"I . . . appreciate your interference," he finally said.

"Again, 'thanks' is really easy to say," Chivarion prompted.

"Thanks," Rotrog said through gritted teeth, sounding in no way thankful.

"Not bad, but keep trying. You'll get there."

Rotrog flashed his tusks in a silent growl, then gathered up what little dignity he had left and walked out through the smoking hearth. He hated that he'd been caught looking foolish, and he hated that the little human had saved him by opening the door for the fighters. Whether she knew it or not, according to his people, he now owed her a life debt, and that was no small thing.

As he sat at the long table that had once felt so comfortable, the spell book pressed against the flesh of his chest like a frog-skinned parasite, and the witch's cackles rattled around in his head like broken teeth.

Something was definitely rotten in Barovia.

And the witch was right; something was rotten in him, too.

13

ALISHAI

Alishai was so furious with the godsforsaken orc that she was certain her blue skin was as purple as Fielle's dress. He had purposefully lied to them, sent them on a wild-goose chase, locked them in a room, and done something absolutely stupid that had nearly gotten himself killed. And if it had, the witch would surely have emerged from the secret room and killed Fielle next. Thank goodness all their banging on the door and screaming had awakened her. Thank goodness the witch had been too busy gloating over the defeated orc to notice the drow barbarian about to ram her like an angry sheep.

It wasn't that Alishai particularly cared if Rotrog lived or died, but she hated being lied to—hated it. Even if he was willing to risk his own life for the possibility of some stupid book, he had taken no consideration for the other lives he was putting in danger. His actions were often proving to be selfish and careless, and he didn't even have the talent and power to save himself.

"We're done in here, yes?" Alishai looked around the small stone room, only then noting a chest in the corner and a random scattering of coins. "Or . . . no." She looked to Kah. "Sense anything dangerous?"

Kah knelt and considered the coins. "Coins are safe. Wouldn't touch the chest."

Chivarion squatted to poke at a skeleton in broken armor sitting against a wall. "Yeah, this fellow didn't seem to do so well in here. Why's he clutching at his neck? Is it charades, do you think?"

"Not a game. Something bad in the chest." Kah stood slightly in front of it, although Alishai wasn't sure if this was to protect them from the chest or to guard the chest from the greed of anyone who might ignore the kenku to seek yet more treasure.

"Well, if the coins are safe . . ." Chivarion shuffled around the room, picking up all the gold coins and shoving them into his pockets.

Kah sighed and grabbed a few tarnished coins that were sitting closer to the chest. Alishai thought about it, but . . . well, it didn't sit right with her. On one hand, it was stealing from their host. But on the other hand, the more she learned of Count von Zarovich, the more she had to assume that any coins in his possession didn't come from honest dealings, and she didn't want to profit from anyone else's pain. Selûne would not approve of her followers filling their pockets with blood money.

Once Chivarion had collected the last of the coins, including a partially hidden one pointed out by the tressym, he stood and stretched, cracking his back. "Shall we find a less dreary place to discuss the fact that this castle wants to kill us?" he asked. "That cozy, witchless study, perhaps?"

He strolled back out through the hearth, and Alishai waited until Fielle was out to follow her. The human still looked like she might swoon again; she had not eaten enough breakfast. She returned to the same couch where she'd lain unconscious earlier but looked too shaken and nervous to even attempt closing her eyes again.

Rotrog had already taken his place at the table and was leafing through a book, while Chivarion, Kah, and Alishai selected chairs in a loose circle. Before she could settle in, Alishai retrieved the poker and returned it to its stand by the hearth. The secret door closed, and Alishai rekindled the fire. The less Strahd and his minions knew about the group's discoveries, the better.

"Aha. Here it is. Gargoyles!" Rotrog exclaimed, holding up a book. "Fascinating things!"

"Eh, not so fascinating when they're trying to kill you, but you missed that part." Chivarion played with a knife, twisting its point against his thumb. "But those are definitely the things that wouldn't let us leave."

"Which means their master doesn't want us to leave," Alishai continued. "He sent the invitation, forced our hand with the carriage, and is now keeping us here. Like Fielle said, we were herded to the castle. But why? What use could a wealthy count possibly have for a group of strangers?"

"He is bored," Rotrog said, sounding quite sure of himself. "His people are not an educated lot, and visitors to these parts are rare. I believe he merely wishes for illuminating company."

"If his people aren't educated, isn't that on him?" Alishai snorted. "If he wanted clever people, he would build schools. Print books. He is their lord, after all, and he has enough coin that he leaves it lying around in the darkness."

Rotrog sat forward. "A ruler cannot be held responsible for the quality of his people."

Alishai, too, leaned forward. "Then what's the point of a ruler?"

"Doesn't matter," Kah said, her hands up to calm them. "What is, is. Trapped, we are. But there must be another way out. Big castle. Lots of doors and windows. Just can't use the front door." She looked at her hands, flinched, and lowered them until they were hidden by the table.

"So we agree that whatever Strahd intends is bad, and we all want a way out?" Alishai looked around the room.

"You know, now that I think about it, he's not trying *terribly hard* to kill us," Chivarion said, leaning back with his arms crossed. "It would be easy. Poison in the food. Stab us in our beds. I can think of dozens of fun ways to go about it. But instead we get little cat-things and silly witches and bloody water. It reminds me more of a tressym playing with its prey. Maybe Rotrog is right. Maybe the count is bored."

"Then he needs hobbies," Alishai snapped. "Not . . . living playthings. We need to leave. Now."

Rotrog stubbornly shook his head. "Have any of you spoken with our host? If you took the time to get to know him, I feel certain he would win you over. He is charming, intelligent, generous. Perhaps the state of this domicile is not his main concern. Perhaps he is a loftier personage who doesn't focus on insignificant, venal, material matters."

Alishai's hands were in fists on the table. "I very much wish to speak with him again. While sober. I will ask him, point-blank, what he wants with us."

"Well, don't be rude," Rotrog said. "We are guests here—"

"This is not how guests should be treated." Chivarion shook his snow-white hair. "Not that I've ever been a guest before. Especially not in a castle. But I thought it would be . . . nicer. Running a place this way seems irresponsible, if he's not doing it on purpose."

Rotrog pointed a finger emphatically in the air. "Castles are inherited! This edifice was built generations ago. No one person could possibly know every intricacy of such a large domain."

Alishai leaned back and stared up at the ceiling, her arms crossed. "Well, then those of us who wish to leave shall look for a way. Even if he's not trying to murder us outright, I suggest no one travel this castle without their weapons."

"My potions."

Everyone looked to Fielle. Only her eyes were alive in her wan face. There was something wrong with her, something possibly magical, but so far, no one was familiar with her malady. Something about it frightened Alishai; it stunk of evil.

"My potions are my weapons," Fielle explained. "I woke up in this dress, and my skirt and bags are gone. All my potions, my artificer's kit, my trinkets. I don't know how or why or where."

Alishai stood. "Let's go look through your room. Perhaps they were put away." She went to Fielle and held out a hand, but Fielle stood on her own. Chivarion and Kah likewise stood, but the little human blushed.

"Please. Don't treat me like I'm made of glass. I don't need an entourage. It makes me feel silly. Like I'm troublesome."

"No trouble—" Kah began.

"Alishai will be with me."

Uncertain, Kah and Chivarion sat back down, and Alishai squired Fielle to the staircase. "You said your room is on the same floor as the dining room?"

"Yes. I can find it. I'm fine, I promise you."

Alishai didn't believe that for a second, so she stayed a step in front of Fielle the whole way down the winding stairwell, waiting to catch her if she swooned again. Back in the main entryway, they found the door to the room with the gargoyles closed. Hopefully, as long as they didn't open that door, the area would remain safe. Fielle led Alishai past the dining hall, down a few twisting stairs, through a long stone hallway, and to the bottom of a turret.

The room within was shaped like an octagon, with arrow slits placed at intervals that seemed both strategic and decorative. Frescoes adorned the ceilings, showing billowing green meadows peppered with flowers and a tall white castle with golden spires. These paintings had once been bright and beautiful, surely, but now they were crumbling and stained, a dream turned nightmare. A grand four-poster bed stood against one wall, draped in filmy white fabric and covered in pillows and a quilted velvet coverlet. Soft rugs covered the floor, and the furniture arrayed around the walls looked fresh and recently polished, the newest things Alishai had seen in the entire castle. There was a wardrobe, a bedside table, a low table by two cozy chairs, and a pretty stand carved with flowers that held a bowl and ewer full of water that Alishai dearly wanted for herself. As Fielle opened the wardrobe, Alishai squinted at the odd juxtaposition of luxurious furnishings and the dingy walls. This place, she thought, had been recently and hastily converted into a bedroom.

"No sign of my skirt," Fielle said, slamming the wardrobe door with what little strength she had. "Just more of these blasted gowns. And nowhere else to look. All my pockets. All my potions and tools. All gone."

Alishai looked at her hands, feeling infuriatingly helpless. "I fear there is something wrong with you, something more than a mere cantrip can solve. I have never had such need of my own meager healing skills. I have little left to give."

"We both need sleep." Fielle's smile was kind. "I'm going to take a nap. You should, too."

Looking around the room, Alishai failed to find a second place where she might comfortably rest. "If I could borrow a pillow, I'll take the floor."

"There is no need."

They both looked up to find the chamberlain, Rahadin, standing there, his posture impeccable and his smile almost cloying.

"Ah, good. Rahadin, I have some questions—" Alishai began.

He waved that away. "And I will of course answer them. But first, Count von Zarovich wishes to speak with you. He is in the chapel. He knows you have concerns, and he would welcome your company."

Alishai's pulse quickened; this was exactly what she needed. "But Fielle—"

"Will be perfectly safe here. She is under the count's protection."

Like that mattered!

"Our party has been attacked several times, and to be quite honest, I'm worried for her safety. She's not well."

Rahadin inclined his head in apology. "The castle is old and drafty, and many parts of it have been closed up for far too long. On behalf of the count, I apologize for any stray creatures that might have taken up residence in its darker corners. But I assure you on the count's word that Fielle will be looked after. Now, please. The count is waiting."

Alishai looked to Fielle, who was clinging to her bedpost like a sailor lost at sea. "Are you sure?"

Fielle did her best to smile. "I'll be fine. Go talk to the count. Get some answers. I just want to lie down."

"Are you *really* sure?"

"I'm sure. Go. And thank you." Fielle kicked off her slippers and blushed. "When everyone leaves, I can take off this blasted dress. I never did like stays and petticoats."

Alishai ducked her head in understanding and walked back down the long hall, noting that there was no door on Fielle's room, not even old hinges. She would have been uncomfortable there herself, but what about this place was comfortable? Nothing about her old life had been comfortable, either, so why would she expect any relief here?

"A right at the entryway." Rahadin's voice echoed down the hallway as if he stood right beside her.

Annoyed by his smug tone, and by everything, really, Alishai turned right and entered a long hallway filled with life-sized statues of humans—fourteen of them, to be exact. What was with this place and statues? As she walked past them, pushing aside hanging curtains of cobwebs and blinking against clouds of dust, she felt as if their stone eyes watched her go, measuring her as she passed. Her hand was on her glaive, and with each step, she waited to hear the scuff of stone on stone as the statues, like the gargoyles, attacked. As she passed between each pair of figures, noting that their armor was in a style she'd never seen before, she braced herself for the swing of a stone mace or the scrape of a stone sword drawn from its scabbard.

No attack came. She pushed open the brass doors at the end of the hallway and beheld the chapel.

Well, it had been a chapel once. Now it was falling apart.

Oh, it must've been grand when it was new. The ceilings soared ninety feet overhead, supported by arched buttresses and flanked by tall stained-glass windows caked in years of filth. Barely any light penetrated the thick glass, which was broken in some places and boarded up in others. The pews were no longer in neat rows but had been strewn around the room like an angry child's playthings. A thick coat of dust lay over everything, and bats chittered in the corners of the ceiling like gossips in a choir. Count Strahd von Zarovich, however, was nowhere to be seen.

A single sunbeam penetrated the gloom, landing on a stone altar carved with angels and vines. Upon the altar lay a figure covered in a dusty black cloth, and a black mace sat on the floor at the figure's feet as if recently dropped.

Every particle of Alishai's body urged her to leave the chapel immediately.

She did not feel Selûne here.

She did not feel any gods.

The gods, if they had any sense, had abandoned this place long ago.

Strahd could rot. This place was cursed.

She was just about to turn around when she heard a low, creaking moan.

It sounded . . . like a person in great pain. Alishai knew this sound well; her commune had worked as a hospice, taking in those who could not afford effective healing. People with wasting diseases and ailments with no cures came to feel the holy touch of Selûne's chosen prophets. The elderly, the injured, the slowly rotting, the cursed—they all begged for release from the endless torture of their existence, or at least for a few, brief moments in which nothing hurt.

Alishai had always been useless in this manner. Her healing talents were minimal, her temper was short, and the Moonmaiden had called her to fight, not soothe. Whoever was here, she had little to offer them.

As she stood in the empty silence, it came again. A soft moan, followed by a sigh.

Perhaps she could not solve this problem, but her oath compelled her to try.

Glaive still in hand, she scanned the area until she found a blanketed lump in a pew up front. It hadn't been overturned, but it was set at an odd angle, and the person in it was lying on their side.

"Hello?" she called.

"Hello? Who's there?"

The voice was old and tremulous. Female, Alishai thought.

"Are you well?" she asked.

Another groan as the figure struggled to sit up. "Can't remember the last time I was well, child. These old bones are a cage."

Alishai had no choice but to walk toward the pew. Up close, she saw a wizened old human woman wrapped in an ancient gray blanket so faded and worn that it might've begun as any color. The woman gazed at her with eyes cast over white, her wrinkled, spotted skin stretched thinly over a toothless skull.

"What is your malady?" Alishai said softly. "For I am a paladin of Selûne, and I am duty bound to help you. My skills are minimal, but I will do what I can to ease your pain."

The old woman's head fell forward. "That which ails me has no cure, for the only one who could help me is gone."

"Selûne tells us we must always have faith." Alishai sat on the bench beside the figure, taking her withered hand. It was dry and papery, the bones delicate and gnarled. "She will bring you courage and strength."

A dusty, humorless laugh, like the cold winter wind whistling down a chimney. "The moon waxes and wanes, and it is clear that I am waning, child. Soon, I shall be just a sharp point, and then nothing. All the faith in the world won't help me. What is the point of prayer and worship when the answer is the same? Hopelessness. Abandonment. Darkness."

Alishai knew that pain made people say blasphemous things, but she could not let such a statement stand. "We are never alone. She is always listening, even when we can't hear her. Selûne teaches us that even though the sky is dark, the moon is still there. The Lady is always with us and ever faithful."

The hand tightened around Alishai's fingers, the grip steely and desperate now. "And what about you? Have you always been so good? So certain?"

The voice was . . . different. Cunning. Alishai's other hand went to her dagger.

"I try to be good. I try to follow her path. Sometimes trying is all we can do."

The fingers clamped down like manacles. "And were you always faithful to your goddess, or did you waver? Did you ever turn from her—"

Alishai whipped her hand away and stood. The old woman's cloak fell back, showing a nearly bald head with straggling gray hair and crusty, weeping scabs. Her eyes were nearly black now, and they were knowing. And cruel.

As if she knew what Alishai was thinking, the old woman smiled widely, showing wet, toothless gums. Her grin curled upward, her mouth opened fully, and sharp teeth sprouted in the pinkness like grubs popping out of the earth. Her canine teeth began to grow even beyond that, out to points. Her nose was elongating, her ears were lengthening, and Alishai stumbled backward away from the pew, away from this thing, this thing that she recognized.

"What's wrong, Paladin? Did you forget your oath?" the old woman said roughly around a wolf's teeth, her face growing into a hairy snout. Her eyes leaked from black to yellow, from sightless to cunning and hungry. She curled her fur-backed hands around the pew, her black claws squealing against the old wood as she pressed up to standing. "Or did you betray it? When did you choose your freedom over the suffering of innocents? What will happen to the cursed, now that you have damned them? Where is your moon? Where is your heart?" She stood, back cracking, breaking through the thin blanket to show wiry black fur. "Where is your goddess now, oathbreaker?"

The old woman—the werewolf, the thing—raised her snout to the sky and howled, and Alishai—paladin, warrior, hero, faithful of Selûne—turned and ran out of the chapel as fast as she could.

14

FIELLE

Fielle stood by her bed, leaning against it for strength, waiting for Rahadin to do something or say something or to please, please go away. He made her feel like a dead bird torn open so that its entrails might be used for scrying, like his sharp eyes were picking apart her deepest inner being.

Rahadin said nothing. He might've been a statue if not for the rise and fall of his chest.

"You may go."

Hearing that voice, Rahadin bowed his head and hurried from the room. Fielle didn't even have time to feel relief before Count von Zarovich appeared before her, reaching for her hands. As if of their own volition, they released the bedpost to be enveloped in his cold white fingers.

"My lady, you have taken a chill. Please, make yourself comfortable so that we might enjoy one another's company." He released her hands, and she shoved them under her armpits, hoping to warm them with her body. They were numb now, half-dead. She watched as Strahd built up her fire until it was roaring and pulled the chairs closer to the hearth. A soft woolen blanket appeared in his hands as if he'd conjured it from nothing. "Please. Sit."

She all but fell into the chair, sinking back, unable to accomplish the alert and ladylike demeanor a count's audience demanded. He draped the blanket over her with tender care and took the other seat, spreading out in the way of men of power, taking up all the available room and giving off an air of almost predatory pleasure.

"Did you already speak with Alishai?" Fielle asked.

Was the count . . . smirking?

"I must have missed her in my haste to attend to you, my dear." His eyes bored into her, drilling into her skull; a small pain pulsed in her temples. "Tell me, where are you from?"

She pinned her lips together, but after a small pause, the words tumbled out anyway. "Baldur's Gate, in the Western Heartlands. My family has long owned a tavern and theater there called the Dancing Dragon."

"And are you a traveler? Do you know much of the world?"

"I have never left the city's gates. I am needed much at home."

Even spoken unwillingly, her resentment simmered in each word.

"Have you ever heard of Barovia before?"

She tried to sit up straighter, but it was as if she were pinned in place, like she was but a marionette and someone else was pulling the strings. "No. Never. No one has. Even Rotrog, who is well educated. It worries us all that we were brought here from such far-flung places. We all wish to go home."

"Do you not feel at home here? Does my land not speak to you?"

Fielle fought the look of disgust that naturally sprung to her features. "Home is more than the land. Home is familiar. Comfortable. I feel . . . disconnected."

"Then allow me to tell you a story." Strahd stood and walked behind her, his fingertips landing heavily on her shoulders, his sharp nails piercing the thick fabric of a dress that did not belong to her and yet fit her as if it had been tailored for her body. "Once upon a time, there was a young man of noble birth who was good and kind and wished to protect his people. He was a warrior and a leader, and he dedicated himself to his duties, ensuring that his nation was strong. When he grew older, he moved to the valley of his greatest conquest and claimed the earth by spilling his own blood. He named the valley Barovia and built a castle there—Castle Ravenloft."

Fielle shuddered, and Strahd's fingers dug in deeper as if to further pin her in place.

"Now in middle age, the man graciously invited his family to come stay with him, including his younger brother. This handsome, friendly, well-loved younger brother, still flush with youth and enthusiasm, had never fought in a war, had never sacrificed himself for his people. He was naïve and sweet and foolish." Strahd practically spit this last sentence. His nails dug in so hard that Fielle gasped, and he removed his hands and returned to his chair, gazing off into the air just over Fielle's shoulder.

"The younger brother was affianced to a local villager, and the older brother grew jealous, for he had fallen in love with this same woman. When she did not accept his love, he delved into the hidden lore of a local temple and believed he had found the answer to all his problems. Lovelorn and desperate, he made a pact to regain his youth and vitality and thus earn the heart of his beloved. But his plan was all for naught. When she saw what he had become, what changes had been wrought, she ran from him. Spurred to a rage, he . . ."

Strahd's mouth hung open, his eyes faraway and misty.

Fielle tried to speak, but her throat was frozen.

Finally he drew himself up tall. "I made a choice for love, you see, and I was rewarded with eternal torment. One innocent mistake, and I have been trapped ever since. The Mists descended, and Barovia was removed from the world, spirited away to . . . somewhere else. It is on no maps. There are no roads that lead away from this place. There is only the land and the blood and the Mists and the Dark Powers who rule over all. In Barovia, I am the land, I am the Darklord, but even I am not the ultimate master. I am doomed to live it all over again, doomed to commit the same errors over and over and over. No matter how hard I try, I am trapped here, just as you are. Here, in my home."

He reached for her hand and kissed it, and she felt the scrape of sharp teeth against her knuckles.

"All I want is a consort to reign by my side. Someone to finally accept my love. Someone to take the burden of rule from my weary shoulders that I might find some small amount of solace. A beloved, an heir. Simply a moment when I am not fully alone."

He still held her hand, and she found that although she could not speak, she could squeeze his fingers with her own. It was a sad story, and she understood what it was like, being overshadowed by a more brightly glowing sibling. She felt certain he was leaving something out, but . . . well, she had not told anyone her entire story, either. She had made one mistake, and here she was. They had that much in common.

"Are you saying . . . we can never leave?"

She had to fight to get the words out, but at least she could speak again.

Strahd's eyes swelled with an old sorrow. "You truly would depart so soon? But I have waited so patiently . . . it's been so long . . ." He released her hand and settled back in his chair. There was a new coldness to him, as if she'd insulted him by asking to go. "Do you not feel any kinship at all with the land here? I thought perhaps I sensed something special about you. You have an old soul."

"I have never liked the thought of being caged," she said softly. "It is difficult to be happy when one cannot leave."

Strahd cocked his head, his lips slowly lifting in a shy smile. "If the cage door is open and the bird remains, that is the real gift, is it not? One must remove the falcon's hood before it can fly, much less hunt. My only hope is that one day, someone as kind and beautiful as you might turn to me and know my love."

A flush crept up Fielle's cheeks.

Had the count . . . just expressed interest in her?

She had lived her entire life in the shadow of her sister, and now a count—a leader! Ruler of this castle! A—Darklord?—was looking at her with desire in his eyes. It was flattering, if nothing else. The poor man was such a tragic figure, noble and lonely and longing.

"How can you say such things to me?" she said, eyes cast downward. "I'm just a tavern girl, and you barely know me."

He reached out, fingertips softly grazing her cheek to pull her face back up. Their eyes locked, and her stomach swooped. It was like falling into a swirling abyss, plummeting through icy air, surrounded by the cold touch of fog, hurtling toward something unfathomable.

"Perhaps I know you better than you think," he whispered.

15

CHIVARION

Without Alishai's passion and Fielle's kindness, the study quickly became a very dull place. Rotrog was mesmerized by his books, and Kah appeared to be quietly praying as she played with a string of beads. Chivarion didn't necessarily enjoy nearly dying, but any fight was better than being bored. Although he did not kill animals for sport, he was happy to kill nearly anything out of necessity. He had been raised from an early age to understand that anyone who began a fight had signaled their willingness to die, and so he felt no guilt over what happened when he was challenged. He'd also learned very quickly that anyone with a price on their head deserved it, and that hunting them down was basically ridding the world of bad rubbish. Feck around and find out, that was his way.

Exploring the castle and exterminating anything nasty was, therefore, a public service on his part.

"Well, this is very boring," he announced. "Murder and I will go and have a look around, and if we encounter something else that wants a tussle, then perhaps the day will get lively."

Rotrog did not deign to respond, but Kah looked up, blinked at him, nodded, and returned to her worrying. Chivarion stood and stretched and poked his head into the room with the rotting cake but saw nothing useful within. He liked weapons, so the dusty harp and lute were of little interest and would likely break if smacked against an enemy. On the other side of the study, he found a long hall full of hideous statues and rubble. The roof had caved in, and oily rain plopped down amidst the cobwebs.

"Yuck," he told the nearest statue. "Isn't rain the worst?"

"No," the statue said, or perhaps Chivarion imagined it, because the statue did not respond to further questions.

Still uninspired, he placed Murder on his shoulder and took the staircase back up toward his room. On the landing, he passed the painting of Strahd and stopped by what appeared to be a trapdoor. He hadn't noticed it last night when Rahadin led him here, and he'd come a different way this morning after dealing with the cat-thing. With his sword in one hand, he knelt and grabbed the ring. The hinges squealed in protest as the ancient wood door lifted from its frame, and Chivarion stared down . . . and down and down and down. This shaft seemed to stretch all the way through the castle, hundreds of feet.

"Hello?" Chivarion called.

Hello, hello, hello, the shaft echoed in a voice that wasn't quite his.

"You're a wretched place," he told the heart of the castle.

Wretch, wretch, wretch, the shaft replied.

"I wish to leave."

Leave, leave, leave.

"So leave."

Murder leaped to the ground as Chivarion bolted to his feet, dropping the trapdoor with a heavy thud and whipping out his crossbow. That last bit had been spoken not by him and not by his distorted echo, but by a third, secret voice—one he hadn't heard before—which seemed to be on the other side of a banded wooden door that hadn't been there this morning. The door was ajar, and Chivarion gave Murder the signal to hold back as he pushed the door further open, crossbow at the ready.

He'd expected to find another guest room, but the sprawling space appeared to be a lounge, as there were couches and chairs to lounge upon and a stranger lounging upon one of them. Overhead, heavy beams ran the length of the dingy ceiling, and three ornate lanterns hung from long chains, swaying gently in a nonexistent breeze and throwing restless shadows that danced and gibbered on the walls like mad imps.

"Who are you?" Chivarion asked the young man strewn upon a divan. He was a handsome human, pale white with long blond hair and misty gray eyes. His clothes were elegant but a little shabby, and his air was one of annoyed boredom. Chivarion could relate.

"My name is Escher," the young man said, looking the drow up and down and failing to conceal his interest. "And who are you?"

"I am Chivarion Dyrr. I was given the chamber next door. Or sometimes it's next door. Sometimes it doesn't have a door. It should be next door, even if it isn't."

Escher raised an elegant eyebrow almost as sharp as Chivarion's own. "Ah, yes. The guest room. No one has graced that chamber in quite some time. How do you find it?"

Chivarion lowered his crossbow but kept his hand on his sword. Murder crept in to sit beside his boots. The tressym was too curious for her own good. And too trusting.

"Dusty and unreliable. A cat-thing attacked me from the wardrobe this morning. Utterly ruined my favorite tunic. Does that happen often?"

Escher threw back his head and laughed. "Not terribly often, but occasionally, just to keep things fun. That was probably a gremishka. Ugly little cat-bat gremlin things made of spoilt magic. They're almost as bad as the rats here."

"I killed it."

Escher gave a shoulder shrug. "Good. The fewer gremishkas, the better. What are you?"

Chivarion bristled at that. "What do you think I am?"

"Not an elf or a dusk elf. Something different."

Ah, so he was only ignorant and not a bigot. "I am a drow. My kind are most common in the Underdark, home of the great city of Menzoberranzan. But I go wherever I like."

"And what are you doing here?"

"Being bored, mostly. I'd like to go home. Not to Menzoberranzan;

they threw me out long ago. But to Waterdeep. There is little coin to be won here, I think, and even fewer good taverns to spend it in and lovers to spend it on."

With an avid smile, Escher curled up from the divan and leaned forward eagerly. "They threw you out? Well, that sounds like a delicious bit of gossip. What for?"

Chivarion cursed himself for mentioning it. So often, his mouth ran ahead of his mind. Most of the time, when people questioned him, he simply hit them about the head until they forgot. But that would be rude, he thought, to concuss a fellow guest.

"For beating up twerps," he said instead. "What are you doing here?"

Escher giggled like this was the funniest thing he'd ever heard. For all that he was very pretty, Chivarion didn't like him. He was like the gremishka: pointy and mean.

"I am here to entertain our host, just like you." Escher gestured at the room. "Here to enjoy unparalleled hospitality in this grand and glorious palace of light and joy. Here to dance for Strahd's pleasure." He stood and did a strange little dance. Chivarion's fingers tightened on his sword. He couldn't anticipate what Escher would do next, and that made him nervous.

"Are you allowed to leave?" he asked.

In the blink of an eye, too fast to follow, Escher was right up in his face, nearly chest to chest. "Of course not," he hissed through clenched teeth.

Teeth that were far sharper than anyone's teeth ought to be.

Chivarion's instincts kicked in, and he threw an elbow into the young man's face, striking him hard on his sharply cut cheekbone. Escher hissed again and ran to the open window, climbing out and disappearing. Chivarion gave chase and stood just inside the leaded glass sill, watching the handsome young man skitter across the roof tiles like a spider.

"That boy is not normal," he said to Murder.

"Normal is highly overrated."

Chivarion spun, crossbow already up, and loosed an arrow. It flew past Count Strahd von Zarovich, cutting a trail so close to his skull that it left a small part in his black hair slicked with acid-green poison. The count did not flinch. He merely smiled as if it were quite amusing to nearly die by poisoned arrow.

"Sorry. You startled me." Chivarion was not in any way sorry, but he'd learned long ago not to say that part out loud.

"You are disturbed," Strahd noted.

Still in the same formal dress from last night, he selected a tall-backed chair, its pattern so worn it was just a jumble of thread, and sat. His eyes: sharp. His posture: sharp. His fingernails: sharp. Everything about this man was sharp. Chivarion had been hunted by all sorts of creatures, from goblins to owlbears to dragons, and the way Strahd's eyes followed him as he selected his own chair marked him as prey. The drow crossed one foot over his knee to feign relaxation and lay his sword across his thighs, his hand never leaving the pommel.

"Well, disturbing things keep happening. Yesterday, we were nearly killed by zombies and dead pigs. This morning, my door was sealed shut, and a gremishka attacked me. And then we encountered gargoyles and the barf-witch. So, yes, I suppose I'm a wee bit jumpy."

Strahd tapped a finger against his chin. "Such a large place, this castle. So old and difficult to keep up. I apologize if my negligence has brought you discomfort." He looked up at the door and curled a finger in command. "Ah, here are my darlings. Ludmilla, Anastrasya. Come meet our guest."

A great black nose pushed the door open, and two giant wolves trotted into the room and went directly to Strahd, their tails wagging happily as they jockeyed to lick his hands. One wolf was black and the other was gray, and their eyes were the yellow of a harvest moon. They looked at Chivarion, and he looked at them, and their gaze was so intelligent and cunning and *knowing*, and he had never felt like such a stupid animal in all his life.

"Pets are a joy to the childless," Strahd said, scratching the black wolf behind her ears. "A relationship cultivated over many years, built on trust and affection. You, of all people, understand what I mean." Strahd smiled a wicked smile. "The tressym is a magical creature. I have long wished to meet one. What is her name?"

Chivarion's mouth had never been so dry, his throat so blocked. "Murder."

The word fell unbidden from his lips like it had been pulled out with a hook.

"Come here, Murder. Come and make friends." Strahd crooked a finger at the tressym, who hid under the chair at Chivarion's feet.

In his head, over and over, Chivarion thought the words, *No, don't go to him.*

First Murder's nose appeared from the dusty shadows, then her bright yellow eyes, then her ears, pressed down flat against her bald skull. Just as her name had been pulled unwillingly from Chivarion's mind, so was the tressym emerging from under the chair as if she had no choice in the matter. Her claws were out as she leaped lightly to Strahd's lap. She did not settle in like she wished to take a nap; she did not curl up into a ball or a comfortable loaf. She sat, face-to-face with Strahd, unblinking.

"I have heard they are mischievous little terrors," Strahd said. He reached for Murder's wing, and although it had been clenched against the tressym's side, at the count's touch, it extended. "An ideal companion for a spellcaster. Intelligent, immune to poison, fiercely loyal." Strahd held one of the delicate wing bones in his fingers. "Tell me, how did you find her?"

Chivarion sat stock-still, a tornado of rage inside him, barely held in check. He knew well enough that if he disappointed the count, that delicate bone would snap between his curious fingers. One word from Strahd, and the wolves might tear Murder apart while their master held her by a fragile wing. Chivarion would've taken an arrow to the eyeball rather than see Murder held in such a precarious position, but now he had no choice. He could not defeat both wolves and their master before Murder was ripped to shreds. Again, it was as if the words were torn unwillingly from not his throat but his heart.

"I lost a fight in Waterdeep when I was quite young. They left me for dead in some rat-stinking alley near the docks. The rest of my team had perished or fled. As I lay there, I heard a man muttering angrily—a wizard, drunk and full of himself, as they so often are. He threw something into the water and said, 'Good riddance to bad luck.' He left, and I thought I was delusional when I heard mewing. The bastard was trying to drown a kitten. I couldn't move for myself, you understand, but something about that desperate sound, about what dirty, lazy, cowardly work it was to kill a young creature—it made me angry. I managed to catch the bag with my stave before it went under. And then Murder crawled out looking like a bald rat, and we've been friends ever since."

"You saved her." Strahd held up Murder's arm, inspected her paw, pressed the pad to extend her claws. The tressym, like Chivarion, was frozen in place, trembling in fear. "No wonder your pet is loyal to you."

"We are loyal to each other," Chivarion corrected. "And she's not my pet. She's my friend."

Strahd leaned back in the chair, pinning Murder in place with a hand between her wings. The wolves on either side of the chair raised their muzzles, sniffing the tressym. Strings of drool dripped from their lips.

"Friends. Yes. What a lovely word. *Friends.*" But the way he said "friends" made it sound more like a curse word. "I used to have friends." This time, it came out as a growl.

You might have more friends if you weren't a terrifying monster who threatened innocent tressym, Chivarion thought but did not say.

"Perhaps," Strahd whispered, and Chivarion wished his head were as empty as he was often told it was, because he knew the monster was reading his mind.

Murder let out a frightened mewl as one of the wolves gingerly took her paw in its mouth. One bite, and those sharp teeth would crush the tiny bones within.

"So delicate," Strahd said, his voice even again. His eyes met Chivarion's, and it felt just like looking down that endless shaft to the bottom of the castle. "Bodies are such tender things, are they not? So easily broken. So easily crushed. I only hope you and your friends are careful as you enjoy my hospitality. Even under my protection, there are so many accidents waiting to happen in this musty old place."

He stroked Murder's head in the hideous pantomime of a fond caress. One wolf had a tressym paw in its mouth, the other had its teeth around Murder's slender naked tail. Chivarion had never felt so helpless in all his long years—

Well, maybe he had felt that helpless once before, but this was different.

This was personal.

And this, he knew, was a threat.

"Tell me what you want," he begged.

Strahd leaned forward. "It is not for you to know. I will take what I wish when I find it. I have no use for you. Your only task is to stay out of my way."

He stood, cradling Murder against his chest like a baby, and Chivarion's teeth ground together as he contemplated what he would do if the count attempted to take the tressym with him. But instead, Strahd suddenly released his grasp. Murder fell to the floor, landing on all four feet with her wings spread. The wolves watched, eyes alight and jaws foamy with saliva, held in check by unseen hands. Strahd snapped and pointed to the door, and the wolves obediently trotted out. Chivarion swiftly knelt and tenderly gathered Murder to his own chest.

"We would be out of your way if we left," he said, perhaps a little too quickly.

Strahd only smiled, wide and cloying. "And deprive myself of your company? Why, I wouldn't trade our time together for all the coins in the world. Just stay a few more days. I insist."

Strahd swept a bow and followed his wolves into the hall. Chivarion clutched Murder to his chest. Only when the door was closed did he allow himself to weep.

16

KAH

The thing about prayer was that it worked a lot better when the god in question was actually listening. Ever since she'd woken up in the forest among these strangers, Kah had been unable to feel her tether to Akadi. Her spells still worked somehow, but when she chanted or fell to her knees, it was like sending a letter to someone who was no longer at that address. She felt lost. Forsaken. And for that, she could blame only herself.

The orc sharing the table seemed happy enough with his books, but Kah was not one for reading. She was a creature of curiosity and experience. Akadi bade her worshippers to follow their dreams to a life of adventure and meaning. Thus far, Barovia was too dreary for an inspiring adventure, too empty for meaning. Back home, Kah always felt as if she were one lucky day away from regaining her wings and discovering flight, one good deed away from her heart's desire. But here? Here, she had never felt so far away from the one thing that would fulfill her.

But maybe . . .

"A question?" she chirped.

Rotrog looked up in annoyance, his heavy brows drawn down in censure. "Can you not see that I am busy?"

"One question only."

He nodded. "One."

"Can magic—can it do anything?"

That, at least, made him pause. "Define anything."

Kah waved her arms in the air. "Anything."

Rotrog sighed heavily and rubbed his temples. "Tell me what it is you wish magic to do, and I will tell you if magic can do it."

Kah looked down, feeling very silly, but . . . well, she'd never had the chance to ask a real wizard this question before. What if the answer was quite easy and none of her kindred had ever bothered to ask the right person?

She held up her arms, with their soft black feathers. "My kind . . . we had real wings. Once. Long ago. Then, we lost them. Some say it was punishment. No one knows why, not anymore. All I want . . . all I want is to fly again."

Rotrog looked at her with pity, like she was a child denied a sweet. "If you were meant to fly, you would fly."

"But the magic . . ." She trailed off. She was too shy to ask again, but he had not answered her question. Still, she knew him to be proud, so perhaps if he couldn't be entreated, he could be goaded. "Perhaps someone more powerful would know?"

The orc sat up straight, baring his tusks. "I am powerful! I was first adept under High Mage Argitau himself!"

She shook her arms. "Well, then?"

Rotrog looked away, snarling. "I have heard of such a thing. Transmutation. Very high level, very demanding. Only lasts an hour. But as you might have noticed, all my spell books were left behind when I was transported to this domain, so unless I find that spell here, I am unable to help you."

An hour.

What good was a dream that lasted an hour? Would it be worse to have wings and then lose them than to never have them at all? Might she find a wizard to cast the spell continuously? Did magic even work like that?

"May I return to my studies?" he asked, nose in the air.

Kah bobbed her head. "Do as you will."

Rotrog's eyes latched on to his book, and Kah stood. She began to understand his obsession with such things. Perhaps if she found a spell book, she could find a spell that might help. Just because Rotrog didn't know about bigger magic didn't mean it didn't exist. This place was different. Maybe the magic was different, too.

Exiting the room, Kah headed for the spiral staircase and considered. She had seen so little of the castle, and there was no one to ask where she might find the knowledge they needed. Her choices were up or down. She knew there were floors above this one and below. Did she want to explore more of the turret or see what was in the cellar? Just the thought of what this place must be like underground made her shiver, her feathers fluffing up. It was already cold, dank, mildewy. There were possibly catacombs or dungeons. Probably lots of bones. She was definitely headed upward.

Up one floor, she paused on the landing. A large portrait of Count von Zarovich glared at her imperiously from the wall. She moved a step to the left, then two steps to the right. The eyes . . . were definitely following her.

Not like they were alive—like someone was standing behind the portrait.

A trick of the light, definitely.

She continued upward. The next floor included the guest room she shared with Alishai, and a strange pairing that was. To think—she'd slept soundly last night while Alishai walked around, or possibly sleepwalked, and got into a bathtub full of blood. If not for the gory evidence, Kah would've nodded along to Alishai's story but personally decided the anxious and angry tiefling had been dreaming. Crusted blood, however, did not just magically appear in someone's hair.

There were two other doors on this floor, and although one refused to budge, the second swung open with a sickly creak. For all that Kah agreed with Alishai that Rahadin had to be lying about the massive castle's lack of available guest rooms, this dreary chamber supported the chamberlain's point. There were no moldering tapestries, no paintings, no ancient armoires, no rugs. It held only an iron chest, a spindly wooden ladder leading up to a trapdoor in the ceiling, and a narrow wooden bed outfitted with rusted metal restraints. The straw tick mattress had been eaten away to rags, and old bloodstains had seeped into the wood.

"Horrid place," she muttered.

"I'm so sorry you don't approve."

Kah spun around to find Count von Zarovich standing in the shadows behind the door, the sharpest thing in a room sagging with age. His eyes flashed as he glided toward her, his cloak stirring the thick dust on the floor. She went stock-still, awed by both his power as a count and his predatorial manner of movement.

"Apologies, my lord, didn't mean to—"

"Insult a count? Think nothing of it. This room does not show off the castle to its best advantage, I'll admit. Tell me: Are your own rooms comfortable?"

He was so tall that Kah had to look up at him; he made her feel small and breakable. How easy it would be for Strahd to toss Kah onto the bed like a sack of feathers and clamp those rusted manacles around her wrists. Maybe there was a key, and maybe there wasn't. The count had asked about her comfort in the most uncomfortable atmosphere she'd ever experienced, and she wasn't sure how to answer. She did not like to lie.

But she also did not like to die.

"I slept well," she said, because it was the safest truth.

"And how do you find Barovia?"

Again, Kah did not like to lie. "I'm accustomed to warmer climes," she told him. "Are we far from Waterdeep, do you know?"

Strahd's eyes bored into her own like he was looking for something deep in her skull, and she felt the thump of a headache begin in her temples. Try as she might, she could not look away. The feathers rose around her face and all up her arms and chest, her body trying desperately to make itself seem bigger than it was in an attempt to scare away a potential hunter.

Finally Strahd sighed sadly. He walked to the only window, a narrow thing with thick, dirty glass, and looked out, his hands clasped behind his back. "Whatever Waterdeep is, my dear, we are farther away than you think."

Every little bit of Kah's body willed her to run away while his back was turned, but she was quite certain that he knew exactly where she was and what she was thinking. And that, somehow, without knowing why or how, she'd disappointed him.

"Can I go, sir?" she asked, clicking her beak nervously. "Did you want—is there something more?"

"No, nothing more. It is clear that you are not . . ." Strahd trailed off. "But I already knew that, didn't I? I simply had to be certain."

With a swirl of his cape, he departed, leaving Kah alone. She hurried to the door and paused just outside it, her back against the cold stone, listening for his footsteps. Whichever way the count had gone, she would absolutely be exploring in the opposite direction. For some reason she couldn't identify properly, he terrified her to her very bones. He had done nothing out of the ordinary, had not threatened her, had not said anything odd in particular, and yet . . .

He was wrong, just as he was—his existence, his eyes, his touch.

Wrong, wrong, wrong.

And he was walking downstairs, judging by the sound tapping up the stone steps.

Kah stood there, her breathing quick, her feathers refusing to smooth out. Only when the footsteps had long given over to silence did she dare to creep away from the wall. As soon as she set foot on the stairs again, she heard a noise from up above, echoing down to her, a noise that made her blood run cold and her eyes dilate.

A baby crying.

She froze, listening to the wails of fear and desperation.

There was no answering shuffle of feet, no mother's murmur of comfort.

There was only the sound of a newborn abandoned and frightened.

She wanted to turn around and run back down the stairs, to rejoin Rotrog in the study and put her hands over her ears, but the sound of the wailing child haunted her dreams. If there really was an infant upstairs, no one was coming to help it.

"Count Strahd," she called down the stairwell. "Is there a baby that needs tending upstairs?"

The only answer was an echo.

Upstairs, upstairs, upstairs.

She said a quick prayer to Akadi and ran upward, her talons clicking on the old, worn stone. One, two, three stories she passed, and the infant's cries grew louder and louder with each revolution.

How did a baby possibly get to the tower's high peak, she wondered?

Why would anyone assign a family quarters there? Who would leave a child there alone?

It made no sense.

But lots of things in this castle made no sense.

Strahd himself made no sense.

Why had he—what had he wanted?

Didn't matter.

Baby crying, baby hurt.

She was acting on instinct now.

Instinct and faith and . . . shame.

She had to make this right.

She had to stop the crying.

The stairs ended on a stone walkway that ringed the tower wall. Overhead, splintered beams held up a cone-shaped roof; part of the structure had caved in to show a patch of cloudy gray sky. Arrow slits provided a scant bit of weak, dull light, and bats rustled in the rafters. Kah looked about frantically for the crying child, its full-throated screams filling the space, but she saw nothing.

Nothing but a deep hole in the center of the tower, a pitch-black arrow going directly into the castle's cold, dark heart. Freezing air rushed upward like a banshee, making Kah jerk away and plaster herself against the mold-slicked stone wall.

"Where are you?" she cried.

She dared not stare into the shaft to see if perhaps the child was—

What?

If the child was *what?*

If a baby had fallen down that hole, its cries would've ended abruptly.

Nothing could survive a fall like that, not if that wretched tunnel went all the way to the foundations of the castle. It had to be nearly two hundred feet. If Kah had had wings, it would have been nothing.

But as it was, a wave of dizziness made her slide down the wall to sit. She couldn't think, not with the screaming. Was the child perhaps one floor down?

It had to be.

But she wasn't standing again. She couldn't.

She scooted down the stairs on her rump, praying to Akadi to silence whatever dark magic was tormenting her. Akadi, of course, did not hear her, or at least she did not respond.

Finally, Kah could take no more.

"Stop it!" she screamed, hands over her ears.

And the crying...

Stopped.

But it was replaced by something worse.

Giggling.

"But I'm just a little baby," said a mocking, childlike voice. "Don't you want to play?"

The voice came from everywhere and nowhere, bouncing off the stone walls and ceiling, swirling around the hole in the floor.

"No!" Kah shouted back. "Leave me alone!"

"Alone, alone, alone," the voice pretended to echo. Another giggle. "I'll keep you company. I'll keep you company... forever."

Something dropped down from the hole in the ceiling and landed on the stone walkway with a sick splat. It looked like a doll, the sort of soft thing little children clutched to their sleeping chests or dragged around by the limp fabric arm. It slowly stood, as if discovering its own body, and turned its stitched-on face toward Kah. Its mouth was a crooked curve of red yarn, its eyes two shiny black buttons. In its dirty beige hand it clutched a needle like a child might carry a play sword, and each of its lumpy legs ended in a filthy little sock.

"Why don't you sing me a song? I like songs. But you don't sing like a bird, do you? You're not a bird. Birds can *fly*. You're something in between, some unholy ragbag mishmash—"

In response, Kah lashed out with a taloned foot and kicked it, but the doll-thing merely tumbled clumsily backward like a wet towel and re-formed.

"That's not a nice way to play. Don't you have any manners? First you insult the count, and now you kick his childhood toy. Tut-tut. So rude!"

Kah did not want to stand, not now that she'd seen what lay at the heart of the tower. She wanted to scoot back downstairs and—

And what?

Spend the rest of her time in the castle waiting for this foul bit of dark magic to chase her down and poke her in the eye with its needle? No, she had to end this now, before it hurt her or someone else. She unhitched her mace, said her prayer to Akadi, and hit the doll as hard as she could. It flew across the tower and splatted against the wall, tumbling down to the stone, where it rose again, the same as before.

"Have you ever wanted something so badly?"

It pulled up to stand and stalked toward her, its needle flashing in the spare light.

"Wanted something so badly that you didn't care who you hurt? So badly you would kill for it?"

It rushed at Kah with frightening speed and nearly got her with its needle. She danced back, panicking, and fetched up against the wall. With solid stone at her back, she couldn't swing her mace. So she said her prayer and punted the thing—directly into the shaft.

"You do know!" it screeched as it fell. "You do you do you do!"

It giggled all the way down, but Kah did not wait to see what happened next. She scurried down the stairs, keeping close to the wall, her mace in her hand. Down and down she went until she was on her own landing. She threw open the door and flung herself into bed, pulling the covers over her head.

"It wasn't real," she told herself. "Bad bit of magic. Liar. Old garbage."

But the thing . . . had spoken like it knew things it couldn't possibly know.

And, somewhere in the castle, she was certain it was still alive, or . . . maybe not alive, but still giggling and carrying its silver needle through the darkness. Hunting her.

17

ROTROG

It was a great relief when Rotrog had finally been left alone in the study. *His* study, as he thought of it, beside *his* grand bedroom and *his* luxurious bathing chamber. He could be happy here, with his amiable host and glorious books, and—

Well, the witch had not been pleasant.

Nor had the gargoyles.

But then again, Rahadin had told them they would know when they weren't welcome, and weren't those transgressions their own fault? The entryway was off-limits; they understood that now. And Rotrog had perhaps not given enough thought to his exploration of the secret room beyond the hearth. He had in fact been attempting to find Strahd's secret grimoires. And he'd been appropriately punished. Like a good student, he had learned his lesson.

He studied the new spell book until his eyeballs ached, and when he stood, his back cracked all down his spine. Perhaps he could get one of the others to use a little cantrip on him and erase all the common pangs of a studious wizard. Outside of the witch and her cursed malady, it had been nearly an ideal day. His stomach gave a mighty rumble, and he went down to the banquet hall to see if perhaps dinner had been laid out. Much to his delight, it had, exactly the same spread as the previous night. He ate and drank with gusto, watching the door to see which of his compatriots might arrive. None did. Full and satisfied, he retreated to his grand chamber and fell into a strange sleep of twisted dreams. He was playing Hawks and Hares with Strahd, but he was a hawk that morphed into a hare, and Strahd chased him, laughing, through the corridor and pounced like a fox, his teeth snapping, the blood—

Such strange dreams.

The next morning, Rotrog rose and brushed his hair and went down to breakfast. He was tired and sluggish, but that was his punishment for studying so late. This time, his repast was not to be so congenial; the long table felt crowded even though there were only three other people there. Alishai had deep purple smudges under her eyes and picked at her sausage roll. Chivarion seemed especially vigilant, almost jumpy. He placed a platter of meat on the table for his tressym and could not take his eyes off the peculiar and, in Rotrog's opinion, unappetizing creature, staring at the beast as if it might disappear if he blinked. Kah, too, was on high alert. Her head cocked to and fro like her avian ancestors as she scanned the ceiling, then the floor, then lifted the tablecloth to look under the table.

"You all appear to be more anxious than usual," Rotrog said, happily demolishing his sausages. "Did you not sleep well? This place brings strange dreams, does it not?"

"No, we didn't sleep well, you dunderhead. This place . . . it gets to you." Alishai bit into a pastry and chewed like it tasted of dust.

Chivarion's eyes flicked to the door. "Have you seen Strahd today? Has he been here?"

Rotrog sighed. "Sadly, no. Our host is a most busy and important personage."

"What of Fielle?" Kah asked.

Alishai's head jerked up, her mouth a firm line. "Has no one seen her this morning? I left her in her room with Rahadin yesterday after the witch imbroglio."

"You left her with Rahadin?" Chivarion's lip lifted in a sneer. "I wouldn't trust him farther than I could throw him, which is honestly a bit far. So I wouldn't trust him farther than Kah could throw him. He's rather . . . oily, don't you think?"

"The oiliest," Alishai agreed. She looked around. "And I don't care if he hears it. So, no one has seen Fielle since then?"

The tiefling looked to each person. When her eyes drilled into Rotrog, he shrugged. "I arrived first, and there was no sign of an earlier diner."

"Fie on this," Alishai said. "I'm going to check on her." She stood and took two steps toward the door before turning back, uncertain. "We should all go. I don't think—traveling alone here . . ." She trailed off as if not wanting to admit the truth.

"Not safe," Kah said with a shiver.

Rotrog sighed and stood, spearing a sausage on his fork to bring along. With his staff in one hand and his fork in the other, he followed the others. Well, actually, Chivarion took up the rear post as usual, his tressym riding on his shoulder. Rotrog did not know where Fielle's room might be but hoped it wouldn't involve too many stairs. Fortunately, Alishai merely led them around a few corners and down a long hall. She had her glaive in hand and scanned the area like they were marching into battle instead of enjoying a promenade through a castle. Even little Kah had her mace out and ready. Rotrog wanted to ask them what they'd encountered here that made them so apprehensive; he'd dealt only with the witch, and he had accepted that when one ventured into hidden spaces, one accepted the consequences.

The hallway emptied out into an octagonal room with furniture almost as fine as his own. The large bed was mussed but not currently in use. Alishai rushed to the bed, pulled back the covers, threw the pillows to the floor, knelt to look underneath the bed skirt. Next she went to the wardrobe and ruffled through the layers of cloth. Chivarion joined her and pressed a hand against the wooden backing.

"No secret door in this one," he said, but he sounded more grateful than annoyed by this fact.

"Nowhere else to hide," Kah said, darting along the walls and pressing a stone that stuck out a little more than the others. "No traps. No doors." She went to an arrow slit. "Too small for even Fielle." She looked to Alishai. "She's not here."

Alishai's hands tightened on her glaive. "We have to find her."

"Now, now." Rotrog knew he did not share her authority, holding a sausage fork as he was. "We don't know that anything has gone awry. The castle is large, and we were given permission to wander. Let us find Rahadin or the count and see if perhaps they can point us in the right direction."

"And where do you think we'll find them, hmm?" Alishai shot back. "They keep themselves well hidden until they wish to be seen."

"I saw Strahd yesterday," Chivarion admitted. "But he was . . . not kind. He had wolves with him. Large ones. And he threatened to pull Murder apart like a roast chicken."

"That cannot be true!" Rotrog protested. "Our host is not some monster! He is educated, a great leader. He has no need to harm your little pet."

Chivarion was in his face in a heartbeat, the tip of his dagger grazing Rotrog's chin. "Murder is not my little pet. She is my friend. She has saved my life a hundred times over, unlike you, who have only risked it!"

Rotrog's hands went up, the sausage waving impotently in the air. "I meant only that there is no conceivable reason the count would wish to harm an innocent animal. I am certain he was just handling the, er, creature a little rougher than perhaps you would prefer."

Chivarion withdrew the dagger. "He was not rough. He was quite specific in his threats. If I see him again, I'll kill him myself."

Rotrog held his staff under his arm as he smoothed down his robes. "You'll do no such thing. It's very rude, to harm a host."

"It's just as rude to threaten a guest."

"He somehow threatens without threatening," Kah said, the feathers around her head at attention. "I saw him yesterday, too. Snuck up on me. Asked odd questions. Disappeared." She shivered. "Felt like he might snap me up in one bite."

Alishai nodded. "He spoke to me as well. That first night, before the bath. I'm certain I didn't dream it." She looked up, met each person's eyes. "So Strahd has sought each of us out individually for a chat but avoids us when we're together. And he asks peculiar questions. It feels like he's . . . looking for something. Doesn't it?"

Rotrog waved his sausage for emphasis. "He is merely being polite!"

"He was not polite to Murder!" Chivarion grabbed the sausage and threw it across the room, where it hit the wall and fell with a sick splat.

"Enough!" Alishai barked, and they all stared at her. "Forget your quibble. We have to find Fielle and see if Strahd questioned her as well. Since she's the only one missing, I'm worried that whatever he's looking for—maybe he found it in her. The rest of us need to stick together. Rotrog, if you could please dispose of that sausage? Yes? Good. Come on."

Rotrog did not appreciate being told what to do, but . . . well, fine, he was somewhat worried for the little human. She was about the size of an orc child and very frail, and he did owe her for saving his life yesterday. He quickly fetched and devoured the sausage, barely tasting it, and hurried down the hallway. If there were things in this castle that had frightened the others, he did not want to stumble into them on his own.

Back in the front hall, Alishai stopped. "That way lies a hall of statues—"

"Another one? Great spiders, this Strahd likes statues!" Chivarion interjected.

"And then a fallen chapel. I don't think Fielle would be there. Has anyone been downstairs?" Heads shook. "How about the next floor up?" More heads shook. "Above that one is the study—"

"My floor," Rotrog said.

"Sure. So, the study. And above that is Chivarion's chamber—"

"And a cursed lounge with a creepy young man who jumps out of windows and climbs across the roof like a roach," Chivarion added.

Alishai rubbed her eyes. "The more I hear, the less I understand. And the less I like. Continuing on, above that is the floor where Kah and I sleep, but the other doors are sealed shut. Has anyone been above that?"

Kah tentatively raised a hand. "Opened one of the doors on our floor; that's where Strahd found me. Nasty bed in there with manacles. Fielle wouldn't like it, not a bit. Then I went all the way to the top of the spire. There was a thing. Child's toy. Attacked me. It fell down a shaft, but it's still . . . around." Her eyes traced every corner of the chamber. "Awful place. Haunted."

"So we either go up or down a floor. Anyone have a . . ." The tiefling's lips twisted. "A good feeling? About anything?"

"If the choice is between a dank castle dungeon and literally anything else, I would vastly prefer we went upward," Rotrog said.

Alishai chuckled. "For once, we are in accord."

She started up the grand staircase, and Rotrog truly didn't believe everyone needed to have their weapons in such an aggressive position. At the next landing, Alishai stepped out and considered the available choices before leading them down a long hall, around a corner, and to a massive set of doors.

"Ready?" she asked.

Rotrog was not ready. He did not want to explore. He did not want to face dangers untold. He wanted to make a tidy pile of sausage and pastry sandwiches and carry them up to the study. There was still an atlas he needed to find. But there was no way out of this situation without admitting cowardice, and he was always hopeful he might find another hidden spell book, so he nodded along with the rest.

Alishai pushed open the doors to reveal a once-elegant hallway, the sort of place where a king might preside over royal matters. Cobwebs draped from the ceiling like gossamer vines, and a heavy layer of dust coated every surface. An aristocratic stone balcony overlooked the lofty room, and two slumped figures sat there upon thrones.

"If Strahd is the count, then who are they?" Chivarion asked, his voice carrying.

Rotrog winced. "Relatives, perhaps? Parents?"

Chivarion looked at him like he was an idiot. "Dead parents?"

"Royalty is peculiar. Perhaps it is some sort of tradition."

A low moan crawled across the room, raising the hairs on Rotrog's arms.

Kah startled. "What was that?"

Rotrog inclined his head. "It came from the thrones, I believe."

"Hello?" Alishai called softly. "Do you require aid?"

The only answer was another moan.

"I hate this place," Alishai muttered. She took off at a jog toward the balcony. After a moment, Kah followed. Chivarion was more measured as he stalked across the hall. Rotrog, again, followed, not because he was concerned for the figures upon the thrones or able to help them in any way, but because he did not wish to be left alone here.

The moment Alishai crossed the center of the room, there was a scraping noise overhead. Rotrog froze in place and looked up. The hairs in his ears twitched at the squeaking of bats, a sound he knew well from long evenings spent in the ancient library at the academy. Alishai and Kah were still running, but Rotrog stood and watched in horror as a cloaked figure erupted from the ceiling and swooped directly for him, arms outstretched. As it neared, a throaty chuckle bubbled up, and Rotrog dropped his staff and sausage fork and dove to his belly as it passed overhead. He felt the air ruffle his hair and covered his head with his hands, peeking out through his fingers.

Chivarion, just behind him, leaped and swung his silver sword in a perfectly timed double-handed downswing. The creature's head bounced away, rolling across the dusty hall like a child's forgotten ball. Rotrog waited to feel the hot spurt of blood across his back, ruining his cloak, but the figure merely swung back overhead in the opposite direction.

"Stupid dummy," Chivarion growled.

"My intelligence is—"

"No," the drow corrected. "That. That was a stupid dummy. A mannequin." When Rotrog just stared at him, he continued, "Did you not hear the head thump? Real heads are less bouncy. There's more of a thump, but with a little squish."

With an annoyed sigh, he jogged over to where the head lay on the floor and carried it back to show a carved wooden facsimile of Strahd's face with mad red eyes.

"Some sort of prank, I am certain," Rotrog said. It was unnerving, how even the painted eyes seemed to follow him.

Chivarion tossed the head over his shoulder, and it rolled away.

The—body? The rest of the mannequin had disappeared among the cobwebs overhead.

"Are you done?" Alishai snapped, having stopped just short of the balcony.

"We are not toddlers engaged in gameplay." Rotrog sniffed. "We were attacked."

Alishai shook her head in annoyance and strapped her glaive to her back, preparing to launch herself up to the stone balustrade. Right before she could jump, a new voice echoed throughout the hall.

"Do not dare disturb them," it said. "For they will surely attack!"

18

ALISHAI

With one smooth motion, Alishai's trusty glaive was back in her hands.

"Who said that?"

A cloaked figure—

So many figures in this castle, so many formless phantoms, so many secretive shadows and slumped shapes!

—appeared at the balustrade right where it met the wall, far from the thrones. Pale white hands pushed back the brown hood to reveal an older human man with a hawklike face and longish white hair swept back from a sharply receding widow's peak. He was dressed sensibly in tall leather boots and smart brown traveling clothes of good quality, and a pair of glasses perched on the end of his nose.

"They are zombies, you see," he explained. His voice had the excitable, bombastic tone of a zealot, but a learned one. "Yet another confounding instance of Strahd's elaborate mummery."

"How do you know that?" Alishai asked, her glaive still at the ready.

He regarded her with bemusement. "How do you *not* know that? A paladin like yourself should easily be able to sense evil."

Alishai's jaw dropped—at least internally. She'd been so consumed by the crawling sense of dread and general reek of age and death that she had somehow forgotten to simply use her senses. She had not been a paladin long, and although the fighting part came naturally to her, this specific application of her talents was not something she'd ever needed before. In her experience thus far, the most evil creatures were of flesh and blood; she'd thought she'd had no reason to scan for fiends here, in the castle of a wealthy lord, and she'd had no time to do so in the butcher's cabin. Feeling like a fool, she opened her senses, and of course the stranger was correct. The stench of rotten flesh was an assault to her very soul. To think: She'd almost walked directly into the arms of yet another zombie.

"Who are you?" she asked the stranger, hoping to draw attention away from her failure.

The man gave a small bow. "Rudolph van Richten, at your service. And who are you?"

Alishai looked back at her three companions. "We're travelers. Guests of the count. But we're missing one of our number, and we're worried she might be in trouble."

Van Richten's gaze sharpened, and Alishai understood then that although he appeared old and somewhat frail, this was a man who did not run from threats. "This is not unusual news for a guest in the castle. Tell me: Did Strahd question your party, and did he take a particular interest in your missing friend, as if he'd chosen a favorite? Was he solicitous, perhaps even fond of her?"

The man's words were so true that Alishai felt them ring in her soul like a bell. "Yes. Our first night here, he did seem to favor her. And he spoke to us all individually."

"That is bad news indeed. And has she been unwell, your missing friend? Weak but restless, pale and dreamy?"

Now it was Alishai whose attention sharpened. "Yes. Yes, to all of that. Is this common? Is it a sickness?"

Van Richten glanced around the hall and sighed in weary resignation, as if he'd lost another soldier in a battle he'd been fighting for far too long. "It is indeed a sickness, but a very specific one. We should not speak here. Come. Let us find a more private place."

Alishai could identify the undead, but she could not divine the goodness of a living creature's heart. Still, she sensed this van Richten could be trusted, and that he had information that would be vital to finding Fielle.

"We'll follow you."

"Wait just a moment, now," Rotrog said. "We don't even know this person!"

Alishai glared at him. "He's here, he's alive, and he knows something about Fielle. Do you not think the four of us could take him in a fight? Have you lost faith in your spells?"

The orc considered his staff and sniffed. "I know my worth."

"Well, then."

Van Richten inclined his head. "Thank you for your trust. I assure you that I only have your friend's best interest at heart, and that your lives are in danger so long as you reside under this roof."

He climbed nimbly down from the balustrade and led them back through the audience chamber and down a narrow hallway, pushing open a creaking wooden door to reveal a sort of barracks. Eight roomy beds were lined up neatly along the oak-paneled walls of a large chamber, with yellowed ivory gauze softly billowing from their canopies in a breeze Alishai could not feel. At first she wondered why Rahadin had not given this chamber to her or Kah, with its larger beds and more convenient placement, but then she realized that something about the room made her skin crawl, as if someone had left mere seconds before they arrived, and that someone had only the foulest intentions and might return shortly.

Van Richten closed the door once they were all inside. Oil lamps lit the space in a way that was almost cozy—but nothing here was cozy, not really. Chivarion lay down upon a bed in a puff of dust, his elbows out and his feet crossed. Rotrog reluctantly sat on the edge of one, but Kah and Alishai stood close to van Richten. Alishai noted the kenku had her hand on her mace but did not seem distrustful of the newcomer.

"So what are we dealing with?" Alishai asked.

The man took off his glasses and cleaned them on his cloak. "We are dealing with only the most merciless and cruel creature in all of Barovia. I take it you have heard of vampires?"

After a brief pause, Alishai, Rotrog, and Kah burst out laughing.

Chivarion, on the other hand, sat up and leaned forward.

"Vampires aren't real," Alishai said. "They're a myth used to scare children."

"Vampires are very real," Chivarion said, far more serious than usual. "I've fought them. Horrid things. They do not wish to die again."

"How can you be in Barovia and not believe in vampires?" van Richten asked. He put his hands on his hips, and Alishai saw a variety of weapons strung about his person, including wooden stakes and a silver dagger. "Surely in your time here, you have seen things that confirm your worst fears. Even if you have never encountered such a monster in your own realm, you must have noticed that this place is . . . different?"

"The zombies," Kah said. "The boneless pig things."

"The carriage that drives itself," Chivarion added. "The gremishka."

Van Richten gestured to the moon sigil on Alishai's glaive. "And in your studies, you must've crossed paths with werewolves."

Alishai's skin twitched at that word. "Werewolves I know. But the undead, rising from the soil to drink blood? It doesn't even make sense. How—"

"In a world filled with magic, the how takes care of itself," van Richten told her, a sparkle in his eye. "Let us move forward. If you accept that vampires are real, then you must understand that it is likely that Strahd's interest in your friend is more dangerous than you know."

"I believe Strahd to be a gracious host," Rotrog began, shaking his staff.

"Is he?" Van Richten cocked his head. "Well, then. If he invited you here, he has a reason. And if he forced your hand to accept his hospitality, driving you here to his lair, he has a reason that is deeply important to him. And if he has been gracious, then he is either testing you or toying with you. Count Strahd von Zarovich is more than just a vampire. He is the original vampire, and his existence is dedicated to a singular task: finding his one true love, Tatyana."

"Our friend is named Fielle, not Tatyana," Alishai said. "She is a human woman."

Van Richten nodded eagerly. "Yes, yes, I thought she might be. Large eyes? Pale skin? Small stature? A kind heart?"

Alishai looked to Kah and Chivarion. It was unnerving, how well this strange man had just described Fielle.

"All that," Kah agreed.

As he nodded, van Richten paced the room, his hands clasped behind his back. "My intelligence was correct, then. You came through the Mists, you were *called* through the Mists, and you woke up here—my friend woke you, I believe, in the guise of a raven—and then Strahd found you. Quite unlucky indeed. And now you are in the castle, and one of your number has grown sickly and then disappeared." He shook his head and spoke as if to himself. "This has happened before. It will happen again."

"But what of now?" Alishai barked. "What has he done to Fielle?"

Van Richten stopped and looked up at her as if he had forgotten she existed. "He has chosen her. He will want her for his own. It is likely he has begun to . . . turn her."

Alishai wanted to grab the loquacious old man by the front of his shirt and shake him. "Speak plainly! Turn her into what?"

Van Richten blinked like an owl. "Well, into a vampire spawn, of course. And eventually, a full-fledged vampire, you see. He will wish her to dwell by his side for always, as his beloved countess. Once upon a time, Strahd fell in love with a human woman who did not love him in return, a woman named Tatyana, and so he made a pact with dark forces so that he might live forever. After sealing this pact with his own brother's blood, Strahd attempted to claim his beloved, but she dove off a cliff, sacrificing her life that she might be free of Strahd and his foul curse. Since then, he has been trapped here in Barovia, searching for the love he felt once upon a time. He wants a consort. Or an equal, an heir. He is a creature of endless hunger and cruelty." Van Richten put a kindly hand on Alishai's shoulder, but she shook it off. "If your friend has disappeared, it is likely she is buried underground and will soon rise utterly changed."

"Fielle is a vampire?" Chivarion asked, dumbfounded.

"Not yet. But soon, perhaps. A vampire spawn shares many of a vampire's baser instincts and powers but is compelled to serve their maker. They are drained of blood, then buried. When they rise, they are something new. They will not become a full vampire until they are allowed to drink from their creator. But most vampires prefer soldiers to equals and hesitate to give their spawn further powers. Strahd will likely keep your Fielle under his thumb until he is certain she is the one he's been waiting for—that she is the embodiment of the spirit of Tatyana. Her mind, in some ways, will still be her own, but Strahd will control her." He pulled a wooden stake from his belt. "It might be kinder to kill her now. Being in thrall to Strahd is not a pleasant life."

Alishai stepped fully into van Richten's space, Chivarion right behind her. "We will not see Fielle harmed," she warned.

Van Richten reluctantly replaced the stake in his belt. "She has already been harmed. It is too late."

"It is never too late." Alishai considered what she knew of vampires, which was almost nothing. "There must be something we can do. If we kill Strahd, will she be free?"

In that moment, van Richten looked very old indeed. He sighed, his head hanging loosely on his spindly neck as he fidgeted with his gloves. "In your world, that might fix things, but here, in Barovia . . . well, I have a hypothesis. This domain—these domains of dread, for there are several bound by the Mists—this place is different. Strahd is bound to Barovia; it is a hell created specifically to hold him. When he is killed, he is fated to always return. This is not the first time our count has claimed a consort, hoping to bind himself to Tatyana's soul. I am in the castle now looking for Strahd's journals to see what he knows of this phenomenon, of his situation, and if there might be a true key to ending his reign. My hope was to save his chosen victim before he could drink from her, but it appears I am yet again too late."

"Surely everything can be killed?" Rotrog asked, sounding highly doubtful.

"Killing him is a difficult and delicate task, and he will always rise again." Van Richten looked off into the distance. "I have killed him before. And yet here we are."

"Then we find Fielle and steal her back," Chivarion said. "Can't we just go outside and look for a fresh bit of dirt and start digging?"

"Can't get outside," Kah chirped. "Gargoyles."

"And as long as Tatyana's soul remains in Fielle's body, Strahd will hunt her to the ends of the world—this world that he controls. There is no escape and nowhere to hide, I'm afraid," the old man said.

"Hmm. If only there were some way to separate Fielle's soul from that of this Tatyana woman," Rotrog said. "If that part of the conjecture is indeed correct."

"Cut her in half?" Chivarion offered.

"Yes!" Van Richten quickly refocused, blinking aggressively. "No! I mean, in a way. Yes. Yes! It's Tatyana he craves, not your Fielle. Fielle is but a vessel. Strahd is a monster who cares only for himself, and he has this one particular goal. If the two souls could be separated, Strahd would have his Tatyana without harming an innocent, and for a while, there might be peace."

"So is Fielle still Fielle?" Kah asked. "Or someone else?"

Alishai nodded along. "She seemed much the same as before, but more tired."

"This is a topic of much curiosity." Van Richten gestured with his spectacles, stabbing at the air as he spoke. "I don't believe the vessel is aware of—another soul. It is like a silent parasite, perhaps. Or maybe your friend has always possessed this soul, and only in this world does that become a problem. Tatyana died long before I was born, and thus far, Strahd has always turned his consorts before I could get involved. It should be painless, severing that connection. And I think I know a way . . ."

"How?" Alishai felt as if suddenly time meant something again.

Van Richten paced the small room, bent over like a shorebird. "We would need a new vessel for Tatyana's soul. And a way to separate them." He stopped and straightened, clicking his heels together and grinning manically. "You know, I've heard of someone who can perhaps oblige in both those areas—Dr. Viktra Mordenheim of Lamordia. Tell me, how do you feel about steamships? And does everyone have a warm coat?"

19

FIELLE

Fielle was cold; someone must've let the fire in the hearth go out. Without the warmth radiating from the chimney bricks in her attic room, she was left shivering. She reached for her coverlet and found fur tight around her neck. One of the mousers from the kitchen, snuggling close for warmth?

No. Not a cat. The fur was just as cold as she was.

She opened her eyes to find the room totally dark. The silence was deafening, like wool stuck in her ears. That was the odd bit—the old tavern's bones creaked at all hours of the day and night, the roof and foundation fighting over which one might settle with louder cracks. It was located in a rowdy district, and there was always a party somewhere in the streets outside her window, and after that party, the drunks argued and fought and sang their way home.

The only reason things might be so quiet was a sudden and unusual blanketing of snow.

Yes, that was it. A rare winter storm, like when she was twelve. Deep, thick snow surely covered the streets, leaned against the window glass, and sat heavily on the roof tiles. A cold wind must've whistled down the chimney, snuffing out the fire. If only Fielle had a thicker blanket, she would merely turn over on her side and snuggle down deeper.

But—

She couldn't turn. There was something right there, just overhead. It reminded her of the bunks in her Uncle Thiero's wagon, back when she was a child and a fire had put the tavern out of business for a year, forcing them to make their coin with a traveling show. But this wasn't the wagon; it didn't smell of tobacco and tung oil and horse.

The odors were sharper: newly cut wood and old, dark dirt.

And everything was still, oh so still.

With trembling hands, fearing what she might find, Fielle reached up. Her fingertips scraped against raw wood, a flat board, so close. Her heart—

It wasn't beating fast. It wasn't in her throat. It wasn't choking her.

She couldn't feel it at all.

Even worse, she discovered she wasn't breathing.

Was she . . . dead?

She felt her face, and that, at least, was the same as ever in shape, muscle and bone flexing as she opened and closed her mouth, but her skin was ice cold. She traced her lips, closed her eyes and skimmed fingertips over their lids. Her hair was there. She recognized the heavy brocade dress with its fur collar.

She could move. She could smell things. She could touch things.

But she was bound somewhere cold, dark, cramped, quiet.

She knew now where she was.

Buried, underground, in a coffin.

"No," she murmured. "No, no, no . . ."

"Who is there?"

The voice was startled, round and deep.

A woman, with the same accent as Strahd and his servant, Rahadin.

"My name is Fielle, and I think . . . I think I've been buried alive. Or I'm dead. You can hear me? Who are you?"

"I am . . . I was . . . I . . ." The voice trailed off, confused and dreamy. "I don't quite remember."

"Are you dead, too? Are you in the box with me?" Fielle felt around to discover the dimensions of the box that held her. She was surrounded by fabric but could find no suggestions of another person. This was a relief, but a small one. The original problems persisted.

It was a long, considering moment before the other voice answered. "I see only darkness. I hear only you. For a while, it was as if I dreamed. I could only watch what occurred, a silent witness. I awoke in a forest, surrounded by strangers—none human—but someone else spoke and made all the decisions. I could not control my body, could not make my mouth speak my thoughts. There were dead things—a butcher, parts of pigs. We fought them. We nearly lost. The dream became a nightmare. Rain. A carriage came. And then—"

Fielle shivered, remembering.

"The castle. The last place I could ever wish to be." A pause. "Strahd's castle."

In the darkness, Fielle's eyes were wide open, hunting for the smallest bit of light to illuminate the situation, but she knew she would not find it. She was trapped here, trapped with this . . . phantom. There had to be an explanation.

"You're describing what happened to me," she said quietly, because her voice was the only sound in the entire world, besides the mysterious other. "I went to sleep in my bed in Baldur's Gate and woke up here, in Barovia, surrounded by four strangers. We fought zombies in an abattoir, and we took the carriage to the castle. Are you . . ."

There was no good way to put this without sounding quite mad.

"Are you a ghost? A spirit? A god?"

Fielle realized she was speaking out loud, but the other person—the new voice—was different. She heard it without hearing it, not with her ears, exactly, but . . .

Closing her eyes, she thought the words, "Have you been with me all along? Are you inside me?"

"Inside you . . ." the voice mused, testing it out. "Perhaps. I see only darkness now, but I hear you in . . . my head, if I had a head. Perhaps I am a ghost. The last thing I remember of my own life was leaping from the cliffs of Castle Ravenloft, my final act of rebellion to avoid an eternity at Strahd's side." A pause. "He is still alive?"

"He is."

A sad sigh. "Even in death I cannot escape him."

"So you were his beloved?" Fielle asked, recalling Strahd's story.

"No!" The vehemence was sudden and fierce. "I remember now. I was to marry his brother, Sergei, the most wonderful man in all the world. But Strahd killed him and drank his blood, all so that he might claim me as his prize. I hated Strahd. He was cruel, selfish, arrogant, violent. I watched him speak to you in your chamber. When he looked into your eyes . . . I felt him hunting for me. I was like a bird in a cage, fluttering away from his certain grasp."

"I thought . . . he might have feelings for me," Fielle said quietly. "When he spoke of wanting someone to love."

"And my heart ached for you, because I knew he could only bring you pain," the voice assured her.

Fielle shifted. She could feel her limbs, her skin, but . . . nothing hurt. If she'd been buried, that meant someone thought her dead, but there were no wounds, no signs of illness. "Maybe I am dead, then. If I am speaking to a dead person. Nothing seems to be wrong with me."

After a long moment, the voice spoke with great gravity. "I remember now. I am—was—dead. After the fall. My name is Tatyana. And we are tied together, you and I."

"It is strange, and yet . . ." Fielle paused, tentative.

"Comforting? I can feel your goodness, your kindness. I have felt everything you felt, your love for your friends and your willingness to sacrifice for them. You do not deserve to be the object of Strahd's affections."

"Neither did you. It's nice, to know that you are with me, Tatyana. Even if I die here, I won't be alone."

"I don't want to die twice . . ." Tatyana trailed off with a soulful sigh.

Fielle was trying to think of a way to offer some sort of comfort when her entire body went on point like a hound. She was suddenly starving, her stomach cramping, her mouth watering. A faint smell reached her, and she bolted upward, smacking her head on the wood.

There was something outside—some kind of food—and it smelled *so good.*

"What is that?" Tatyana asked, just as avid. "I have never wanted to eat something so badly in my life."

A crunch overhead as something passed by; even through six feet of loose dirt, Fielle could sense it. A human. A peasant, judging by the scent of unwashed body, soured linen, and muddy boots. But underneath those unsavory odors was the promise of nourishment, a thirst slaked after a torturously long time without satisfaction. Even from here, Fielle could smell the man's blood, and her craving overtook her like a wave, crashing over her body, making her muscles contort with longing.

"We have to break out of here," Tatyana said, desperate.

"But . . . the food I smell . . . it's not . . ."

Fielle did not want to accept what she understood on an animal basis.

It wasn't possible, this feeling that washed over her.

These new senses, so sharp and strong.

It couldn't possibly be—

"It is the blood." Tatyana's voice was ragged, uneasy.

Fielle shook her head, the rough wood scraping her cheek. "No. No! I am not the kind of person who hurts people! I do not eat people—or drink blood, or whatever this is. The idea is ridiculous. This is madness. That can be the only explanation."

"Then we are both mad. Because I am not that kind of person, either, but we need that blood." Tatyana was practically begging now, and Fielle shared her need.

"And anyway, I'm not strong enough to break out of a coffin. This is solid wood. I would shatter every bone in my hand if I tried. And surely I am buried at least six feet underground in frozen soil. What would I do—claw my way out like a mole? It's insane."

In her mind, Tatyana whimpered.

The man was moving farther and farther away.

Fielle was not a strong person in body or mind, a fact that her family loved to remind her of whenever possible, but she was an artificer, and she was clever. Even without her kit, she always had resources at her disposal; she understood how things worked, how they were put together. Did she have any makeshift tools? Perhaps the bone from her corset's stays, or the heel of her boot? No, the whalebone would snap, and she couldn't reach her boot. She felt around the coffin, testing its construction, seeking a weak spot. When she pressed on the lid with both hands, she felt a nail give way.

Could it be that easy?

She pushed with all her might and felt nails pop loose. She had enough room now to kick the end up with her feet. More nails gave way, and dark dirt flooded the coffin, filtering down to cover her face. She briefly worried that she would suffocate before she remembered that she was not currently breathing. Pinning her lips closed, she pushed with her arms and legs, forcing the coffin lid up and away. With her sharp new senses and cravings came an extraordinary strength the likes of which she'd never known before. The coffin lid was free now. She ignored the falling dirt, black and loamy with the tang of iron, and shoved the coffin lid aside. When she sat up, her hair pressed into packed soil and met resistance. She felt grains of sand scratch across the thin skin of her eyelids, the dry ridges of her lips.

"He is walking away," Tatyana urged. "We must reach him!"

With renewed vigor, Fielle thrust her body upward as if swimming through the loose earth. Then she was standing in the coffin, every inch of her encased in soil. Her teeth were slicked with grit, her nostrils full of loam. She climbed toward the surface, clawing, clambering, the heavy dress weighing her down. Like Tatyana, she, too, could sense the man walking purposefully away. She did not know the extent of the castle's grounds, but she knew that when he saw her rising from her own grave, he would run.

When she heard a new set of feet crunching over the grass nearby, she grinned fiercely. Dirt coated her teeth, thick and powdery, but she did not care. All she could think about was hot, pulsing blood, refreshing and nourishing, falling into her mouth like rain on parched flowers. Finally a hand broke through the crust of soil, and she felt the cold wind of Barovia on her muddied palm.

"Yes!" Tatyana urged, still with her, the voice in her head now part of her. "Yes, keep going! Gently, gently."

Fielle understood. They were hunting now, and it would be better not to spook their prey. She slowly dragged her body out of the hole, kicking with her booted feet. The earth squeezed against her, and she fought it, pulling the long dress after her until she lay on her stomach, birthed from the wretched clutches of Barovian soil. She dusted dirt off her eyelashes and opened her bleary eyes.

The world looked different. More distinct. It was nighttime, but she could see perfectly well even with the heavy cloud cover she'd come to expect here. Every detail was sharply cut in a thousand shades of gray, each touch of light gleaming like it had been kissed by a star. The man who'd most recently crossed near her grave had not noticed her; he was walking toward the stable holding a bit of oiled leather. She could hear his heart beating from here, see a haze around him, almost an aura, like her senses wanted to make sure she could not miss him.

"Run," Tatyana urged her.

So she did.

She picked up the hem of her skirts and sprinted directly at the man, faster than she'd ever run before in her life. He only realized something was happening at the last minute, turning his head in surprise as she launched herself like a cat pouncing on a mouse, her fingers curled into claws as they caught his shoulders. Fielle rode the man to the ground and straddled his waist, the dirt-dusted brocade of her dress billowing around him, swallowing his body.

"What—" he started.

Her hand slapped over his mouth, forcing his head down and to the side, further exposing the thick veins on the side of his throat. Fielle swallowed hard and lowered her mouth. Her teeth were suddenly too big, forcing her lips back.

But she couldn't! She shouldn't—

"Do it," Tatyana urged.

With a feral lunge, Fielle sunk her teeth into the man's neck, felt their sharp points piercing his skin and inserting themselves neatly into his flesh. He bucked underneath her, and she resettled, pinning his arms with her knees. She felt something warm and soft and wet and realized that in her haste to hold him down she'd accidentally stuck her thumb into his eyeball. She winced but did not pull away.

"Just drink," Tatyana said. "That is all that matters now."

The blood—it was exquisite. Hot, salty, sweet, sparkling like champagne as she gulped and gulped and gulped it down. She tried to be neat, not because she cared about appearances but because she didn't want to lose a single drop. It filled her, swelled inside her, burned like a candle that shone through a lantern to light an entire room. She had never felt so satisfied, so certain that she was doing exactly what she was meant to be doing. This was her calling, to drink and rejoice with fullness.

And then suddenly he came up dry. She pulled, sucking, and there was nothing left. He was empty and completely drained, and the scent of him repulsed her. Unwashed skin, greasy hair crawling with lice, sweat-stained clothes rimed with salt, a crotch that stank of old goat. She pushed him away and stood, stepping away from the crusted husk.

"More," Tatyana declared.

"Yes. Yes. More," Fielle agreed. She didn't have to speak with her mouth to communicate with Tatyana, which was good, as she wasn't sure how to talk around her new fangs. As she stood there, scanning the area for prey, the teeth fit themselves back into her gums like a cat's claws retracting. She licked her lips and wiped off her chin. Her fingers came away slicked with dead blood.

"Ah, there you are. Turn around and let me see you, my dear."

Hearing Strahd's voice, Fielle felt Tatyana's disgust and rage as if it were her own. He was behind her; he'd snuck up on her. And now he was commanding her.

"I should kill him for what he did to you," she told Tatyana in their new way of speaking.

"No. Not today. You are not strong enough." Tatyana hmmed. "For now, do not let him know that I am here, or all is lost. Try to be yourself. Your old self. You were different, before this. I remember. The shape of you inside has altered, somehow. He need not know."

Fielle swallowed down her fury and tried to remember how to smile. She lifted her heavy skirts and turned around. Count Strahd von Zarovich stood there in his beautiful suit and cape, his eyes afire with delight and desire. Fielle smiled demurely and curtseyed, bowing her head. Black dirt fell from her short hair and rimmed her fingernails.

"My lord, what has happened to me?" she asked him, feigning an innocence she no longer felt. "I feel strange."

Strahd held out a hand, and she had no choice but to take it. He pulled her close and tucked her fingers into his elbow before leading her toward the castle. She glanced back to the mound of dirt, which still showed the marks of her passage. There was no tombstone, just a gentle curve of disturbed soil. It was not the only such mound, although the others had been compacted by time and rain, making darkened divots instead of gentle hills.

"You have been transformed," he told her with a paternal sort of fondness. "You will never again know illness or shrink from some outside threat. You are stronger now, faster, a predator uniquely suited to a life in Barovia. You will no longer eat food but will crave blood, and I will keep a fresh supply available to you. You found your way to the surface faster than I anticipated; I have a better meal waiting for you in your chamber."

"I am something unexpected," she thought. "I am more than he thinks I am."

"*We* are more," Tatyana corrected.

20

CHIVARION

The strange human talked more than anyone Chivarion had ever met. Van Richten buzzed around the moldering room like a brass bee visiting every dusty flower, explaining this and that. Chivarion wanted to grab him by the front of his brown shirt and demand he hold still and use simple words with only one syllable.

"Now what's this Lamordia place you won't shut up about?" he asked.

Van Richten was alight with—whatever made people want to teach other people facts. He loved explaining things. It was exhausting. Chivarion never wanted anyone explaining anything to him at all unless it was "how to kill more bad guys for coin."

"Lamordia is another domain. Where we are now—Barovia—is one of the Domains of Dread, you see?" van Richten said, gesturing at the air as if there were a perfectly reasonable map drawn there, which there was not. "And then there's Lamordia, Kartakass, Dementlieu, et cetera. Unlike your home, these places do not share a landmass. They are not bordered by the same seas, and there are no roads that connect them. They are almost like a series of ponds, all separated by mist. And yet one is not next to the other, you understand."

"I don't," Chivarion told him.

Undeterred, the man continued. "They are connected by the Mists, which means that the only way to travel between them is to understand the Mists, as the Vistani do, or to have a token that allows you to navigate these strange liminal spaces. And I have such an item, you see?" He reached into the interior of his coat and withdrew a heavy ring bearing a family crest. Something about it made Chivarion want to throw it into the deepest lava-filled crevasse he could find.

"This is a Mist talisman—an object especially attuned to Barovia. If you are in another domain and you enter the Mists, hold this, and concentrate, it will direct you back to its home."

"But we're already here," Alishai said as if speaking to a child.

Van Richten was all wound up now, flapping his arms and jumping about. "Yes, yes. I'm getting ahead of myself. First we must get you to Lamordia, so here is what will happen. A ship waits for me at Tsolenka Pass. The captain is an old friend—Larissa Snowmane. She is one of the chosen few who can navigate the Mists. I will send you to Larissa, and she will take you to the realm of Lamordia. There, you will find a way to travel to Schloss Mordenheim, the home of Dr. Viktra Mordenheim. She is the only person in all of creation who might be able to perform this separation of souls—and create a vessel to house Tatyana's soul. Dr. Mordenheim is a maestra of the flesh, you see. A doctor of death."

"That . . . does not sound welcoming," Chivarion said. "And you keep saying 'you see,' and I keep not seeing at all."

"Time is of the essence, my boy, time is of the essence! Now . . ." Van Richten stopped his frenetic pacing and considered them, lowering his spectacles. "Are you up to this task? It will not be without dangers. Life is cheap in Lamordia, and people are often worth more dead than alive."

"Why?"

Van Richten waved the question away. "It is a question of raw materials, you see."

Again, Chivarion did not see.

"So, if you are amenable, we can begin immediately. The longer your friend remains a vampire spawn, the less you will recognize her as a kind and caring soul. And what's more, I believe . . . well, I have a hypothesis that she is not the only one in danger." He lowered his spectacles and gave them all a concerned look. "Do any of you feel... different?"

Chivarion raised an eyebrow. "Different how? Because my shadow is definitely not behaving lately."

Van Richten nodded in understanding. "There's that. And paranoia. Sometimes rage. Are you overly tired? Drained? Having strange dreams you only half remember?"

They all looked about, met and then studiously avoided one another's eyes.

"I have been staying up too late in my study," Rotrog said, baring his tusks. "It is all easily explained by lack of sleep."

"Forgive me . . ." Van Richten darted forward and tugged at the collar of Rotrog's robe, showing two small red marks on his neck. The human sucked in a breath as the orc yanked away and fussed with his robes. "The marks of a vampire's fangs. He's been feeding from you."

Chivarion's fingers went to his own neck, and he found them—two tiny scabs. But when had Strahd—a vampire!—attacked him?

Of course. While he was trancing.

He did vaguely recall a hazy and mesmerizing vision involving a shadowy, handsome paramour nibbling along his neck—and other places. Perhaps it had not been a vision after all.

He hurriedly checked Murder but thankfully found no such marks. She purred and rubbed against him as if in apology for allowing an undead fiend to sup upon him.

"So we all have these marks, it seems," Alishai said tiredly. "What does this mean? Are we doomed to become—whatever he is?"

Van Richten shook his head. "Oh, no. A vampire, after all, does not wish for competition. He was likely testing each of you, searching for the unique flavor of Tatyana's soul. Now that he has her, he is likely to turn you into thralls. He has already fed from you. If he then feeds you his blood, you will be bonded to him, a mindless, hungry creature under his command."

"Don't like the sound of that," Chivarion murmured.

"But . . . he is our host!" Rotrog cried. "A great man! A count! Surely he wouldn't—"

"He would. He has. Please stop giving your trust to a monster.

You're smarter than that." Alishai sounded exhausted. "Again, can we just kill him and stop all this nonsense?"

Chivarion held up a dagger. "Yes! Killing! *Love* the sound of that!"

"As I said—kill him and he will return. And likely kill you for betraying him—kill you permanently. I have never found a way around it. Until now! I believe that separating your friend's soul from that of Tatyana could give us a chance to break the cycle. Do you wish to undertake this task?"

Alishai looked around. Her face was determined and angry, but it was that way most of the time. "It would appear we have little choice. We must do this not only for ourselves, but for Fielle. We all owe her. Are we ready? Does everyone have everything they need? Because I, for one, do not wish to be in thrall to a vampire."

"Well, we don't know—" Rotrog began.

Chivarion reached out and put a finger to the orc's lips, startling him into silence. When he spoke, his voice was low and deadly. "Shush, wizard. Listen. You will do this. You will do it because your only choices are becoming a vampire's thrall or dying, and you will do it because you owe Fielle a life debt, and you will do it because if you don't, I will beat you to a bloody gray pulp. Agreed?"

The orc bared his teeth and snapped the air where Chivarion's finger had recently been. "I will do it for my own reasons," he growled.

Chivarion shrugged. "Don't care why you do it as long as it gets done."

Rotrog grumbled to himself as he and Kah performed a sort of personal inventory, poking at pockets and bags. Chivarion needed no such performance to know that he carried everything he owned on his person. He had Murder, he had his weapons, he had his coin, and he had his belt bag, and that was it. It struck him as entirely foolish, the idea of leaving one's belongings in the unlockable room of an enormous castle, especially when strange spider-boys were crawling in and out of windows at their leisure.

"I could use some more books," Rotrog began. "And I'm not even sure I—"

"We have everything we need," Alishai told van Richten. "What else do we need to know about this Lamordia place and the person we seek?"

"Details, details. Come along."

Van Richten nodded repeatedly as if to reassure himself and led them out of the room and through the castle, down the stairs and to the area below the banquet hall. Chivarion generally felt quite at home in dungeons, but this place felt . . . wrong. The walls closed in; the shadows whispered and shivered over the grimy stone, flickering with the flames of torches that burned with no smoke. The human scuttled and paused, listened and peeked around corners, moving with the energy of a busy rabbit who knew dangers lurked everywhere but was dedicated to making progress. Finally they stood in a strange room with two life-sized statues of men on horseback and a large brazier glowing with white fire. Chivarion stepped forward to warm his hands, but the fire, oddly, offered no heat. An enormous hourglass hung overhead like a chandelier, which seemed like a bad decision for an hourglass, as such things required turning to be useful.

A selection of seven stones sat in little carved cups around the brazier, and van Richten pointed at the violet one, which winked in the fire's crisp white light.

"I will put this stone into the fire. When the flames turn purple, anyone who touches them will be transported to Tsolenka Pass near Luna Lake in the western reaches of Barovia. There, you will encounter the Mists. Call out to Larissa Snowmane, captain of the good ship *River Dancer,* and a paddleboat will appear. Tell Larissa I sent you. Ask her to take you to Lamordia, as close to Schloss Mordenheim as she dares to go. Larissa will worry about leaving me here in the castle, but you must assure her that I know my way around and will take pains to guard my safety." He focused on Alishai. "Do you understand?"

Chivarion certainly didn't; it all sounded magical and melodramatic and overly complex. But Alishai stepped forward, her chin up. "I understand."

"When you reach Schloss Mordenheim, demand to see Dr. Viktra Mordenheim. Come up with a convenient lie if you must—she's always looking for mercenaries. And then ask her for a machine that can separate two souls and a spare body to act as a vessel. She will likely demand payment, but that is a problem for another day."

"A problem for us, you mean!" Rotrog spluttered.

Van Richten shook his head. "Yes, and that is how heroes work, is it not? You can watch your friend fall permanently to evil and lose herself entirely until she is an undead monster who craves your blood while each of you becomes a mindless thrall, or you can go convince a mad doctor to create a machine that has never yet existed to do something impossible. But I assure you: Here, in this place, anything is possible." His owllike face took on a dark and serious cast. "It is also a surety that now that Strahd has selected his Tatyana, you will all become either playthings or supper. He will tire of you soon if he hasn't already, and believe me: You are not strong enough to fight him."

"Wait." Alishai held up a hand. "Why are you not going with us?"

A brief flash of pain suffused the wrinkled face. "Adventuring is a young man's game. I will be of better use to you searching for Strahd's journal here. My hope is that when you return, I will be better equipped to help you find a way to escape Barovia."

Chivarion would've argued, but he had grown bored of the old man's monologuing and was no longer paying much attention. "Then let's get on with it."

Van Richten clapped his hands, ignoring Chivarion's impatience. "Excellent! Here we go."

He picked up the purple stone and placed it in the fire, quickly pulling his hand back. The flames shot upward in a haze of purple sparks.

"On three," Alishai said.

"On three or after three?" Rotrog asked.

"On. Three." An annoyed pause. "One, two—"

Chivarion picked up Murder and held her tightly with one arm. "Three."

Chivarion put his hand into the flame like everyone else and the world swirled around him like he'd just taken a particularly hard punch to the nose, albeit without the exploding pain. After a soft pop, he heard nothing, and the world went totally dark. His eyes squinted shut, and a moist chill settled into his bones, making him shiver. When he opened his eyes, the group stood in a hexagonal stone room. There was a hearth on one side, cold and blackened, with the wind howling down it like a pack of wolves. Three windows looked out at a still, dark lake that clearly hungered to drown every soul it could consume. Chivarion was at first concerned because the only door was barred shut, but then he realized it was barred from the side he was on, and so he simply lifted the rotting wood from its place and opened the door.

An angry gust of wind buffeted him hard enough to make him stumble. Murder struggled against his chest, and he murmured sweetnesses to her as he stepped outside. They had emerged on the shore of the dark lake, its waters deadly still and the color of a dead drow's flesh. An enormous boat bobbed nearby, completely at odds with their surroundings. From the bright red paddle wheel to the gilded gryphon figurehead and three terraced decks, this jolly boat seemed to defy the dreary darkness of Barovia simply by existing there.

"Larissa Snowmane!" Alishai called, cupping her hands around her mouth so the cruel wind couldn't snatch her words away. "We are here on behalf of Rudolph van Richten!"

After a few moments, a figure appeared on the deck of the ship—a woman. She wore a dark green cloak, and her hair fell in a long white braid over one shoulder.

"And why did van Richten send you to me?" she asked.

"We're trying to save our friend," Alishai called. "He also said you would worry about leaving him alone in the castle, but he wanted us to assure you he knew his way around."

At that, the woman threw back her head and laughed; her voice was musical, and her movements were graceful, as if every step were part of a dance. "That is exactly our Rudolph. Well, then. Come aboard and tell me more."

She disappeared from the deck, and before anyone could ask how they were expected to get to a ship that was at least thirty feet offshore, they heard a splash on the other side of the paddleboat, and a dinghy zoomed around the larger ship and toward them. There were no paddles; it appeared to be powered by magic. The small craft beached itself upon the shore as eagerly as a good dog and went still.

"Seems safe enough," Alishai said.

"As safe as anything else," Chivarion muttered.

The tiefling cautiously stepped into the boat and sat in the center of the last of three benches. Rotrog went next and began poking around the boat as if hoping to find a magic spell carved into the wood. Kah sat beside the orc on the center bench, and Chivarion murmured encouragement to Murder as he climbed in and sat on the front bench. Although the tressym enjoyed larger vessels, she could sometimes be prissy about smaller ones. She hated to get her feet wet.

As soon as Chivarion was settled, with the tressym's claws digging nervously into his knee, the boat pushed itself away from shore, turned neatly, and made a beeline for the far side of the paddleboat. Larissa stood on the lowest deck, regarding them.

"You are welcome on the *River Dancer*, but I warn you: She is a magical vessel, and I do not suffer fools. Do you swear you mean us no harm?"

"We so swear. We only want to save our friend," Alishai responded. "Her name is Fielle. Strahd is trying to . . ." She paused, shook her head. "It sounds ridiculous. He's turning her into vampire spawn."

But Larissa did not laugh. She looked deadly serious. "Then we must hurry. I, too, have lost friends to monsters." She threw a rope ladder over the rail. One by one they climbed up the ladder and hoisted themselves over the side and onto the paddleboat.

"Would you rather fly?" Chivarion asked Murder, and she leaped up from his knee, spreading her wings to fly to the deck on her own. Kah watched wistfully from above, her feathers raised as the tressym landed neatly on the railing. Chivarion hissed at his new puncture wounds and climbed the ladder. As soon as he was out of the boat, it attached itself to nearby chains and was hoisted up out of the water by invisible hands. It must've been quite handy, having a ship that thought for itself.

Larissa, as it turned out, was the only person on the *River Dancer*; her ship was imbued with magic and required very little work from its captain. Once Alishai had explained the details of their quest, Larissa invited them to enjoy the ship's hospitality as she navigated their route to Lamordia.

"When we are in the Mists, do not be disturbed," she warned them. "It may be silent and still, or you might hear sounds that frighten you. Remain calm and place your trust in me and in the *River Dancer*.

We'll get you to Lamordia." She shuddered. "Not that you'll enjoy it there. I can take you as far as the Forest of Rust, but you'll have to complete your journey over land. I don't dare take my ship into the Sea of Secrets."

"Pirates?" Alishai asked.

Larissa laughed her musical laugh. "Not in Lamordia. No; there, I worry about blizzards, radiation, kraken, and worse—tax collectors."

She left them to enjoy a hearty meal. Although Strahd's table had been opulent, this food felt more . . . real. More filling. The loaves of bread were still warm, the butter fresh, the water crisp and tasting of faraway mountains. Even Rotrog exclaimed over the perfectly spiced sausages, and the chicken was so fresh Chivarion wondered if it had been alive and clucking just this morning. It was filling, is what it was, and it only served to highlight how uncomfortable everyone had been in Castle Ravenloft. For the first time in days, Chivarion was . . .

Relaxed.

Soon the calliope settled on the stern began to play a merry song, its many shiny brass whistles streaming colorful steam that was almost immediately whipped away by the cold, harsh wind. The ship moved at a quick pace, swiftly traversing the eerily still lake and funneling into a sluggish river that cut a stark line through a forest of heavy green fir trees. Chivarion was well accustomed to the cold and spent most of his time shirtless in even the fiercest weather, yet he wished he'd brought a heavier cloak.

"Mists ahead!" Larissa called from the ship's wheel.

Chivarion stood and walked to the bow. Up ahead, a wall of white spread along the river and obscured the rustling trees. The boat moved inexorably toward the thick Mists, and Chivarion closed his eyes as he slid into their clammy embrace.

INTERLUDE:

THE MISTS

Five new hearts beat like drums, echoing through a place that wasn't a place, a time that was timeless. The Mists had no borders, no edges, no signs. Only a few canny characters could find their way through the solid blanket of white, and even they did so at their peril, for what could ever be safe and known in a place that was nowhere?

The drow was as tough and thick as an old scar, his body a weapon and his mind an empty fist. As the steamship entered the Mists, he picked up the tressym and settled her firmly on his shoulder.

"Stay with me," he whispered to her. "Or we could be lost forever."

He had begun life in the Underdark and been cast out for failing to live up to the expectations of his family. Outside of his proficiency as a warrior, he was everything they despised: soft, kind, good-humored. Tossed out into the sun, he'd quickly learned that such softness would lead only to betrayal or entrapment. He grew a hard skin, stopped smiling so much, covered his body with sharp tattoos and sharper weapons. Only his heart stayed soft, just the right shape for a tressym kitten to curl up in—and a lover, every now and then, but only when he was about to leave town.

And then he landed here, among strangers. He wanted to trust them, but he had long ago forgotten how to trust. He wasn't worried about the journey ahead, did not anticipate failure. That was the beauty of his dense skull: He was not imaginative enough to conjure a world in which something could beat him.

The little kenku, on the other hand, was terrified. She had never been without her flock, never been more than a few blocks away from the abbey where she'd been fledged. Her goddess was gentle and patient, and Kah was certain that one day, her dream would come true and she would fly among the clouds.

She was creative enough to picture a thousand ways in which this adventure could go wrong, most of them due to some error of her own. But she was determined to help Fielle, for just as Chivarion's heart was wary, Kah's was as open as the sky she craved. If she died trying to help a friend, there was no greater way to please Akadi, Lady of the Winds.

But Kah did not want to die.

She just wished she was enough for whatever storm was coming.

Had she wings, she would've flown directly into any tempest to help her friend.

On Kah's other side stood Alishai. The tiefling's heart held a storm of its own as she glared into the Mists, daring this new world to defy her. She was possibly the most broken of them all, a once-bright creature snatched from a world of safety and trust and thrust into a life of punishment and torture in the name of her beloved goddess. Having finally seen her cult's messiah for what she truly was, Alishai now wore her anger like a brand. She did not blame Selûne for the cruelties of her priestess, and her oath drove her forward, urging her to save Fielle's innocent soul before evil could befoul it.

For someone so hurt, she was loyal as a dog. She wanted to help, wanted to believe. She would bring these ragtag strangers together or die trying.

And then there was Rotrog. On the outside, he was an erudite orc scholar, powerful across multiple axes. On the inside, he was a pile of quivering pudding, poisoned by his own self-doubt and guilt. The Mists swirled into his body, licking at him like fire crawling hungrily over a log. His dread was delicious, his uncertainty a feast. He held himself away from these strangers not because he actually disliked them or doubted them, but because he doubted himself. He was a coward at heart, and if he let them get too close, they would see right through his arrogance and learn the truth. Possibly while watching him run away, right when they needed him the most.

As for the tressym, she kept her thoughts to herself. She was smarter than she let on, and she did not open herself to the Mists.

This place, she knew, was designed to torture.

She would not give it that satisfaction.

21

ROTROG

Lamordia was a strange place—just as strange as Barovia, and yet entirely different. In Barovia, the sky was always smothered in low, heavy gray clouds, the air either on the verge of snowing or storming so hard that a person felt they might never be dry again. The shadows seemed to move just a moment too slowly, as if badly pantomiming the bodies they followed. Dead things came alive, and fires always seemed on the cusp of going out, leaving one in utter darkness. Or perhaps that was just Castle Ravenloft, but Rotrog's time in the castle had definitely colored his feelings for the land in general. Now that he knew what Strahd was, now that he'd accepted that the count's interest in him was a farce, he had no love left for the place. He exhaled, and it felt as if he expunged all the air of Barovia out of his lungs. He was almost surprised dust and bats didn't fly out, too. When he took his next big breath, he opened himself to Lamordia.

The forest was . . .

Well, now that he was standing in it, it was not so much a forest. It was a sea of rust.

Larissa had apologized that she could not take them farther and had given them some provisions, but now that they stood on the dusty red ground, they were on their own in a place unlike any Rotrog had ever seen before.

The trees were not exactly trees. They were metal hulks that jutted up from the earth like tusks, each towering trunk exploding with iron spikes that resembled needles when seen from the safety of the *River Dancer*. Perhaps there was dirt somewhere, but the top layer of substrate was rust. It filtered down from the trees, a gentle rain of powder that made Rotrog squint just thinking about it.

Alishai led the group along, the forest on their right and the sea on their left. Larissa had told them to follow the coastline to the east until they found the city of Ludendorf, which would take approximately a day and a half. Rotrog felt as if he walked a tightrope. On one side, the cold gray water lapped at the shore, and any number of watery beasts might venture forth at any time to claim an easy prize. On the other side, the forest of soughing pipes and razor-blade leaves gently undulated in a wind that seemed formed of ice. Each gust bit through Rotrog's cloak, nipping at him like dogs with icicle teeth. The air smelled of salt and iron and the sick, fishy odor of rotting seaweed, which mounded up on the beach in lumps that resembled drowned corpses.

His imagination was galloping away. And how could it not, with so much sensory input that he could barely take stock of his bearings? Even his hearing was useless. The sea pounded against the shore, battering itself into the hard, cold sand, while the trees swayed and scratched nervously against one another, screeching and creaking. Every now and then, a branch fell with a heavy clank, making Rotrog spin in place, imagining enemies carrying weapons tipped with yet more spikes of rust.

"The orc is jumpy," Chivarion noted.

Rotrog sniffed, showing his tusks. "And who wouldn't be jumpy, I ask you? Kraken on one side, certain impalement on the other. Can't hear, can't smell, so cold I can barely feel."

"At least it's not Barovia," Alishai said grimly.

"I rather liked Barovia!"

He knew the lie even as he said it.

Alishai turned to sneer at him over her shoulder. "Of course you would. It's as gloomy and stuffy as you are. Wait."

She went into a fighting stance and drew her glaive. Behind him, Rotrog heard the snicker of Chivarion's silver blade. Kah had her mace in hand, and Rotrog did his best to stay directly behind her, his staff clutched firmly in his fist as he repeated his best spell over and over in his mind.

There was something headed toward them—something strangely shaped. It was walking along the shore, dragging a leg awkwardly behind. It did not appear to be attacking, or even aware of them. At regular intervals, the misshapen figure stooped to pick something up and toss it back into the sea. As it came within hailing distance, the entire party around Rotrog prepared for an attack.

"Can't save them all," the figure said forlornly in Common, slow and slurring.

It was a person—

Sort of. Almost like several people stitched together. Rotrog could see the black sinews that circled his head in neat Xs, roughly attaching a crown of sickly blond hair with a pale pink bald spot to a face with brown skin and a thick black beard. One leg was longer than the other, and even the hands were different sizes and colors. Clad in a ragged fur vest and torn pants without shoes or a shirt, the figure passed by them, laboriously tossing starfish from the sand back into the water. The party turned to watch the flesh golem until he was out of sight and only then did they relax their hold on their weapons.

"Strange fellow," Chivarion said. "D'you think the little star things are grateful?"

"They're all dead," Kah said. She went to a nearby one and poked it with a toe.

Rotrog rubbed at his nose. "That explains the smell."

Alishai led them on, and very little about their surroundings changed for quite some time. The sea remained the sea, and the forest persisted in being made of metal instead of the usual greenery. No birds roosted among those bristling branches, and no deer stepped daintily among the trunks. There were no flowers, no chipmunks, no mushrooms. The sky was as thin and clear as skim milk tainted with mold.

Far, far away, on the edge of the world, a dark city of spires and smokestacks rose to pierce the clouds, belching smoke in a thousand shades of black and gray, plus colors that no smoke should be: acid green, urine yellow, and a grotesque purple that reminded Rotrog of the bruised smudges under Fielle's eyes when last he'd seen her.

"We're making good time," Alishai said. "That'll be Ludendorf, and once we're in the gates, we should have no trouble finding a ship that will take us to the doctor."

When he'd first met her, Rotrog might've reminded her that she was simply parroting what Larissa had already told them. But now he was beginning to understand her. He was a student of history, and he recognized the qualities of a leader. She was trying to keep them together, working toward a common goal. She was tired and short-tempered, but Rotrog noticed the way she slowed down when Kah started panting or paused when the tressym stopped to eat a dead shrimp. She didn't mention that every such stop would hold up their quest; she genuinely cared about their individual needs. Rotrog was beginning to respect her, for all that he found her somewhat annoying.

He did his best to keep up with the others. He was not an organism dedicated to the physical arts, and his legs and back were already aching at so much drudgery. His place in life was at a table, reading a book, occasionally standing to practice a spell. An adept named Orglor had once called him Chicken Legs, but Orglor didn't use that epithet again after he found his bed full of grease. The pen was mightier than the sword, Rotrog always told himself. And occasionally, the pen had to do more work than usual, and then the pen would eat more sausages at dinner than usual and sleep harder than usual.

He was going over spells in his head when Chivarion quietly asked, "Am I hallucinating, or is that a giant flea?"

The party turned as one to face the woods. A creature emerged, galloping toward them. It was about the size of a small pony, rust brown and hunched over, with overlapping carapace segments and long, feathery antennae.

"What is it?" Alishai called.

"I believe it is called a rust monster, but I can't remember why—"

The thing was upon them, and the time for taxonomic identification was past. Chivarion ran to meet it, leaping up to thrust down with his sword. The gleaming blade skittered uselessly off the hard shell, and he landed behind it. It spun and slammed into him. The drow went flying, as did at least three blades hung about his person. The monster, oddly, ignored Chivarion. Instead, it turned to his wavy-bladed dagger and swallowed it down in one clanking gulp.

"Hey!" Chivarion shouted, furious as he stood. "That thing—it's eating my favorite dagger! And it rusted my short sword! But not my good sword! Use your—something else!"

Just like the drow barbarian, to forget the word "magic." But Kah was ready. She'd hooked her mace onto her back to protect it from rusting, and she threw her arms out, screeching a prayer to Akadi. Flames burst from her hands, billowing around the creature and making it shriek and writhe. Before it had recovered, Alishai was already launching toward it with her glaive. Rotrog opened his mouth to call her off, but then he remembered: Her glaive was magical, so perhaps it was immune to this creature's rusting powers. As she slashed down, the now familiar thunder pealed across the beach, and the rust monster fell to its side, legs churning in the air.

It was Rotrog's turn, but he'd been so busy watching the fight and searching his mind's catalogue for the correct genus that he'd forgotten to focus. He aimed his orb at the creature and opened his mouth to speak, but the beast rolled over and over, tumbling directly toward him.

In that moment, he forgot his spell.

He forgot all his spells.

He turned to run.

But the rust monster scrambled to its feet and bounded after him.

As it happened, he was running toward the forest, and as the rusted spikes reached for him, he realized this was not a good idea. Perhaps the thing couldn't swim and the sea was a better option. He changed course, hoping to outrun it.

"Use your greasy spell!" Chivarion called. "Metal and grease go together!"

Chivarion was right. Rotrog knew that spell best. He mumbled it to himself softly a few times and then spun, raising his staff and making the proper gesture as he screamed the invocation. Grease flew out of his staff and splashed all over the rust monster, which slipped and fell, scrambling like a dog on a patch of ice.

"Yes!" he shouted. "Yes!"

The monster got its front legs under it and shakily stood.

"Now do the fire one!" Alishai called.

He hated that she was right, but he again pointed his orb and called on his faithful firebolts. The monster, coated in grease, was subsumed by flame. The heat made Rotrog step back, his cheeks sizzling. The air smelled of fried fish and scorched metal. Burning like a torch, the beast screeched and rolled around madly.

Another screech answered it from the forest, and then another. Two more rust monsters galloped out from among the trees, shaking rust and spikes loose with their passage. As if seeking retribution for their fellow, they both aimed directly for Rotrog.

"Do you wear a metal chastity belt or what?" Chivarion called. "Because they like you better than me, and I'm wearing at least ten more metal weapons."

Rotrog took a step backward, then another.

He . . . had an idea what they wanted, if they craved the taste of iron.

And they couldn't have it.

They couldn't!

"It's none of your concern what I keep under my robes!" he bellowed. "Do your job and busy yourself with fighting. It's your turn to do something useful, you hulking ignoramus!"

Chivarion was not put out by this epithet. He grinned. "Good point." He ran at the nearest beast, catapulted himself into the air, and stabbed downward, but this time he knew better what he was dealing with. His adamantine blade found the juncture between two of the rust monster's plates, and it cried out in pain as a spurt of rusty fluid sprayed out of the hole Chivarion had left in his wake. The drow landed neatly—just in time for the second creature to latch on to his arm. He shrieked and batted at its antennae with his sword, severing one of them. It fluttered to the ground like a feather.

Kah enveloped the bleeding rust monster in her sacred flame, and Alishai attacked the one missing an antenna with her thunder glaive.

With each step, the two remaining rust monsters were doing everything in their power to reach Rotrog. Two more of the creatures burst from the forest to join them as they eagerly jockeyed around him. He fiddled nervously with his red ring, watching the stronger fighters face off with the bear-sized monsters who wanted nothing more than to take the one thing he prized above all others. He knew he couldn't run faster than these beasts, couldn't make it to the city before he collapsed. He almost asked Chivarion to carry him, but he was too proud, and the drow was injured. The rust monsters were faster than they had any right to be.

"We recently passed a structure in the forest," Alishai said. "It didn't look like much, but perhaps we can barricade ourselves within, heal up, and decide on a better plan. Especially if we give them whatever Rotrog has that they want so badly."

She was beside him now. "Magic Missile," she told him. "Cast it now. You can hit both of the injured ones."

She was right again, damn her. He cast the spell, and both animals took a hard hit, screeching their pain and rage. But before Rotrog could lower his hands and revel in his success, Alishai reached out and grasped his arm in an iron grip.

"This is what they want, isn't it?" she asked him. "Give them your rusty bauble, and I'll buy you something nicer if we live to see the city."

"No! It's mine! An artifact! You don't know its value, and it cannot be replaced!" Rotrog snarled, showed his tusks, and stomped his feet, indulging in a display of rage that he would've considered gauche back home at the academy.

But Alishai had not released her grip, and he was not strong enough to throw her off. She punched his arm in some sort of nerve cluster, forcing his hand open. The moment he wasn't clutching the ring, she slipped it off his finger and threw it toward the sea. The rust monsters all galloped toward it, ignoring the party completely.

"Come on, fool," Alishai said coldly, yanking him toward the forest.

Rotrog fell to his knees and unleashed a howl at the smoky sky. His arms fell to his sides as his head fell forward, his eyes hot with tears. He had no choice but to watch longingly as the rust monsters fought over his ring. He looked at his staff but didn't dare attempt a spell or even a cantrip. Not now. Who knew what might happen?

"Come, come!" Kah urged him, tugging at his cloak.

Alishai was already running toward the forest. Chivarion was collecting his dropped blades—the ones that had not rusted. All Rotrog could do was stand on numb feet and follow the others toward a forbidden forest of rusty blades and a future where he'd lost everything.

22

FIELLE

Time passed differently when one was dead.

That first night, Strahd taught Fielle a little, but not all that she needed to know. He walked her around the castle, showing her various rooms at her disposal. There were galleries, banquet halls, dungeons. He pointed out various traps and explained that the gargoyles in the foyer were indeed magicked to prevent visitors from leaving against Strahd's wishes.

"So they would attack me?" she asked.

He looked sternly down his nose at her. "If you attempted to leave our home without my permission, yes."

Fielle no longer had need of the banquet hall but was welcome to play the organ within or the harp or lute upstairs in the guest hall, Strahd told her.

"I do not play," she said coldly, thinking about all the times back home when she'd begged her father to let her learn from the musicians always draped around the tavern.

"Your job is behind the scenes," he'd always told her. "You're an artificer, not a bard. You weren't born to be a star, not like Zerina.

Your gift is your creations. Your potions. That's what we need. Focus on that and leave the music to people with talent."

Fielle bared her teeth as she followed Strahd down the stairs.

She might be a new creature, but she felt all her old wounds and betrayals just as deeply as she ever had. Even though she could now pursue music on her own terms, they'd poisoned it for her long ago.

"Why did they treat you so poorly?" Tatyana asked.

"Zerina was the golden child, the firstborn, and they told me I was born to serve her. I didn't have her voice, her grace, her ability to bewitch with her music. I wanted so badly to dance and sing—not because I thought I could ever best her, but because it brought me joy. But my father hated my voice. He said I was always off-key. He beat me when he caught me singing in the kitchens."

Her hands made fists courtesy of Tatyana's rage. "You did not deserve that. You deserved so much more."

Fielle considered this as she paced beside Strahd, who had no idea of her internal conversation. Although he was always watching her, still he did not truly understand her, and she worked to continue this deception.

"I tried to punish them," she silently told Tatyana. "The day before I arrived here, Zerina was displeased with a new effect I'd rigged on the theater set to lift her in the air. She cast a spell on me, silencing me. I couldn't speak, couldn't defend myself. My father watched with approval, said he enjoyed the silence. That night, when I made my sister's special tea, the one that kept her voice smooth and strong, I mixed in something else. A tasteless magical elixir that would shred her vocal cords and destroy her lungs permanently. I left her tea steaming in its usual place by her bed and went to my own tiny attic to sleep. And I woke up here."

After a moment's pause, Tatyana said, "That was cruel."

"I felt shame at first, but now . . . now I wonder if perhaps she deserved worse."

After their tour, Strahd showed her the elegantly carved coffin built just for her and placed in her room; he ran his palm across the cushioned velvet pillow and showed her how to work the lock installed on the inside.

"What is that?" she asked, pointing to a small velvet bag slumped in a corner.

"A bit of soil from your grave. You must always keep it with you so that you will slumber peacefully. A vampire cannot sleep without a bit of grave soil, but you needn't climb back into the earth again."

"I am a vampire now?" She looked down at her hands; they were paler than they'd once been, her fingernails harder and pointed.

"Not yet, but soon," he promised her. "For now, let us get to know each other."

Although she'd risen from the grave earlier than expected, there was not much time left to explore the castle before dawn. Some spawn, he told her, took days to rise, but for her, only a few hours had passed. He spoke of this with surprise, and Fielle was pleased with herself. She did not like Strahd, but she liked to see that he was impressed with her. She was, she realized, impressed with herself. This was a new feeling, and one she wished to explore more fully.

As they walked together, he asked her questions about herself: He wanted to know about where she'd been born, her education, her family, her likes and dislikes, and any little trinkets she might enjoy.

"Blood," she wanted to tell him. "Just give me blood."

But she told him instead that she liked garnets and clockworks and horses, and he nodded and continued to probe her as if feeding on her memories.

"Stop giving pieces of yourself to him," Tatyana snapped in her head.

"I gave him nothing. Everything I told him was a lie," she calmly replied. "It's not difficult."

"Oh." Tatyana seemed surprised. "I did not know. That is clever."

Just before dawn, when she would be compelled to sleep, Strahd had a young woman brought into Fielle's room, a village girl scrubbed clean and still smelling of lavender soap. She was trembling as she sat on the edge of the massive bed, her dark eyes huge in her drawn, sallow face. Even the wealthiest and most well-kept Barovians, Fielle understood, were not bursting with good health. The poor girl, nearly a child, was underweight and pale, but that did not make her blood any less compelling, any less musical where it swirled through her veins like the round tones of a viola. Fielle stood primly, her hands clasped. Strahd was watching her carefully, studying her.

"Are you not hungry, my dear?" he asked.

"He's expecting us to pounce," Tatyana said. "It might be best to let him think we have less control. He is already suspicious of how early we rose from the grave."

"True," Fielle agreed. "Let him see our hunger, then."

"I didn't know if I needed permission," she said, looking down shyly. "Back home, I was punished if I ate before dinner had been served."

Strahd smiled like a doting father and gestured grandly toward the girl.

"Dinner is served."

Fielle crossed the rug in two steps. The girl startled, her eyes wide, and Fielle took her hand. "Do not worry," she said sweetly. "This is just a dream." Clutching the bird bones of the girl's hand with both her own, Fielle clamped her teeth down on her wrist, where the bluish veins swam toward the surface. Blood filled her mouth, sweeter than that of the man she'd taken outside, heady with innocence and hope. The girl tried to yank her hand away, and Fielle tightened her grip hard enough to hear the crack of bone on bone.

"It tastes better if they aren't in pain," Strahd said, a teacher lecturing a student. "That's one reason the neck is preferable. With wrists, they so often fight, and they are so very fragile. Not like you. Not now."

Fielle glanced back at him, considering, and released the girl's wrist. Blood spurted across the coverlet as the girl surged upward, but Fielle stopped her with a hand to the chest, pressing her down into the pillows. As she had with the man outside, she spread her fingers over the girl's turned cheek, holding her head down to expose her throat. Her fangs gamely sunk in, and she drank in steady gulps, careful not to pop the girl's eyeball and trying to ignore Strahd's eyes fluttering over her like dusty moths hungrily battering a lantern.

"He's right, the fiend," Tatyana complained. "I can taste the difference!"

"We're learning," Fielle reminded her. "And still, it is not bad. Just not as good."

Before the girl was properly dead, Fielle lifted her chin and turned to Strahd, daintily wiping the blood from her mouth. "Is it better to drain them dry?" she said. "How do I keep her from becoming whatever I am?"

If there was one thing Fielle didn't want, it was dozens of vampire children in the castle, following her or wanting things from her. Now that she had left the Dancing Dragon, she was enjoying a life without chores and backbreaking work. She would not willingly create unwanted burdens from strangers, binding herself to them and their expectations.

"Drink as much as you like. They can be kept like pets, fed and allowed to rest before you drink from them again. If they die, it is no great loss. There are many such villagers, and all dance at my whim. They only arise as spawn if drunk dry by a true vampire and then buried. Once you are a full vampire, you can kill them and have them burned so they won't return. Or bury them and allow them to rise as spawn. They do make lovely servants, with no choice but to do one's bidding."

She looked at the dying girl as she processed that last bit.

So that was her life now: She was a vampire spawn.

A servant to her maker, Strahd.

No wonder she had felt compelled to do everything that he had asked. And yet, there was rebellion in her, a spark that turned from him. Could he really force her to do *anything*?

She wanted to know, she needed to know, but she did not need to know right now.

She would have to discuss this with Tatyana later; unless she "spoke" to Tatyana in her head on purpose, her thoughts thankfully remained her own.

The girl on the bed stared up at her with pleading, glassy eyes, her dried lips open, breathing in small pants.

"So she will live? You will make sure she lives?"

"I will have Rahadin care for her. But it will be morning soon, and you should sleep now," Strahd told her. "The sun will burn you, in your new form. Although there is generally cloud cover in Barovia, you still must guard yourself. You will require a full day's rest to maintain your powers. You cannot cross running water or enter where you are not invited." He smiled, his dark eyes dancing. "But you are welcome in Castle Ravenloft. It is your home, now and always."

He kissed the back of her hand with his cold lips, bowed formally, and departed. Seconds later, Rahadin strode in, gave his own, much colder bow, and removed the gasping girl on the bed. Fielle did not like the way the blood had soaked into the coverlet and pillows; she would not make the mistake of feeding so messily in her quarters again.

"We should sleep now," she told Tatyana.

"I do not wish to do what Strahd tells us to do," Tatyana retorted.

Fielle gave an enormous, jaw-cracking yawn, which seemed a strange action when she did not need to breathe. An old habit, perhaps. "I am tired. Climbing out of my own grave was exhausting." She looked at her long nails—nearly talons now and crusted with black dirt. "Although perhaps bathing would be a better choice." She walked out into the hall. "Rahadin!"

The elf soon appeared. "Milady?"

"I wish to bathe."

He looked her up and down, the corner of his lip lifting. Most likely, he found her present state as disgusting as she did.

"The master has wished you good night. The sun will rise soon. We will have a bath prepared for you tomorrow night when you wake. If that is all?"

"Yes, thank you." She bobbed a curtsey, although it almost felt as if Tatyana fought against the movement.

"He expects us to be a pliant servant, and we don't want him to suspect anything else," she reminded Tatyana.

"Yes, yes. So you say."

"He does not know you are with me. We need to keep it that way."

Fielle did not know why she sensed this, but she believed it with all her—

Well, her heart no longer served a function, did it?

She believed it, and that was enough.

With Tatyana mollified, she considered the coffin, grateful that the one she'd been buried in was not so thick, so carved, so polished. She had pried her way out of a simple pine box, judging by the scent and the thickness of the wood; Strahd had chosen it, she thought, to make it easier for her to rise. This coffin was more like a luxurious jail cell, the wood several inches thick and offering far more room in every direction. All the interior surfaces were covered in rich pink velvet, and a pillow had been thoughtfully provided. Looking down at the dirt crumbs clinging to her dress, she stripped it off, along with the fur-lined cloak, and removed her stays and boots. Bending at the waist, she ran her fingers through her short hair, dislodging as much earth as she could.

Clad only in her chemise, she climbed into the heavy box and lay down, testing its comfort. Would this be like sleeping, she wondered, where she could expect to awaken every so often at a noise or dream? Would she even dream at all? If her body was dead, or undead, or at the very least not alive, was her brain still . . . doing whatever living brains did?

There were so many questions, and the only way to get answers was to ask Strahd and hope he might indulge her when it would likely benefit him to keep his new spawn utterly in the dark.

Feeling the tug of something like sleep, her body growing cumbersome, she pulled down the top of the coffin, which was heavy and yet she had no trouble maneuvering it. She was faster and stronger now, it seemed. She found the lock and latched it as Strahd had taught her, which gave her some comfort. At least while she lay here, insensate or dead, no one could harm her body.

Well, unless they burned the coffin, or threw it in the ocean. Perhaps she would be safer in the ground, or hidden in a crypt, or—

No. Strahd loved her and foolishly hoped she might return that love. He would not allow harm to come to her.

Swaddled and swallowed in complete darkness, she crossed her arms over her chest.

"Good night, Tatyana," she thought.

"Good night, Fielle," Tatyana responded. "It is . . . nice, not being alone."

And then the world fell away into utter nothingness, and in many ways, it was a kindness. When she slept, she did not hunger. She did not rebel. She did not rage. When she slept, she felt the true peacefulness of death.

23

KAH

The silly orc—he just kept standing there, staring at the rust monsters like he was on the verge of politely asking them to return his ring. Kah knew what it was to lose something valuable, but she also knew that there wasn't a ring in all of Faerûn that was worth dying for. After another tug on his sleeve, Rotrog seemed to collapse inward, letting her pull him toward the forest. There was no fight left in him, no fire. He seemed . . . desolate.

Kah knew something of that, too.

She was behind him now, pushing him forward, but he was like a sulky child having a tantrum. Chivarion, as always, was behind them both.

"If you don't run," the drow said menacingly, "I'll either poke you with a knife or pick you up, whichever one displeases you more."

The threat was sufficient, and the orc began to jog. He was breathing heavily, but at least he was moving. The forest wasn't terribly far away, but at any moment, the rust monsters might end their dispute over Rotrog's ring and turn to give chase. One rust monster wasn't so bad, but there were too many to fight just now. Although Kah did not like the look of the spiky metal trees, she was glad to have some cover—and to see that Alishai had been right about the hidden structure.

A destroyed castle, perhaps?

But not like Castle Ravenloft, no. Not big and intricate chockablock with creepy shadows and trapdoors and terrifying dolls. Kah would've chosen the dead forest full of rusty nails and terrifying monsters over the thought of sleeping in Ravenloft again knowing the doll was hunting her with its shiny silver pin—or that Strahd himself might sneak up in the night to suck her blood. In this castle, there was no place to hide. Any turrets or spires that had once existed had long ago fallen to ruin. There were sturdy stone walls veined with moss and lichen and piles of blocks suggesting exactly where various parts of the castle had fallen off like necrotic tissue. The only windows were arrow slits, and there was an arched hole where a metal door had once stood, proudly—or paranoically—facing the sea. The rust monsters had likely stripped this architectural carcass long ago, but its bones of tumbled rock offered shelter for the swiftly falling night.

Alishai held up a hand, bidding them wait—

But Kah held up her hand, too. "Traps," she said simply, and Alishai nodded once.

Kah did not want to enter the castle alone, but she had to make sure it was safe. She stepped under the arch and into a space that felt like a frozen grave. Tall stone walls rose on every side, slightly off-kilter as if sagging with exhaustion. One corner was blackened, the stones cracked and jagged, suggesting a lightning strike. She whispered her cantrip but did not sense any threat; she doubted this place had ever known the touch of magic. There were no snares, no trip wires. It was exactly what it looked like.

"Safe," she said.

The others joined her, and they all looked around. Most of the inner walls, built thinner than those protecting the castle from without, had fallen. Piles of tumbled boards and chunks of wood suggested that every ounce of metal had been devoured long ago. Kah could almost imagine the rust monsters tearing the place apart, sucking out nails like birds pulling worms from trees in fairer lands.

A spiral staircase wound upward into nothingness, each swayback step furred in moss.

Alishai began to collect the fallen wood into a pile in the center of the main room. For a long moment, Chivarion just stood there, rearranging the knives on his belt and muttering about the loss of a dagger as his tressym explored the castle's furtive corners.

"Chivarion, that large, round table might make a good door, don't you think?" Alishai said.

Chivarion looked up, annoyed. "Not really into interior design, but if you say so."

She chucked an armful of wood onto her pile. "If you roll the large, round table in front of the open door, it might keep the rust monsters from devouring us whole while we sleep."

The drow sighed. "I'm still angry about my dagger."

"You should be angrier about what that thing did to your arm."

He looked at the bite covering most of his left arm from his elbow to his shoulder. "Someone can fix that, but my daggers are gone forever. Several eaten, one rusted! And daggers don't grow on trees." His eyes shot upward. "Even here. Those are just spikes. Their balance is probably all off for stabbing."

She stared at him a moment longer, and he growled in annoyance and went to heft the enormous table, a solid cross-section of a very large tree, the sort that no longer existed here. Or perhaps the trees had been turned into metal by some strange act of magic or science, or by an angry god extracting vengeance. Kah did not like this place; it felt unnatural. A place where no birds flew was not a place a kenku could ever feel at home.

Chivarion wedged the table into place across the empty doorframe then mounded several large stones behind it so that it could not simply be pushed over or aside. There was a much smaller doorway in the back corner, and he piled stones to block it, then walked the perimeter of the space to make sure there were no holes big enough to admit a rust monster hungry for daggers. Kah felt silly just standing there, but she had performed her duty; everyone had their role, and hers was complete. Well, almost. She went to Chivarion, bade him bend down, and healed his shoulder.

The drow summoned a smile with some difficulty and moved his arm around. "Another excellent job. If only you could fix daggers, too."

"I can mend?"

He felt around his waist. "I didn't bring the rusted one. Maybe—"

"Do not go back outside," Alishai warned him. "If it's there in the morning, fine. But no one is dying for a bauble tonight." She turned to Rotrog. "How about a little firebolt to get things toasty?"

But Rotrog, usually so pleased to be able to perform a spell under ideal circumstances and when not under fire, did not respond. The orc stared vacantly into space, his eyes red and his shoulders drooping. He was the most un-orcish orc Kah had ever seen, but he was currently also being a very un-Rotrogish Rotrog.

"Rotrog! Fire! Now!" Chivarion pantomimed pointing a staff at the wood and creating a firebolt.

But even that goading did not hit home.

"Cold," Kah said, tugging at Rotrog's sleeve. "Please, fire."

At that, he shook his head and looked at her as if he'd never seen her before. "I'm afraid I can't make a fire, little Kah," he said sadly, as if she were a child he hated to disappoint and he was a sad old grandfather. "All my powers . . . were in that ring."

Alishai looked to Kah, who could only shrug. "Not how wizards work, I thought?"

"If anyone has a traditional way to start the fire, I would be grateful for the warmth." Rotrog sighed heavily and sat on a block of stone near the pile of wood. "And then I suppose I have no choice but to tell you my tale of woe."

Chivarion gamely produced a flint and steel and set about gathering what tinder he could find, mostly bits of dead moss. After a few moments, he was blowing on a spark; it would take a while to build to a proper fire, unlike a simple spell even the most basic wizard could handle. The drow began pulling foodstuffs from his bag, preparing a light supper. Throughout all these preparations, Rotrog stared into the tiny kernel of flame as if looking for an answer.

"As I told you," he began, "I was an adept in the magical academy of High Mage Argitau in the city of Silverymoon. From my earliest days, I longed to be accepted there and become a great wizard. When

I came of age, I passed my exams and interview with flying colors and studied diligently. I soon learned that competition among the adepts is fierce, and the friendships and alliances I at first welcomed became betrayals and indignities. Closing myself off and recommitting to my studies, I eventually was called to act as personal adept to the High Mage himself. My dream had come true."

He chuckled sadly.

"Or, more accurately, my nightmare. The High Mage treated me as chattel. He was cruel, demanding, exacting, and he destroyed my sleep and my spirit. He did not teach me the promised magic; he feared the possibility of anyone becoming as powerful as he. Only when he was busy elsewhere could I steal a glance at his grimoire. I had mere moments to study the simplest of cantrips and spells, and I could only practice them in rare moments alone. They . . . rarely worked."

The fire was crackling merrily enough now, and Chivarion was working on one of his stews. There was nothing additional to add from their packs, as the forest was utterly lacking in the usual ground mammals that provided stringy meat and the greens and mushrooms that offered texture. There was still some dried fish from the *River Dancer*, and some old potatoes and rubbery carrots, but it would be a thin meal that night. Overhead, the sky had turned the sour purple of the bad livers witches used to tell fortunes in the dingiest back alleys of Waterdeep. Alishai had her glaive at her feet and was staring at Rotrog as if willing him to speak.

"And then one day I found a drawing in an ancient tome in the library, a compendium of magical artifacts. I recognized it immediately as the ring the High Mage wore. He slept with it on his finger, his hand in a tight fist, and he never, ever removed it. I began to wonder if perhaps his power came from the ring, but I knew that if I asked, he would not tell the truth. I had to know for myself. And so . . . I took action."

The orc looked up at the sky, but if Lamordia had stars, they were hidden behind layers of smoke and smog. Kah had never realized before how comforting the stars were, how pleasant it was to sleep in her hammock in Waterdeep and watch the little lights blink out the window. Alishai, too, was looking up and frowning; she likely missed the moon. Kah wondered if the tiefling felt as disconnected from Selûne as Kah felt from her lady Akadi, but she was too shy to ask.

Rotrog had gone silent as he stared into the fire. Now his eyes jerked up nervously, met Kah's, and returned to the flames. His head hung limply, his staff across his knees.

"One of my duties was to pack the High Mage's evening pipe, a concoction of herbs to help him sleep and quiet the complaints of his joints. It was messy, and he did not like the way it made his fingers smell. He watched me make this concoction, for he never trusted me. He never trusted anyone. But what he didn't know is that on that night in particular, I had rubbed his pipe stem with something else, earlier in the day, something that would paralyze him in his sleep. He stood over me, criticizing me as I measured out the greenery and flowers. I remember I was sweating and hoped he wouldn't notice. Perhaps blinded by his arrogance, he never thought me smart enough to fool him. He puffed away at his pipe, fell asleep, and was rendered utterly comatose. As he lay before the fire, I slipped the ring from his finger and onto my own and felt its power flow through my veins."

He held out a hand, then made a fist and dropped it. "The first spell I attempted had never worked before—"

A long, painful pause.

"Grease. It went everywhere. The fire spread swiftly, for the academy was crafted entirely of wood. I knew the spell for controlling flames, but I was so frightened I couldn't remember it. On a different day, the High Mage would've awakened and easily smothered the conflagration, but by my own hand I had rendered him unconscious. I shook him, shouted at him, all to no avail. The fire spread, and I began to cough. I fell to my knees to crawl toward the rest of the dormitory to warn them, but at some point, I passed out . . ."

He looked up, his eyes wet.

"And I woke up in Barovia, in the Mists, with you. Hence my confusion in the moment." He cracked his knuckles and wrung his hands. "And now you see why I couldn't start the fire. That ring was the source of my magic. Without it, I am again just a bumbling fool. And I am almost certain that back home, the High Mage is dead, possibly the entire academy. At the very least, the building must've been burned to cinders. We were in a dry season, and it is likely the fire spread farther throughout the city."

Rotrog let his head fall forward and his staff tumble to the ground.

In the utter silence that followed, Chivarion cheerily called, "Stew's ready!" When no one immediately responded, he added, "If you're not hungry, I'm happy to eat it all."

"No, we're hungry," Alishai said through gritted teeth, "but I believe we're also concerned about Rotrog's broken spirit. And the practicalities of moving forward without a wizard. It drastically reduces our ability to function as a team."

"Leave me behind, then," Rotrog wailed. "It is what I deserve. I am a creature of ill omen. I bring tragedy to all who meet me."

"So that's a no on stew?"

Alishai flapped a hand at the drow. "Rotrog needs his stew. We all do. Dish it up, if you will, while we talk this through."

"There is nothing to discuss." Rotrog sniffled around his tusks. "What is done is done."

"Folderol," Kah said, perhaps more forcefully than she meant to.

Everyone stared at her.

She ducked her head, wanted to sink back into her cloak so that they might see only the tip of her beak.

But no. She'd said what she meant, and she meant what she'd said.

"Was that a sneeze?" Chivarion asked.

"It means nonsense," Rotrog explained.

"We all know sneezes are nonsense, I'm just trying to keep up."

Kah shook her head, feathers fluffing in annoyance. "You don't need the ring."

"You don't understand—" Rotrog began.

"No, *you* don't. That ring was just metal here. Maybe magic at home, maybe a crutch. But here? No." She felt the gazes around her sharpen. "I didn't feel it. It was just metal. Not a magical artifact at all."

"Then how do you explain the fact that I couldn't make a single spell work before I stole the ring, and after, my magic was so powerful that I probably killed everyone in the academy?"

She drew back her cloak so that he could see the stern will in her eye. "Confidence."

"That's ridic—" he blustered.

"You thought the power came from the ring, so for you, it did. I've watched you fight. Lots of times. You don't believe in yourself. Get flustered. But when someone commands you to do a spell, it works. Trust yourself like we trust you." She shrugged. "That's all."

"She's got a point," Alishai said with the tiniest hint of a smirk. "You're almost like a crossbow that just needs someone else to pull the trigger. The more you think about a spell, the less able you are to cast it. But when someone shouts at you, you simply do the spell. You just need to be yelled at."

"I beg your pardon—" he began again.

"They're right," Chivarion said. He held out a small bowl. "Stew?"

"I am not hungry," Rotrog said with great dignity. "I am grieving."

"Then you're an idiot." Alishai snagged the bowl. "You need to keep up your energy, and you need to open your bloody ears and listen to us. Now, cast Grease."

"No."

The tiefling put down her bowl and stood menacingly. "Cast Grease. Now."

"No!"

Alishai looked to Chivarion. "Attack him."

Chivarion's eyebrows rose, his attention captured. "You're giving me permission to beat the orc silly? Finally!"

The drow stood, grinning, and took a menacing step toward Rotrog.

"No. Please—you don't understand," Rotrog muttered, his hands raising defensively in front of his face.

"I'm going to enjoy this," Chivarion muttered.

"If there is no power, there is no—"

Chivarion's fist reared back, his eyebrows up.

Alishai's grin was a fierce and feral thing. "You'd better cast Grease before he hits you."

With an orc's war cry, Rotrog raised his hands and gallons of grease splashed over the tiefling and drow. Alishai's hair was slicked down to her head, and she wiped grease out of her eyes and thumbed it out of her ears.

"Disgusting," Chivarion grumbled, slipping and sliding as he chased his grease-coated tressym and the slippery beast slopped out of his hands.

Kah was glad that she had chosen to sit next to Rotrog, and she was overjoyed that she'd been right. She didn't often speak her mind, but she had been so certain. And now Rotrog was changed utterly, grinning and wiggling his fingers.

"I can't believe it," he crowed.

"You should believe more," Kah told him.

After a bowl of stew and a cleaning spell, they all fell asleep around the smoldering fire, surrounded by trees that whispered in the voice of needles and rust monsters restlessly prowling and scratching at the makeshift door.

24

ALISHAI

Waking up on the frozen ground of Lamordia was no treat, but at least the grease had been banished and they would soon be in a proper city with proper food. Chivarion was fine enough as a camp cook, but they had not expected to find the forest so inhospitable, and dinner had been scant. Alishai would've suggested a quick fishing trip if not for the rust monsters. She could already hear them on the other side of the makeshift barricade, prodding it with their armored claws and making unbearable clicking sounds.

When she stared up at the sky, she finally saw a sliver of moon hanging in the limpid dawn—a strange moon that she did not recognize. It was like looking in the mirror and seeing the face of a stranger. No wonder she felt so far from Selûne. This was just some empty curl of stone, meaningless and silent. She shivered, the enormity of her predicament settling in.

This was not her world. It never had been.

As Kah worked at waking Rotrog, Alishai climbed up the castle wall until she stood on the derelict ramparts above the door, looking down to see what waited outside. Five rust monsters rumbled around like armored ponies, waving their antennae together and clicking their awful mouthparts like old gossips. Five wasn't too terrible, and provided the rest of her crew was nimble, they could assault the beasts from up here while out of reach. She considered the barricade and the crumbling walls, then thought about what a pain it would be if Rotrog fell and broke his neck. After last night's confession, she understood him better—a lot better. And she knew how to use him as a weapon simply by telling him which spells to use and when. Now she just needed to memorize his full roster and prepare to shout at him more than usual. She could do that.

"Only five," Chivarion said, having joined her at the top of the wall, his tressym landing lightly beside him. "Not so bad. A little grease, a bit of sacred flame, and perhaps we'll be cracking open crab claws for breakfast."

Alishai watched the creatures mill about; they did not look appetizing. "They probably taste of iron."

The drow shrugged. "Good for the blood." He looked down. "Kah, can you climb?"

The kenku, who had finally succeeded in getting Rotrog's eyes open, nodded and scurried up the stone wall to join them. The rust monsters couldn't look up, but they were acting agitated, which meant they could probably sense that their prey—or at least the nearest vehicle for fresh iron—was on the move.

"How are we going to get Rotrog up here?" Alishai asked quietly.

"Rotrog can hear you," the orc grumbled.

"And can Rotrog climb?"

The wizard stood and fussed at his robes. "I am always eager to acquire new skills."

Unfortunately, he was not a dexterous sort, which Alishai had already assumed based on his general physical ineptitude. He often bumped a hip against a table or stubbed a toe, and when they'd run yesterday, he'd quickly been out of breath and panting.

"You're looking for footholds," Chivarion coached from above. "Just a little ledge for your foot, or a stone that sticks out just enough to grab."

"I am staring at a flat wall." Rotrog glared up at them. He scrabbled at the wall like a cat on ice before giving up. "It is hopeless."

"Yeah, I suppose you are."

"You could probably stack up rocks to get him here," Alishai said.

Chivarion glanced around the jumbled castle interior. "I suppose that might get the blood pumping." He climbed back down and cajoled stones into a makeshift ramp. The wall was perhaps ten feet tall, so for someone of his strength and restless nature, it didn't take long. There were stones aplenty, after all, and each of them had been cut neatly. Soon Rotrog stood with them on the ramparts, hunkered down and clinging to the stone wall like he was lost at sea.

"Grease and fire?" he suggested.

Alishai nodded. "And you definitely know how to make grease."

Rotrog lifted his staff with great gravitas, but Alishai could see his arms shaking. He still didn't believe in himself. She almost wanted to push him over the wall and into a fight so that he might be forced into service. He cleared his throat, and—

All five rust monsters raised their antennae in alarm and galloped around the castle and deeper into the forest. Their shells crashing through the metal trees sounded like two portcullises rutting.

"Well, that was neatly done!" Rotrog said, chin up. "They must've seen me and remembered what happened yesterday."

But Alishai knew better. When they'd gone on alert, the rust monsters had all turned in the same direction, and they had run away in the opposite direction. This suggested that the beasts feared something more than a few adventurers and their magic. Alishai drew her crossbow and squinted toward whatever had caused the rust monsters to flee. A harsh and guttural sound, half caw and half growl, echoed through the forest.

"That doesn't sound good," she muttered.

Kah cocked her head, her pupils dilating as she listened. "Never heard that sound before. Not ever, not once."

"It almost sounds like an owlbear." Chivarion stuck a finger in his ear. "But more like a—"

"Raven," Kah finished for him, her voice husky with . . . pain? Anger? Something. The little kenku was almost always congenial, and it was strange to see her hunch over and ruffle her feathers in misery.

As if called from the forest by Kah's foul mood, two enormous shapes appeared, glossy purple-black and galloping at full speed.

"Ravenbears?"

Alishai felt silly even saying the word, except that . . . well, these bear-shaped beasts had the heads of ravens and a distinctive call that started with a caw and ended with a prolonged growl. The pair stopped short at the makeshift door, and the bigger one stood on its hind legs, placing a heavy paw tipped with black talons against the old wood table, testing its resistance. The wood wobbled, and the beast added its other paw, pushing with full force.

"Rotrog, grease. Kah, sacred flame," Alishai said quietly.

"Do you really think—" the wizard began.

"Rotrog, grease. Now!" she shouted.

Startled, he muttered his spell and seemed yet more startled when it worked. Grease splattered over the nearest bear, which stumbled back, pawing the slick liquid off its bright yellow eyes.

"Kah, sacred flame!"

The cleric said her prayer and sent a whoosh of fire at the ravenbear—

And missed.

The fire vented harmlessly between the beasts, making the first one drop to all fours and the second one bat at its beak with a feathered arm.

"Sorry," Kah said. "I—it's hard. They look like me."

And they did, a little, aside from the lack of intelligence. Of course, that didn't mean Alishai consented to lose the fight and become a pile of bones in a ravenbear den. She had one spell she hadn't used that often, but, well, no time like the present. Hefting her glaive, she leaped to the ground and swung, calling on the power of Selûne. Her glaive struck the grease-covered ravenbear and erupted in white-hot flame. The bear went up like a torch, shaking its head and then falling to the ground, rolling back and forth. Its fellow bellowed rage and focused on Alishai.

A flash of gray fell from the sky, and Chivarion struck the attacking bear with his silver sword, his bellow equally loud and furious. Murder swooped down from the ledge on outstretched wings and dealt a vicious slash at the ravenbear's face, right across one eye. The beast opened its remaining angry eye, stood on its hind legs, and brought a heavy paw across Alishai's upper arm, catching under her armor and tearing it away. Red-hot pain was swiftly followed by numbness, and she stumbled back. Now the castle wall was behind her and one of her arms was useless, which meant she couldn't climb back up. Even worse, the ravenbear that had been on fire had managed to roll back and forth until it was merely smoking. Its fellow nuzzled it and moaned, and it struggled to its feet.

"Rotrog, Magic Missile!" Alishai cried.

The wizard obediently performed the spell, and three glowing darts shot from his staff, pelting the injured bear one after the other. The beast fell over, groaning, its huge black paws churning the air.

"Yes!" Rotrog shouted.

But in his moment of triumph, he must've tripped or somehow lost his balance—not unusual in the least—because the next thing he shouted was a very rude word as he tumbled off the wall and landed directly on the wounded bear. Flailing, the orc rolled away from the beast—and kept rolling, then crawling. He fetched up around the corner of the castle, and then Alishai didn't know if he was hiding or running away. Either option was equally possible.

"Kah! Do something!" she shouted.

The kenku raised her arms, opened her beak—

Then snapped it shut without speaking.

Kah jumped down off the wall, fluttering her arms like her feathers might actually help slow her descent. She landed on the ground, cocked her head at the ravenbears—

And ran around the same corner of the castle as Rotrog.

"Well, that's two cowards," Alishai grumbled to herself, disappointed as she rubbed the deep scratches on her arm. She looked to Chivarion. "Think we can finish this together, just the two of us?"

His brow wrinkled down angrily. "Three of us. Do not discount Murder."

"Oh, I never discount murder."

Alishai raised her glaive, preparing to call down thunder and end the dying beast, but then she heard a sound that made her blood run cold: the caw-growl of a third ravenbear in the distance.

"Oh, hells. Not a fresh one?" she grumbled.

"I also prefer the not-fresh ones. The barbecued one is definitely my favorite," Chivarion responded. He, too, raised his weapon.

But the ravenbears were no longer paying any attention to the fight. Their heads were lifted, their beaks open, their thick tongues tasting the air. The one on the ground struggled to stand, and the mostly unharmed one nuzzled it affectionately as if in apology.

The caw-growl sounded again, followed by a second sound—a higher pitched, less guttural scream.

Hearing it, the bear on the ground wailed in distress, and the fit bear nuzzled it one last time before charging away, galloping full speed toward the noise and bellowing its own furious caw-growl. The moment it was out of sight, Chivarion ended the dying beast with one well-aimed slash, putting it out of its misery.

"Rotrog, Kah!" Alishai called. "Hurry, before it returns!"

Rotrog scrambled around the corner of the castle, dusting rust powder off his robes. "Kah ran into the forest, directly toward the new ravenbear. The poor creature. She was strange, but she was—"

"Right here. Now, run!" Kah chirped as she appeared from the forest.

In situations like this one, it was always better to follow the person who was running and ask questions later, so Alishai took off after Kah. Rotrog fell in behind her, muttering about his heart rate, while Chivarion as always took up the rear, his tressym briefly loping by his side before hissing at a bit of metal and launching into the air. Kah led them back to the beach and set the course toward Ludendorf, which they would surely reach in a few hours if there were no further fights to the death.

When they were a sufficient distance from the abandoned castle, Alishai said, "I believe we can resume walking now. I would imagine the ravenbear is too busy fighting his challenger to worry about us."

"No challenger," Kah said, slowing to a walk. "Just me."

Alishai's head whipped around. "Just you?"

Suddenly shy, Kah ducked her head. "I heard the adults. I've heard ravens. I made the sound of an adult ravenbear, then the sound of a scared cub. Wanted to draw them off." Her beak clicked sadly. "Too bad, one had to die. The father."

"Okay, wait." Chivarion tried to catch up. "So you attacked a baby?"

"Fascinating," Rotrog murmured. "And rather clever. A baby might not call them off, and the challenge of an adult might not be sufficient, but the sound of an adult attacking a baby . . ." He nodded. "Yes, yes, quite cunning."

"I thought you'd run away, you know," Chivarion said.

A sigh. "I did, at first. Couldn't hurt them. Almost like—"

"A cousin?" Alishai offered.

Kah shrugged. "Ravens, kenku, ravenbears. All alike, you know? A common ancestor, maybe. We don't know why kenku are different. Our history is lost, lost. All we know is . . . once we had wings like ravens. Long ago, we lost them. Don't know why. But it's all I ever wanted. To fly again. To be in the sky. I can almost . . ." She raised her arms, flapping them like they were lined in long feathers, like if she wished hard enough she might soar into the clouds. And then her arms fell.

"Like Rotrog, I have a confession."

"Oh?" the orc asked, suddenly interested.

For a while, Kah simply trudged forward, her taloned feet leaving runes etched in the wet gray sand as the cold, endless sea spit dingy scum onto the shore.

"We're listening," Alishai urged her.

"Rotrog told us—he did a bad thing. That brought him here."

"I didn't—" the orc began.

"Shut your piehole," Chivarion snapped. "She's telling a story!"

"Me, too," Kah admitted. She pulled her hood up to hide her head so that only her beak stuck out. "Wings. I just want wings. So badly. Heard there was a hag in Waterdeep who owned a bookshop and could help people, for a fee. Went to see. She asked me to do one thing for her. Didn't want to do it, but . . . wings. Real wings. She promised them."

"What did she want?" Alishai asked, because every time Kah stopped talking, it seemed as if she might never speak again.

"A baby," Kah said softly. "Just a baby. So I went to the orphanage. Peeked inside. Lots of babies, all wrapped in white. Stunk of piss and worse. Bad place for babies. Told myself maybe the hag would give it to someone else, someone who dearly wanted a baby but couldn't have one." A sad shrug. "Lied to myself, I did. Crept in at night and listened for a baby with a rattling chest, sick baby. Might die anyway."

"You could've healed it!" Chivarion blurted out, and Alishai shot him a quelling look.

"I know," Kah muttered. "By Akadi, I know. But the moment I lifted the baby up, the decision made, all went dark. Woke up in the forest with you."

"And the baby?" Chivarion asked, horrified. "Is it here somewhere? Did you leave it in the Mists?" He shuddered. "Gods, can you imagine? An angry ghost baby stuck in the Mists?"

Alishai wanted to strangle him, but instead, she said, "It's okay, Kah. The baby is fine. It's back in Waterdeep, I'm sure. No harm was done."

"Don't know that," Kah said. She looked out toward the sea. "I was going to give it over. Give it to the hag. My mam . . . she would be so ashamed."

Alishai's throat went dry, and she wanted to walk into the sea herself. But instead, she shoved down her own feelings, her own past, and went to put an arm around the diminutive kenku's trembling shoulders.

"Everybody makes mistakes," she said. "And maybe those mistakes are what doomed us to this place. But we're going to make up for it. We're going to save Fielle. And maybe kill Strahd. We have a chance to do good here."

"Do good, yes," Kah said, nodding a little. "I want . . . I want to do good."

So did Alishai. But what she wanted even more was to make sure no one here ever found out her own secret—and how bad it truly was.

25

CHIVARION

Ever since waking up in Barovia, Chivarion had been vaguely amused at the ragtag bunch of weirdos he'd been stuck with. The paladin, Alishai, was a good fighter, but she had repeatedly rebuffed his advances, which meant she had no taste. The clumsy wizard was handsome but pathetic, and the kenku was a functional healer but so small and quiet that he often forgot she existed. And now he'd witnessed two embarrassing confessions. It was startling to realize he was traveling with people who seemed quite innocent but had actually done terrible things. Chivarion was hired muscle, brute force, a killer, but he'd never set a school on fire or stolen a baby, and he certainly never would. He definitely wouldn't abandon a baby in the Mists, which hopefully Kah had not done. He had secrets of his own, but he did not plan to go blurting them out while strolling along the beach.

He glanced at Murder, who was trotting by his side with her wings folded tightly against her goose-bumped body and her ears flat to her head to shut out the freezing wind. The tressym wasn't put out by their change in circumstances; she seemed a little cold but otherwise none the worse for wear. Chivarion had been surprised to learn that

Murder enjoyed traveling, but then again, he'd started carrying the hairless kitten along with him on journeys immediately after saving her from a certain death. They could communicate, in a way. Not with words; they just understood each other.

"We might need to find you a jacket," he said to the tressym. Murder looked up, dubious, and said, "Mer." Which meant that maybe they did, or maybe they didn't. Perhaps tressym didn't like clothes. Chivarion had once spoken to a smith about forging a small set of armor for his friend, but the surly dwarf had explained that first of all, cats didn't need armor and probably didn't need wings, either, and second of all, a creature weighed down by armor might not be able to fly. Chivarion had looked to Murder then, and the tressym had spread out her wings with a decisive flap, her decision made. That was why they got along—they listened to each other.

By lunchtime, they were nearing the tall stone wall that encircled the city of Ludendorf. Chivarion had seen many cities across Faerûn, from the big ones like Baldur's Gate and Waterdeep to the smaller towns and tiny villages, but he had never seen a place like this. For one thing, most big cities started with an inn, then a village, with towns and farms scattered around to raise the food and animals that the people crammed cheek to jowl didn't have room to raise. Ludendorf sat alone, hunched like a vulture. There was the city, then the wall, then . . . nothing. Dead grass for miles, faded to the yellow-gray of an old man's teeth.

Then there was the smoke. In most cities, you could expect pleasant little curls of smoke rising from homely chimneys with darker, smellier smoke issuing from the chimneys of forges and tanners and other businesses. Ludendorf seemed like it was 90 percent smokestacks. The entire thing bristled with pipes like the horrible bleaty organ in Strahd's dining hall, and from these pipes issued smoke in a rainbow of ugly colors that corresponded to the stages of a wound going from bloody to bruised to putrid to dead. Red, purple, blue, green, yellow, gray, black. No wonder the sky looked like it had been punched. When the sun did show, it was more white than yellow, anemic and sickly and with no real warmth. Chivarion wondered what the people within the city ate, because the countryside did not appear capable of sprouting even the most determined weed.

Alishai led them toward a tall gate, and Chivarion was surprised to see it held together with iron in a land where rust monsters roamed—until he noted all the guards standing at the top of the wall taking aim through specially made holes in the stone. There were a few crossbows, because a crossbow was always useful for threatening undesirables, but many of the guards wore backpacks with tubes attached, almost like very aggressive bagpipes. Chivarion didn't want to find out what came out of those tubes until he was on the other side of the wall.

When they reached the door, a man called down to Alishai. "State your business!" He pointed one of the tubes at her, and she glared at it and hefted her glaive.

"We are a party of—"

"Yes, fine, for Dr. Mordenheim. Come on in. Hurry up. Don't try anything funny."

Alishai looked to Chivarion, who shrugged. How did these guards know they were here to see Dr. Mordenheim? And what did they consider funny?

The doors cranked open through the use of chains and some sort of machinery that belched yet more foul gray smoke into the already smoke-filled air. As the doors parted, smog drifted out lazily to pool around their feet.

"Hurry up. Don't let the rusties in," the man complained.

They hurried through the doors, which didn't even open all the way—just enough to allow them passage before slamming behind them with a heavy clank. There were no guards on this side to further interrogate them, so Alishai did what any good leader did: She kept walking as if she knew exactly where she was going.

"What—" Rotrog began, but Kah jerked on his sleeve and shook her head.

"You're going to stretch the fabric," he complained.

"And you're going to get us killed or arrested, you are," she shot back.

The streets of Ludendorf were filthy, greasy cobblestone, and all the buildings had a similar look dominated by sharp lines, dingy cream walls with black sills, and pointed burgundy roofs. The grimy windows gleamed as dully as oily puddles. There were the usual wagons and carriages, which Chivarion expected, but then there were strange conveyances pulled by neither horse nor ox. Some simply looked like boxes on wheels that shat smoke, while others resembled metal pumpkins or enormous bicycles. The streets were not terribly crowded, and Chivarion doubted there could be more than a thousand people living within the city walls.

"Considering the scholars in matching robes carrying books, we can safely assume that big cluster of tall buildings up ahead is some sort of academy or university, yes?" Rotrog murmured with the eager, hungry eyes of a child watching a pie cool on a windowsill.

Alishai glanced at him, narrowing her eyes. "Obviously. But we don't have time to go to school."

A sad sigh. "First you make me leave a castle full of books, and now I must pass by a university full of learned people. This place was truly designed to torture me."

"Well, maybe you and Dr. Mordenheim will speak the same language."

"And which language is that?"

"Annoying smarty-pants."

Chivarion was more than happy to avoid the university. Anyone who would choose books and learning over swords and fighting couldn't possibly be much fun, in bed or out of it. Unless the book was about things to do in bed, but Chivarion didn't know if books like that existed. If they did, he hoped they were mostly pictures. He prodded Rotrog in the back to get him walking again.

A river wound through the downtown, but it looked more like mining runoff than an actual living body of water that supported fish and fishlike things. Instead of having one main street with many offshoots, Ludendorf was more like a V hugging the docks, and this river seemed like it was in quite a hurry to escape to the sea. Quaint bridges made it possible to navigate the filthy water, and below them, the dirtiest ducks Chivarion had ever seen paddled around sadly.

The people, at least, seemed cheerful. They were a sturdy folk, clad in heavy furs or the dark robes of the university, carrying woven baskets or pulling wagons behind them as they moved through town. Most of them were relatively normal, for humans, but some of them, like that fellow on the beach throwing the sea stars, were . . . off. Put together wrong. Which is to say, someone had put them together, and they'd made a bad job of it. Excess arms and legs, metal parts riveted to flesh, altogether too many perambulating organs in jars. Chivarion tried not to stare, but it was difficult. Luckily, either these creatures were accustomed to being stared at, they didn't care, or they didn't notice. One, a muscular fellow who had a glass jar full of brain where his hair should've been, even complimented Chivarion's sword.

He'd forgotten he was holding it.

He thanked the man and hung it back on his belt.

Just because this place felt odd and hostile didn't mean he needed to be waving Liversliverer around like they were still out in the wilds. It just made him uneasy, this Ludendorf. Like there was something hidden in the thick metal guts of the place, burping smoke like a citywide case of indigestion, a powder keg constantly about to explode.

It was not a large city, and soon they arrived at the docks. The wood was old and splintered and gray, the boats bobbing in the same dull water they'd been walking along for two days. A steamship sat heavily in the harbor as if sulking.

"You there," a man called. "Going to Schloss Mordenheim? You're late." He held a clipboard and had a very impressive mustache. Chivarion always thought mustaches were impressive because growing one was one of the few things he couldn't do no matter how hard he tried.

"You're expecting us?" Alishai asked.

The man looked from the clipboard to her, confused. "Dr. Mordenheim put out a call for mercenaries, and I would be very much mistaken if you are not, in fact, mercenaries?"

Alishai recomposed her face. It seemed like she was going for "confident and winning," but Chivarion thought it came across as "murderous and lying."

"That's us. Mercenaries. Hence all the weaponry and such."

The man tapped his clipboard. "Well, get on board, then." He pulled on a chain, and a bit of jewelry popped out of his pocket. After staring at it pointedly, he tucked it back into his pocket. "Five more minutes and the ship would've left without you."

"Come on, mercenaries," Alishai said, clearly enjoying the pantomime. She swaggered up the gangplank and onto the ship, followed by Kah, then Rotrog, then Chivarion, who picked up Murder to ride on his shoulder. The tressym had been on boats many times before and generally enjoyed sailing due to the vast number of rats with nowhere to go.

Once they were on board, Alishai paused, uncertain. The deck was mostly empty, aside from sailors doing sailor business, but rowdy voices could be heard from within the . . . the inside of the ship. Chivarion didn't know what it was called.

"Let's stay outside." The comely but easily angered tiefling led them past an open door, through which Chivarion noted nearly two dozen Lamordians in their heavy furs and beaver pelt hats. It was almost like a saloon, complete with the odors of beer and grain spirits, and the people seated within were bristling with weapons and hungry for a fight. Chivarion liked liquor and gambling but was glad to avoid this particular gathering. Normally, he would've known many of the mercenaries within, as it was a limited circle in any given city back home, but here, he knew no one. That meant that his reputation did not precede him, and it was likely that Murder would become the butt of a joke about someone's supper, and then he would go into a rage and start throwing much bigger men overboard.

They found some benches at the front of the ship and sat down. Rotrog clutched the metal seat like he was afraid it might come unbolted and toss him into the water, while Kah held up her arms and closed her eyes, enjoying the sea breeze in her feathers. Poor Alishai, though—she looked nervous. As the sailors cranked the anchor on board and the ship's motors began to churn, her face went from its usual twilight blue to a sort of turquoise.

She had, in effect, turned green.

"Seasick?" Chivarion asked. She nodded. Even her tail was green and droopy. "Look at the horizon. A fixed point. And pinch your wrist, right here. Then plug one ear. And hold your nose. And tell yourself, three times, 'I'm not seasick, but Chivarion looks very kissable.'"

A snort. "Punchable, maybe." Alishai tried to follow his more serious directions and failed. "You know I've only got two arms, right?" She squeezed her eyes shut, stuck a finger in one ear, and held her nose. "Kah, could you perhaps . . . ?"

She trailed off, unable to ask for help. Kah performed her healing spell, and Alishai waited, blinking rapidly . . .

And burped. It smelled of fish.

"Well, that didn't work," she grumbled. "It's going to be a long trip, isn't it?"

"You can pray," Kah reminded her. "The goddess always listens."

Alishai's eyes popped open. "Yes. Yes. Selûne is the goddess of navigators, after all." She pulled her amulet from under her armor and clutched it close to her heart. "Selûne, Moonmother, She Who Guides, hear your humble daughter, I entreat you, let your moon be my light—" She broke off and ran to the side of the boat, losing what little Chivarion had managed to scrape together for breakfast.

"What's this?" called a gruff voice—one of the Lamordian sailors. "Little lady's already yarkin', and we're barely away from the docks!" The man grinned with teeth like old wooden pegs. He wasn't the healthiest specimen, old and wrinkled and bald with white caterpillar eyebrows, his legs bowed and spindly. He reminded Chivarion of a string of snake jerky he'd seen once in a questionable vendor's snack cart.

Alishai turned, glaring fire—

Then spun back to the railing as she heaved.

The sailor only laughed all the harder. "Oh, Moon Lady, stop me from borfin' up me fish stew," he sang in a mocking voice. "Oh, woe is me!"

Alishai turned slowly, wiping the back of her hand across her lips. "Don't you know that mocking Selûne on a ship is bad luck?" she asked, her voice ragged. "She is a kind goddess, but those who abuse her on board a ship will never complete their voyage."

"Don't you be threatening me, missy!"

"It's not a threat. To Selûne, it is a promise."

The man flapped a hand at her and blew a raspberry. "Pfft. Selûne? *You're* a loon. Never even heard of her. Heathen blasphemy won't last long on this ship, I tell you that. If you mess on the deck, best you clean it up."

Alishai's hands went to fists as she watched the sailor strut away. "He will live to regret that," she muttered.

"Or he won't live, if you're right," Chivarion corrected.

Her eyes flicked to him, but she couldn't argue the point. At least her anger had replaced her seasickness. She sat down on the bench, head hanging as she prayed—silently, this time. Chivarion watched the sailor as he joined two of his fellows, obviously recounting to them what had just happened. The sailor's eyes seemed like they were always squinting into the sun, and yet they narrowed with hate when he looked at poor Alishai sitting there, trying to keep her insides on the inside.

Chivarion pulled one of his remaining daggers and twirled it contemplatively in his fingers. He didn't know much, but he knew one thing.

There was going to be trouble.

26

KAH

Kah had never sailed the ocean before, but she felt right at home. There was a nice breeze on the open deck, whipping around her as if urging her to spread her wings and fly. She tried it several times when she was sure the sailors weren't watching. She'd seen the mean one mocking Alishai as he told more and more of his friends about their exchange, and she didn't want to attract similar attention. Kenku weren't terribly rare back home, but they were apparently rare enough in Lamordia that the common folk stared at her with unhidden curiosity. One of the mercenaries, seeking some fresh air on deck, did a double take and hurried up to excitedly ask her if she was a wereraven.

"Kenku," she said.

"You're welcome?" he replied, too confused to realize his mistake.

The boat was terribly slow, and Kah was surprised that a city that seemed to have such advanced technology couldn't devise a better way to get from Ludendorf to the castle just across the bay. She could see it, rising from a rocky island battered by the iron-gray surf. It wasn't looming and shadowy and pointy, like Castle Ravenloft, but seemed instead to be orderly, humble, and foreboding. She didn't particularly like either place, and together, they had destroyed her interest in castles utterly.

Uncertain what to do with herself, she rejoined Alishai on the bench.

"Feeling any better?" she asked.

"Oh, yeah, truly superb." Alishai burped, a long, frog-like sound. "Never better."

"Odd that you were fine on the *River Dancer*."

Alishai was too sick to glare at her. "Rivers are thick and still, but the sea goes up and down, or haven't you noticed?"

Kah had noticed, and she liked the sea, but that information wouldn't help the tiefling feel any better, so she kept it to herself. She was just about to ask if Alishai might feel better if she closed her eyes when the ship shook underneath them, shuddering up through Kah's talons and directly into her spine. Had they run aground on rocks or sand? The ship was no longer moving.

A bell began to ring, over and over, and the sailors abruptly stopped their idle chatter. There were several stations around the ship, almost like metal cupolas with chairs and tubes, and now some sailors ran to sit in the chairs while other sailors ran to and fro distributing enormous spears with wicked hooks.

"What are those?" she asked.

"Harpoons," Alishai said quickly before another long, drawn-out burp and a moan of displeasure. The boat rocked a bit while moving, but it rocked even more now that it was held still.

"What is happening?" Rotrog asked one of the soldiers.

"Kraken!" the sailor barked. "Get inside!"

"Cracking? What is cracking?" Rotrog asked, but the sailor was already gone. "Oh, what I wouldn't give for the right books!" the orc moaned before sitting back down on his bench.

"We really should go inside," Chivarion urged, but Alishai shook her head.

"S'worse inside," she mumbled. "One of the nicer sailors said. No air. I can't—"

She stood, lurched to the rail, and made horrible noises but didn't produce anything new.

"Out of stew," she croaked. "Thank goodness."

The ship juddered again, and Alishai clutched the railing as the ship began to tip to one side.

"Starboard!" a sailor screamed. "Three o'clock!"

All the sailors on that side aimed their pipes downward and shot their harpoons into the water in quick succession. One of the harpoons must've struck something, as the rope attached to it went taut and the ship convulsed and gently keeled in that direction.

"Come," Kah chirped to Alishai, trying to guide her away from the railing she was about to fall over.

"Don't touch me, I'll—" She heaved again.

Kah didn't know what the big deal was; regurgitation was, after all, how kenku fed their babies, and no one seemed to complain about it.

Chivarion joined them and put a hand on Alishai's arm before wisely withdrawing it when she glared at him. "We need to get inside. Barfing is bad, but being swallowed by sea monsters is worse."

"Not moving," she croaked. "Would honestly rather die."

"Your funeral," the drow said before retreating to the door, where he stood, half in and half out, with the tressym at his feet. As for Kah, she was rooted in place, her hands wrapped around the rail. She wanted to help Alishai, but now she wanted to run, and yet . . . the water was not her realm. She was terrified of the foaming sea and certain that if she released her grip, she would tumble down into the waves below and drown.

The sailors, who were all humans in matching uniforms, had gone from coiling rope and gutting fish to all-out war with the undersea creature. A thickly built man with sunburned skin and an enormous mustache appeared, barking orders and pointing a lot. Kah didn't know most of the words he was using, but she understood well enough that he wanted the sailors to kill whatever was in their way and kill it fast.

"Conrad, keep hitting it with harpoons. Pavlovich, you, too. I want that sea to run black with blood. Mirian, Ama, more harpoons. Everyone on port side move to starboard. Double grog tonight if we live!"

At the word "grog," the sailors redoubled their efforts. All the harpoons were brought to the side tipping toward the sea, and the sailors worked together to load the machines that could shoot them.

One of them must've struck home again, as the sea churned and a long blue-gray tentacle shot up out of the water before sliding over the edge of the boat railing. Great white suckers felt along the metal floor of the ship, and the sailors carrying their harpoons screamed and scattered, throwing the weapons to the ground in their haste to escape the range of that curious, hungry appendage from the deep. Alishai abandoned the railing and ran for Rotrog's bench on the other side of the ship, pulling Kah along with her. Kah's feet were finally able to move, and together they scrambled across the deck, slipping and sliding, to clutch at the bench.

The orc's eyes were screwed closed, his fingers turning white where they grasped the cold metal. "Is it going to eat us?" he asked.

"I'd like to see it try," the tiefling rasped. She was breathing hard, still pale, her glaive in one fist and her tail wrapped around a leg of the bench.

Kah watched the tentacle pick up a sailor and drag him down the deck, the man's pale fingers scratching for any handhold as he screamed for help. It was the very sailor who'd mocked Alishai earlier, and he certainly sounded different when he was terrified for his life. Kah wanted to help him, but judging by the size of the tentacle, hitting it with her mace would've been like stabbing a dragon with a toothpick.

The captain, on the other hand, didn't seem at all put out. Pulling out a cutlass as he slid across the deck, he slashed at the tentacle, but his sword appeared to be more for show than for fighting; it was, at the very least, quite dull.

"I call dibs!" Chivarion said.

He sprinted across the deck to where the captain was impotently hacking at the tentacle and swiftly severed it with one powerful slice of his silvered sword. Black blood sprayed across the deck, splattering Chivarion and the captain and his sailors as the remaining stump of tentacle withdrew into the water with an offended plop. The part Chivarion had cut off flopped around as if unaware that it was no longer attached to the greater beast. At first, the sailors cheered, but then the ship listed hard to the side, the harpoon ropes creaking.

"Cut the ropes!" the captain shouted. "We taught 'im a lesson. Let the bastard run!"

The sailors, emboldened by the floppy, impotent tentacle, pulled out smaller knives and cut their ropes, and the boat sprang upright, wobbling back and forth until the deck was flat underfoot again. A great, dark shape moved away through the water at a troubling pace, trailing a river of black ichor. All around the ship, the sailors cheered and clasped shoulders and slapped backs, congratulating one another on a job well done. But the sailor who'd recently escaped the kraken's clutches was not celebrating. He was shaking, covered in inky blood and staring hatefully at Alishai.

Kah walked up to him, shoulders hunched up. "Need healing?" she asked shyly. "I—I can help."

"Don't want help from the likes o' you," the man spat. "Got a ship's healer, don't we? Get your blasphemous hands away from me, outlander."

Hurt, Kah withdrew. She'd hoped to smooth things over, but perhaps she had only made them worse. Instead, she went to where Alishai sat with Rotrog and watched the sailors move about the ship, coiling their ropes and replacing harpoons and butchering the tentacle for meat. She hoped that the rest of the journey would be quick and peaceful.

As it turned out, the kraken had done something to the ship's engines, and so they were dead in the water for some time. The boat drifted, bobbing gently, and the other mercenaries left the hall to wander about the deck. Kah suggested they find Alishai some water—and make sure Chivarion wasn't causing trouble, now that he was in high spirits from the kraken fight. They found the drow at a table playing Mucklebones, and Alishai stared daggers at him until he gave up and abandoned the game.

"How much did you lose?" she asked him.

The drow looked away. "Just a few of Strahd's coins. Just passing the time."

"Well, don't. We might need supplies."

"It's my money, not yours! I earned it! And I can spend it however I wish!"

Alishai wagged a finger in his face. "This is why I hate gambling. It makes people angry. Angry when they lose. Angry when they leave.

We can't get in a fight here, not with each other and not with anybody else. So let's go."

Chivarion's beautiful face wrinkled up in a snarl. "You are not my boss."

Alishai snatched up the bones and shook them in her fist. "Okay. We'll play one round. I win, you leave. You win, I never bother you about gambling again. Hells, I'll even give you a gold piece."

At that, Chivarion grinned. "Deal."

Alishai threw the bones, and Chivarion threw the bones, and Alishai laughed and told him to get off his rump and get out, and he did, and that was that.

Kah was fairly certain Alishai had cheated, but she didn't know how, and she didn't know how to prove it—or why she'd want to do so. Instead, she followed the tiefling around as she secured a cup of water, an old bucket, and a few hours in hammocks for the entire party.

"Might as well rest now that I'm out of puke," she said. "Who knows how long until they fix the blasted ship?"

They fetched Rotrog and followed a young sailor down into the bowels of the ship. Before, the engine had growled like an angry manticore, but now there were only the clanks and thumps of annoyed men fixing something that should not have broken. The room they were offered was small and cramped, but it had two open portholes that let in a healthy breeze and ten net hammocks strung from the ceiling, and it was relatively quiet. Kah liked sleeping in hammocks; she liked being in the air, off the ground, floating. It was lovely, actually, being rocked to sleep by the ship. The sailor assured them someone would wake them when they reached Schloss Mordenheim, if that should happen sooner than anticipated, and Kah happily wrapped herself up in her cloak, pulled her hood over her eyes, and went to sleep.

She was dreaming of the sky when a sound woke her, and she whipped back her hood and sat up. The light had changed, headed toward dusk, and the engine was still annoyingly silent. Two of the hammocks were occupied, and Kah immediately noted that one person was missing.

Outside in the hall, she heard the sound of a struggle.

Silently, Kah slipped from her hammock and tiptoed over to Chivarion, rousing him from his trance with a hand on his shoulder and a finger to her beak. His eyes flew open, startled, but he saw her point at the empty hammock and nodded his understanding. The drow gingerly lifted the sleeping tressym from his chest and slid out of his own hammock, pulling a dagger and heading for the closed door. They left Rotrog behind, which was probably for the best, as Kah had to assume that his magic spells might do more damage to the steamship than to whatever enemies had attacked Alishai.

Chivarion slid the door open, and Kah heard the muffled grunts of someone struggling but silenced.

"Put her down," the drow said, low and deadly.

"We're throwing her overboard. She's bad luck. Jinxed the boat." Kah knew that voice—that same sailor from before.

Peeking out the door, Kah saw two more sailors behind him, their faces covered in bandannas, attempting to carry the struggling tiefling down the hall and toward the stairs. She was giving them more trouble than they'd bargained for, and now one had a whittling knife to her side while he held her legs and the other had an arm around her neck and a huge, filthy hand over her mouth. Both men were splattered with bile.

"Not bad luck," Kah said. "Here there be monsters."

"She is so bad luck," the sailor argued. "She cursed me. She told me I wouldn't finish the voyage, and then a kraken attacked!"

Alishai smacked the filthy hand away from her mouth with a sharp rap of her tail. "You were trying to hurt it," she said. "What did you think it was going to do?"

"The beast went right for him," one of the other sailors said. "We all saw it."

"I don't intend to die because you have bad luck." Alishai wrapped her fingers around the man's arm and sunk her teeth into his skin. He dropped her, howling in pain, and she lashed out with her tail, striking the ringleader across the face. Before he could do anything about it, she grabbed his ankles and yanked, pulling him off-balance and making him fall over. The sailor still holding her legs was the biggest one, and he pulled her down the hall, dragging her toward the stairs.

"Really?" she asked, sounding tired. She looked to Chivarion. "Wanna punch this guy or what?"

"Yes, please!"

The drow hadn't taken two steps before the sailor dropped Alishai's legs and backed away. All three of the sailors, with their bandannas pulled up over their noses so that only their eyes showed, glowered at the tiefling as she stood and dusted herself off. She pulled a dagger from her belt and pointed at the sailor who'd mocked her. She'd nearly taken out his eye.

"This is between you and me, little man," she growled. "Come fight me, then."

"I ain't scared of you, girl." He held out his whittling knife. "Crazy, moon-worshipping witch. We kill you, the engine'll start again."

"I'm not crazy, and I'm not a witch." Alishai's voice was low and feral. "And killing me won't make your engineers more talented. Are you that ignorant?"

"Oh, Moon Lady, save us!" the sailor sang. "Oh, S'loony! The moon ain't a god, and your bad luck don't belong on this ship."

Alishai sprung at him and pinned him against the wall with a heavy clank, her dagger to his roughly shaved pink throat and his feet dangling.

"Do. Not. Speak. Of. Her."

"Witch," he whispered. "Crazy witch."

Kah saw the blade bite into the razor-burned skin, the tiny dribble of blood.

"Don't!" she chirped. "Or they will throw you overboard. Superstitious lot. Captain, too, probably."

"He has blasphemed against my goddess—"

Kah crept close and put a hand on Alishai's knife arm, tugging gently until the blade left the man's neck.

"Blasphemy only hurts the blasphemer. He doesn't know better. You do. Selûne does."

At that, Kah felt the fight leave Alishai's body as the shame rushed in. She released the sailor, and he dropped to the floor and skittered back toward his friends.

"If any of you touch her again, I'll kill you," Chivarion warned them.

Alishai chuckled. "Unless I get there first."

"I hate mercenaries," the biggest sailor mumbled. "Not worth it."

After he turned to head down the hall, the other sailors realized they'd lost.

"Mark my words—if anything else bad happens, it's on your head," the first sailor said.

"If Selûne wants to punish you, she doesn't need me to do it. You've chosen a dangerous profession, and you're an idiot. Mistakes are bound to happen."

The sailor gave her a crude hand gesture and retreated. Alishai sighed heavily and returned to the room. Kah followed her, and Chivarion checked up and down the hall before joining them and closing the door, hooking it closed this time to ensure no one else attempted to barge in. Rotrog had slept through the entire thing and still snored gently in his hammock.

"Why?" Kah asked simply.

Alishai lay back in her hammock, avoiding Kah's eyes. "Why what?"

"Why'd you let him get to you?" Chivarion asked. "The little rat."

A long sigh. "Because he mocked Selûne."

But Kah didn't buy it. "No. Something more."

Alishai sat up and glared at her reproachfully. "Is it not enough to hear one's goddess mocked, to be nearly killed for following the right path?"

As if on cue, a beam of silvery moonlight pierced the room, glowing through a porthole. It landed on Alishai, and to Kah's absolute surprise and horror, the stony tiefling began to cry.

27

FIELLE

When she next woke, Fielle did not experience the pleasant languor she'd known as a human, that urge to stretch and resettle, to pull the coverlet up higher and take a few more precious moments of comfortable rest. Her eyes were open in the darkness, her entire body alert. There was no way for her to know if the sun had set, and yet *she knew*. She undid the latch to her coffin, pushed it open, and leaped out to find exactly what she wanted most in the world: food and a bath.

It made sense to eat first and then bathe, rather than fuss with yet more blood and create more laundry. Another young Barovian woman was in her room, fluffing the pillows on her bed. The woman spun and, seeing Fielle, gasped, her eyes wide—did they all have big eyes, like frightened rabbits, or was that just malnutrition? The woman said nothing, and Fielle said nothing. She had no need to playact with her food. She pulled her chemise over her head, tossed it away, and had her fangs in the girl's neck before she could react to this strangeness. In her previous life, Fielle had rarely been naked, and then only to dress or bathe, but now she did not care at all who saw her or judged her; they were all her lessers, and anyone who disagreed could do so with teeth sunk into their jugular. She was tidy this time, not a drop of sweet blood spilled or wasted.

Once the girl swooned, Fielle maneuvered her onto the floor before slipping into the tall copper tub that sat in a corner—well, do hexagons really have corners?—of her room behind a screen. The water within was close to boiling and was steaming gently, scented with fragrant herbs that still floated on the surface. She lay back, luxuriating.

"This is pleasant," Tatyana said. "I . . . feel what you feel. Even more today than yesterday."

Fielle hummed. "It is pleasant. And I feel more myself than ever."

When she'd finished bathing and had dressed in a clean gown, Fielle followed Tatyana's directions up to the study, where she stood before the roaring fire. She'd noticed this painting before, but now she understood it. Now she recognized the eyes, so similar to her own, the violet dress that she'd woken up wearing her first night here. It was Tatyana. Her hair had been red . . . just as Fielle's hair was naturally red. Back home, her father had forced her to keep her hair shorn and bleached blond so that beautiful Zerina with her waist-length red tresses would remain the star of the Dancing Dragon. Whenever Zerina saw Fielle's red roots growing out, she would claim a sore throat and pout and swear she would never sing again, threatening to stop the flow of gold that poured in every night when she stepped onto the stage.

"We are both objects to Strahd, then," Fielle said. "Just things to possess."

"That is so. But together, perhaps we can find a way to deny him that pleasure."

To that end, Fielle looked more closely at the books strewn across the table. The room still smelled of the lavender with which Rotrog perfumed his robes. She could also catch the scents of the others—Alishai, Kah, Chivarion, even the tressym. But where were they? It was not like Rotrog, she thought, to leave books behind, and the scent was not terribly fresh.

She walked along the shelves, dragging her fingers along the books' spines. Unfortunately, these books seemed to have been chosen for their uselessness. They were all beautiful volumes but in no way helpful to Fielle's position. There certainly was not a book titled *How to Be a Vampire Spawn*, much less *How to Escape Your Vampire Sire*. There were books on obscure laws, dead religions, extinct animals, basket weaving. Not even spell or recipe books.

And then there was something else, something that called to her.

She felt its pull, so like a magnet. After yanking several heavy tomes from their shelf and tossing them on the floor, it was revealed.

"A Tarokka deck," Tatyana said softly. "*My* Tarokka deck."

The packet was almost invisible in the shadows at the back of the shelves, wrapped in a bit of dark gray silk, but the moment Fielle touched it, she felt a jolt of familiarity.

"I used to play at telling the future," Tatyana confessed. "These cards only ever showed me despair. I wondered if I was using them incorrectly, but . . . perhaps they told the truth. There are fifty-four cards representing four suits. Swords, stars, glyphs, and coins. Plus the fourteen High Cards, the most powerful cards in the deck."

Fielle slipped the cards from their box and flipped over the first one. The Darklord.

That word—Strahd had used it. He'd said he was the Darklord of this place, its ruler, but tied to it eternally. He'd seemed sad when he used this epithet—not proud. Fielle's nose wrinkled up in disgust. If she were a Darklord, she would do things differently. She would revel in it, not moan about it. The card was disturbing: a withered visage wearing a tall crown, seated at a skull throne, one hand up in a sickening benediction. She flipped through the rest of the black-and-white cards, noting that there was nothing cheerful or hopeful to be found among the painted figures. Beast, Executioner, Torturer, Necromancer. Even the most innocent cards held a certain threat.

"I see what you mean," she said.

"Hide them," Tatyana told her. "Strahd cannot know."

As Fielle slipped the cards down the front of her corset, she thought briefly of her colorful skirt with all its many pockets and wondered if perhaps it had been burned. These new dresses—they did not feel like hers; she felt like an animal wearing clothes.

When she returned to her room, she found Strahd sitting in his usual chair. A game board sat before him on a low table, and he shook a handful of shiny gray stones. To his side stood a crate about four feet tall, sparking her curiosity.

"And where have you been, my dear? I'd hoped to be here when you woke."

He had the cold, hard eyes of a predator, and she could tell that, yet again, she had disappointed him, or at least failed to please him. Perhaps tomorrow she would force herself to lie in the coffin for several minutes, just to make sure she was behaving as expected.

"You said the castle was my home, so I was exploring." She dropped a curtsey, which she'd noticed made him smile. "Was that wrong?"

Strahd reached out and cupped her face. Inside her, Tatyana shivered with revulsion, but Fielle was careful to remain stock-still. "Not wrong, no. Just unexpected. Was the maid not sufficient?"

Fielle shrugged. "I am still hungry, but I am always hungry now, it seems."

To her surprise, Strahd laughed. "She was to be your lady's maid—did she not tell you? To help you bathe and dress and do your—Well, your hair will never need a maid's attentions, I suppose."

"She said nothing, so I attacked. I do not require aid in my toilette, but thank you for the kindness. I am unaccustomed to the ways of a castle."

Strahd cut a hand through the air as if banishing the thought. "It is nothing, my dear. I have a game I'd like to teach you, but first, a gift. You said you like clockworks, I recall?"

"Yes," she said cautiously. She had neglected to tell him of her extensive training as an artificer, of her kitchen magic and clever way with small machines, but she had allowed him this one small bit of truth, and it would seem he had latched firmly on to it.

"Come out, Pidlwick," Strahd said. "Come out and meet your new mistress."

There was a muffled thud from the crate, and the door fell down to reveal the strangest construct Fielle had ever seen. He—she was almost certain it was a he—was about four feet tall with skin of burnished leather stitched carefully together and jointed with oiled wood. His fool's costume of black-and-white stripes with red bauble buttons was bracketed by shoes that curled to long points and a four-pronged red hat with bells at the end of each peak. Soot had been rubbed over his eyes and mouth to give him the mockery of a jack-o'-lantern's jolly grin, and his eyes held an uncanny light. The sprightly, round little man bounded out of the crate and did a front flip, landing in a deep bow with all his bells jingling. Fielle was at once unsettled and oddly charmed. Within her, Tatyana recoiled. The thing radiated wrongness—and a desperate need to be seen, to be loved. Fielle understood that feeling.

"Hello, Pidlwick," she said, holding out a hand. "I'm Fielle."

Pidlwick shivered like a pleased dog and reached to shake. She felt the strength in the wooden joints as his smaller fingers squeezed her own.

"Pidlwick does not speak," Strahd informed her. "But he understands. He knows the castle inside and out and is an excellent guide."

"I look forward to a tour," she told the clockwork man, and he spun around in a circle, kicking his feet with joy. "Thank you for such a thoughtful gift, Count von Zarovich."

"It is an abomination," Tatyana said in Fielle's mind. "It is nothing like the true Pidlwick, who was human and warm and kind. It is a cruel and false facsimile. I abhor it."

"I do not," Fielle told her smartly. "The circumstances of his creation are not his fault. And we need all the allies we can get. If he has lived here a very long time, perhaps he knows things about Strahd that can help us escape him."

Already Strahd had moved on from his grandiosity and was explaining the board game. Fielle had not liked board games before her transformation, and she learned that she liked them even less now. Strahd was terribly pleased with this little entertainment he'd created, and he clearly wanted Fielle to be impressed. She told him it was clever, admired the stones, and did not try too hard to win, although she did give him somewhat of a fight so he wouldn't think her stupid. The count seemed delighted to have a gaming partner and promised they would play every day. Internally, both Fielle and Tatyana groaned, but outwardly, she smiled and nodded. This smile did not reach her eyes, but Strahd was not the kind of man who noticed that in a woman, or anyone—or perhaps he had simply never seen a woman truly happy and thus had no comparison.

They were well into their second game when a polite cough issued from the hallway outside Fielle's chamber; it still had no door, she noted.

"Speak," Strahd demanded.

"Master, there appears to be an issue." Rahadin's voice was so quiet that Fielle likely would not have heard it before her senses had all come alive in her undeath. "A private one."

Strahd sighed his annoyance, moved one of his game pieces, and stood. "Forgive me for abandoning you prematurely. Barovia demands her leader." He bowed neatly and left. He did not ask Rahadin for further details within her earshot, and as curious as she was, she did not attempt to follow.

Grateful to at last be out from under her captor's watchful eye, she turned to Pidlwick. "Well, it is just us now. Will you show me your favorite places in the castle?"

Pidlwick capered about and nodded vigorously, setting the bells on his cap ringing. It should've been a cheerful noise, but the sound was atonal and slightly off. He scampered toward the door, awkward and ungainly, and looked back to make sure she was following.

"It will try to push you down the stairs," Tatyana warned.

"And I am already dead. If he tried such a thing, I would tear him in half with my bare hands. Surely Strahd has given him firm orders to treat me well." Tatyana couldn't argue that, so Fielle followed the dancing little man down the hall. He led her up and up and up to a guest chamber that smelled vaguely of cat piss and angry drow. The bed was empty, however, and Chivarion and Murder were nowhere to be seen. Pidlwick went directly to an armoire and showed her a hidden door.

"Ah, so you like secrets, do you?" she asked.

He nodded vigorously.

"I like secrets, too."

And so the little clockwork man ran excitedly up and down the stairs, looking back periodically to confirm that Fielle was still following him as he showed her closets, secret rooms, and trapdoors. Before waking up in the coffin, she'd been too weak to properly explore the grand edifice—most likely, she understood now, because Strahd had been drinking from her. Not too much—not enough to kill her, not enough to turn her. Just a taste. Testing her, most likely, until he was certain she was what he thought she was. Could he taste Tatyana's soul, she wondered? Or had he immediately known, the moment he saw her eyes?

No matter. She was here now, and she was changed, and her entire focus was to escape Strahd's grasp and live this new life on her own terms. To that end, she needed more than just a childish tour. She needed weapons.

"Pidlwick, darling, do you know if there are any books in the castle about vampires?" Pidlwick put his head to the side like a confused dog; he was so quiet she could hear the gears turning in his head. Fielle extended her fangs and pointed to one. "Strahd is a vampire. I am a vampire spawn. I want to know more about how I'm different from a human. Can you help me? I would be ever so grateful."

The clockwork put his fist under his chin and pantomimed thoughtfulness for a moment before nodding enthusiastically and doing the awkward little jig he did when he was happiest. He took off at a run, and Fielle followed him. He led her to a floor she had not yet visited and did cartwheels down a hallway and into a study, or perhaps an office. Dusty scrolls and tomes lined the wooden bookshelves on every wall, and even more books covered the floor in piles like snowdrifts. A wooden chest sat in each of the four corners, each bearing a heavy iron lock. At a massive black desk in the very center of the room sat a human man feverishly scribbling in a ledger. His quill scratched against the vellum, and he gave a weary sigh before looking up. He did not seem surprised to see Fielle, but then again, he looked so old and worn that perhaps nothing could surprise him anymore.

"Can I help you, miss?" he asked. Then, pushing up his pince-nez, he sneered at Pidlwick and said, "Ah, you brought that thing."

"I am a guest of Count von Zarovich, and he has asked Pidlwick to give me a tour. Tell me: What is it you do here?"

The man drew himself up tall. "I am Lief Lipsiege, the count's accountant. I account for the count. Ha!" Fielle realized he expected her to chuckle, so she did. "The count counts on me, you see. So I am not to be fed upon."

Fielle could smell the man, as well as the iron manacles that chained him to the desk. His odor suggested he had not bathed in a century.

"I had no such plans. But I am curious. Would you happen to know about—"

She looked to Pidlwick, who mimed opening a book and writing in it, then performed Strahd's courtly and old-fashioned bow. Fielle immediately understood.

"A journal? I am curious about the count's history and am interested in his many altruistic deeds." Just saying the words made Tatyana growl in her head, but even if she had changed—*they* had changed—still Fielle could sweet-talk anyone.

"Ah, yes. A fascinating tome, I'm sure, although I only have time for numbers." Lief gestured around the room. "In one of the chests, I believe. None of them are mimics, if I remember correctly, but it's been a long time. The key is—" Again, he gestured vaguely around the room. "Somewhere. I forget."

Fielle thanked him warmly and began her quest as he returned to his mad scribbling. The books appeared even duller than those in the study, all centered on ancient accounting techniques and surveying. She scanned them for something sized strangely or with a peculiar title, but all the titles were boring. Closing her eyes, she breathed in deeply and immediately knew where to look. Tucked behind a massive book on taxes was a smallish tome of leather wearing an old bloodstain that had called out to her ever-hungry senses. Within, the pages had been hollowed out to hold a heavy iron key. In the first two chests, she found only gold, which was currently useless to her. But in the third chest, she found exactly what she was looking for. Pidlwick danced and spun around her, bells jangling madly, as she picked up a smallish leather journal labeled TOME OF STRAHD.

28

ROTROG

Rotrog had been awake for quite some time—ever since Alishai had left her hammock to find the facilities and had instead been seized by the waiting sailors. He'd feigned sleep because he knew he was useless in such confined quarters. If he used acid, he'd leave a hole in the hull. Same for fireballs and missiles. Grease would send even his own party slipping and sliding and breaking all their bones against the steel walls with each swell. Perhaps he could've walloped someone upside the head with his staff if he were lucky, but thus far, to be quite honest, he had not enjoyed that kind of luck. So he waited and listened, and then the others awakened of their own accord and did what they needed to do.

He wouldn't have let the sailors hurt her. He would've done something before then.

That's what he told himself.

But deep down, he knew the truth.

He was a coward.

And that's why he still feigned sleep.

The tiefling was terrifying when she was angry and fighting, but he was even more frightened of whatever could make her cry.

"I was raised in a cult of Selûne, behind tall walls," she began, her voice soft. "The leader, Narelle, told me she'd found me on the road one day, alone and in rags, sitting quietly in a puddle of moonlight when I was barely old enough to walk. We lived off by ourselves in a commune near the Sea of Fallen Stars. A simple life, completely self-sustained. The reason we were so far off the beaten path was that everyone but me was . . . a former werewolf. Narelle had healed them all of their affliction through Selûne's grace and was considered a very powerful leader and healer. Everyone loved her. Except me."

Somewhere deep in the bowels of the ship, the engine spluttered. Everyone waited, breath held, for it to power up, and when it didn't, Alishai continued as the beam of moonlight played over her tearful face.

"Narelle was cruel to me. I was treated like a servant and told this was because I was different, that everyone else in the community was a victim of great evil, healed by Selûne. They had all suffered dearly, and yet I alone was untouched by tragedy. I had been discovered, adopted, my every need attended to. I was spoiled. Nothing I did was ever good enough for Narelle. I wasn't fast enough when running errands. The food I cooked wasn't properly seasoned. Narelle tried to teach me to heal, as people came from all around, hoping Selûne's grace might offer succor for their incurable diseases and wounds, but I was rubbish at it. I was taught to fight to channel my anger that I might help defend the community if Selûne's chosen were ever threatened, and even then, I was too brash, too haughty, too welcoming of the violence.

"Of course, Narelle's cruelty only happened in secret. In public, she treated me as her moon-chosen acolyte. She appeared kind and motherly with her gentle smile. But in private, I was her punching bag and scapegoat. Anything that went wrong was my fault."

Alishai sniffled and chuckled sadly. "I can see now that she was an angry old woman, jealous of my youth and beauty and freedom to live without the curse of the wolf. But all I saw then was that I had been carefully selected for abuse, even though I had tried my hardest to please both Narelle and Selûne. First I prayed every day to Selûne to help me become the best version of me that I could, a version of myself that Narelle could love, or at least not despise. As time went on and those prayers were not answered, I begged Selûne to deliver me to freedom, that I might be sent beyond the walls of our compound or find some way to escape, some moment when I wasn't watched. Those prayers were not answered, either. And as Narelle grew older and I was no longer a child, she became even more cruel. Most of her magic was dedicated to healing, but secretly, she could hurt. Fill me with fire or ice, blind me, cause my body to quake and contort in a rictus of pain. When she used that last one, she told me she was shaking the Shar out of me, for only Shar could make me such a terrible acolyte. And I heard her."

Again, the engines cranked and whined.

Again, they did not catch.

Rotrog kept his breathing steady. Alishai was casting a spell with her words, and he knew that soon, he would find out why the paladin was . . . well, the way she was.

"And so I decided that Selûne had given up on me, if she had ever cared about me at all. I tried to call down her power, and nothing happened. So instead, I prayed to her twin sister, the Lady of Loss. Shar."

The engine's whine cut through the darkness, almost begging.

"I knew nothing of Shar save that she was Selûne's opposite, her greatest foe. And I fell to my knees and begged Shar to hear my prayers and allow me my freedom. In that moment, a cloud covered the moon, and the door to Narelle's locked room gently swung open. I picked up my glaive and went inside to stand over her sleeping body. I was filled with fierce joy. Finally, after years of begging Selûne to help me, I had found a goddess who heard my plea—and who acted upon it. I raised my glaive and prepared to give myself to Shar, to break my oath to Selûne, and . . ."

She held up a hand, twirling her fingers through the beam of moonlight.

"That's when I woke up in the forest with you."

In the silence that followed, the engines yet again cranked and whined, and this time they caught and growled to life. The ship shuddered and began to move. Rotrog's hammock swayed gently, and he nearly revealed his position by asking a question. Fortunately, Alishai answered it for him.

"My oath remains unbroken. Whatever brought me here made sure of that. I came very, very close. The worst part—the part I did not consider in that moment—is that if I had succeeded in killing Narelle, it would've doomed the rest of our community. Sixty-three people would've been afflicted with their original disease. Do you know what harm sixty-three werewolves can cause? Those poor, innocent people. They were happy with Narelle, happy to live safely together and know that they would never become hungry, murderous monsters, and I would've taken it all from them, just so I could be free."

"Freedom is important," Chivarion said.

"But I would never have been free of my shame. It would've made a different sort of cage. And I think Shar would not be such a kind mistress."

"If it makes you feel any better, it was a lie." Kah's voice was soft and tender.

"What was?"

"The werewolves would not have reverted. The cure is permanent. Narelle lied."

Alishai snorted. "I'm not surprised. She had to keep her standing, her importance, at all costs. And she had to keep her sycophants so that she might always be adored."

After a few moments of silence, Rotrog asked, "So when you called on Selûne's powers here, that was the first time your magic manifested?"

Alishai snorted. "Ah, so now you're awake. Just in time to hear my tale of embarrassment and faithlessness. Of course. But to answer your question, yes. My first thought upon waking in this new world was to apologize to Selûne and wholeheartedly render myself to her in body and mind, and I felt her power flow through me and understood that she had extended her grace. Not that the shame of nearly breaking my oath will ever leave me, I am certain."

"But do you feel her? Your goddess?" Kah asked, uncertain.

A thoughtful, humming sigh. "No. I did not feel her there, and I do not feel her here. But I have faith. I believe, really believe, and I think that must be the difference. I was angry at Selûne for a long time because someone hurt me in her name, but . . . I see now, with distance, that the goddess is not the same as her worshippers. Narelle was not good to me, but she was a savior to many. She was just one person, one flawed and complicated person. She cannot define my relationship with my faith. Or with myself."

Rotrog nodded, chewing on this thought. Until this moment, he'd felt very little kinship with Alishai, and he was startled to realize they had been in very similar situations, held in thrall to a more powerful being. Rotrog had not broken any oaths, but he had certainly done something shameful. She had called shame a cage, and he was beginning to think he would always wear his own bruises from clutching those bars.

"Everyone makes mistakes," Kah said. "We can move on."

"Yes," Rotrog agreed. "We are in a new place with new rules."

"But we're still trying to get home, right?" Alishai sat up and looked around. "Not right now—we have to help Fielle—but in general?" She focused on Rotrog, who suddenly wished he were still pretending to snore. "These Domains of Dread . . . have you heard of them?"

"No. Never. And there was nothing in Strahd's study that sketched even the simplest map. Van Richten said this place has no real borders, that it is a separate plane of existence. Our experience thus far suggests that is accurate."

They were all silent for a moment, and Rotrog wondered if the others felt as lost and faraway as he did, as if home were thousands and thousands of miles away, unreachable and amorphous, like smoke that eluded capture. He hadn't particularly liked his previous life, but that didn't mean he was ready to accept that his entire existence had shifted to a different plane with different rules. There was something about the feeling of home, of being centered, of knowing everything about every day, that was deeply settling and solid . . .

And there was something about not being able to reach home that left one feeling untethered and unreal.

A fist banged on the metal door, shattering the moonlit peace.

"Landfall shortly!" someone called. "Prepare to disembark!"

Rotrog unwrapped himself from his cloak and stood on shaky legs. He'd gotten some sleep but not enough; sea voyages were apparently exhausting. The party trudged down the hall and up the stairs, mixing with other groups of mercenaries, all giving one another shifty-eyed looks of distrust and evaluation. They stood out, Rotrog realized; all the other groups were mostly human and clad in clothes of similar styling, in dark colors and trimmed with fur. A few gnomes could be seen here and there, smaller and more spindly than their human associates—and looking even meaner and more unhinged to make up for the size difference.

Stepping up onto the deck, Rotrog found the sea changed by night. The sky was a deep indigo, the moon doing her best to shine through a hole in the clouds. The water was an endless field of black aside from the soft white waves made by the boat itself. Up ahead, a castle stood stark against the clouds, blocky and forbidding, rising up from a whispering forest that clung stubbornly to an island of stone. White threads of smoke curled upward from the castle, far more of them than might be expected from the usual coterie of chamber fires.

From what he could see, there were five other groups of mercenaries. These people had chosen to come on this journey because they needed work, and apparently working for Dr. Viktra Mordenheim would pay the bills. None of the mercenaries seemed well off; their clothing sported frayed hems and patched elbows. Despite the near-freezing temperatures, several people were barefoot or poorly shod for the weather. Rotrog had no idea what this doctor might want from them, but he knew that even among these desperate killers-for-hire, their little group of misfits had to fight to the front of the line. They had to plead their case.

They had to get there first.

Their only other option was to return to Barovia, where their host, the local ruler, was a monster himself. The totem that would ostensibly take them back to Barovia was still in Alishai's possession. As unpleasant as Lamordia was, Barovia was not Rotrog's first choice. Although Strahd had been kind to him at first, he did not wish to build a life in a place of eternal darkness, ruled over by a vampire and at the mercy of whatever dangers the count might randomly wish to spring upon him. He did not wish to be a thrall or a corpse.

"I need to wash before our interview," Chivarion murmured. "The squid blood was fun at first, but it's getting awfully itchy, and I look unkempt."

"No!"

Everyone turned to stare at Rotrog, who did not usually make exclamations.

"You like 'em dirty, eh?" Chivarion gamely quirked an eyebrow.

"No! I mean—what? It's just—you saved the ship. It's obviously kraken blood, and anyone from this place will recognize it. Let the doctor see that you are worthy of her attention."

Chivarion's face screwed up in annoyance.

"Also, it makes you look quite dangerous. Rakish, in fact," Rotrog continued.

"Like a rake?"

Rotrog pinched the bridge of his nose. "No. Not like a rake. Not that kind of rake. It makes you look . . . saucy."

"Like a sauce?"

"Jaunty."

"Like a jaunt?"

"It looks good!" Rotrog all but roared.

"Oh. Well. Thank you." Chivarion tipped his head and grinned, highlighting the black smears over his light eyes. Rotrog realized that the dense drow had understood him just fine but was fishing for a compliment, which he had actually given. He blushed, grateful that it was likely hidden by the darkness.

The other mercenaries did not appreciate this outburst and were glaring at him, but then the boat bumped up against the dock and the groups began to jockey for position by the gangplank. Rotrog noted that there was a solidly built road of smooth stone that led up to the castle. He'd expected a hike, as the island looked quite wild from far away, but up close, he saw this was an orderly place where ships were docked and unloaded in an organized manner. Beside the road, there were two metal tracks that led from the dock to the castle, plus a crane just the right size to unload heavy cargo from the ship and place it in metal carts with wheels that fit neatly over the tracks. Lampposts stood at handy intervals along the road to light the way, their fires burning a toasty orange in a landscape dominated by gray.

This place—it was very, very different from Barovia.

Both were inhospitable, stark, dangerous.

But Lamordia had a stolid, tenacious determination about it, as if no matter the cold, the wet, the smoke, the despair, still it would find a way to march on. Much like that odd, stitched-together fellow they'd seen on the seashore, tossing the dead sea stars back into the uncaring ocean, this place seemed like it considered death a mere inconvenience it was determined to ignore.

The other mercenaries fought their way down the gangplank and hurried up the road toward the castle, with their group going last. Alishai scanned the immediate area as if hoping to find a wagon or a helpful hostler waiting there. Instead, they saw only masses of fish being unloaded into one of the carts waiting on the track. A gnome sat in the crane, carefully maneuvering the catch into the waiting receptacle. The moment it was settled, someone must've flipped the right switch, as the cart of fish zoomed up toward the castle on its tracks, a pipe behind it belching smoke.

"The cart," Rotrog whispered to Alishai. "We need to ride on that cart."

She barked a laugh. "That we do, wizard. That we do. How much to ride in a cart up to the castle?" she called to the gnome.

He stared down at her, dumbstruck. "How . . . much?"

She nodded. "We need to get to the castle."

"So walk."

"We need to get there first."

The gnome thought about it, laughed, and named a price. Alishai haggled with the gnome until they were both happy, then put several bits of metal in his hand.

"Is it safe?" Kah asked, cocking her head at the cart.

"Nothing about this place is safe. You're a healer. What are you scared of?"

To that, the kenku had no proper answer. Alishai leaped into the cart and helped Kah in, then Chivarion boosted Rotrog over the edge and jumped in to join them. The party stood in an open metal box the size of a carriage; fishy-smelling water swished around the floor. Before Rotrog could complain, the gnome pulled his lever, and the cart jerked to life, sending them all knocking into one another before they fell in a heap. The trees overhead zoomed past as they untangled their limbs and weapons and squatted down, clinging to the sides of the cart. The ride was smooth, if loud, and honestly not much worse than Strahd's carriage, except for the fish water.

When it jerked to a stop, Chivarion caught Rotrog before he could fall, steadying him with a—yes, *saucy*—wink. This kindness did little good, as the cart immediately tipped them all out into a massive pile of fish, some still flapping angrily.

"What the—?" another gnome called.

Alishai leaped to her feet and grinned fiercely. "We're way ahead of them. Come on!"

Rotrog stood with as much dignity as he could muster, removed a fish from his robe, and followed her around to the front of the castle. Twelve tall stone steps took them to an imposing entranceway.

"Halt!" called a tinny, echoing voice.

They stopped, but there was no one visible—until they looked down. The odd but dignified creature that perched on the top step was even smaller than Murder, who raised her haunches as she prepared to pounce.

"We talked about this," Chivarion said, catching the tressym in midair. "Don't eat guys who talk. Unless they're rude."

"Ahem," the creature said. It was about the size of a squirrel and resembled nothing so much as a toad crossed with a small gargoyle. A face with floppy, alert ears, glowing yellow eyes, a pug nose, and a wide mouth topped muscular shoulders, a round belly, and widespread wings. When it spoke, its mouth did not move, and Rotrog noticed that it wore a small metal box on a collar around its thick neck—the source of the tinny voice.

"Apologies," Alishai said. "Is this Schloss Mordenheim?"

"So you're stupid. That is unfortunate," the creature's voice box said with a Lamordian accent and the cultured, annoyed tone of a powerful woman accustomed to disappointment.

"Not stupid, merely unfamiliar with the local customs. We were smart enough to take a cart from the ship to the castle instead of walking, unlike the other mercenaries," Rotrog said.

Alishai shot him a glare, but he felt kinship with this small but aristocratic being, or at least with whoever controlled it. He continued. "As you appear to be in charge, I will divulge that we wish to speak with Dr. Mordenheim, if you please."

The creature raised its chin, preening. "So, someone has manners. Thank goodness. I was beginning to lose hope. You are in fact speaking with Dr. Mordenheim. Please follow the homunculus to my laboratory, and we will see if you can indeed help me."

29

ALISHAI

They followed the homunculus through the hulking entryway and into a round foyer with none of the detail they'd seen in Strahd's castle. It was a simple square room formed of rough-cut blocks of gray stone, utterly devoid of moth-eaten rugs, billowing tapestries, or cursed paintings of long-dead relatives. Instead of torches, there were glass-encased lanterns, their flames steady but low. In the center of the room hung a bulky chandelier, and under that chandelier sat an elegant, wheeled table topped with a glass bell jar, and inside of that bell jar was what looked like a human brain with two bright blue eyeballs attached by stringlike nerves.

"Morvel, I'm taking this group to the lab," Dr. Mordenheim said through the voice box worn by her homunculus. "Please ask the other mercenaries to wait here until called."

"Yes, Doctor." The voice was masculine and proper, as if it were perfectly normal for a brain-topped piece of furniture to accept orders from a homunculus. The light pink organ, a mass of glossy pink curls, pulsed gently as it floated in milky fluid, attached to several wires that connected it to machinery within the table, including a small speaker. The blue eyes gently rotated to follow the group as the homunculus led them away.

This castle, at least, had been designed sensibly, all sturdy rectangles and firm corners. As the homunculus led them up a short set of stairs, Alishai approved of the no-nonsense nature of the space. Castle Ravenloft, in her opinion, had been overwrought and aggressively decorated, with nearly every surface covered in tchotchkes and every wall stuck with paintings and tapestries. She'd found it . . . in bad taste.

Her approval of Mordenheim went down a notch when they encountered a small, yappy dog that was actually two small, yappy dogs sewn together down the middle so that it had two small, yappy heads that seemed to be competing to learn which one might be louder. They passed a patchwork man like the one from the seashore—or perhaps he was made of the opposite bits of that other man, as he had a pink-skinned face and curly black hair with brown ears. This man was sweeping and making a terrible job of it. The deeper into the castle they ventured, the more horrified Alishai was. Schloss Mordenheim was bedecked not with art and furniture, but rather with living creatures stitched together with firm black sinew or captured in jars of opaline fluid. Many of these creatures hurried away impatiently on errands, while others sat in place as sentries or servants, and yet others wandered around as if in confusion. They all stank of magic and metal and oil, and Alishai found them rather creepy, edging on blasphemous.

This Mordenheim woman was a doctor—

But of what?

The homunculus stopped before a large metal grate that resembled nothing so much as a cage. It flapped its wings and rose just high enough to press a brass button set into the stone wall before landing neatly on all four feet. The sound of heavy machinery whirred to life, and the grate slid aside to reveal a box with handsome wood paneling and a tall, thin man whose brain was clearly visible through a glass fishbowl turned upside down, upon which sat a small, neat cap that matched his hunter-green coat. What's more, the man's torso sat upon a long brass pole that ended in four small wheels, as if a coatrack had been shoved somewhere very unfortunate. He did not seem too put out by this reality.

"The lab, please," the homunculus said.

The coatrack man pulled a lever with his white-gloved hand, and the grate slid closed before the metal box began to rise. Alishai hated how the floor shook under her feet, the unnatural way that they were hefted into the air on what she suspected was an enormous chain. She vastly would've preferred even the tightly spiraling staircase of Castle Ravenloft. Something about this place was horribly unnatural, as if it fought life itself to continue existing. She began to worry about Dr. Mordenheim in a way that Strahd had not worried her at all. What kind of person could make a paladin wish for the comfort of a vampire?

Finally the coatrack man threw a lever, the box stopped suddenly, and the grate slid open. The room beyond was brightly lit, the walls washed thickly in white and glowing a strange, otherworldly green thanks to a row of glass tanks fitted with bright lights. A human head floated in each of these amniotic cages, their eyes blinking and their mouths twitching as if they couldn't quite decide what they thought of the laboratory. Every bit of space was taken up by either shelves covered in jars full of body parts and creatures or machinery bristling with levers, dials, and buttons. Bright blue-and-white electricity crackled here and there like restless cats that couldn't stop bickering. Wires and tubes hung from the ceiling, roved along the walls, and snaked along the floor among puddles of fluids that, well, it was better not to think about.

Most worrisome of all, a large table held the majority of a powerful human man's body, the black stitches now horribly familiar. He was missing a leg at the calf, an arm at the shoulder, and everything above his neck. The flesh was purple and mottled, streaked here and there with the bright red of infection. A pustulant puddle had formed underneath it, pooling on the metal table. The scent of rot rode the air, smothering the other smells of hot metal, rancid oil, and medicinal tinctures.

"Ah. There you are."

A figure appeared from behind one of the green tanks, a tall and almost cadaverous woman who shared the coloration of elves—white skin, short white hair, lavender eyes—but not the pointed ears. She wore a tightly fitted suit of stained white under a heavy leather apron bristling with instruments. Black gloves went up to her elbows, and in one hand she held a glass tube filled with glowing green liquid.

"Dr. Mordenheim, I presume?" Rotrog said with his annoying brand of gallantry.

The woman smiled and tilted her head. "And the mannered mercenary. Yes, I am she. Welcome to Schloss Mordenheim. I will get quickly to the point. I require bodies."

That, at least, gave Rotrog pause. He glanced at the mostly-man falling apart on the steel table. "Bodies?"

Dr. Mordenheim shook her head and hurried about her lab, twisting dials and inspecting the contents of beakers. "Yes. Bodies. That's why I've called you here. Without raw materials, my experiments are stalled. My last group of mercenaries did not return, and so I am without the constituent parts I require."

"So you want us to kill people?" Chivarion asked, warming up to the idea. "Because that's kind of my specialty."

She looked him up and down as if wishing he had already been deboned like a chicken and laid out upon a slab. "If that is what it takes, but I offer a simpler solution. The morgue in the basement of Ludendorf University is positively stuffed with bodies. Every pauper in the city foolish enough to sell flesh rights is immediately sent underground to await study. I am currently at loggerheads with Dean Quinbil, and he is withholding sale of those bodies to me as punishment." She looked each of them in the eyes. Alishai did not enjoy it; she felt as if Dr. Mordenheim were constantly seeing everyone around her as potential component parts.

"I need you to go to the morgue and steal as many bodies as you can." Dr. Mordenheim lifted the lifeless arm on the table and dropped it with a wet thunk. "The freshest, most complete, least damaged, least diseased, least rotted bodies. I want them pristine." She pointed a finger at Chivarion. "Including the heads! Not nearly enough heads these days. Ah, those juicy student brains." For a brief moment, she actually looked happy. But her face swiftly reconfigured itself into irritation as soon as Alishai spoke.

"And what payment are you offering?"

Dr. Mordenheim rolled her eyes. "Payment. As if being part of the grand exploration of science, innovation, and life beyond death is not enough! As if supplying the rudimentary media from which I will create consciousness is not a great privilege. You mercenaries and your payment." She tugged at her gloves. "What do you want?"

"Two things," Alishai began, but Rotrog stepped forward to silence her.

Seeing Dr. Mordenheim's sneer, she allowed it.

"This is indeed an inestimable passion," Rotrog began. "I have never witnessed such incredible creations. Why, just in this glorious castle I've seen wonders beyond my understanding! To wit, I wonder if you have ever considered how a soul might be extracted from a human body? We've a friend, you see, with two souls sadly fighting over one body, and we wish to separate those souls and provide a vessel for the, er, extraneous soul."

Dr. Mordenheim stared off into space over Rotrog's shoulder, her light violet eyes bright and her lips pursed. "Fascinating! And how do you know this human contains two souls? What is the empirical evidence?"

"Well, she wasn't acting like herself—" Chivarion began, but Kah silenced him with a hand and pointed to Rotrog, who seemed like the only one who spoke the doctor's language.

"A tragic tale. A vampire seeks his lost love, and he has determined this soul resides in our friend's body. It has been corroborated by a local expert in such things. If you were to create a machine that could extract that spare soul and place it into a waiting body, why—"

"It has never been done," Dr. Mordenheim continued. "Bring this person here, and I will attempt this extraction."

Rotrog winced. "Sadly, she is on the other side of the Mists. If you could travel there—"

Dr. Mordenheim slashed a black-gloved hand through the air. "Impossible. I am tied to Lamordia. But if I create this machine for you, will you bring me word of the experiment's conclusion? This information is vital for my continued experimentation."

Rotrog closed his eyes and placed his hand over his heart, a protective gesture that seemed valuable around Dr. Mordenheim. "I give you my word. If the transfer is successful and we are able, we will bring you this knowledge."

"Excellent. Excellent. Now the bodies." Dr. Mordenheim paced the room, easily navigating the snake pit of tubes and wires. "I need at least five spotless, beautiful bodies from the morgue—including one that will be suitable for your purposes, as a repository for the spare soul. My personal ship will take you to the university under cover of night and await your return. If you are caught, I will disavow you. And if you mention my name, I will send assassins to kill you as you wait in the Ludendorf jail. Do you understand?"

"Of course. Quite reasonable," Rotrog allowed.

"You will—"

Dr. Mordenheim gasped and squatted, her eyes focused on Murder with an unholy interest.

"This creature. Who created it?"

Chivarion swiftly scooped up his tressym and stood, holding the winged cat close to his chest. "Murder is a tressym. She was born this way to a tressym mother. They are—well, not quite common in our homeland, but reasonably so."

"Half cat, half bat," the doctor murmured as she stood and stepped close enough that Murder put her ears back and hissed. "Or half bird?"

"All tressym," Chivarion reiterated stiffly, turning away slightly. "And she has claws, so I would not suggest you get any closer."

Dr. Mordenheim hadn't blinked in a solid minute. "I will give you everything you ask in exchange for this creature. There are many groups of mercenaries who can bring me bodies, but this natural conglomeration deserves thorough study." Her hands were up, her fingers twitching toward Murder.

Chivarion's jaw dropped, but Alishai was already reaching for her glaive. "Murder is a member of our band, not some object that can be bartered. She is not for sale at any price."

"Yeah!" Chivarion barked.

Dr. Mordenheim eyed Alishai's glaive, one sharp white eyebrow up. "Very well. I will put out word, and someone else will bring me a—tressym? This is a poor place, and money talks."

"Not to you, it doesn't, does it, sweet lass?" Chivarion murmured to Murder, cradling the tressym like a baby until her bat-like ears perked up again.

Sickened by this display, Dr. Mordenheim made shooing gestures toward the door. "Go, then. The homunculus will take you to the ship."

"Tonight?" Kah asked. "Now?"

Dr. Mordenheim apparently hadn't noticed her before and now bent over to inspect the kenku, who, like Murder, was probably a little too intriguing to someone interested in unusual bodies. "Tonight. Corpses don't get fresher with time. It's an hour there and an hour back. Perform well, and you'll return well before daylight. But you! Feathers, and yet quite humanoid. Are you—"

"Leaving," Kah said, backing away.

Dr. Mordenheim sighed, and this time, Alishai went last. Chivarion usually took up the rear, but he was too concerned for Murder, which was an appropriate reaction to the way the doctor's eyes roamed greedily over nonhuman creatures.

A damp glove landed on Alishai's shoulder, and she stopped. "And what are you? I've seen your kind before but never had a chance to study the intricacies . . ."

"A person."

The fingers squeezed, hard. "My interest is a compliment."

Alishai reached back to remove the glove, and not gently. "We are all people, not the ingredients of a recipe."

As she followed her group toward the metal cage, her fingers wrapped around her short sword, she heard Dr. Mordenheim softly call, "My compliments to the chef anyway."

30

KAH

The trip to Ludendorf University was a breeze compared to the steamship. Dr. Mordenheim's personal watercraft was smaller, swifter, and had only two sailors, both of whom seemed totally disinterested in their passengers and any prayers offered to unusual gods. The ship's deck was small and busy, and so the group was asked to remain in the deckhouse where they wouldn't get in the way. There were several open portholes and a fresh enough breeze, which felt delightful ruffling through Kah's feathers. Benches were bolted to the walls, and the group found seats and tried to get comfortable on the cold metal. Kah did not particularly want to raid a university basement for dead bodies, but it seemed almost pleasant compared to spending one more moment with Dr. Viktra Mordenheim staring at her like a clockwork with a missing spring.

Chivarion was hunched over in a corner, curled protectively over Murder as if suspecting an ambush at any moment. "I can't believe she wanted to take you," he murmured.

"She wanted me and Kah, too," Alishai reminded him, looking only a little greenish.

The drow looked up. "Yes, but you're . . . normal-sized. Murder is just an innocent little baby."

Kah had seen the tressym attack the undead and slice smaller creatures to ribbons, but she did not comment. Murder had only ever been helpful in a fight, and she, too, was insulted by the doctor's attitude. She also did not seem to appreciate the coddling. The tressym gently fought her way out of Chivarion's hug and leaped to the floor, where she groomed herself in annoyance, slurping at her bare shoulders and paws. With a loving but exasperated look over her shoulder, she strode out onto the deck and went into stalking mode. As soon as she was out of sight, Chivarion put his head in his hands.

"I—I need to tell you something," the drow said, his voice low and shaky. He didn't look up; his face was hidden by his hair. He took a deep sigh. "I almost—I almost did a bad thing. And I need to confess. It's eating a hole inside me."

Kah sat beside him and put a hand on his arm but said nothing. The drow sunk down deeper, fingers in his hair, and shook his head.

"You might be surprised to hear this, but I am very bad with money."

Kah was not surprised to hear this, but she made a sympathetic noise before Alishai or Rotrog could say something that would derail Chivarion's confession. It festered inside him, poisoning his soul, and the healer in her wanted to urge it out.

"And I like to gamble. It's fun. I thought it was harmless. But, well, I got in deep. In a gambling hall. I kept losing, but I felt so lucky, as if at any moment I would win big, double or nothing. Even when I knew it was hopeless, I kept going. I was desperate. I bet everything." A meaty pause. "I lost."

Kah looked up and saw two green lights blinking from the darkness outside the deckhouse door, but she did not interrupt.

"I was taken to the boss. He owned the gambling hall and a traveling circus besides. He explained that I was so deep in debt that I could never repay it. He gave me a choice. They would cut off my hand unless I gave him what he wanted. Murder." A sad sigh. "They'd never had a tressym before. He just saw Murder as another curiosity, as an exhibit. But she has feelings! She understands things! More than me sometimes."

"So what happened?" Alishai urged, and Kah shot her a quelling look.

Some things needed patience, and that included convincing a barbarian to unload the heaviest burdens of his soul.

In the smallest voice, Chivarion said, "I agreed."

And Kah knew that he did not mean his hand.

"I rescued Murder when she was a kitten. Since then, we've been family. And I agreed to give her over, even knowing that she would be bred over and over to produce kittens for that monster. A life of captivity and worse. All because I wanted to gamble and because I was too vain and scared to sacrifice a hand." He held up one of his hands as if he could lop it off with his eyes, then let it drop. "I asked for one more night, and I took Murder to the docks, bought her a nice fish, played all her favorite games, then curled up to sleep, knowing that the next morning, I'd have to hand her over. And we woke up in the Mists."

"And he gave you one night? How did he know you wouldn't run?" Alishai asked.

Chivarion looked at her like she was an idiot. "We were followed. Watched. A constant reminder that it was a farce. Still, I wanted it to be the best night of her life. I hope . . . I hope she never knows it wasn't real."

A meow issued from the darkness outside before Murder strolled into the room. Everyone stared at the tressym, likely wondering the same thing Kah was: Did the clever creature understand every word? She daintily stepped across the deckhouse floor and rubbed against Chivarion's legs, purring. He reached down and picked her up, putting her forehead against his. To Kah, it looked like he was holding a dead chicken to his face to test its freshness, but the cat's rumbling purr told a different story.

"I'm so sorry," Chivarion whispered. "It's the worst thing I've ever almost done."

The tressym stopped purring and reached out with one paw to slap the drow across the face. Her claws left red welts across his gray skin.

"Yeah, I deserve that," he said. "But I'll wear your scars with pride if it means you forgive me."

For a long moment, the drow and the tressym stared into each other's eyes, and then a golden glow consumed them. A look of absolute wonder suffused Chivarion's features, and his eyes, once lavender, shifted to the same lambent gold as those of his pet, complete with slashed pupils.

"She said she forgives me," he whispered. "I—I understood her. She forgives me!"

Murder purred again, and Chivarion hugged her to his chest. Kah looked away. She'd never felt that kind of bond with another living creature, and it sent a shock of intense loneliness through her heart. Perhaps Chivarion had done something terrible, but he had been forgiven, and it looked as if their bond would be stronger than ever.

With Chivarion's soul unburdened and filled with a new kind of magic, the rest of the party was left feeling awkward. There were six hammocks in the back room of the deckhouse; Kah claimed the farthest one from the door, again wrapped herself in her cloak to sleep, and said her usual prayers to Akadi. Although she was far from home, she somehow felt . . . at peace. Everyone in their party, she realized, had held some dark secret in their heart, a thorn festering in their soul. And one by one, they'd had cause to share their shame and find kinship within the group. They'd all been brought here on the cusp of a horrible, unforgivable decision—or having just made one. Did that mean this plane was meant as punishment—or perhaps it was a place to find forgiveness? Their shameful pasts, after all, had brought them together, and now they were working as a team to prevent a good-hearted soul from becoming a monster against her will.

If this was an afterlife, it was a strange sort of afterlife.

And if it was an opportunity for redemption, well, perhaps when they saved Fielle, they would be returned to their proper world and allowed a chance to start over.

Some time later, she was awakened by a blue hand on her shoulder. "We're here," Alishai said. "Ready your weapons."

Kah landed on the cold floor right as the boat bumped up against the dock. Rotrog steadied her with a hand. The orc seemed nervous, but he almost always seemed nervous when there was a fight involved. Alishai and Chivarion, at least, looked grim and effective, although Alishai was clearly still feeling the effects of the sea. They had not been given a map and had no idea what they'd be up against; Kah suddenly realized she had a hundred different questions for Dr. Mordenheim about this proposition but no way to ask them.

Where was the morgue? Was the university defended? Would they be facing innocent students or paid security? Were there wagons, or was she expected to carry a corpse on her back? Hopefully, the corpses would be in a variety of sizes because Kah was not adept at carrying heavy things.

"There's plenty of doors, but the side door is closest to the morgue," a sailor said. "We'll be waiting."

"And where—" Rotrog began.

"Don't know, don't want to know." The sailor stuck a pipe in his mouth and disappeared into the deckhouse.

"We get in, we get what we need, we get out," Alishai said. "With as little loss of life as possible."

"But wouldn't killing people actually make the job easier?" Chivarion argued. "I mean, if she wants fresh corpses . . ."

"The people in charge get angry when you start killing willy-nilly," Alishai reminded him. "Steal a couple of dead guys? No big deal. Murder a few paying students? Someone's going to be in trouble."

"But maybe just one teensy-weensy little death . . . ?"

Alishai dragged a hand over her face. "This isn't a market. We're not haggling over plums. Let's just go steal some corpses."

She lifted her glaive, and Kah said, "Perhaps—fewer weapons? Until we see what's there."

Alishai hooked her glaive on her back. "Good point. Nobody expects to see a glaive in the university halls." She looked around. "Not that we look like students. Or Lamordians. We should've asked for coats or something."

Chivarion nodded, gently placed Murder on the ground, and marched into the deckhouse. After two disturbing slams, he returned carrying two heavy and familiar fur coats.

"Did you kill the sailors?" Alishai asked.

"No. I just borrowed their coats."

"Did they agree to that?"

He grimaced. "Kind of."

"Whatever." Alishai accepted one coat and gave the other to Rotrog, who reluctantly put it on. "Hood over head," she said. "No one here looks like us. Kah and Chivarion, you've already got hoods. Let's all try to blend in."

Kah thought this highly unlikely, but arguing the point wasn't going to help anyone. She pulled her hood down over her face, almost completely hiding her beak, and held a knife in each hand, hidden by the deep sleeves of her cloak. Alishai pulled up her coat's hood, which didn't quite cover her horns, and jogged toward the side of the building. They were close to a corner, and the shadows soon swallowed them whole. Overhead, the university loomed as the sky stood grim witness, dark and starless, smothered in thick clouds. Their path had no outdoor lighting and no guards, but why would it? This was, after all, simply a university in the wee hours of the morning. The students might be returning home from carousing, but they would use more approachable entrances.

The side door was, to their surprise, unlocked. The wide hallway beyond was painted a sterile white and lit by the same kind of gas lantern Dr. Mordenheim favored. Doors marched along at regular intervals with lights between them and neat signs that made it especially easy for a group of thieves to find what they were looking for.

Operating Studio 1 and 2. Supplies. Laboratory 3 and 4. The offices of several professors. None of these doors was the correct one. Alishai scouted around the next corner, and Kah heard a thump, followed by the shattering of glass. When she turned the corner, she struggled to make sense of what she saw in the next hallway. A brain quivering on the floor with a boot print in the raw pink softness. Shattered glass and pink liquid spread around it. A metal contraption that looked almost like a cart on legs. Had it been some sort of . . . four-legged brain conveyance? Whatever its former use, it was now broken and useless, thanks to Alishai.

This new corridor had two sets of broad doors labeled Morgue 1 and Morgue 2. How many dead people were there, that the school required two morgues? The air was frigid and carried an unpleasant chemical smell that made Kah's eyes water. Alishai stood between the two sets of doors, and before she could make her choice, a man came around the next corner and stopped.

"You there!" he said, brusque and accusatory. "State your business."

Alishai seemed at a loss for words, so Chivarion said, "Um . . . not getting caught?" And then his elbow crunched into the man's nose.

"We talked about this," Alishai said.

"He's a guard. He would've raised the alarm. And look! He's not dead, and now we have another coat."

The unconscious man had fallen face-forward onto the ground, and now Chivarion pulled the coat from his limp arms and handed it to Kah. It was a good enough fit and definitely helped with the distinct chill that seeped out of the basement walls. As Chivarion stuffed the man into a broom closet, Kah felt around in the pockets and found two small metal boxes, one of which featured a big red button.

"They have alarms," she said, considering the button. The other device had a series of holes that suggested it had a speaker. "And . . ." She held it up. "They can talk to each other."

Chivarion closed the closet door, which required kicking and shoving various body parts back in when they wanted to flop out. "Ha! You see? Knocking him out was a smart move. Although I still say he'd make a great corpse."

Alishai sighed. "We're not killing innocents. Our foul deeds brought us here, and I for one don't need more reasons to be kept here." Standing before Morgue 1, she asked, "Everyone ready?" When they all nodded, she put a hand on the door and pushed; it swung inward.

"Oh, hells," she said.

31

CHIVARION

Still annoyed by the free body he'd been forced to leave behind, Chivarion pulled Liversliverer out before advancing through the swinging morgue doors. Alishai stood there, facing off with the scene she'd interrupted. A large and corpulent man was in the midst of an operation, holding a blood-wet scalpel and wearing a leather apron and a strange hat that magnified his eyes. Flanking him were two younger and smaller figures—students, probably. Bright lights shone down on their subject, a corpse that had been sectioned off like a cow in the butcher's window. The back wall was covered floor to ceiling by two rows of identical metal doors. There were several silver tables gleaming around the room, plus cabinets and rumbling machinery and yet more tanks full of bubbling liquid with various fleshy things bobbing around inside. Lamordia definitely had a *look*.

"This is a private session," the man with the scalpel barked. "Can I help you?"

"Oh, don't mind us," Alishai began, hands up. "We're just here for the—"

"Corpses," Chivarion finished, because honestly, anyone in this university was bound to be pretty smart and would soon notice he was holding a large sword.

"Grave robbers!" the man shouted in an accusatory fashion, ignoring the fact that he happened to be desecrating a corpse.

In response, Chivarion dropped his sword, picked up the nearest glass barrel of brains, and lobbed it at the shouting man. Even with such a clumsy object, Chivarion's aim was excellent, and the jar landed hard against the man's chest, walloping him over onto his back on the floor and miraculously not breaking. The two students briefly stared at each other before picking up scalpels and waving them threateningly. A shuffle of feet alerted Chivarion to the fact that Kah and Rotrog had joined them, and the four of them fanned out to block the double doors.

What happened next was so strange that Chivarion could only watch in fascination. Two machines that had been standing against the wall now advanced forward menacingly like soldiers in lockstep. They were men made of metal, gangly collections of pipes and tubes and joints. Where they should've had a head, each one featured a fishbowl, and in each fishbowl was a large white rat with bright red eyes like candy buttons. The rats sat in small chairs, using levers to drive their mechanical bodies, and their coordination and grace were slightly terrifying.

One of these rat machines advanced on Alishai, swinging up an arm and spraying flames directly into her face. The tiefling fell back screaming, her hair on fire like a candle; she dropped to the ground and rolled around. Rotrog already had his arms raised, but Kah said, "No grease, no fire, no acid," and he paused. The orc's mouth hung open for a moment, and then his lips curled in a smile. He murmured something guttural, waved his staff through the air, and aimed a sickly chartreuse ray of light at the bigger of the two students. At first, nothing happened. But then the human's face went mossy green and she doubled over, vomiting what looked like blood but smelled like borscht. The other student sidestepped the puddle and took aim, flinging his scalpel at Kah. The small blade stuck out of the kenku's shoulder, and she gasped and clicked her beak as she staggered backward. Chivarion reached over and yanked the blade out, then hurled it right back at the student. It landed in his belly, and it was his turn to gape like a fish.

"Okay?" Chivarion asked Kah.

"Don't like being stabbed, but I'll live," she replied. "Angry now."

Chirping aggressively, she raised her mace overhead, and light radiated out of it as she swung it into the guy who'd stabbed her. Fire enrobed his body, and he screamed and ran to a corner of the lab, where he pulled a lever that caused water to rain down on him.

"Don't kill students!" Alishai snapped.

"He stabbed Kah!" Chivarion snapped back. "That's just rude!"

While Chivarion was focusing on the student, another lab rat steered its machine toward him and raised its flamethrowing arm. Chivarion felt the rage flow into his body like rain wetting the desert sand. He welcomed it, that feeling of rushing fullness, and he swung an arm at the rat-machine, flinging it into the wall. The fishbowl burst in a shower of glass, and the rat leaped neatly to the floor, chittering in annoyance.

"Faster, Murder! Kill! Kill!" Chivarion screamed, and his tressym darted across the lab, leaping from table to table before landing on the rat and digging her teeth into its neck, shaking it back and forth until it went limp.

One rat down, one to go.

The slightly singed student who'd stabbed Kah was in action again and must've thought himself quite stealthy as he crawled across the lab behind a row of tables. As Alishai healed herself in a corner, Rotrog gleefully hopped over to block the human from leaving. After reaching into his cloak, the orc threw something and muttered a guttural word, and the human—

Broke out into laughter.

Sick, twisted . . . weird laughter.

Laughter that he was unable to control.

The man couldn't stand. Every time he tried, he fell over, rolling around on the floor, giggling and guffawing. A few small tarts and a feather were tangled in his hair.

"What did you do to him?" Chivarion asked.

"New spell I picked up from the witch book," Rotrog said. "I've been meaning to try it, but I needed the tarts. Thank goodness for the *River Dancer*'s hospitality, eh? Now, please hit him while he's down."

Chivarion grinned, and it was not pretty. "Gladly."

As the human rolled back and forth, tears squeezing from his eyes, Chivarion picked up one of the nearby tanks of liquid, tearing it away from its moorings in a spray of sparks and fluid. He slammed the tank on top of the man hard enough to bust the glass and send green glop and intestines all over the floor.

"If you have to kill, at least try not to mess up the bodies!" Alishai snapped, now fully healed and no longer singed.

"Dr. M wanted perfect corpses," Chivarion argued. "He was not what I would call perfect. Not after I stabbed him."

"Well don't bust up the other two!"

The student who had been vomiting must've understood this exchange, as she crawled for the door as fast as she could, heaving with every lunge forward. Chivarion neatly caught her by the back of the lab coat and held her up like a large kitten.

"What's the best way to kill someone while not busting them up?" he asked the room in general.

"Suffocation, probably," Alishai said. "But again—don't kill innocent students!"

Chivarion groaned in annoyance, and the woman vomited all over his arm; he dropped her, cursing at the smell. She landed on the floor and grabbed something, slamming it into his foot.

A scalpel.

She'd stuck a scalpel into his big toe!

Chivarion screeched and pulled out the scalpel, throwing it across the room. As he reached for the woman, who was definitely no longer innocent, one of the lab rat machines swung its arm down and stabbed him in the back with something he barely felt.

"Was that even a knife? Like, a tiny little rat knife?" he said, throwing his head back to laugh.

And that's when the room started to go all warm and swimmy. Chivarion exhaled and closed his eyes. It was like being drunk but without having to pay for or pee out all that meddlesome beer.

"Chivarion!" someone called from quite far away. "Chivarion!"

"He's over there," he said. "Nice fellow. A bit brutish, just between us rats."

"Can you heal him? I've got to—gugh!"

Chivarion was sitting on the floor now, leaning against something large and cold and soft. It felt a little like a bear that had been shaved, and they were both sitting in a puddle of gravy. A strange way to pass the time, but Chivarion had traveled widely and encountered many strange cultures. It was best just to give in, honestly.

Clank!

He looked up and saw a spindly metal man chopped in half. The metal man had a rat for a face, which was not a particularly nice face, although Chivarion had seen worse. As the metal man fell, the rat beat its tiny pink paws against the glass that contained it.

"You want out? Yes, well, no one likes a cage." With one tap of his fist, Chivarion broke the glass and released the rat. In response, the rat ran up his chest and tried to kiss him. Except it bit him. Quite near the jugular. Everyone here was *so rude*.

"Stop that," he said, swatting at the rat. "That's no way to say thank you."

Murder suddenly appeared and tussled with the rat. They hissed and spit and bit at each other, and Chivarion wanted to help but he couldn't move his arms at all. Only his eyeballs still moved. Something hurt at his neck, and there was a wet, hot sensation, a pinching there.

"Chivarion, come on!" someone called.

"I'm good, thanks. Just enjoying the show."

Someone cursed at him, and then he felt the loveliest, warmest glow, like sunbathing on the deck of a sailboat in the Shining Sea. He found that he was able to twitch his toes, then wiggle his fingers.

"Get up, you loaf!" someone said irritably. Alishai held out a hand, and he took it and stood. His entire body was tingling, and the front of his tunic was wet with blood.

"That rat injected you with something," the tiefling told him, her tail twitching. "But Murder got it."

He looked around to find both of the lab rat machines toppled and Murder licking blood off her paws. The two students and their instructor were nowhere to be found.

"Is the fight over?" he asked. "Did they get away?"

Alishai sighed and looked away. "We . . . we couldn't kill them. They're innocents. So we trussed them up and stuck them in empty drawers—that's what all those little doors on the wall are: body drawers. The man's still laughing, and the woman is still vomiting. We need to get our corpses and get out of here before someone notices."

"I don't mind killing them," he told her. "I've taken no oaths."

But she shook her head. "There's plenty of dead here without us adding to the work. Just start opening doors and pick a good one."

Kah and Rotrog were already working at it, opening the metal doors and pulling out rolling tables and their contents. Each door held a body, and each body was covered in a white cloth. It was the worst possible game of chance, opening a frosty-cold door to examine the frostbitten toes waiting under a sheet.

"Here's a good one," Kah said. "Female."

"I have one, too." Rotrog cleared his throat. "No, wait. Missing a head. Ick."

They eventually found four more workable bodies with most of their parts intact, but only then did they realize the error in their plan.

"There are four of us and five of them," Alishai noted.

"And one of us is a tremendously powerful barbarian," Chivarion reminded her. "I can carry two. I have two arms and two shoulders, after all. Also, really nice lats. And abs."

"And what of me?" Kah said. She'd healed her scalpel wound, but she was still significantly smaller than the smallest of the corpses, which had to weigh twice as much as she did.

"We should've brought a wagon. Did we see a wagon?" Alishai asked.

"The tables have wheels," Chivarion said. He'd noticed this while he sat on the floor, bleeding to death as a rat gnawed out his poison-filled jugular vein.

"So?" Alishai snapped.

"So we just treat the bodies the same way they do," Rotrog said, catching on. "Put each one on a table, cover it with a sheet, roll it out. If we put on the lab coats, we'll be less noticeable."

"You're an orc," Alishai reminded him.

"And you have horns, but we're all doing our best."

Kah kept her furry coat, while Chivarion, Alishai, and Rotrog struggled into lab coats. Rotrog wore the strange headgear that magnified eyesight, while Chivarion tied the leather apron on over his prominent bloodstain. They soon had their corpses neatly laid out on metal tables, covered with coats and draped with white cloths. Murder was curled up on Chivarion's table, which held two of the smaller bodies, although the woman was the lightest and reserved for Kah.

"Are we ready?" Alishai asked.

"Let's deliver these corpses to the crazy doctor," Chivarion said, then after a chuckle, "Wow, I didn't realize how absolutely unhinged that was going to sound. Whatever. Let's go."

Alishai pushed her table out the swinging doors and into the hallway. Kah followed, then Rotrog, then Chivarion—their usual formation, but hindered by carcasses. The tables rolled smoothly, their wheels recently greased. They rolled a lot of corpses up and down this hallway, apparently. Chivarion was fairly certain they were going to get away with it.

At least until they rounded the last corner to find the very thing they didn't want to see: a short man in a white lab coat who looked like he was accustomed to wielding authority, and beside him, a hulking monstrosity of a man that had to weigh as much as all of them put together.

"No, no," the smaller man said tiredly, flicking his fingers at them. "Back into the morgue. Come on. Turn around. You've got the time wrong."

From the very back, Chivarion couldn't quite see what was happening, why the little man wasn't sounding an alarm or shouting or throwing more rats at them.

"You heard him. Turn around," Alishai called gruffly. She purposefully strode to the other end of her table and pushed it toward Kah.

Confused, Chivarion went to the other side of his table and obligingly pushed it back into the morgue. Rotrog followed him, then Kah, then Alishai. The room was becoming quite crowded again. Chivarion checked that his corpses were well covered and moved to a defensive position, his hands grasping daggers but hidden behind the large mound of two dead bodies. The little man came last, huffing in annoyance while the large man beside him remained silent. Now Chivarion could see that the small man was very old and wore terribly thick glasses—and that he was exceedingly drunk.

The large man beside him was not actually a man, but another construct of flesh, as if all the biggest, most muscular men in the land had been stripped of parts and stuck together with rage and razor blades. His eyes were flat white and unseeing, but his hands were in mighty fists riddled with veins.

"Now, I told Professor Florence to get an early start, but this is ridih—"The small man hiccupped a few times. "Ridih! Ridih! Ridiculous. S'not even dawn yet! So put the lads back in the freezer and get out!"

Chivarion looked to Alishai, who shrugged. "Yes, Professor."

"Dean! I am no mere professor! I swear, no respect these days, none at all." He looked around the room, squinting, nearly falling over as his head swung. "And where has Professor Doth gotten to? He was doing a little experiment in here tonight, I'd thought. I was going to look in. Transplanting something or other. A giant centipede was involved. Doth! Doth, my friend, are you here?"

A muffled thump and a few giggles issued from one of the doors in the wall, and Chivarion cleared his throat and stomped a foot to cover it up.

"Can't count on anyone these days," the dean grumbled. He looked up at the hulk beside him. "Well, except those created to do our bidding, ha ha! Now, let's get going, you lot. I've got to lock up. Zacharias and I will wait outside. Never did like the smell of the—the—when you open the doors."

Wobbling, the little man walked a curving path toward the double doors, leaned on one, and fell out into the hallway. The hulking man did not help him but merely walked just behind him as if following secret orders.

"Can I—"

"You can't kill him," Alishai told Chivarion. "He's important, and I'm fairly certain the big one will attack if you try."

"Maybe just concuss him a little? Put him in a door? I could use a decent fight."

Alishai grinned. "He's blind and drunk, and the construct does not appear to be sentient. Let's just sneak out. Surely we can do that. All we have to do is get past an old, blind drunk and we're home free. If we pretend these fellows are our friends, and we've been carousing?"

Chivarion considered his two corpses and looked around the room. "Well, there are plenty of lab coats."

"And I've a spell I've been meaning to try," Rotrog said. "It could be fun."

"Fun," Alishai repeated, staring at the corpse under her sheet. "Yes. Such fun. Tra la." She looked to Kah. "Any ideas about your lady?"

Kah chirped a laugh. "Have a spell myself. Time to try it, as Akadi wills."

Chivarion found it challenging, shoving the stiff, cold limbs of his corpses into the arms of the lab coats, and he did not enjoy fastening the buttons over the jiggling bits of two strange men, one of whom had already been cut open once and sewn roughly back together. Still, he picked up one with his left arm and one with his right, hefting them up like two drinking buddies who'd had a few too many.

"Ready," he said, and he pushed out the door.

32

FIELLE

The *Tome of Strahd* was the key to everything.

Fielle read it cover to cover, concealing it within a larger book and sitting in a corner in case Strahd, as was his wont, crept up to surprise her. For all that he was cunning and powerful, he seemed to think her an idiot, or at least childlike in her intelligence. He was not aware that with two sharp minds living in one body, she was now twice as clever as he was. She humored him because it suited her. She simpered and blushed, or tried to, as she no longer had a pumping heart. She avoided him whenever possible, and Pidlwick helped her. He, too, was not as foolish as he seemed. She studied Strahd's story, she learned every inch of his castle, and she watched, and she waited, and the clockwork clown gamboled and danced in her wake.

While exploring the castle's spires, she followed her hunger to find a human rummaging through piles of junk. When she attempted to attack him, he fought her back with uncanny quickness, and they ended up facing each other like a cat and dog about to go another round. He had a stake in one hand and a silver dagger in the other, and yet he did not strike.

"You are Fielle, are you not?" he asked.

She hissed in surprise at being identified. "Perhaps. Why?"

"I have recently spoken to your friends. Alishai and the rest. I am Rudolph van Richten—an ally. I wish to aid in your escape."

Fielle allowed her fangs to retract and took on a less aggressive position. "My escape?"

"From Strahd. It is my understanding that he believes you are the current vessel of his once love, Tatyana, and that he wishes to make you his."

"This man knows too much," Tatyana whispered in her head.

"We need to learn what he knows," Fielle assured her. "We can use him."

Perhaps once, she would've focused on this man's kind face and the earnest way he blinked at her. Now she could only catalogue the places where his pulse beat nearest his skin and count the stakes hidden under his cloak.

"I will never belong to Strahd," she warned him. "I will end him."

"That is my goal as well," van Richten assured her. He peered at her face; it made her want to squirm. She was quite sick of men gazing into her eyes, looking for something they had no business finding. "Do you contain Tatyana's soul, my dear? Are you aware of it?"

She drew back. "What I contain is my business alone. Will you help me kill Strahd or no?"

"I have been hunting Strahd these many years, you understand. Even now I am searching for his journals, hoping they might inform me of some hidden weakness that might be exploited. If we could rid this world of his foul presence once and for all, I believe . . . things might be better. And you would be free. Your friends are on a quest to make that happen."

"Free," she mused. "What is that like, I wonder? I have always been caged. First by my father, now by Strahd. I would do anything to know true freedom."

Van Richten smiled, looking very much like a kindly grandfather, if a kindly grandfather were armed with dozens of weapons. "Then perhaps you can help me find his journal. I hear it is an old book with a leather cover, and—"

"Do not trust him," Tatyana growled.

But Fielle was willing to use every weapon she could find. She withdrew the book from a deep pocket she'd sewn into her skirts. "The *Tome of Strahd*," she said simply. "I know it well by now. So here is what you must do. In these pages, Strahd discusses several items steeped in magic that might be used to cause him harm. I cannot use any of them myself, but if you can find them, we can work together. I have a spell that will ensnare him, but I need someone living to wield any such magical weapon. In my current state, anything that would harm him would also harm me."

Van Richten's eyes shone like a small boy at his first Shieldmeet. "Yes! The tome! I've been looking for it for so long. I've heard tell of such weapons. May I?" He held out his hands for the book, and Fielle snarled.

"I will not give it up, but I will tell you what I know. Our best chance, I think, is the Holy Symbol of Ravenkind."

He nodded eagerly. "I have seen this totem before. Its effigy lies around the neck of a statue in the hallway. But where is the original, I wonder?"

It was Fielle's turn to blink at him as if he were the idiot child. "Did you not consider that perhaps the effigy you saw is the true symbol? Go and see if you can take it. Why would there be a copy?"

The old man shook his head as if he were trying to shake loose a thought. "I will go and see, yes. But how does it work?"

And so Fielle told the old man her plan, or part of it, and he believed every word. She laid out every step and told him which parts he might play. She interrogated him on his strengths and weaknesses, his spells and weapons. Together, they worked through the details of a very specific plot, and he assured her that he was willing and able to perform every service she requested.

"If you betray me, I will kill you," she warned him. "I see you—monster killer, vampire hunter."

"But you are no monster," he protested. "You are an innocent. A victim. Your friends spoke highly of your kindness, your sweetness, your generosity. They want to help you, and so do I."

"You are very brave, to help us," she said, forcing her lips into a grateful smile.

Van Richten bowed. "And you are brave, to face such a foe. Now, let us go together and see if the Symbol of Ravenkind is true."

Fielle drew back. "Oh, no. If the count found us together, he would kill you and doubt me. We cannot meet again until it is time to destroy him. I will do my part, and you will do yours, and we will meet tomorrow at dusk in the chapel."

"But there are so many ways this could go wrong!" The old man began to pace, and it only made Fielle want to chase him and pin him down like a skittering rat. "Perhaps it isn't the real symbol. What if I can't obtain these other objects you require? This stratagem requires more planning. And it would definitely be wise to wait until your friends return—"

"No!"

He blinked at her, again startled.

She recomposed herself, laced her fingers together to keep them from growing their claws. "It must be tomorrow night," she said sweetly. "I cannot live in this purgatory any longer. I must be free of him or die trying."

"Just a little patience—"

She was on him in a heartbeat, his throat clutched in her talons. "*I have been patient.*"

She felt a tiny point of heat against her belly and looked down to see a silvered knife pressing into the cloth of her dress.

"I, too, have shown great patience," van Richten said. "And I do not wish to die so easily. But I will do as you ask. Not because I believe it is the correct course of action, but because the longer you are under his spell, the less you are yourself. I can see it—your humanity leaving you."

Fielle released her hold on his neck, and he removed the tip of his magicked knife from her belly.

"You're not as sweet as you look," she said.

He tipped his hat. "And I think, perhaps, neither are you. Barovia tends to do that to a person, my dear."

Fielle turned on her heel and left, faster than any human could run. She had traps to lay and servants to drain and vampire spawn to kill. If this van Richten fellow could follow directions and fight as well as his weapons suggested, she just might have a chance.

"Do you think we can count on him?" Tatyana asked. "I seem to think . . . there's something familiar about him. He has tried to help before."

"And did he succeed?"

A long silence.

"I can't remember. We should ask the Tarokka."

Fielle did not go to her room, which had no door. Rahadin and Strahd often appeared there suddenly as if trying to catch her unawares. Instead, she went to the very top of the tower, a place where Pidlwick always seemed happiest. She took the old, worn deck from her pocket and shuffled the cards, thinking about the battle to come. Now that she had the tome, she knew more about Strahd than he did about her; not only that, but she suspected that the moment he learned she had his journal, he would fly into a senseless, bestial rage unlike anything she'd seen of him so far. She smiled to herself, picturing the smooth, controlled count rendered an animal.

The first card was the Master of Swords.

The second card was the Master of Glyphs.

The third card was the Tempter.

Fielle's sharp smile was genuine. That was exactly what she'd hoped to see.

33

ROTROG

Yes, Rotrog was an orc, and yes, he was stronger than most creatures, even if he rarely used his muscles. But that didn't mean he wanted to carry a corpse around, forced to smell its weeping fluids and rotting flesh. He didn't know how Chivarion could stand being draped with two of the disgusting things. Instead, he pulled a bit of string and wood from a pouch in his chatelaine, spoke the right words, and mentally commanded his unseen servant to carry the corpse. He hadn't used this spell before, but . . . well, it helped that there wasn't currently an emergency. As long as he could think clearly, his magic was straightforward.

"It should look like the corpse is walking," he told the servant mentally, because saying it out loud would've been completely deranged. "While you carry it with ease. Any passersby should believe the dead body is alive and acting perfectly normal for an alive person."

He had no idea how the spell worked or what unseen force might be obeying his command—or how clever that unseen force might be. Luckily, it did exactly as he'd asked. The corpse sat up suddenly, hinging at the waist, and hopped off the table to stand on its two bare feet. Its arms hung loosely, and its upper body turned from side to side with curiosity.

"Act normal," he reminded it. "Walk casually. I'll follow you, you follow the drow."

The body nodded in a jolly fashion and walked out the door, neglecting to push it open with an arm but rather allowing the door to bounce off its face. Yes, well, Rotrog had not given it directions for opening doors.

"If you must open a door, use your hands," he reminded it.

Just outside the morgue doors, the corpse turned to the opposite doors and pushed them hard with both hands, making them swing away and then back, knocking the corpse, again, in the face. Its head flung back dramatically, and its upper body turned to face Rotrog as if to say, "Now what?"

"No more doors. Follow the drow. *Act normal.*"

The corpse bobbed its head and walked down the hall with an almost bouncy motion. It got so close behind Chivarion that it trod on the back of his boot, and he turned around to glare at it.

"Don't step on the drow. Walk behind him."

The corpse obediently waited before walking again.

Satisfied that his spell was successful, Rotrog stopped to hold open the morgue door and see if Kah could handle her corpse. The kenku was doing a spell of her own, and soon her corpse jumped off the table and gave a soft, zombielike moan as it staggered toward the orc.

"What spell is that?" Rotrog asked her.

She ducked her head as if embarrassed. "Animate Dead. A new one. Not my usual, but necessary."

The corpse—the sort-of-zombie—roughly shoved Rotrog with its shoulder as it lurched down the hall. Kah followed it, chirping directions, but it wasn't nearly as eager and obedient as Rotrog's unseen servant. As for Alishai, she hoisted her female corpse's arm over her shoulder as Chivarion had and dragged it out the door, its feet scraping along the stone. Convinced that everyone could keep up, Rotrog jogged back to his corpse right as it sloppily rounded the last corner toward the door that led outside. They were so close—so close!

And now they just had to get past the drunken dean and his pet monster.

Chivarion shoved his corpses through the door and into the night, and Rotrog hurried ahead to hold the door for his unseen servant before it could draw attention to itself. His corpse tripped on his foot on the way out and fell flat on its face, flipping up the lab coat and revealing its shiny white buttocks.

"Get up! Get up and cover the corpse's personal areas!" Rotrog thought.

The corpse bounced up to standing and put two hands over its crotch.

"Not like that. Just—just walk. Don't do anything weird with the hands."

The corpse's hands went to its sides and flopped back and forth as it walked, following Chivarion. The dean sat on a nearby bench, his enormous guardian standing beside him.

"I say, is that Olenko? I thought he had an accident," the dean called.

"Uh, a small one," Chivarion said.

"He got kicked in the chest by a horse, didn't he?"

Chivarion could only say, "Um," so Rotrog called out, "Bah, nothing the healers and half a barrel of wine can't fix. He's not feeling a thing after a night of carousing!"

"Hear hear!" The dean held up a silver flask and kicked his feet. "Wait. That one looks familiar, too. Is that my Uncle Yusef?"

He pointed to Rotrog's corpse, and Rotrog mentally commanded his unseen servant to walk with some decorum.

"He didn't tell me his name," Rotrog said. "But he sure can put down some, er, human alcohol liquor!"

"My Uncle Yusef doesn't drink." The dean hopped up and wobbled a bit before marching toward Rotrog, who hoped the magnifying lenses and surgical headgear hid his more orcish features.

"Go on along, friends, I'll meet you there," Rotrog called to the rest of his party. They were so close—he could see the boat, its gangplank waiting welcomingly. Kah's zombie slogged down the hill, tripping and groaning, but that only served to highlight her supposed drunkenness. Alishai picked up her pace and swung her corpse into a full child's carry, and even though Rotrog's heart was thumping like crazy, he knew that once Chivarion and Alishai had deposited their corpses on the boat, they would return to save him. They wouldn't leave him, or even leave him alone to deal with the dean.

This—

This was a new thought.

Rotrog had friends, and he trusted them.

They wouldn't leave him behind.

He knew this with a surety that stunned him.

"Uncle Yusef?" The dean peered up, adjusting his thick glasses.

"Hold very still," Rotrog commanded his servant. "Try to give the corpse some dignity."

In response, the corpse went very stiff and threw up a hand in a salute, nearly slapping the dean in the face.

"Once a military man, always a military man," the dean said. "But you certainly smell pickled. When did you take up drinking?"

Rotrog grimaced, wracking his brain for a spell, but he did not know how to make a dead man speak. He did know one spell, but . . .

Oh, this was about to get messy.

He moved behind the corpse, made a subtle gesture, and . . .

Grease flew from Rotrog's fingertips over the corpse's shoulder and splattered all over the dean. To anyone watching, and not too closely, and definitely drunkenly, it certainly looked like a drunk man in a lab coat had vomited all over the dean, his fancy black robes now positively covered with goo.

As the dean flapped at his robes and dropped his glasses from oiled-up hands, Rotrog commanded his unseen servant to run to the boat.

But the unseen servant, unfortunately, was just as careless as anyone else, and the corpse slipped in the puddle of grease and landed on its back, the lab coat flying up to expose—

Well, there went its dignity.

"Run!" Alishai shouted from the gangplank.

"Run!" Rotrog mentally screamed at his unseen servant.

The corpse slipped and slid as it tried to regain its feet. "Pull the dean down," Rotrog commanded it, and it reached for the tangle of robes, and the dean, too, fell down in the puddle of grease.

"Zacharias, help me!" the dean called, and the enormous flesh golem stomped toward him, huge hands reaching. Rotrog kicked his corpse, causing it to roll away from the reaching giant, and then, as he doubted he could properly stand and run, he, too, rolled away in the grass.

"Crawl!" he commanded the servant, and the corpse skittered obscenely on hands and feet, its white bottom glowing in the night and its rucked-up lab coat wet with grease. Not trusting himself to stand, Rotrog rolled over and over toward the ship. The grease shed onto the grass, and soon he felt steady enough to stand and run the last few feet. When he again commanded the unseen servant to run, it galloped toward him on hands and feet. He pointed at the ship, and it trotted up the gangplank and onto the deck like a faithful hound. Rotrog was the last one up, and he felt an immense shiver of relief roll over him as his feet hit the gangplank.

Right up until something grabbed his robes and jerked.

His fists tightened on the railing, and he looked back to see the enormous flesh golem clutching the hem of his robes. The dean was hurrying toward the boat, shouting, "Stop! Stop right there! I see what you're doing! Thieves! Hold him, Zacharias!"

"Rotrog, use fire!" Chivarion called. "They hate fire!"

And once, Rotrog would've growled at anyone who dared tell him what to do, anyone who thought they knew more than he professed to know. But now he stopped panicking and raised one hand from the rail, and a bright ball of fire emerged from his fingertips and slammed Zacharias in the face. The flesh golem released his robes, and Rotrog ran up the gangplank as fast as he could. Zacharias swatted at his enflamed face and danced around like an angry baby, and the dean jumped up and down and shouted, but the boat dropped the gangplank and took off at a quick clip. Rotrog sat down on the deck and drew in a deep breath. The corpse collapsed beside him on its back and went totally limp, the unseen servant apparently quite done with its work.

"Will they send ships after us?" Alishai asked one of the sailors.

He laughed, showing sharp rat teeth. "Nothin' they have at the university can catch the doctor's ship. And they know that if they tried, we'd blow 'em out of the water. The doctor's got munitions they can't even imagine. The only danger is gettin' the corpses out. You did better than most. Zacharias usually tears a few folks in half, at least." With a sullen glare at Chivarion, he hunched up his shoulders. "You'd best be glad the doctor pays us well and needs bodies or else you'd be tastin' our steel. That purple feller gave me a black eye."

"And it looks terribly dashing," Chivarion told him with a wink. "Sorry about that, by the way."

"Apology not accepted." The sailor spit over the railing and gestured for them to get off the deck.

Rotrog was uncomfortable with how close he'd come to being torn in half, but they were already so far away from the university that the flesh golem was just a pale lump against the darker city. With the corpses dumped in something like a heap, everyone went to sit on the metal benches. Rotrog could barely hold his eyes open, but he gave it his best effort. Before he knew it, the boat was shuddering to a stop, and he woke up with his head pillowed on Alishai's shoulder. Little Kah was slumped against him, and Chivarion was on his back on the ground, his white hair flowing over Rotrog's feet and the tressym curled up on his chest. They'd all fallen asleep in a pile, and . . . well, it was honestly kind of nice. Rotrog didn't want to wake anyone, but the sailor had no such compunction.

"Ahoy-hoy!" he called in the door. "Landfall!"

Kah bolted off Rotrog's side, Chivarion bounced to standing, his tressym in his hands, and Alishai shifted her shoulders and stretched as if pretending they had not all been snoring together. Pretending they had not all been recently sweetly entangled, they went out to the deck, where the rosy fingers of dawn painted their pile of corpses in delicate pastel tones of pink and lavender. The sailors were tying the ship up to the dock, and the gangplank was already attached. Two carts had been thoughtfully placed beside the dock, rolling tables much like those in the morgue, which seemed safer than the swiftly rolling boxes of fish juice.

"Shall I?" Rotrog pointed his staff at the corpses, but Alishai shook her head.

"Nah. Save your magic. We can use muscle for now."

She and Chivarion carried the corpses to the carts, piling them on awkwardly, all except for Kah's corpse, which walked on its own. Alishai and Chivarion pushed the carts, and Kah walked between them, shoving an arm or leg back onto each cart as needed, her corpse marching along behind her and Rotrog walking last of all. Once they reached the castle proper, the homunculus met them at the door and led them through the foyer.

"You were successful, it seems." The voice box sounded pleased. "An excellent haul. Did you have any difficulties?"

"We interrupted an operation in the morgue," Alishai said. "Three university people. We left them mostly unharmed. And then the dean gave us a spot of trouble—"

"The dean." The homunculus scowled, baring its teeth, before flying up to press the call button for the lift. "Horrid little man. I had a deal with his predecessor. Please tell me you put this one to sleep. I should very much enjoy having access to his brain. Is he among your collection?"

Rotrog didn't want to know what Dr. Mordenheim would've done with the dean's corpse.

"No. He was drunk, so we used . . . subterfuge to slip past him."

The metal doors opened to reveal the same coatrack man. Alishai and Chivarion maneuvered the carts into the car. Along with four people, a homunculus, and the coatrack man, they just barely fit, and the smell in the small, enclosed room was not pleasant.

"To the lab, please." The homunculus looked up at them. "It was I who created the dean's bodyguard, you know. And unfortunately, as usual, I performed my task all too well. Perhaps your next mission will be an assassination. If you escaped Zacharias unscathed, I'd like to see you go back and . . ." Another scowl. "Scathe him."

The coatrack man pulled the lever to open the doors, and they stepped out into the lab. Rotrog drew a deep breath before remembering that the lab air was no better, scented as it was with the odors of rancid flesh, pickling fluids, ozone, and chemical tinctures. Dr. Mordenheim looked exactly as she had before, down to the same stained lab suit and heavy leather apron. Did she sleep, Rotrog wondered? Or was she perhaps more like her creations than it appeared?

She examined the bodies with brisk efficiency, holding up an arm, pushing back an eyelid, and prodding the stitches on one corpse's chest. "Yes, this is good," she said. "I take it you've chosen the vessel for your friend's second soul? Put that one on the operating table." Then she made a face. "A zombie. You've brought me a zombie."

Kah's beak clicked. "Can't you . . . unzombify it?"

Dr. Mordenheim closed her eyes and shook her head. "Idiots. Why is the world so full of idiots?" She pointed at Chivarion. "You. Cut her head off."

"Kah? No! She's my friend—"

"The zombie. Cut the zombie's head off. The cleaner, the better."

Before anyone could protest, Chivarion had pulled out Liversliverer and sliced off the zombie's head, one clean cut through the neck. Rotrog flinched away from the blood, but there was none. Dr. Mordenheim caught the head before it fell.

"Put her on the pile," she said patiently.

Chivarion placed the body of the ex-zombie on the pile, to which Dr. Mordenheim added her head. Dusting off her hands, she returned to the operating table where the female corpse Alishai had collected now lay, and she reached for an apparatus that included a face shield, magnifiers, and copious wires. After fitting it over her cropped white hair, she picked up a saw.

"If you do not wish to watch this part, I can have my servants bring tea to the salon."

"Tea?" Chivarion made a face. "Is there anything stronger?"

The doctor started up the saw, and flecks of blood sprayed the room.

"We'll take tea." Alishai grabbed Chivarion's arm and steered him toward the lab door, where the homunculus waited. Rotrog swiftly followed, plugging his ears as the saw bit into bone.

The salon was a pleasant room one floor above the lab. They couldn't avoid hearing the various machinery the doctor employed, but it was thankfully far enough away that they didn't have to see anything or smell anything—or get splattered by anything. Several elegant couches and tall-backed chairs surrounded a low table, and Rotrog claimed a chair and immediately began to doze. Kah gently shook his arm when a servant entered with a tray of triangular sandwiches and dainty cookies. The servant, a young girl with two beautifully formed mechanical arms, deftly poured tea and coffee as requested and bobbed a polite curtsey before disappearing. Rotrog selected a tiny triangle of sandwich and before long had devoured an entire mound of such delicacies. He'd never tasted anything like it, pillowy bread encasing odd cheeses and creamy vegetable whips, but it was pleasant to eat something other than Chivarion's fish stew. Once he was full, he fell asleep again and did not wake up until Murder screeched in his ear. By this time, the tressym's customary greeting was no longer startling.

"My creation is ready," the homunculus said smugly. "Please join me."

Back in the lab, Dr. Mordenheim stood beside her table, stitching up the corpse's neck with small, careful sutures. The body had been dressed in the sort of thing human women wore, a greenish dress with lots of lacy bits that made Rotrog vaguely nervous.

"The vessel is ready," Dr. Mordenheim said, biting off a bit of thread and drawing a hand grandly over the woman's body. "A device resides in her chest—a vessel for the vessel, you might say, a box designed to contain a soul. The only tricky part will involve connecting the vessel to the person who currently contains two souls and pumping the second soul into the new body."

Dr. Mordenheim held up a strange machine riddled with tubes and wires. One particularly long wire led to the corpse, and another ended in a very large glass syringe.

"You will place the vessel and the living body side by side. It will be best if the living body—if she closes her eyes or looks away, or perhaps if she is asleep. You must insert the syringe into the living body's heart and then press this button." She pantomimed ramming the enormous syringe into the corpse's heart, then pointed to a very large and obvious button on the upper chest of the corpse. "That will begin the transfer. The living person will not be harmed. Well, if you insert the needle correctly. If you insert the needle incorrectly, she could absolutely be harmed. But there is always a risk to such procedures. Once the two bodies are connected and the button is pushed, the device will operate accordingly, and the second soul will travel into the new vessel via this tube." She showed them the tube running from the syringe to the corpse, slipping under the neckline of its dress. "It could not be easier."

Rotrog thought that there *had* to be a way that was easier, but as he didn't know it, he did not argue. He was also fairly certain that

Alishai would be the one to perform this procedure, which meant that he could stand in a corner and try to ignore what was occurring while pretending to be occupied with something erudite.

"And now, our bargain complete, I have one more question. Or perhaps a better word is . . . requirement."

The doctor's smile was cold as a dead slug. With one gesture of her hand, all the doors slammed shut, their latches ramming home. Bars slammed down over every window. Flesh golems, previously hidden in the shadows, emerged menacingly to stand, swaying, waiting, their mouths hanging open and their hands twitching.

"I want you to go on one more quest for me," the doctor continued. "There is someone I very much need to find, a woman named Elise who stole something precious from me. You have proven you're more than capable."

"We don't—" Alishai began.

"I wasn't finished," the doctor snapped. "Accept this quest, or you won't be leaving Schloss Mordenheim alive."

34

ALISHAI

The flesh golems moved to flank them, slopping and oozing all too much like the boneless monsters they'd encountered in the abattoir in Barovia. The homunculus watched, its tail twitching. The doctor's hand moved to her bone saw, but her smile did not change.

Alishai knew what she had to do. She stepped closer to the operating table and gave Kah a significant look, hoping the clever kenku would understand what was happening.

"Tell us more of this quest," Alishai said. "We make all our decisions as a group."

"You have little choice, but very well; I shall indulge you. I once loved a woman with an incurable disease," the doctor began with cold precision. She put down the saw and stepped toward one of the closed windows, the glass showing a sudden snowstorm. The temperature in the room dropped, and Alishai shivered. "Her name was Elise, and she was dying, and no doctors could help her. On her behalf, I worked feverishly to create a device that might keep her alive forever: the Unbreakable Heart. It required many . . . sacrifices."

The rest of the group crowded close as if drawn into the doctor's story, and Alishai had to stop herself from smiling; they were waiting for her. Chivarion had his tressym against his chest, and he looked to Alishai and raised his eyebrows. She jerked her chin at the corpse-vessel, and he winked at her and nodded knowingly; she gave that a 50 percent chance that he understood and a 50 percent chance he thought she was flirting. Next she looked to Rotrog, then at the various golems and machines surrounding them. When she wiggled her fingers, he nodded and grinned, showing his tusks. Kah simply wrapped her fingers around her mace.

Dr. Mordenheim was caught up in her own tragedy, ignoring them all as she stared at the snow beyond the window glass. "But as my grand creation sat cold in my beloved's chest, the constables infiltrated my lab, accusing me of various foul deeds. I barely had time to pull the lever. Electricity arced into the device as they pulled me away, and I watched Elise rise from death and spring from the table, the Unbreakable Heart glowing golden in her rib cage. I had succeeded, but I was dragged from my laboratory before I could speak to her. I fell unconscious, and when I awakened, I was here in Lamordia, and Elise was gone. She has recently been spotted in the icy wastes of the Sleeping Beast. I want you to bring her to me, and then you can claim your prize here. I will keep the tressym as collateral."

She looked to Alishai. "I will assume you agree?"

"No."

The doctor's head jerked back as if she had been slapped.

"No one in Lamordia tells me no. No one *can*."

"Looks like she just did," Chivarion said.

The doctor again reached for her bone saw, her smile curving into a sneer. "We'll see how far—"

She did not finish that sentence, because Kah's mace caught her square in the temple in a fiery flash of light. The doctor's body flew through the air, knocking over a deeply confused flesh golem.

"Rotrog, Lightning Bolt!" Alishai called.

The orc grinned ferociously as a wave of lightning blossomed from a crystal rod wrapped with a bit of fur in his hand, and he waved it like a conductor's baton. Bright blue-white light enrobed the three nearest constructs, exploding onto the wet ground at their feet and spreading out to a second wave of victims. Several machines and tubes burst into flame. The flesh golems that remained unharmed by this electric wave huddled back as if terrified of the dancing fire.

"The up-and-down box," Alishai shouted as Chivarion carefully hefted the vessel, draping the tube and syringe around his neck like a scarf. "We've got to get out of here!"

She ran, and they followed. Any creatures left alive in the lab were too frightened to give chase and instead huddled around their fallen mistress. In the hall, Alishai pressed the button for the box repeatedly and took her glaive in both hands as the machine laboriously rumbled upward. When the cage doors opened to reveal the coat-rack man, she smacked him sideways with her weapon. He landed heavily and, as she'd guessed he would, struggled to stand again.

Kah pointed her mace at him and said, "Don't move." He quivered and obeyed.

At the elevator controls, Alishai pushed the lever downward and readied her weapon for whatever they would face in the foyer. She had to get her friends safely out of the castle and into the Mists, and they had to ensure that the vessel remained unharmed or all this work and seasickness had been for nothing.

The box dinged cheerily on the ground floor, but when the doors opened, there stood the worst thing Alishai could imagine, something for which she had not planned—

Zacharias the angry flesh golem and the dean, now sober and flanked by two constables.

"You there!" the dean shrieked. "Stop right now and get arrested!"

Alishai slammed the lever back upward right as Chivarion said, "Um, no thanks."

Zacharias attempted to reach into the box, but Murder leaped into the air and slashed at his outstretched fingers with her claws, making the giant man rear back with a screech of pain. The doors closed successfully, and the box again chugged upward. But this time, Alishai did not stop it on the floor containing the lab; there was neither safety nor egress to be found there. Instead, she let it take them as far up as they could go. She did not know what they might find in the castle's heights, but it had to be better than an angry doctor and an angrier monster.

When the doors opened, a wild wind licked at her hair and sleet drove into her eyes. They were on the roof, and as they advanced out onto the snow-covered stone, they scanned for a new wave of Dr. Mordenheim's monstrous servants. The area was flat and empty but for several bulky shapes covered in ragged tarps.

"Is this where she keeps her extra body parts? On ice?" Chivarion peeked under the fabric of one such lump. He turned back and grinned. "Even better, actually. I mean, most things are better than piles of body parts, but . . . well, look."

Still hefting the vessel in her heavy dress, he whipped off the tarp to reveal a machine. But not the sort of machine they'd seen thus far, merging living body parts with metal limbs and glass jars. No, this was a vehicle—

A flying vehicle.

Alishai hurried over and inspected it more closely, and her hopes sunk. "It's missing a wing," she said sadly. "And it's too small."

"But there are four more tarps," he pointed out. "So don't get sad yet."

Her heart filled with hope, Alishai moved to the next lump and found another flying machine, this one with a sort of whirligig on top instead of wings on the sides. Rotrog uncovered one that looked like a giant cone attached to a harness.

"Here!" Kah called. "This one—it could work!"

They hurried to look at her discovery, which appeared to be a gliding machine with taut skin wings shaped like those of a bat. It was going to be a tight fit, especially with the extra corpse, but the passenger compartment was shaped to fit several flesh golems the size of Zacharias.

"This does not appear safe," Rotrog said, running his fingers along a fragile wing.

"Nothing here is," Chivarion argued. "Why would this be any different?"

Alishai checked the final lump, which was indeed a pile of frozen body parts, before walking to the castle wall and looking out. The sky overhead was filled with swirling snow, but thick white fog pressed against the stone walls below as if the Mists had crept close to hear Dr. Mordenheim's tale of woe. "All we have to do is get into the Mist together and van Richten's ring should guide us back to Barovia. Remember how there didn't seem to be an up or down when we were on the *River Dancer*? Perhaps time and space work differently when you're . . . inside."

"And then perhaps we won't crash and die," Chivarion finished cheerfully. "Maybe. I mean, I'm willing if you are."

Rotrog sighed. "If it's Zacharias, the law, and an army of flesh golems or a possible plummet to the sea, I also choose the possible plummet."

"I choose wings," Kah said quietly. "I always choose wings."

They loaded the corpse in first, strapping her down carefully, then crowded into the wooden contraption. Alishai took the pilot's seat, experimenting with the two controls until she understood how they moved the wings and tail. She slipped van Richten's mist token onto her finger, hating how the metal ring's cold started spreading into her flesh and up her wrist like ice freezing in her veins. Chivarion tucked Murder against his chest, murmuring to her in a baby voice, and Kah and Rotrog took their seats.

Across the roof, the roof door slammed open and Zacharias unfolded to stand defiantly in the snow, the dean and two constables squeezing out to stand around him.

"I said stop!" the dean called. "Stop them!"

"So how do you get this thing going?" Chivarion asked.

Alishai couldn't find a button for that sort of thing and belatedly noted there were no wires or machinery attached. "Um . . . brute force?"

He laughed and placed Murder on the floor. "Rotrog, come on. Help me heft it. Use your muscles for once."

But Rotrog didn't budge.

He did, however, grin.

"Who needs muscles when unseen servants exist? Just pretend I'm doing the work."

With a shrug, Chivarion got out and gamely lifted one side of the glider as the other side magically rose up as if hefted by someone not nearly as strong but trying very hard. As Chivarion walked toward the ledge, Rotrog fiddled with a little stick man, and Zacharias stalked across the roof, trailed by the dean and the constables.

"A little faster," Chivarion murmured, and the unseen servant struggled to keep up with him but did not fail, and then the glider sat balanced on the ledge. Zacharias was almost upon them, too close a call for Alishai's taste. "This is going to be awkward, but what isn't?" the drow murmured.

Alishai wrapped her hands around the controls, her feet braced, and Chivarion leaped into the glider. With his weight added, the wooden contraption leaned forward, nose down, and fell off the edge of the castle.

INTERLUDE:

THE MISTS

Few creatures found solace in the Mists.
They had been specifically designed to inspire confusion and breed fear, to swallow hope, to disappoint all who craved clear borders and happy endings. The tiefling, the orc, the drow, and the tressym were appropriately and deliciously fearful.

And yet—

One bright soul entered the Mists and, for a brief and shining moment, was filled with joy.

As the glider plummeted downward, Kah felt her tummy swoop, and she raised her arms and flapped them, her eyes closed as she imagined diving like a falcon, falling with the surety of a creature designed to soar again, the wind streaming through her feathers. In the pilot's seat, Alishai grunted and pulled on her controls, and the glider pulled out of a dive and into an upward climb.

It was the most beautiful feeling Kah had ever experienced.

"I'm flying," she whispered. "I have wings, and I'm flying."

And then they were swallowed by opaque white.

As quickly as Kah's dream came true, it shattered.

In the Mists, there was no up or down, no past or future, no east or west or north or south. The Mists would happily deny the little kenku further access to her life's dream. White fog enveloped the glider, and then Kah might've been wrapped in a coffin's fine velvet for all the sensation she was allowed.

No more swoops, no more wind, no more floating.

"Oh," she groaned.

Unable to see a single thing, still the creatures around her understood her sadness. The drow reached forward, putting a hand on her shoulder. The orc patted the space between them until he found her arm, and then he patted that, too. The tiefling didn't dare release her controls, but her heart went out to Kah, a pulse of pain on behalf of her friend flashing from her heart like the beam of a lighthouse. Even the tressym left the safety of the drow's lap to twine around the kenku's ankles, lending the comfort of her warmth and the rumble of her purr.

Kah's light could not be dimmed.

She had flown—for just a brief moment, she had flown.

And now she had friends who cared about her.

That was a lot more than she'd ever hoped for before she came to this place named for dread. This was her great adventure.

35

ALISHAI

It was a most peculiar feeling.

The Mists held Alishai suspended, as if she'd fallen into the ocean without getting wet. Her eyes saw only opaque white. Strange sounds echoed from the nothingness—howling wolves, trees thrashing in a thunderstorm, screaming children. The only reliable sensation was the Mist talisman on her finger, the frozen ring drawn to its home. She allowed it to guide her hand like a compass pointed to true north.

All at once, the Mists cleared, and the glider emerged in the chill, gray skies of Barovia. Castle Ravenloft was just ahead, and Alishai fiddled with the controls, trying to choose some safe place to land amid the rocky outcrops and stone spires. Nowhere was safe, and they were losing altitude, so she made a grim decision and aimed for the biggest stained glass window.

"You're not thinking about—" Rotrog began.

"Shut up and hold on. And close your mouth if you don't want to eat glass."

The glider crashed through the window, plummeted downward,

and landed hard. The machine somehow remained intact as it skidded across stone, fetching up against a solid wall and smashing apart. Slightly dazed, Alishai opened her eyes and realized they'd somehow crash-landed in a crypt.

She immediately recognized their surroundings.

They were back in Castle Ravenloft, although she had never seen this part of the castle before—it must've been the catacombs, judging by the coffins. The deep chill suggested they were underground, and the ceiling appeared to be old, tarnished gold that might've been worth a pretty penny to anyone able to climb thirty feet, fight through a haze of bats, and pry the aged metal away.

She stood among the wreckage of the glider. "Is everyone okay? How's the corpse?"

"Nice of you to inquire about the living first," Rotrog said, standing and rubbing his rump.

Chivarion unbuckled the vessel and gave it a brief inspection. "She appears to be, well, still dead of course, but the machine is intact." He looked to Kah, worry written in his features. "Kah, are you . . . ?" He trailed off, as if unaware how to ask about feelings.

Kah stood, looking down at the feathers on her arms. "At least I got to feel it. Once." After a moment of what felt like mourning, she looked back up. "I'll be fine. But what of Fielle? Where are we?"

"In the crypt of King Barov von Zarovich," Rotrog read before moving to the other coffin. "And the queen, Ravenovia van Roeyen. Strahd's parents, do you think?"

"Barov and Ravenovia," Kah chirped. "Barovia."

"I've been in here before. Well, almost." Everyone looked to Chivarion. "There's some kind of magic in the antechamber that zaps you right back to the stairs. So I looked in here and thought, wonder who those fancy people are? And now we know."

"Kah, are there—"

The kenku had her eyes closed and held up a finger as she murmured a prayer to Akadi. "No traps," she finally said. "Not in here."

"Good. Chivarion, if you'll carry the, uh, lady, and we'll take her to . . ." Alishai paused. Where? Where was safe? Now that they knew their host was a vampire, and supposing he and his servants knew every inch of this castle, where might a doctored corpse escape his notice?

Nowhere. They just had to hope that Strahd was away or distracted. Actually, now that she thought about it, he had to be away. No one who heard the cacophany of a flying machine crashing through a very expensive window could keep away from surveying the damages, especially someone so interested in keeping tabs on the comings and goings of his domain.

Chivarion hefted the vessel. "Let's take her to Fielle's room. She has to go there at dawn, if not before. That's how vampires work. Unless anyone has any better ideas?"

Rotrog opened his mouth and raised a finger—

And then shut his mouth and nodded. "A reasonable suggestion."

Alishai went first, walking up several steps and through a series of crypts that she had no interest in investigating further. There had to be dozens of wide columns laid out in a checkerboard throughout the enormous catacombs, holding up the arched ceiling, which was furred with thousands of bats, shivering like a living velvet carpet. Each column contained a crypt, and many had plaques dusted with cobwebs. A thick gray fog clung to the floor, and each step suggested the ground was covered in putrid waste, with skittering bugs and the scrape of tiny bones underfoot. The smell was so bad Alishai wanted to pinch her nose, but after Dr. Mordenheim's lab, it was almost a relief.

She turned, a finger to her lips. Once, Rotrog would've challenged her, or perhaps Chivarion would've mocked her or at least questioned her, but now they simply nodded. They trusted her. Somehow, against all odds, throughout their strange adventure, they had become a unit. It was a new feeling but a welcome one.

The long walkway through the catacombs brought them to a spiral staircase. Alishai pulled her short sword and dagger as she crept upward. Behind her, she heard the clank of Chivarion's sword and Kah's mace, noises that were now familiar and comforting. Although she had been in this twisting staircase many times, it had always been above ground level, and now the chill stole into her bones. The shadows between the torches seemed to shift and extend long claws up the stone blocks. Alishai took each step with care, sending out her senses, knowing well how many dangers the castle held. She came upon a landing and swiftly hurried upward, recognizing that it was still underground.

Thankfully, the next landing was one she knew: the main floor, and the site of Fielle's chamber. Alishai stepped off into the hall of statues and waited for the rest of her . . .

Well, what was the right word?

Party?

Team?

Friends?

Family?

Dare she even think that word?

It had never held meaning for her before. Narelle had made it clear they were not family, and Alishai had always been made to feel like she was outside the cult, a servant, a lesser. But here, with these people, she felt seen. She felt known. She felt heard. She would give her life for any of them, and she knew now that they would likely do the same for her. And that's why they were here—to save Fielle. So it was time to finish the plan that had taken them through the Mists and into another world. It was time to give Fielle her freedom—and to reclaim their own.

Kah, Rotrog, and Chivarion joined her in the hall. The statues around them seemed to leer, their mouths mocking, their eyes cruel. Lightning cracked outside, loud enough to make even a seasoned warrior startle. It was often difficult to tell if it was day or night in Barovia, but when it stormed, the world went dark. They had to hurry before Strahd realized they were here and came to stop them.

Alishai turned left, toward Fielle's chamber, but Rotrog put a hand on her arm, tapped his ear, and pointed in the opposite direction. She went very still and sent out her senses.

Something was happening in the chapel.

A fight.

Alishai traded her short sword and dagger for her glaive and paused while the rest of her party prepared to enter the fray. She pointed at the corpse, still over Chivarion's shoulder, and then at the ground.

He nodded and carefully deposited the body behind a statue. It wasn't an elegant hiding place by any means, but at least it wasn't out in the middle of the floor. As soon as he had Liversliverer in hand, Alishai turned toward the chapel and led the charge.

Once the double doors to the chapel were thrown open, the scene came into focus. Before the altar, Strahd held Fielle by the throat, her feet off the ground and kicking. She wore a voluminous white wedding dress, now singed and stained, draped in dirt and cobwebs. She fought like a cat, hissing and spitting, her claws and teeth bared. Strahd—

To Alishai's surprise, she realized he was barely holding on.

His hair was mussed, his suit torn and burned. Black veins riddled his pale white skin, and his hair, usually perfectly slicked back, was a mess. He was panting, his arm shaking as he struggled to hold Fielle. Several stakes protruded from his chest, and his other arm had been broken in several places and hung at odd angles. Rudolph van Richten sat slumped against a pew nearby, his eyes closed. In his lap were a crossbow and a vial of water; he sat crookedly, limp and boneless, and looked like he, too, had been in the scrap of his life. A small automaton had fallen beside him, a roundish, clownish mannequin of metal and wood half-burned to ashes. Four vampire spawn lay around the room—three elegantly dressed women and one young man.

"Fielle!" Alishai cried, right as Chivarion ran toward Strahd with his crossbow out.

Thwip thwip thwip!

Three new bolts stuck out of Strahd's body: one in his head, one in his shoulder, and one in his side. He dropped Fielle and snarled. Rotrog hit him next, his magic missiles striking their target in quick succession and driving Strahd back. Fielle, who had landed on her feet, surprised Alishai by casting a spell that slammed into Strahd like a wall, freezing him in place.

Her glaive in both hands, Alishai raced down the aisle between the ancient pews, calling on Selûne and preparing for a massive hit.

"Stop!" Fielle screamed, and Alishai skidded to a halt, her glaive overhead, a foot away from what she felt sure would be a death blow to their common enemy.

At first, she didn't understand. Why wouldn't Fielle want to see Strahd die? Just a few more hits, and he might be gone.

But Fielle . . . she smiled.

With fangs.

The little human stalked toward Strahd like a cat that had cornered a mouse, reaching up to grab his hair with both hands and pull him down to her. He could not move, but his mouth opened and closed stupidly, his entire body shaking as he tried to resist her. Slowly, grinning, her red eyes alight, Fielle brought her lips to his cheek and kissed him softly . . .

Before she viciously buried her teeth in his throat.

Alishai heard the soft pop as they punctured the skin, heard the fierce suck as Fielle tasted his blood, or whatever a vampire had in place of it. Her lips clamped down on his neck and her eyes closed in bliss as she drank and drank and drank. The black veins in his skin pulsed and grew like roots spreading in pale dirt. Fielle did not stop drinking, did not pause. She rode him to the ground, straddling his chest as he landed with his back on the stone floor of his cathedral. Her white skirts billowed around her, red drops flung across the silk like a constellation.

"I . . . forbid it . . . you may not . . ." Strahd whispered, every word thready and weak.

"You can forbid Fielle all you like," she said, barely lifting her fangs from his neck. "But Tatyana does not obey you." The voice that came out of Fielle's mouth was deeper and tinged with the same accent that Strahd had, Alishai was horrified to note.

Having spoken her piece, Fielle—or the thing inside Fielle—redoubled her efforts, taking deep pulls from Strahd's neck. The longer it went on, the more work it took, as if she were trying to inhale the last bit of wine from a bottle with a reed straw. They could hear it, the fierce sound of her sucking the life out of his weakening body. Strahd was smaller now, diminished, crooked, shriveled and wizened. Finally, she closed her eyes, pulled away, and groaned, dragging her fingers in red stripes over her face and licking the blood off them one by one.

When she opened her eyes, what Alishai saw there . . .

It wasn't Fielle.

It was some sort of monster.

Alishai took a step back, and then another.

Fielle stood and smiled. "Thank you," she said. "For setting me free."

And then, with the next breath, she attacked.

36

CHIVARION (AND MURDER)

Chivarion had lived a long life and had been surprised many, many times. He had come to expect the unexpected, and he had learned that he could handle most unexpected things through either extreme violence or sheer dumb luck. Then again, "unexpected things" were usually a seagull stealing his sausage roll or a treasure chest actually being a mimic. When the unexpected thing was Fielle flying at him, claws curled and fangs outstretched, he was momentarily stunned.

"But—friend!" he managed to bark before she slammed into his chest and knocked him to the ground, her teeth clicking close enough for him to feel hot spit fleck his neck. He caught her by the shoulders, holding her away as he lay on his back on the filthy, bone-riddled floor of the chapel. His instinct was to be gentle with her even though she was doing her best to tear out his jugular. "A little help?" he called, looking around for someone else who wasn't currently trying to kill or be killed.

Alishai grabbed Fielle from behind, wrapping her up in a bear hug that pinned her arms to her sides. "Fielle, stop. Strahd is dead. You're free," she said. "We're here to save you."

Chivarion leaped to his feet as Fielle easily tore free of Alishai's grip and faced off with them.

"Save us? From what? Strahd is no more." Fielle's eyes were red, her body hunched over like a predator on the hunt. All of her softness and sweetness had fled, leaving behind a ragged creature of sharp lines and taut muscles.

"She is a full vampire now," Rudolph van Richten called from nearby. "She has drunk from her maker, and she possesses all his powers. And all his hungers." He looked to Fielle. "Fielle, we can restore your humanity—"

"No!" she shrieked. "We do not wish to be weak again. To be the scapegoat, the servant, the underling, the small and pitiful nothing. We are powerful now. We are strong. We will rule this place in Strahd's stead. He has fallen, and we are the Darklord this world deserves!"

Chivarion looked to Alishai, who shrugged.

"We?" Chivarion asked.

"We!" Fielle looked back and forth as if gauging who to kill first. "We are stronger together."

"Yes," Alishai agreed. "We are. And we have a way to separate your soul from Tatyana's. We went to a doctor and had her create a machine to help you. If you'll just calm down, we can give Tatyana her own body—"

"It's a very nice body!" Chivarion added helpfully. "Very fresh!"

"And then we can all go back to normal," Alishai finished.

Fielle straightened her posture. She licked her lips and let her fangs withdraw. Her eyes were the wrong color and her skin was pale, but at least she looked like Fielle again.

"This is why you left?" she asked. "To go find a cure? For me?"

"Yes," Kah chirped eagerly. "To help you."

Fielle smiled her old smile . . .

And then kept smiling, the corners of her mouth stretching wide and bloody. She threw back her head and cackled, the mad peals of her laughter echoing so loudly that the bats on the ceiling chittered and shifted like a living blanket.

"We don't need your help! We don't need anything. I finally have the sister I always longed for, always with me. I finally have a strong body that no one can harm. Together, we have a home, servants, wealth, an entire country to obey us, all the blood we desire. Why would we give all of that up?"

"For . . . friendship?" Chivarion said weakly.

Fielle shook her head at him. "You bumbling idiot. We don't need you. We are all that we need." She raised her hands and then slammed them down as if playing a chord on an organ, and a giant black cloud of bats fell shivering from the ceiling and swirled around the room like a living tornado. Chivarion saw what was coming, and he felt the ancient rage sing in his heart.

He had given everything to help Fielle.

He had gone to another world, fought monsters, carried corpses.

He had nearly seen his greatest friend stolen by a mad doctor.

He had shared his deepest secret shame with these people.

He, a brute, a killer, his sword arm for sale to the highest bidder, had been willing to do anything to help Fielle, and now she was throwing bats at him? And worse, at Murder, who had never done anything wrong, ever, in her whole life to deserve this?

"Get behind me," he told Murder with only his mind, and the tressym ran behind his legs.

The bats were coming at him now, a living cloud of teeth, and as he reached for Liversliverer, Chivarion felt a new magic take over his body, that same golden shimmer he'd felt when his eyes changed and he gained a new understanding with Murder. His fingers shot out and became curling black claws, actual talons, each one four inches long and sharp as a knife. The bats screeched like a chorus from hell, and he slashed through the air with his new claws, shredding the cloud. Squealing screams erupted in a hot splash of bat blood as he tore through the fog of tiny bodies. Nearby, Fielle screamed as if she felt their pain herself. While he swiped at the last of the bats with his claws, the rest of the colony hastily fluttered back into the eaves, settling down nervously in a corner.

"So you have also evolved," Fielle said.

Chivarion stared at his claws. "Looks like it."

She snarled. "We are not intimidated."

Chivarion was gearing up to attack her when Rotrog muttered under his breath and held up something hanging from his chatelaine. A beam of sunlight burst from the orc's palm and shone on Fielle in a spotlight that radiated the warmth of the hottest day in the most unforgiving desert. Her skin sizzled, making her screech and rear back. She twisted, turning her face away from Rotrog and shielding her head. Smoke rose from her neck and hands as she shook and spluttered, and the bats overhead squealed in complaint.

"What are you doing?" Alishai asked.

"She wants us dead," Rotrog said. "Did you not hear her? She has Strahd's powers. She is a vampire, and if Fielle is still within her, we can't reach her until the monster has been neutralized. It must be Tatyana—she is tainting Fielle. They should be separated. We must incapacitate her and use the machine before she can fight back."

"So to help her . . . we have to hurt her?" Chivarion asked. "Because that sounds wrong."

Alishai closed her eyes. "It's the only way. Go get the vessel while we . . ." She sighed heavily. "Handle this." Chivarion nodded and ran back the way they'd come.

Chivarion had bid her stay under a pew, so Murder watched and waited while he fetched his charge. She could feel the power roiling off Fielle and was content to wait until she was needed.

While the human—no! the vampire—continued to burn, Kah raised her hands, apologized to Fielle, and said a prayer to Akadi. A sphere of sunlight bloomed from her indigo palms and filled the chapel with the searing golden brightness of a spring day. Every dark corner was revealed, and the light struck the stained glass like a benediction, sending rainbow colors shimmering around the cobweb-dusted walls. The bats overhead fretted and roared and took off as one, flying out through the eaves.

Fielle, still on the ground, shook and writhed like a rag doll in the mouth of a dog. Every inch of visible skin sizzled and smoked, peeling back over wet red flesh. Her short hair burned off her scalp, and a fog of smoke enveloped her. Alishai knelt, holding down Fielle's arm, and Rotrog did the same on her other side.

"I'm sorry," Kah said softly. "Only way to help."

The moment the spell faded away to darkness, Fielle wrenched away from her captors and launched herself at Kah, knocking the kenku to the ground and tumbling over and over until they fetched up against a broken pew. Kah thrashed her beak and tried to hold Fielle off, but physical strength was not the cleric's best feature. With a fierce growl, Fielle sunk her teeth into Kah's arm and ripped out a chunk of meat, spitting it out and laughing while blood streamed down her chin. Kah screamed and struggled, but Fielle sat firmly on her chest, heavy skirts pooled around them.

On her feet now, Alishai lifted her glaive overhead, said a quick prayer, and slammed it sideways into Fielle. Thunder filled the room, along with a burst of light, and Fielle went flying. She landed on a pew, which exploded in shards of wood, sending Murder running for cover. Shaking uncontrollably, Kah sat up and healed herself, rubbing at the sore place on her arm.

After hurrying across the room, Chivarion gently placed the vessel on the ground beside Fielle where she lay amidst the wreckage of broken pews. Her skin was charred black and gently smoking, her dress torn and stained. She certainly appeared limp and lifeless, but Chivarion had felt the iron in those muscles, the hate in those teeth. Any second now, she would rise and look at him with fury and disgust.

And still, everything in his soul urged him not to hurt this innocent.

Not to hurt his friend.

The huge syringe was in his hands, but he couldn't plunge it into her chest.

Chivarion was sick of Barovia. Sick of this castle. Sick of vampires. Sick of everything that had the bad manners to rise again after it had been properly beaten and destroyed. He wanted to return to a land where people were people and monsters were monsters and everything made sense and no one wanted to kill his tressym. And that meant he had to help Fielle by nearly killing her, and so that was what he would do.

"I'm sorry about this," he told Fielle. "But I need you to hold still."

She certainly appeared weak and wounded, but she turned her face away, sobbing. "No. Please. Please don't. Don't hurt me. You don't know what I've been through. If you have any love for me in your heart, don't do this."

Her voice was sweet again, her eyes deep brown and wet with tears. Chivarion held the enormous needle over her heart . . .

But he couldn't bring himself to stab her.

37

KAH

Kah could still feel Fielle's teeth in her arm. Her body pulsed with fear and rage and hurt. What had happened to Fielle that could make her behave this way? The human woman had been the best of them—the kindest, the most trusting, the most generous, the most positive. The first one who tried to bring them together. The only one who didn't carry a secret shame, a reason they had been expelled from their past life into this strange and purgatorial world.

Well, that Kah knew of.

Maybe Fielle had secrets of her own.

It didn't matter now.

The only way to help her was to separate her from the foul soul tainting her own, and this version of Fielle had more than proven that she was willing to hurt them. Chivarion couldn't bring himself to stab her, but . . . someone had to.

"Listen to me," Kah said, swiftly meeting the eyes of Rotrog, Alishai, and Chivarion. "We were brought here as punishment, but what if . . . what if we can earn redemption? The only things we have in common are these: that we almost made selfish mistakes in a different life, and that we would all do anything to save Fielle and each other in this life. We have fought, failed, sailed to new worlds, discovered new talents. We have made ourselves vulnerable, shared our deepest shames, and found forgiveness. No one wants to hurt Fielle, but we must use every skill we possess to put Dr. Mordenheim's machine into motion. Let's evict the monster that has taken our friend and change her destiny and ours."

Alishai's eyes shone. "Oh, so now you can talk in complete sentences?"

A quick laugh. "When there's something worth saying."

"Well, I'm convinced." Chivarion raised the syringe and brought it down toward Fielle's chest.

But she was too fast. Fielle rolled aside, laughing, and the needle missed her entirely. Of course it had been a ruse. Fielle scrambled to her hands and feet like a twisted spider and again focused on Kah, who held her mace and braced herself for the onslaught. She was so focused on Fielle that she didn't hear the subtle groans behind her, didn't notice the approaching zombie until it clamped its teeth down in her shoulder. Of course—of course there were zombies in the castle. This one had probably been one of Strahd's allies in the earlier fight.

Furious, Kah dropped her mace, said a prayer to Akadi, and pressed a ball of fire into the zombie's face. It screeched and flailed as the flame took hold and forced it to release Kah's arm.

Now that Kah had no weapon in hand, Fielle ran right past her and raised her arms. Thorn-covered vines shot out like whips, wrapping around Rotrog and digging into his robes. The orc screamed as blood bloomed where every little thorn dug in, a cocoon of viciously growing green, a rosebush with no roses. His arms were pinned to his sides as the vines twined around him, and Fielle strode calmly up to him and grabbed his face.

"Let's see what orc blood tastes like, shall we?" With a hiss, she sunk her fangs into Rotrog's neck. His eyes flew wide, his mouth opened in a howl. He turned his head to snap at her with his tusks, but she snapped it right back into place.

Chivarion was already there with his sword, stabbing it directly into Fielle's back. He tried to pull it out, but it was firmly stuck. Fielle released Rotrog and turned around, the blade of the sword poking obscenely from her stomach.

"You think a sword can hurt us now? Even a magic sword? Please."

Alishai raised her glaive, and Fielle burst into a cloud of mist to evade the strike, leaving Chivarion's sword to clatter harmlessly to the ground. The cloud floated several feet away and re-formed into Fielle.

"We have more power than you. More strength. More servants ready to do our bidding. And what do you have?"

"Um . . . friendship?" Chivarion said again.

Behind Fielle, Rotrog was quietly cutting at the thorny vines with a pair of scissors that hung on his chatelaine. He had his one arm free and kept working away, even as the blood rose fresh from each puncture.

"You have *friendship*," Fielle said mockingly. "You have pluck." She snarled in disgust. "You're just food that doesn't know it's dead yet. Barovia is our realm, under our control. It's a playground where we can toy with you, where every rule bends in our direction, where the Tarokka cards always flip in our favor." She pointed at Alishai. "We are playing with you now, but we are growing bored."

Alishai wasn't moving; Fielle had cast a spell on her like she had with Strahd, pinning the tiefling in place. Kah looked desperately to Rotrog, hoping he had a spell of his own. A tangle of green vines curled on the stone floor.

But Rotrog . . . was gone.

38

ROTROG

Rotrog had practiced this spell a few times privately but had never attempted it in a moment of great need. It was fascinating, really, blinking into another ethereal plane. He could still see everything in great detail, down to the charred curls of Fielle's eyelashes, but everything was cast in shadowy shades of gray, and no one could see him. He watched as Fielle bit Alishai, driving the powerful tiefling to her knees. He heard Fielle talking with the royal "we," explaining her many skills and talents and what she would do to each of her once-friends.

He grew bored of her pontificating.

At least Strahd had been engaging.

Now Rotrog moved past Alishai as the tiefling fell to the ground, unconscious. Fielle stood, her skin charred dark gray and peeling back over wet meat, her eyes glowing. She moved to Kah and drank from her as well. Chivarion could only stand there stupidly; Fielle had frozen him in place. Rotrog hurried to the corpse Chivarion had abandoned on the ground. He had only seconds before the spell was done, and then he had one chance to finish this.

Not with magic.

With only the strength of his body—the strength he had never bothered to cultivate because he cared only about spellcraft.

He picked up the syringe with his right hand and dragged the corpse toward Fielle with his left. Step after step he moved toward her in another plane as she arrogantly outlined how she would desecrate the bodies of his friends after she'd drained them dry. He was tired from the fight, left depleted by the blood she'd taken. But he had enough strength to do this. Just this.

"And that is why you will all die now," Fielle said.

Rotrog's spell ended.

Reality descended in every shade of the rainbow.

He slammed the huge needle into his friend's heart and pushed the button on the box nestled in the corpse's chest.

Fielle gasped and fell to the floor.

39

From the Diary of Rudolph van Richten

The fight is over, and yet again I have survived by the skin of my teeth. I'd like to think that Strahd has been killed permanently, and yet I suspect he will return soon; perhaps he already slumbers in his secret tomb, regaining his strength. As I told the adventurers, the cycle is doomed to repeat itself, over and over. But now I have the Tome of Strahd, and perhaps I will learn something that might release this world from its Darklord permanently. Only time—and further study—will tell.

The adventurers succeeded in separating the two souls—of that much I am certain. Dr. Mordenheim's device somehow returned Fielle to her sweet and human self, leaving her mortified by her past behavior and grateful for her salvation. When Tatyana awoke in her new body, she was panicked, terrified of Strahd and of the chance that she might yet again fall into his foul hands. She was relieved to see Fielle, and together, healed by the clever cleric, we all made haste to the brazier room and hence to the River Dancer, where we dined with Larissa Snowmane and did our best to convince the poor girl that she is safe.

We entered the Mists, bringing the adventurers with us—

But then the Mists lifted!

Perhaps it is a sign that, for some small while, Strahd really is dead. There is time enough to research this phenomenon, as I myself go where I please. For the adventurers, however, this was a rare and precious gift. They disembarked and entered an unfamiliar forest, disappearing among the trees and taking Tatyana with them. Moments later, she returned to the shores of the river, confused and alone. The Mists would not let her go. I do not pretend to understand the Dark Powers, but this seemed an especially cruel punishment for an innocent woman. The poor creature does not appear to have retained any of the violence and rage of a vampire spawn, but is instead consumed with despair at the loss of Fielle and a happy future elsewhere.

I had hoped that she might escape, but it appears that she, too, is doomed to repeat the same cycle. The hawk must chase the hare, I suppose. She is safe with Larissa and me for now, but I can only hypothesize that eventually, she will be drawn to Strahd's periphery again, whether in this body or another.

For now, the hourglass is reset in Barovia.

Our cycle begins anew.

For the daring adventurers, perhaps, a new cycle is likewise begun.

I pray I will never learn the truth, for that would mean they, too, are prisoners of the Domains of Dread.

40

FIELLE

Fielle was in a forest, walking as if in a dream. The moon shone down through the leaves, familiar stars twinkling overhead. She startled at a sound in the leaf litter, but it was only a doe and her fawn, their eyes wet and black in the darkness. The doe stared at her, continued chewing, and slowly walked away among the trees, unbothered. Her fawn blinked curiously before following. Neither animal had shown any ferocity or fear. That was enough to convince Fielle that they were no longer in Barovia.

Everything in that accursed realm was either a monster or a monster's prey.

There, toward the end, she herself had been a monster.

But not now.

Now Tatyana was gone and Strahd was dead and she was simply Fielle, and she was eager to be home.

"Wait, I know this forest," Chivarion said, perking up. "I've been drunk here! We are just outside Baldur's Gate."

Alishai looked to Fielle. "That's where you're from, is it not?"

Fielle's heart lifted. "It is! The Dancing Dragon is near the Black

Dragon Gate. It's a tavern and inn, and the food is good. At least it is when I'm in the kitchen."

"Are you not worried?" Kah asked, clicking her beak. "Your family . . ."

Fielle laughed lightly. "After all that I've been through, I doubt my sister's tantrums and my father's chiding will have much power over me. It will be nice to have a warm bed again. And a locking door. And my own clothes."

"A warm bed," Chivarion said. "And perhaps someone to share it with. And food. Lots of food. That sounds perfect. Alishai—"

"For the last time, I will not share your bed, you brawny goat!"

"I was going to ask if you'd cover my bill. I'm afraid my coin purse is empty."

A weary sigh. "Yes, I will pay for your room and board. At least for one night while we figure out our next move."

Kah scurried forward. "Our next move. So we stay together?"

Alishai stopped, and they gathered around her. "I had hoped . . ." the tiefling began somewhat shyly, ". . . that we might travel together. We've learned to work so well as a team, and we could earn plenty of coin, I think, as a party of . . . well, not quite mercenaries."

"Aw, why not?" Chivarion griped.

"We're good at finding things and saving people," she continued. "At helping. And we all need a new start away from our old lives. We all want to make up for our sins. Why not?"

"I do not wish to return to Silverymoon," Rotrog said. He called up a small flame and grinned as it danced along his fingers. "And my magic appears to work here. I'd be glad to travel with you as I collect more spell books and artifacts."

"My sword arm is always for sale," Chivarion said. "As long as Murder is welcome."

"Murder is always welcome," Alishai assured him. "Kah?"

"Akadi bids me fill my life with adventures." The kenku trilled happily. "So I will adventure with you."

Alishai looked to Fielle. "And what will you do? In our haste to leave, we missed so much of your story. We could always use an artificer, if you'd like to join us."

"You'd fit right in," Chivarion agreed.

"Especially if you can cook more than fish stew," Rotrog said. At that, Chivarion stuck his tongue out, and the orc returned the gesture.

Fielle fidgeted, wishing she weren't in a ruined wedding dress. "I think I'd like that. I need to have a heart-to-heart with my family—some closure—but then a life on the road might be just the change I need."

Alishai nodded decisively. "Well, then. Take us to these warm beds of yours."

Chivarion got them to the city gates, and Fielle led them through the streets she'd known all her life. Everything looked so different to her now, so quaint and bursting with life after all that she'd seen in Barovia. The closer she got to the Dancing Dragon, the harder it was to remain calm. She was a new person, but her family would not see her that way. They would see the same old second-born scapegoat, the inconsequential kitchen maid, the unwanted nobody who wasn't worth the spotlight.

But for the first time, she had confidence in herself.

She was worth something.

She would change their minds. She would make them see her.

They turned a corner, and there it was. Her home.

The streets were warmly lit, not bustling but still filled with a certain energy as late-night carousers staggered between taverns, vendors hawked their wares from carts, and pickpockets waited in the shadows for unwary victims. Zerina's voice carried even beyond the glass windows of the Dancing Dragon, but this time it didn't make Fielle's throat ache with jealousy. She didn't want what the Golden Zerina had. She had everything she needed now, all on her own.

The others waited for her to open the door and followed her inside. Within, the tavern was exactly the same as the day she'd disappeared. It was like she'd never left, never even existed at all. Her sister sang on the stage in a dress covered with a thousand tiny beads, the reflected footlights throwing glittering stars onto the walls. Her father stood in the back by the bar, arms crossed, nodding appreciation as coins thumped onto the stage and men called Zerina's name, vying for her attention, begging for her regard. Her weary, graying mother carried heavy tankards through the throng and returned with the empties balanced on an arm.

Sighing, Fielle led her friends to a long table kept in reserve for a local gang boss. They sat, and her father immediately thundered over, furious.

"What is all this?" he bellowed. "Who do you lot think you are?"

"They are friends of mine, Father." Fielle's head hung; it was muscle memory by now. "Please, I can explain."

"Disappear for a month and then show up with a bunch of ruffians on our busiest night? Take up the most valuable table we have? The nerve on you, girl. I should beat you senseless."

Zerina's final note strung out unnaturally long, and then she bowed to thunderous applause. Fielle watched her sister sashay backstage holding dozens of roses tossed by her admirers as the red velvet curtain fell. "If you and Mother will meet me in the dressing room, then I can tell you all where I've been. It will make much more sense when you hear the full story."

"I doubt it." He looked around the table and sneered. "They'd better have coin. With an extra fee for the prime seating."

"I'd like the biggest ale you have," Chivarion said grandly. "And you'd best bring two, little man. I'm feeling thirsty."

Fielle noted Chivarion's daring tone, Alishai's hateful glare, Rotrog's twitching fingers, Kah's hand on her mace. These people—they had her back, and that wasn't nothing.

"I'll return shortly," she told them. "Order whatever you like when the serving girl finds you. Enjoy yourselves. The lute player always puts on a good show." Giving them a tight smile, she trailed meekly behind her father. He gestured for Mother, and the three of them trudged up past the stage and into the wings.

Fielle knew the Dancing Dragon like the back of her hand, had designed the sets, placed the spotlights, crafted the machinery that moved around Zerina as she sang, making it appear as if she were a mermaid among the waves or a goddess riding a Pegasus in the clouds. She knew the smells of the tavern, the seasonal spicing of the sausages, the exact sweetness of the sticky mead and wine mixed in the cracks in the floorboards. Part of her loved this place, and even if her father thought her a mischievous child who'd selfishly run away, soon he would see the truth of what she'd undergone.

"Well?" he said.

He stood between Zerina and Mother, the three of them forming a solid wall of disapproval. Sweat dripped down Mother's temples, her hair straggling out of its bun, white-streaked after a lifetime of servitude. Zerina's lovely eyes narrowed, her stage makeup smeared from the hot lights.

And Father—

Well, she recognized what she saw in his face now.

Hate.

He *hated* her.

And all she'd ever done was everything he'd ever asked.

"Well?" he asked again, louder this time, uncrossing his arms and rolling up his sleeves as if preparing to beat her.

But Fielle could only smile.

And when she smiled, her fangs extended.

She'd told the others she'd been cured, but . . .

Tatyana was gone, taking all the sweetness and humanity with her, and only the vampire remained.

She liked it this way. No one would ever hurt her again.

"What—?" her father began, but if he had more to say, it remained unsaid. She didn't even bother drinking from him; she simply tore his throat out with one wild and joyous swipe of her claws. Her mother stared in horror, frozen and useless as usual, and was easy enough to dispatch.

And Zerina—

Fielle took a little more time with Zerina. She sunk her fangs into that golden neck and swallowed her sister's blood, gulping it down hungrily, taking into herself all the songs that the Golden Zerina would never get to sing again, the songs Fielle had not been allowed to sing herself.

When she was done, the dressing room was splashed in red and blessedly silent.

She went to Zerina's fancy dressing table, took up her favorite silk scarf, and used it to clean the blood from her mouth and chin. Stripping out of the ruined white gown, she selected her favorite of Zerina's dresses, slipped her feet into Zerina's softest slippers. When she looked in the mirror, she saw herself, truly saw herself. Beautiful. Powerful. Unstoppable.

The Dancing Dragon was hers now.

Soon, Baldur's Gate would follow.

The others could join her or die.

This world needed a Darklord of its own.

ACKNOWLEDGMENTS

I was a weird kid, and I didn't have any friends to play D&D with. Instead of playing, I read the *Players Handbook* and the *Monstrous Manual*, much as instead of having a horse, I read every horse encyclopedia I could find. I watched the Saturday morning D&D cartoon and wished I could end up in a new land with a pet unicorn, although I was too scared to go on any roller coasters. I eventually found the drama kids and a social life when I was sixteen, but I never got to play any RPGs until I was in college. My now-husband killed me with a Noghri in my very first game of the Star Wars RPG because I was playing too conservatively. I refused to take any risks because I was so scared of "doing it wrong."

A lot has changed since then.

I have to make safe choices in life, but in books?

Oh, in my books, I am a complete idiot. I am every single one of these characters: Fielle's optimism, Alishai's seasickness and desire to belong, Rotrog's hunger for magic, Kah's shyness around strangers, Chivarion's whimsy. And I'm probably their worse qualities, too, but that's between me and my therapist.

As with most of my books, writing this story has actually been a form of therapy—and an absolute joy. My life walks the tightrope between whimsy and darkness, so a wacky dungeon party plunged into their worst nightmare is really my bailiwick.

Huge thanks to Elizabeth Schaefer and Alex Davis for bringing me on board, and to Paul Morrissey, Sarra Scherb, and everyone at Wizards of the Coast who made this project such a delight. Thanks to my agent, Stacia Decker, for always checking for traps. Thanks to Katerina Ladon for a glorious cover that really nailed my Boo Crew, as I privately call them, both because the Domains of Dread constantly attempt to scare them, and because they are all my boos. Thanks to the copyediting team for fixing all my errors, and to the PR and marketing teams for getting the book out into the world. Thanks to R. A. Salvatore for being so kind and welcoming. They may say "don't meet your heroes," but sometimes you do and it's beautiful.

And thank you, dear reader, for going on this adventure with me.

ABOUT THE AUTHOR

DELILAH S. DAWSON is the author of the *New York Times* bestseller *Star Wars: Phasma*, as well as *Star Wars: Galaxy's Edge: Black Spire*, *Hit*, *Servants of the Storm*, the Blud series, the creator-owned comics *Ladycastle*, *Sparrowhawk*, and *Star Pig*, and the Shadow series (written as Lila Bowen). She lives in Georgia with her family and a fat mutt named Merle.

delilahsdawson.com
Bluesky / Threads / Instagram: @DelilahSDawson

ABOUT THE TYPE

This book was set in Caslon, a typeface first designed in 1722 by William Caslon (1692–1766). Its widespread use by most English printers in the early eighteenth century soon supplanted the Dutch typefaces that had formerly prevailed. The roman is considered a "workhorse" typeface due to its pleasant, open appearance, while the italic is exceedingly decorative.